NEWS FROM NOWHERE

NEWS FROM NOWHERE

or

AN EPOCH OF REST, BEING SOME CHAPTERS FROM A UTOPIAN ROMANCE

William Morris

edited by Stephen Arata

broadview literary texts

National Library of Canada Cataloguing in Publication

Morris, William, 1834-1896
    News from nowhere, or, An epoch of rest : being some chapters from a utopian romance / William Morris ; edited by Stephen Arata.

(Broadview literary texts)
Includes bibliographical references.
ISBN 1-55111-267-1

1. Utopias.   I. Arata, Stephen D. (Stephen David), 1958–   II. Title.   III. Title: Epoch of rest. IV. Series.

HX811.M67 2002   321'.07   C2002-904252-6

Broadview Press Ltd. is an independent, international publishing house, incorporated in 1985. Broadview believes in shared ownership, both with its employees and with the general public; since the year 2000 Broadview shares have traded publicly on the Toronto Venture Exchange under the symbol BDP.

We welcome comments and suggestions regarding any aspect of our publications–please feel free to contact us at the addresses below or at broadview@broadviewpress.com.

North America
PO Box 1243, Peterborough, Ontario, Canada K9J 7H5
3576 California Road, Orchard Park, NY, USA 14127
Tel: (705) 743-8990; Fax: (705) 743-8353
email: customerservice@broadviewpress.com

UK, Ireland, and continental Europe
Thomas Lyster Ltd., Units 3 & 4a, Old Boundary Way
Burscough Road, Ormskirk
Lancashire, L39 2YW
Tel: (01695) 575112; Fax: (01695) 570120
email: books@tlyster.co.uk

Australia and New Zealand
UNIREPS, University of New South Wales
Sydney, NSW, 2052
Tel: 61 2 9664 0999; Fax: 61 2 9664 5420
email: info.press@unsw.edu.au

www.broadviewpress.com

Broadview Press Ltd. gratefully acknowledges the financial support of the Government of Canada through the Book Publishing Industry Development Program for our publishing activities.

Series editor: Professor L.W. Conolly
Advisory editor for this volume: Michel W. Pharand

PRINTED IN CANADA

For my daughters, Emma and Haley

Contents

Introduction

News from Nowhere is William Morris's most important work of prose fiction and a vital document in the history of late-Victorian socialism. It is also an immensely entertaining novel. Composed in 1890, at the close of Morris's most intense period of political activism, *News from Nowhere* is a compelling articulation of his mature views on art, work, community, family, and the nature and structure of the ideal society. In addition, it is a clear-eyed meditation on the processes, as well as the costs, of radical historical change. Unlike previous utopian writers, Morris was as interested in "How the Change Came" (the title of Chapter XVII) as in the society that change finally produced. Like Sir Thomas More's *Utopia* or William Blake's prophetic books, *News from Nowhere* is firmly tied to its specific historical moment, yet speaks forcefully to issues still alive today.

Morris was 56 when he completed *News from Nowhere.* He was arguably the most prominent and respected artist of his generation, one whose range of endeavor had helped redefine art and its potential place in a well-ordered society. His fame as a poet was of long standing. His major volumes of poetry—*The Defence of Guenevere and Other Poems* (1858), *The Life and Death of Jason* (1867), *The Earthly Paradise* (1868-70), *Love is Enough* (1872), and *Sigurd the Volsung* (1876)—enjoyed both popular acclaim and critical esteem. In addition to his own verse, Morris published well-received translations from the classical languages and, more importantly, from the Icelandic sagas. He was instrumental in bringing the saga tradition to the attention of late Victorian readers, primarily through his translations and retellings of traditional tales but also through the original prose romances he began writing in the mid-1880s. While *News from Nowhere* differs significantly from them in tone and style, it does share important thematic material with these romances, especially those written immediately before and after the novel: *The House of the Wolfings* (1888), *The Roots of the Mountains* (1889), and *The Story of the Glittering Plain* (1891).

The quality and variety of Morris's literary output were in themselves enough to merit the high regard in which he was held.

(In 1892 he turned aside the chance to succeed Alfred Tennyson as Poet Laureate, just as, fifteen years earlier, he had declined to be considered for the position of Professor of Poetry at Oxford.) To the first readers of *News from Nowhere*, though, Morris was if anything even better known for his practice of what were—largely thanks to him—no longer called the "lesser arts." As Morris argued in 1877 in his first public lecture, the clearest sign of modern society's ethical and aesthetic bankruptcy was that traditional crafts such as "house-building, painting, joinery and carpentry, smiths' work, pottery and glass-making, weaving, and many others" had, with few exceptions, devolved into "trivial, mechanical, unintelligent" activities shaped by the needs of industrial capitalism.[1] He decried what he considered the artificial and debilitating segregation of the "higher" arts—painting, sculpture, poetry, architecture—from the "lesser" ones. He likewise deplored the segregation of artistic labor in all its forms from the other activities of life. Morris devoted much of his adult life to reviving moribund crafts, most notably weaving, dyeing, furniture-making, and printing, and to arguing for their reintegration into the texture of a well-knit life.

For Morris, the making of art was by definition a public activity—public in that it connected its makers at every stage of their work with the wider community that used, enjoyed, and benefited from the made object, and public in that the vitality of the arts depended entirely on the health of society. Like his great teacher John Ruskin, Morris believed that modern civilization had fatally compromised its health, falling into what Ruskin had called "illth": and with that fall the arts had fallen too.[2] Morris rejected the idea, familiar enough by the end of the nineteenth century, that art existed in a realm somehow apart from the common world of women and men. In his view, it is impossible to talk about art "in itself," since art is intrinsically social. And so, again like Ruskin, beginning in middle age he committed himself to a thorough and uncompromising critique of the world around him.

Unlike Ruskin, though, Morris pursued his critique within a

---

[1] "The Decorative Arts" (1877), in May Morris, ed., *The Collected Works of William Morris*, 24 vols. (London: Longmans, Green & Co., 1910-15): 22:3-4.

[2] *Unto this Last* (1860), in *The Works of John Ruskin*, ed. E.T. Cook and Alexander Wedderburn, 39 vols. (London: George Allen, 1903-12): 17:89.

specific ideological framework, that of late-Victorian socialism. From 1883 until his death, Morris was among the most visible and vocal, and certainly the best-known, spokesman for socialist ideas in Great Britain. All of his political work was done in the name of the organizations he successively associated himself with: the Social Democratic Federation (1883-84), the Socialist League (1884-90), and the Hammersmith Socialist Society (1890-96). His many publications and lectures on social issues were intimately personal, articulating his deepest beliefs, yet Morris always connected those beliefs to the larger movement he had joined. He invariably spoke and wrote as one who does not write or speak only for himself. Morris considered his personal ideals to be realizable—indeed, to be fully coherent—only if they were linked at every point with the ideals of a socialist society.

Which is not to say that his ideals always coincided with those of other socialists. Or that other socialists always, or even very often, agreed with one another. *News from Nowhere* opens at a meeting "up at the League"—the Socialist League, where, says the narrator, "a brisk conversational discussion, as to what would happen on the Morrow of the Revolution," leads each member present to offer "a vigorous statement" of his views "on the future of the fully-developed new society." There being six members present, six divergent views are offered, and "if they did not listen to each other's opinions (which could scarcely be expected of them), at all events [they] did not always attempt to speak all together" (53). The tone of genial tolerance in these opening pages barely masks the narrator's despair as he contemplates, just as William Guest will do later in the novel, the fissures that divided and subdivided the socialist movement into ever smaller factions during the last half of the 1880s.

Morris continually tried to heal the rifts, though he was himself hot-tempered and impulsive and would, like Guest in the opening chapter, continually resolve to avoid contention only to end up "roaring out very loud, and damning all the rest for fools" (53). Though he remained open to persuasion on certain issues, throughout his adult life Morris held to a handful of core beliefs which never changed and which he refused to compromise. By 1890 he found himself out of step not just with late-Victorian society at large but also with the main movements of British radicalism. At the heart of *News from Nowhere* is Morris's vision of what he often referred to as the "true commonwealth": a world "in which all men may live at peace and free from over-burdensome anxiety, provided with work which is pleasant to them and produces results useful to their neighbours."[1] As a century's worth of readers can attest, it is a vision whose appeal does not depend on a knowledge of the intricacies of late-Victorian social debates. Yet in its details as in its larger conceptual patterns, the novel continually engages those debates, and does so in ways that draw heavily on Morris's personal experiences within the socialist movement.

Morris and the British Socialist Movement

Morris joined the Democratic Federation, soon renamed the Social Democratic Federation, in January 1883. Founded in 1881 by Henry Mayers Hyndman, the Democratic Federation was the first political organization in Britain committed to Marxist socialism. After running unsuccessfully for Parliament as a Liberal candidate in the 1870s, Hyndman read *Das Kapital* in French translation—there being no English one yet—and was converted to socialism. He immediately sought out Marx himself, who at first offered encouragement but later called his would-be disciple "a 'weak' vessel" for carrying Marx's ideas to the English.[2] In 1881 Hyndman published *England for All,* in which he drew heavily on Marx's ideas while somehow neglecting to mention his name, an oversight he rectified two years later in *The Historical Basis for Socialism.* Together, the books introduced Marx-influenced social analysis to the British reading public. The Democratic Federation began as an assembly of radical working-men's clubs, but under Hyndman's leadership the groups quickly coalesced under the banner of Marxism.

The decision to join the Federation marked Morris's final break

---

[1] Norman Kelvin, ed., *The Collected Letters of William Morris*, 4 vols. (Princeton: Princeton University Press, 1984-96): 2:173. Subsequent references, by volume and page number, are given parenthetically in the text.

[2] Karl Marx and Friedrich Engels, *Correspondence, 1835-1895: A Selection with Commentary and Notes*, trans. Dona Torr (New York: International Publishers, 1934): 397.

with middle-class Liberalism. In "How I Became a Socialist," written near the end of his life, Morris offers an account of his slow progress towards what he calls "practical Socialism." A sense of massive alienation from the ideals of mid-Victorian culture defined Morris's life. "Apart from the desire to produce beautiful things, the leading passion of my life has been and is hatred of modern civilization."[1] From early adulthood Morris counted himself among those who felt "a vague sentiment of repulsion to the triumph of civilization, but were coerced into silence" by what seemed the near universal worship of "progress" in the culture at large (23:279). Reading the works of Thomas Carlyle and especially of Ruskin helped "give form to [his] discontent" without, however, indicating a viable way out (23:279). By the early 1860s Morris's rejection of modern civilization was complete, yet he struggled to find suitable ways to enact that rejection, to turn ineffectual grumbling into effective action. His effort to revive traditional crafts—and to revive, if only in local and approximate ways, the social relations among workers that enabled those crafts—was one such enactment. Another was his work for the Society for the Preservation of Ancient Buildings. For Morris, architecture was the fundamental human art, and through the Society he helped raise public awareness of its importance to the overall health of a community.

Despite a deep distaste for politics (he disliked even the word, which he seldom used), Morris began in the 1870s to take public stances on political issues. Primarily through his involvement with the Eastern Question Association, which loudly and with some success protested against British foreign policy in the Balkans, his name became linked with the Liberal Party's more radical elements. Yet disillusionment with established forms of radicalism came quickly. "I used to think," Morris wrote in an 1883 letter, "that one might further real Socialistic progress by doing what one could on the lines of ordinary middle-class Radicalism: I have been driven of late into the conclusion that I was mistaken; that Radicalism is on the wrong line, so to say, and will never develope [sic] into anything more than Radicalism" (Letters, 2:199).

---

[1] "How I Became a Socialist" (1894), Collected Works, 23:279. Further page references to this essay are given parenthetically in the text.

Radicalism's limitations lay in its emphasis on political rather than economic oppression. Morris believed that political freedom was of little use to those condemned to live sordid, impoverished lives. Moreover, he shrewdly recognized that those in power would always be willing to tolerate Radicalism's "*political* development, if they think they can stop it there; but as to real social changes, they will not allow them if they can help it" (*Letters*, 2:199–200). Real social change was what Morris was after, and so, despite his sympathy with the radical cause, he came to consider radical politics as part of the very system he wanted to see overturned. The ultimate aims of the radical movement extended no further than reform, when what was needed was revolution.

In late 1882 Morris read *Das Kapital* in French. It did not change his views, since he had already arrived by different routes at many of Marx's conclusions. Marx did, however, provide a compelling theoretical grounding for Morris's visceral rejection of modern capitalist culture. He also sharpened Morris's sense that change was possible. In "How I Became a Socialist" Morris wrote that by the summer of 1882—that is, shortly before he began reading Marx—he could still see his "ideal clear enough, but had no hope of any realization of it." In the fall he began to attend meetings of the Democratic Federation, and in January he joined. "The meaning of my joining that body was that I had conceived a hope of the realization of my ideal" (23:277). After joining the Federation he began to read diligently in political economy. He learned much, too, from talks with more theoretically-minded members such E. Belfort Bax and Andreas Scheu.

The years 1882–83 saw Morris define himself fully and irrevocably as a socialist. He embraced that self-identification until his death. His ties to the Social Democratic Federation, on the other hand, lasted only two years. He quickly clashed with Hyndman over tactics and goals. Charismatic and tireless, Hyndman nonetheless struck Morris (and not just Morris) as mercurial, self-promoting, and, in the last analysis, untrustworthy. Many suspected him of nursing political ambitions which he was using the S.D.F. to further. "That political ambition," Morris wrote to a sympathetic fellow member, "has I think driven the S.D.F. into somewhat *showy* tactics: we have neglected the educational for the agitational.... [W]e have hinted threats of forcible revolution which are merely ludicrous at present, since as yet there is no movement among the workers, bitterly as many intelligent people feel the idiocy of the plutocratic system: in a word we have been theatrical, and have advertised ourselves into a notoriety which has no proportion to our numbers or organization" (*Letters*, 2:364).

Educate and organize: these were to Morris's mind the essential tasks at hand, which Hyndman had put aside in favor of "theatrical boasts, and warnings about immediate violent revolution" (*Letters*, 2:368). A few weeks on the lecture platform had convinced Morris that socialism was almost exclusively a middle-class affair. His first encounters with working-class audiences revealed that they were far from being natural socialists. Their sense of oppression and injustice was acute, but unaccompanied by a clear understanding of its causes or potential remedies. Without such understanding, no lasting change could occur: the new boss would be the same as the old boss. Morris argued that the role of the middle-class intellectual was not to lead or even to incite a workers' revolution but instead to help produce conditions that would make such a revolution inevitable, self-generated, and irreversible. Hyndman, Morris thought, was less interested in such a role than he was in being one of the new bosses.

In addition, he was alarmed by Hyndman's willingness to abandon the revolutionary ideals of socialism in favor of pursuing legislative reform, a course Morris considered futile: simply middle-class radicalism by another name. Indeed, despite the S.D.F.'s inflammatory rhetoric, Morris believed it was finally working against the kind of change he desired.

> I cannot stand all this; it is not what I mean by Socialism either in aim or in means: I want a real revolution a real change in Society: Society a great organic mass of well-regulated forces used for the bringing-about a happy life for all. And the means for attaining it are simple enough; education in Socialism, and organization for the time when the crisis shall force action upon us: nothing else will do us any good at present: the revolution cannot be a mechanical one,

though the last act of it may be civil war, or it will end in reaction after all. (*Letters*, 2:368)

By the end of 1884 Morris had decided to break with Hyndman. Along with other disaffected former members of the Social Democratic Federation, he founded the Socialist League. Morris hoped the two organizations would make common cause, though he recognized that their pursuit of shared goals would often follow divergent paths. "Those whose tendencies lead them toward politics and parliamentarianism," he wrote in January 1885, "will fall naturally towards the Social Democratic Federation; those who are more of purists will fall towards us" (*Letters*, 2:366).

Morris's most important work as a socialist took place during his six years with the Socialist League. In his writings Morris habitually portrays himself as a pragmatic socialist, unversed in political theory, "careless of metaphysics and religion, as well as of scientific analysis," and "blankly ignorant of economics," as he put it in "How I Became a Socialist" (23:280, 277). He was indeed impatient with theoretical discussion. "I do not believe in the world being saved by any system" (*Letters*, 2:202). Yet he was far from being the "sentimental Socialist" that Friedrich Engels, sneering, called him.[1] Morris had a firm grasp on the historical dimensions of Marx's argument. He also recognized that, disconnected from a rigorous economic critique of Victorian society, his "ideal" was no more than utopian dreaming. But unlike Engels and many other socialists, Morris shouldered the difficult task of communicating the insights of socialism to those who had not the time, means, training, or inclination to learn them unaided. Initially a reluctant public speaker, Morris made himself into a highly effective one. He came to see public speaking as the form of social action he was best qualified to perform, a way of intervening, perhaps decisively, in the lives of others. "To do nothing but grumble and not to act—that is throwing away one's life," Morris wrote to his lifelong confidant Georgiana Burne-Jones. "But I don't think that words on our cause that we have at heart do nothing but wound the air" (*Letters*, 2:65).

---

[1]   *Correspondence of Friedrich Engels and Paul and Laura Lafargue*, trans. Yvonne Kapp, 3 vols. (Moscow: Foreign Languages Publishing House, 1959): 2:370.

From 1882 until his death in 1896, Morris sent innumerable such words into the air. Eugene D. LeMire's "Calendar of William Morris's Platform Career" lists over 600 speaking engagements during this period, apart from the regular business meetings (at which Morris often spoke) of the various organizations to which he belonged. In all, Morris composed nearly one hundred lectures and speeches on topics related to socialist issues, though only a handful were published during his lifetime.[1] The prose he cultivated for these works, which is also the prose of *News from Nowhere*, remains one of the marvels of nineteenth-century writing: limpid, lucid, passionate, never condescending, its arguments carried along powerful yet concise rhythms and illuminated by homely though compelling figures of speech:

> Friends, this earthly hell is not the ordinance of nature but the manufacture of man; made I will believe not by their malice but their stupidity; and it is your business to destroy it: to destroy it, I say, not each man to try to climb up out of it, as your thrift-teachers tell you, but to make an end of it so that no one henceforth can ever fall into it.[2]

Passages such as this are fully informed by the tenets of what Marx and Engels called scientific socialism. Those tenets—the materialist understanding of history, the inevitability of class struggle and the call for class solidarity, the critique of the ideology of self-help, the commitment to revolutionary change—are offered "untheoretically," though with no less sophistication and power.

Almost from the moment it was founded, Morris found himself struggling to keep the Socialist League from breaking into factions as the Social Democratic Federation had done. His desire to keep the League the home of "purists" was bound to encounter resistance, and it did. The resistance came from two directions. From one side came pressure to abandon the League's policy of abstention

---

[1] Eugene D. LeMire, ed., *The Unpublished Lectures of William Morris* (Detroit: Wayne State University Press, 1969).

[2] "Misery and the Way Out" (1884), in May Morris, ed., *William Morris: Artist Writer Socialist*, 2 vols. (London: Longmans, Green & Co., 1936): 2:162.

from voting, from supporting candidates for public office, or from working to reform the system from within through legislation. Morris opposed Parliamentarianism in all its forms, believing that it could not lead to the kind of radical change he envisioned. He had left both the radicals and the Social Democratic Federation as soon as they began to pursue what Morris always referred to as "mere palliative measures." As early as 1886 Morris was warding off attempts by some branches of the Socialist League to pass resolutions calling for "Parliamentary agitation" to be recognized as an acceptable form of socialist action. Morris blocked all such resolutions, primarily by threatening to withdraw from the League. "We should treat Parliament as a representative of the enemy," he wrote to John Bruce Glasier in May 1887, and so "we ought not to put forward palliative measures to be carried through Parliament, for that would be helping them to govern us.... If the League declares for this latter step it ceases to be what I thought it was, and I must try to do what I can outside it" (*Letters*, 2:656).

Morris's resistance to electoral politics effectively isolated him from the main movements of British socialism. By the late 1880s the increasing success of the Fabian Society, which aimed to spread socialist principles by infiltrating local, municipal, and national governing bodies, stood in stark contrast to the dwindling influence of the Socialist League. Within the League itself most members, including some of Morris's closest associates, favored or were willing to tolerate some form of Parliamentarianism. Morris persisted in his opposition. Palliative measures, he argued, failed to address the root causes of oppression. Pursuing such measures simply distracted socialists from their true work. For the same reasons, though he never actively resisted the trades union movement or efforts to establish a Labour Party, Morris declined to support either. By the last years of his life, Morris recognized that, as he told the Fabian leader Sidney Webb, "the world is going your way at the present," though he maintained that "it is not the right way in the end."[1]

---

[1]   Quoted in R. Page Arnot, *William Morris: The Man and the Myth* (London: Lawrence and Wishart, 1964): 108. See also Morris's 1887 lecture, "The Policy of Abstention," in *Artist Writer Socialist*, 2:434–53.

The second pressure on the League came from the anarchist side. From 1888 onward anarchists comprised a significant portion of the League's membership. Morris drew on their support in his campaign against the Parliamentarians, but that was their sole ground of agreement. Though Morris counted among his friends the exiled Russian anarchist philosopher Prince Peter Kropotkin, who took up residence in London in 1886, and though he also professed grim admiration for Sergius Stepniak's accounts of the Nihilist movement in Czarist Russia, he was never persuaded by anarchist arguments. Morris's ideal society was still a *society*; the need for and pleasures of communal action, the beneficial interdependence of individuals, were central to Morris's vision. The radical individualism preached by anarchists was no more palatable to him than were the existing forms of individualism under capitalism. "We consider them dangerous," he wrote of anarchists as early as 1883, "for you see they have no program but destruction, whereas we are re-constructive" (*Letters*, 2:210). As Michael Holzman has pointed out, Morris's insistence in *News from Nowhere* on the "communal organization of the society of the future" is an implicit critique of anarchism.[1]

An explicitly anarchist position is voiced only once in the novel, and it provokes derisive laughter. At one point during their long colloquy, William Guest and Hammond discuss how disagreements on issues of public concern are resolved. What if opinion is evenly divided, or nearly so? Does a simple majority rule? In theory yes, says Hammond, though in practice "reasonable" men and women (and in this new world all have become reasonable) will always prefer consensus to conflict. Thus, on some occasions the minority will abandon its claims once it becomes clear that they are not widely supported, while on other occasions the majority will decide not to exercise its prerogative if doing so will lead to lasting divisions or animosities. When Guest expresses mild skepticism about the workability of this system, Hammond replies that he sees only two alternatives, neither acceptable: either to give over authority to "a class of

---

[1]   Michael Holzman, "Anarchism and Utopia: William Morris's *News from Nowhere*," *ELH* 51:3 (1984): 596.

superior persons capable of judging on all matters without consulting the neighbours," or else to "revert to a system of private property" in order to safeguard "the freedom of the individual will." "There is a third possibility," Guest replies, namely "that every man should be quite independent of every other, and that thus the tyranny of society should be abolished." At this point the two men "burst out laughing very heartily" (135).

By the time Morris wrote that passage, control of the Socialist League had passed into the hands of anarchists. In the summer of 1890 Morris relinquished most of his authority in the day to day running of the organization. He resigned as editor of the League's journal, *Commonweal*, which he had run and almost single-handedly funded since early in 1885. In November the Hammersmith Branch of the Socialist League, of which Morris was a member, severed its ties with the League and renamed itself the Hammersmith Socialist Society. Deprived of Morris's financial support, *Commonweal* suspended publication before the end of 1890. Shortly afterwards the Socialist League itself collapsed in disarray and was disbanded. Morris continued his work through the Hammersmith Socialist Society, though as his health declined after 1892 he took a less active role.

News from Nowhere was serialized in *Commonweal* between January and October of 1890. Its appearance thus coincided with the tumultuous last months of the Socialist League, when work for "the cause" had largely ceased, replaced by factional strife and internal bickerings. *News from Nowhere* is Morris's response to that situation, just as it is his response to the anarchists, parliamentarians, Fabians, trades unionists, radicals, and others who diverged from the "pure socialism" Morris espoused. But it is a response in the special sense of that term we reserve for works of the imagination. Though it is filled with arguments, *News from Nowhere* is not an argument. It makes no claims to completeness or consistency in its depiction of utopia. The novel moves the discussion of socialist ideals into a register wholly distinct from the one Morris uses in his lectures and essays. It aims less to persuade than to seduce. The question Morris addresses here is not: why should we work to create a socialist society? but rather: how would it *feel* to live there?

How would it *feel*? The appeal of the world Morris creates in

News from Nowhere is sensual: a matter of touch, taste, scent, desire. It is a world filled with yearning, but yearning that knows the possibility of fulfillment. We will know we inhabit utopia, Morris says, not because it conforms to the intellectual systems we have made but because it meets our longings and realizes our pleasures and capacities across the whole spectrum of human activity. As Krishan Kumar notes, "what matters most" for Morris "are not institutions but the habits of mind and body generated in the people by their whole way of life, as daily lived."[1] Modernity has corrupted those habits, Morris believed. We thus must learn to desire anew, must work to recover what we are capable of. E. P. Thompson has pointed out that in his utopian writings Morris's goal is precisely "*the education of desire.* This is not the same as 'a moral education' towards a given end; it is, rather, to open a way to aspiration, to 'teach desire to desire, to desire better, to desire more, and above all to desire in a different way.'"[2] Such an education does not supplant—indeed, it supplements—the more formal education in socialist principles that Morris endeavored to impart elsewhere in his writings. What distinguishes *News from Nowhere* is, in Thompson's words, "its *open*, speculative quality, and its *detachment* of the imagination from the demands of conceptual precision.... [It is a] challenge to the imagination [of the reader] to become immersed in the same open exploration."[3] Morris recognized that no one is persuaded by reason alone. The appeal to reason may well be a necessary, but it will never be a sufficient prelude to establishing utopia.

Work, Art, Work of Art

How would it feel? In "How Shall We Live Then?" (1889), a lecture composed shortly before he began writing *News from Nowhere*, Morris urged his listeners to learn to reinhabit their bodies:

---

[1] Krishan Kumar, "A Pilgrimage of Hope: William Morris's Journey to Utopia," *Utopian Studies* 5:1 (1994): 97.

[2] E.P. Thompson, *William Morris: Romantic to Revolutionary*, rev. ed. (New York: Pantheon, 1977): 791. Thompson is in turn quoting (adding his own emphases) from Miguel Abensour's *Utopies et dialectique du socialisme* (1977).

[3] Thompson, 790. Thompson's emphases.

We shall not be happy unless we live like good animals, unless we enjoy the exercise of the ordinary functions of life: eating sleeping loving walking running swimming riding sailing. We must be free to enjoy all these exercises of the body without any sense of shame; without any suspicion that our mental powers are so remarkable and godlike that we are rather above such common things.[1]

Of the "ordinary functions of life" the most important, in Morris's view, is work, which, as he says in "How We Live and How We Might Live," we experience at a deep level as the pleasure of "moving one's limbs and exercising one's bodily powers."[2]

Nearly everything Morris wrote and did grew out of this one belief: there is joy in work. Faith in the redemptive power of work was part of Morris's Victorian inheritance, of course, but he made of that inheritance something new. "The latest Gospel in this world is, Know thy work and do it," Carlyle had written.[3] Morris secularized this gospel, relieving it of the weight of Christian moralism with which Carlyle and his successors, including Ruskin, had burdened it. Where Morris departs from them is in his emphasis on work as joy not duty, creativity not discipline. No other writer of the nineteenth century, certainly not Marx, so thoroughly removes work from the realm of spirituality. Work connects us to our bodies, and our bodies to the physical world, sensually. For Morris work is aligned with art, and both with genius, yet he never speaks in terms of transcendence. Work is life-enhancing rather than soul-enriching. Morris thus urges us to seek fulfillment instead of salvation: to strive, in other words, to be happy like good animals rather than good like stern gods.

---

1   Paul Meier, "An Unpublished Lecture of William Morris," *International Review of Social History* 16 (1971): 261.
2   See Appendix A, 261. Page references to the three lectures by Morris excerpted in Appendix A—"Art and Socialism," "How We Live and How We Might Live," and "The Society of the Future"—are to the present edition. Citations for other works by Morris are given in the appropriate footnotes.
3   *Past and Present* (1843), *The Works of Thomas Carlyle*, ed. H.D. Traill, 30 vols. (London: Chapman & Hall, 1897): 10:196.

To "demand the utter extinction of all asceticism" ("The Society of the Future," 268), as Morris did, is to run counter to Victorian moralism. But it is also to run counter to the cultural movements that grew out of Victorianism, namely aestheticism and Modernism, each of which continued to affirm the value of the ascetic ideal. (This shared affirmation binds together figures as unlike one another as Friedrich Nietzsche, Walter Pater, and T.S. Eliot.) That Morris's writings were seldom taken seriously during the era of High Modernism was due in part to his refusal of asceticism. During his own lifetime he was repeatedly scolded for what many considered an unseemly sensuality. In a long review-essay published in 1891, Maurice Hewlett complained that *News from Nowhere* offered readers "not an earthly, but an earthy, Paradise."[1] Hewlett objected to Morris's dismissal of religious or spiritual pursuits in favor of "the humanism of a sensuous temperament which sees the beauty of appearance and is too indolent or too indifferent to look deeper" (345). The "real remedy" to our current suffering, writes Hewlett, lies in the Christian virtue of "renunciation. Pare off what is clay and clogs aspiration; foster what is ether and strains towards its fount" (346).

Morris indeed renounces renunciation, but Hewlett is mistaken when he calls that gesture a sign of either indolence or hedonism. Instead, Morris's utopia fosters what he calls a "non-ascetic simplicity of life" ("The Society of the Future," 272). Asceticism's opposite is not luxury but *its* opposite, simplicity. As that formula suggests, Morris saw asceticism and luxury as the equally inevitable by-products of industrial capitalism. Each represents a deformation of the senses, an estrangement of the body from the body of the world. The descriptions of the "old world" William Guest hears in *News from Nowhere* invariably focus on this estrangement, as well as on the rehabilitation of the senses that their new world has enabled. "The spirit of the new days, of our days," says old Hammond, is "delight in the life of the world; intense and overweening love of the very skin and surface of the earth on which man dwells, such as a lover has in

---

[1] See Appendix F, 343. Subsequent page references to this essay are given parenthetically in the text.

the fair flesh of the woman he loves" (174). Near the close of the narrative, Ellen exclaims: "O me! O me! How I love the earth, and the seasons, and weather, and all things that deal with it, and all that grows out of it" (241). This exultant cry is rightly taken as the climax of the novel. For Guest, as for Morris, it expresses the deep sense of integration that marks this world: an integration of self and body, body and world, self and others.

As Hewlett recognized, such a world would not be prologue to another. *News from Nowhere* is resolutely secular in outlook. Though Morris remained nominally a Christian throughout his life, he was uninterested in religion. This fact separated him not only from believers such as Hewlett, but also from many socialist critics, for whom a refutation of the tenets of Christianity was central to their critique of late-Victorian culture. Morris engaged such issues by ignoring them. The topic of religion, largely missing from his essays and lectures, comes up not at all in *News from Nowhere*. The novel depicts a world from which religious practices and beliefs have evidently vanished. The story closes at a harvest-feast in a church, but the building's original purpose has been forgotten. Given the time and place in which he lived, Morris's indifference to Christianity is striking. In some ways it must have been more provoking to apologists than the overt denunciations of a Bernard Shaw or an Annie Besant.

With only earth to make their paradise in, men and women need new commandments to live by. Morris offered only one, which he rephrased for different occasions but whose central message was always the same. Here is the version that appears in his lecture "Art and Socialism" (1884):

> *It is right and necessary that all should have work to do which shall be worth doing, and be of itself pleasant to do; and which should be done under such conditions as would make it neither over-wearisome nor over-anxious.* (253)

"Turn that claim about as I may," Morris continues, "think of it as long as I can, I cannot find that it is an exorbitant claim." Yet if its truth were accepted, "the face of the world would be changed."

Implicit in this formulation is the distinction Morris insisted on between "useful work" and "useless toil." Throughout his life Morris censured the thoughtlessness (and the heartlessness) of those who celebrate labor as an intrinsic good and leave it at that. One "article of the creed of modern morality [is] that all labour is good in itself," which is "a convenient belief to those who live on the labour of others."[1] Morris was acutely aware that for most of those who came to hear his lectures, work was not a blessing but a curse. To the suffering and privation endured by many workers was added the degradation and demoralization attendant on all "toil" that does not engage the full capabilities of the worker and that results in products that neither give real pleasure nor render genuine service to others. "I tell you I feel dazed at the thought of the immensity of work which is undergone for the making of useless things" ("Art and Socialism," 253). Morris lived through the historical moment in Great Britain in which the lineaments of modern consumer culture came fully into view, and the vehemence of his response is testimony to the shock of the encounter. He was among the first to recognize the human consequences of an economic system predicated on the ceaseless production of consumer desires for artificial necessities. Early socialist reformers such as Robert Owen and Charles Fourier had focused attention, rightly, on the appalling plight of workers under industrial capitalism. Two generations later Morris widens the view in order to show how worker and consumer alike had become enslaved to the gimcrack. Here indeed is Morris's version of Hell: "many thousands of men and women making Nothing with terrible and inhuman toil" so that "not over happy people [can] buy it to harass themselves with its encumbrance" ("Art and Socialism," 254).

Morris is eloquent on the degradations of consumer culture in Victorian Britain, though other observers were equally so. What finally distinguishes Morris is—to borrow from the title of his best-known lecture—the intensity of his vision not just of "how we live" but of "how we might live." At the focal point of that vision is the concept of useful work. To have redeemed work from drudgery and pointless toil is the great achievement of the new world

---

[1] "Useful Work *versus* Useless Toil" (1884), *Collected Works*, 23:98.

William Guest finds himself in. "This change from the conditions of the older world," Guest says to old Hammond, "seems to me far greater and more important than all the other changes you have told me about" (137). In Hammond's world all that is made is needed, and all making is pleasure. Thinking and doing are integrated, a state of being Morris associates with the medieval guilds:

> Men whose hands were skilled in fashioning could not help thinking the while, and soon found out their deft fingers could express some part of the tangle of their thoughts, and that this new pleasure hindered not their daily work, for in the very labour they lived by lay the material in which their thought could be embodied; and thus, though they laboured, they laboured somewhat for their pleasure and uncompelled, and had conquered the curse of toil; and were men.[1]

As this passage suggests, in Morris's view the desire to make beautiful things is innately human. Art is simply the material form we give to the satisfaction we feel in exercising our physical and mental energies. As Norman Kelvin points out, "the psychological connection between the human desire for pleasure and the human desire to make or enjoy art is at the heart of Morris's socialism" (*Letters*, 1:xlvi). Released from the disfiguring forces of modernity, men and women are free to achieve their humanity, which is always bound up with "making" of one kind or another. For Morris, writes Kelvin, "the 'wanting' of art and the gratifying of the want is as *primary* as pleasure-seeking in sex is for Freud. The desire for art is in no sense, for Morris, a sublimation of a drive for sexual or any other gratification. Moreover, for Morris it is *rational* to seek pleasure in art ... [so that] the primary human instinct is always a constructive and life-enhancing one; never, indeed, is it in conflict with the needs of a rational society or with another part of the self" (*Letters*, 1:xlvii).

Individual desire and communal need are indistinguishable in Nowhere, as are pleasure and beauty. Guest finds that the joy he

---

[1]   "The Lesser Arts of Life" (1882), *Collected Works*, 22:236.

takes in contemplating the beauties of this new world is unalloyed, precisely because beauty no longer exacts a price. "Here I could enjoy everything without an afterthought of the injustice and miserable toil which made my leisure" (183). Everything made fulfills a need, or rather, needs, since maker and user are equally fulfilled, and in multiple ways, by the very activities of making, using, contemplating, enjoying. Morris is nearly alone among late-Victorian social critics in asserting that every document of civilization need not also be a document of barbarism. More common is the view expressed by Hyacinth Robinson in Henry James's 1886 novel *The Princess Casamassima*. Having pledged himself to a mysterious political group committed to violent revolution, Hyacinth repents once he convinces himself that, tragically but inalterably, social justice is incompatible with culture. It cannot be denied, Hyacinth concedes, that "the monuments and treasures of art, ... the conquests of learning and taste, the general fabric of civilization as we know it" are based "upon all the despotisms, the cruelties, the exclusions, the monopolies and rapacities of the past." Yet thanks to them "the world is less impracticable and life more tolerable."[1] For Morris, this seeming truism—that beauty comes into the world only at a profound cost in human suffering—is indefensible in its intellectual complacency. Where James allows Hyacinth's recognition of the historical conjunction of art and oppression to conclude his social analysis, Guest's identical recognition is Morris's starting point, precisely because it articulates the "intolerable" problem to be overcome.

At the same time, Morris is perfectly willing to let go of art, or at least the conception of art implicit in Hyacinth's formulation. Morris believes that "genuine Art is always an expression of pleasure in Labour" (*Letters*, 2:329). That definition effectively eliminates "the artist" from the roster of human types. Northrop Frye points out that Morris "has nothing of the romantic elitism that regards the creative person or 'genius' as a special form of humanity."[2] Creativity is not the distinguishing mark of a special class but our

---

1   Henry James, *The Princess Casamassima* (1886; rpt. Harmondsworth: Penguin, 1986): 396-97.
2   Northrop Frye, "The Meeting of Past and Future in William Morris," *Studies in Romanticism* 21 (1982): 310.

common inheritance. In a similar vein, Morris resists the distinction between so-called "low" arts (the product of "mere" skill or craft) and "high" arts (the product of genius or inspiration). This resistance is most apparent in Morris's views on poetry. In contrast to the received view of poetry as the art-form most closely aligned with genius, Morris invariably describes his own poetry-making as an acquired skill, analogous to the skills needed to weave a carpet or dye a fabric. Frye correctly notes that this "determination to treat poetry as though it were a 'minor' or 'useful' art has a political reference: he wants to see the major arts democratized, made the possession of everyone like the arts of design" (310). It is also the case that Morris wants to distance art-making from the idea of alienation. For him true art does not originate in alienation from the social world but is instead the sign and expression of integration. The tortured genius model of artistic production, so familiar in this period and afterwards, has no place in Morris's system.

If for Morris art is another name for the products of unalienated labor, and if all labor under capitalism is alienated, then it should follow that Morris believed that no true art was being produced in his time. This is in fact what he believed. He included his own labors in this indictment. "I regard my work as far as it pretends to produce anything as absolutely worthless," Morris wrote to Thomas Cobden-Sanderson in 1885, "and what I say of my own work I feel of everybody else's that has in it any pretence to art or sentiment. Society is to my mind wholly corrupt, & I can take no deep-seated pleasure in anything it turns out" (*Letters*, 2:381). Two years earlier, in a letter to Georgiana Burne-Jones, he had put the case even more bluntly:

> The arts have got to die, what is left of them, before they can be born again. You know my views on the matter; I apply them to myself as well as to others. This would not, I admit, prevent my writing poetry any more than it prevents my doing my pattern work, because the mere personal pleasure of it urges one to the work; but it prevents my looking at it as a sacred duty. (*Letters*, 2:217)

In *News from Nowhere* it is not quite accurate to say the arts have been reborn, since the inhabitants of Nowhere do not recognize a separate category of activity called artistic labor. "The production of what used to be called art" Old Hammond tells Guest, "has no name amongst us now" precisely "because it has become a necessary part of the labour of every man who produces." He suggests that a new name for art might be, simply, "work-pleasure" (176). Indeed, in Nowhere all activities that are pleasurable and useful are valued the same. Little or no distinction is made between activities that result in "artistic" objects (for instance, tapestry-weaving, metal-working, or mural-painting), activities that produce useful objects (cloth-spinning, glass-blowing, cooking, house-building, pipe-carving), and activities that provide service of some kind (cleaning, teaching, road-mending, water-ferrying, shop-keeping, harvesting), in part because everyone practices several of these skills without specializing in any. There are no professionals in Nowhere, though accomplished amateurs are everywhere. At the same time, the "fine" arts have apparently disappeared from the world. In Nowhere we find builders but no architects, musicians and singers but no composers, carpenters and carvers of wood but no sculptors, dramatic performers but no playwrights, painters of frescoes but no portraitists or landscape artists, book-makers and scribes but no poets. In Morris's utopia creativity is generally expressed through doing; it is closely tied to the expenditure of physical energy. More sedentary or contemplative activities are viewed with muted but discernable mistrust, while "book-learning" is not encouraged.

This revaluing of the fields of artistic and intellectual activity is Morris's implicit comment on the fetishizing of art that was so prominent a feature of the later nineteenth century. While he values highly the products of the imagination, Morris is never tempted to call them sacred or transcendent. In any case, the desire for the transcendent and the sacred does not exist in Nowhere, the world itself being sufficient. This sufficiency accounts in a different way for the absence of novels in Morris's utopia. Itself the closest thing to a novel Morris ever wrote, *News from Nowhere* conducts an extended (though in many places ambivalent) critique of the genre. Morris himself felt lifelong affection for the works of Walter Scott and Charles Dickens (Guest recalls "many pleasant hours passed in reading Dickens" [71]), but for the most part he did not read novels. He recognized that, as the preeminent art form of the Victorian middle class, the novel was among that class's most powerful tools for perpetuating its own values and interests. The genre was thus in Morris's view symptomatic of modernity's "illth." Its chief task was to naturalize the oppressive social and economic arrangements of the modern world, Morris claimed, and make them seem therefore inevitable. Alter the arrangements, and the novel would have no purpose. Just as there were no novels prior to the rise of the middle class, so there will be none once that class has gone. In "The Society of the Future," Morris prophesized, "you will no longer be able to have novels relating the troubles of a middle-class couple in their struggle towards social uselessness, because the material for such literary treasures will have passed away" (273).

Such material *has* passed away in Nowhere, and with it the novel. Strangely, though, a residual longing remains. The novel, it seems, is the sole art form in this new world about which it is possible to hold differing opinions. Ellen voices the majority opinion when she says that "there is something loathsome" about the attention given in novels to the "sham troubles" and "dreary ... feelings and aspirations" of middle class characters while ignoring the real world, which "dug and sewed and baked and built and carpentered round about those useless—animals" (193). On the other hand, the apologists for the genre—Boffin and the "old Grumbler"—are comic characters, and their enthusiasm for such "antiquarian" pursuits is a clear sign of their eccentricity. Yet their passion persists despite all rational objection. Everyone agrees that the novel is outworn, possessing no organic relation to the new society, but novels continue to be read and (albeit rarely) written. The implicit justification for the genre's continuance is that it offers windows into alien ways of life. For old Hammond, novels are historical documents of life before the change came. For Boffin, they are opportunities to revel in the "local colour" of bygone times. Most important, for the Grumbler they are testimony to the creative value of conflict and competition. Weak as it is, the Grumbler's objection to the peace of Nowhereian society is the one sustained effort within the narrative to imagine values which that society cannot encompass. In the Grumbler's view, conflict is invigorating, life-enhancing, productive—and interesting. His position finds a partial advocate in Clara, who expresses muted dissatisfaction with the placidity of their lives. "I wish we were interesting enough to be written or painted about," she says (147). Conflict is also, the Grumbler suggests, innate to human nature, not to be repressed without cost. One cost is the disappearance of novels, which trade heavily in conflict to such good effect. The Grumbler takes great pleasure in reading "a good old book with plenty of fun in it, like Thackeray's 'Vanity Fair.' Why don't you write books like that now?" he challenges Dick, who has no answer (199).

Another cost, more difficult to articulate perhaps, lies in a diminishing of the range and complexity of human emotional response. "Do you know," Ellen teases Guest near the end of their time together, "I begin to suspect you of wanting to nurse a sham sorrow, like the ridiculous characters in some of those queer old novels that I have come across now and then" (237). Guest silently acknowledges the truth of her charge and resolves to sigh no more. He recognizes that the emotion he feels—a complex amalgam of self-pity, anxiety over the future, and sexual yearning for Ellen—marks him as a product of the world he came from. The very complexity of his emotion distinguishes it from any likely to be felt by the inhabitants of Nowhere, whose desires are always frank, whole, self-evident, and capable of being met. In Ellen's view, Guest's sorrow cannot be other than a "sham sorrow" because there is no objective reason to feel as he does. He has, she implies, simply worked himself into a state—just like the "unreal" characters in novels do. Yet as readers of Morris's novel we are likely to feel that Guest is the only "real" character in sight, the only one whose depth and range of emotional response has a touch of verisimilitude. The psychological flattening of the other figures in the book serves a purpose for Morris: among the other appeals of a world so thoroughly committed to "non-ascetic simplicity of life" is the non-ascetic simplicity of the desires such a life calls forth. Yet it is one of Morris's achievements in *News from Nowhere* that he is also able to suggest the affective diminishments such simplicity may lead to.

Eros, Gender, and Domesticity

Such diminishments aside, the directness with which the citizens of Nowhere feel and express sexual desire is among their most appealing traits. "For a political blueprint," Jan Marsh comments, "*News from Nowhere* is a surprisingly sexy book."[1] Because a yearning for beauty is for Morris the fundamental form taken by Eros, aesthetic desire in Nowhere is often directed at men and women. Nearly everyone is physically beautiful. In his lectures Morris often claims that under modern economic conditions people cannot be other than ugly. Wage slavery makes physical comeliness impossible for oppressed poor and idle rich alike. In Nowhere, "work-pleasure" in all its forms has produced a society of men and women whose bodies are, to use one of Morris's favorite praise-words, "well-knit." Guest's delight in the loveliness of those he encounters forms a significant portion of the pleasure he takes in being in this new world. His openly sexual daydreaming discomforts some readers, who feel that Guest (and behind him, Morris) considers the women he encounters as no more than occasions for erotic reverie. Yet in the no longer shame-filled world of Nowhere, men are just as likely to be the objects of such reverie. On the journey up the Thames to the haymaking, for example, Clara gazes "fondly" at Dick as he pulls at the oars of their boat, and Guest speculates that "she was seeing him in her mind's eye showing his splendid form at its best amidst the rhymed strokes of the scythes" (187). The forthright pleasure she takes in contemplating his "man's beauty" (188) is shadowed by no embarrassment or self-consciousness. Like the other women in Nowhere, Clara is a desiring subject and not simply an object of desire.

Such a change in sexual relations could occur only in a society in which marriage and the family had been transformed. *News from Nowhere* descends from critiques of marriage such as John Stuart Mill and Harriet Taylor's *The Subjection of Women* (1869), Engels's *The Origin of the Family, Private Property and the State* (1884), August Bebel's *Women and Socialism* (1885), and

---

[1] Jan Marsh, "*News from Nowhere* as Erotic Dream," *The Journal of the William Morris Society* 8: 4 (1990): 19.

Eleanor Marx's *The Woman Question* (1885). Morris follows Engels especially in insisting that the bourgeois family be recognized for what it is, namely, an economic unit continuous with the larger structures of capitalism. The modern family, Engels wrote, "is founded on the open or concealed domestic slavery of the wife," a slavery which provides for the husband's freedom to pursue his economic interests in the public sphere.[1] Enforced monogamy (at least for women) in addition helps ensure the smooth transmission of property from one generation to the next. Engels explicitly likened the wife's position in marriage to that of the proletariat under capitalism. The comparison, unnuanced as it was, nevertheless helped focus attention on domestic labor *as* labor—uncompensated, unvalued labor that was indispensable to the capitalist economy.

Engels was among the first to call for an end to "domestic slavery" arising from the sexual division of labor. Yet he, as well as many subsequent socialists and feminists, continued to equate domestic work—cooking, cleaning, child-rearing, and so on—with mere drudgery. Morris departs from this valuation, arguing that the drudgery arises not from the work itself but from the social relations under which it takes place. Like other forms of work in Nowhere, domestic labor is no longer alienated. Once people can give free play to their "sense of interest in the ordinary occupations of life" (108), as Guest puts it, household chores accrue dignity. "Perhaps you think housekeeping an unimportant occupation, not deserving of respect," Hammond challenges Guest. "I believe that was the opinion of the 'advanced' women of the nineteenth century, and their male backers" (107). Guest is admonished not to condescend to those whose interests and skills find expression in housekeeping.

On the other hand, in Nowhere those whose interests and skills find expression in housekeeping are almost exclusively women. Morris's revaluation of domestic work leaves more or less intact the sexual division of labor. In his disquisition on housework,

---

[1]   Friedrich Engels, *The Origin of the Family, Private Property and the State, in Light of the Researches of Lewis H. Morgan*, trans. Alex West (New York: International Publishers, 1942): 65.

Hammond still equates "domestic work" with "women's work," and it is not hard to hear the patronizing note. Morris himself seems usually to assume that women are naturally fitted to perform certain tasks better than men, and vice versa. This is not to deny that there are wide areas of overlap—tasks done equally well by women and men—but it does indicate the extent to which Morris adheres to conventional gender stereotyping. In general, his pronouncements on women's issues tend to be muted or in passing. Florence Boos and William Boos have suggested that Morris felt constrained from speaking openly on women's rights by his close association with Belfort Bax, with whom he frequently collaborated in writing for the Socialist League.[1] Bax's anti-feminism was virulent, as was that of other members of the League. Morris almost certainly found their misogyny distasteful, but was unwilling to risk public dispute on the issue for fear that it would further fracture the League. Even apart from such tactical considerations, though, Morris tried to justify his avoidance of women's issues by claiming that they were subsumed within the larger project of socialism.

On one aspect of the marriage question, though, Morris was in advance of most of his contemporaries. From early in his career he was an outspoken advocate for women's right of sexual choice. Like Bernard Shaw, Morris argued that for women bourgeois marriage was just legal prostitution or, as he put it in a letter to Charles Faulkner, "simply a form of ordinary market exploitation" (*Letters*, 2:584). Lacking economic power, women do not have the luxury to pursue "genuine unions of passion & affection" but must instead marry to ensure their financial security (*Letters*, 2:584). Thanks to the double standard regarding promiscuity, "under our present circumstances [marriage] does not burden men of the world at all since there are plenty of whores in the market owing to our system of industrial exploitage," while women remain bound to the code of sexual fidelity (*Letters*, 2:585). Once released from economic bondage, men and women will be free to form unions based solely on what Morris

---

[1]   See Florence Boos and William Boos, "*News from Nowhere* and Victorian Socialist-Feminism," *Nineteenth-Century Contexts* 14:1 (1990): 3-32.

engagingly calls "decent animalism plus ... human kindliness" (*Letters*, 2:584).

Even those unions will be dissolvable, as they are in Nowhere. As Hammond explains to Guest, once marriage is no longer primarily a means to securing property and capital, it need not be legislated:

> We do not deceive ourselves, indeed, or believe that we can get rid of all the trouble that besets the dealings between the sexes. We know that we must face the unhappiness that comes of man and woman confusing the relations between natural passion, and sentiment, and the friendship which, when things go well, softens the awakening from passing illusions: but we are not so mad as to pile up degradation on that unhappiness by engaging in sordid squabbles about livelihood and position, and the power of tyrannizing over the children who have been the results of love or lust. (104)

Like Thomas Hardy, Morris draws attention to the folly of basing sexual unions on the illusion that affection and desire never fade. In the same letter to Faulkner quoted above, Morris complains that current mores dictate that "once 2 people have committed themselves to one act of copulation they are to be tied together through life no matter how miserable it makes them" (*Letters*, 2:584-85). Unlike Hardy, though, Morris does not punish his fictional women for rebelling against such strictures or for exerting their right of sexual choice. The most quietly revolutionary aspect of *News from Nowhere* lies in the equanimity with which everyone (including the author) treats Clara's desertion of and eventual reunion with Dick. Though the complexities of the situation are fully acknowledged, no shadow of moral censure or even of social impropriety is allowed to hang over Clara. The obvious contrast here is with the tortures Sue Bridehead is made to suffer in Hardy's *Jude the Obscure* (1896). Sue is severely punished by a hypocritical society and (less candidly) by a disapproving author for the fluctuations in her affections. Similar changes in Clara's feelings simply mark her as human. As Dick remarks with studied understatement, "love is not a very reasonable thing" (84).

With marriage thus reformed in Nowhere, the family no longer has the ideological prestige it enjoyed in Victorian culture. In the absence of any "bond of coercion, legal or social," families are held together only "by mutual liking and affection" (127), which means that sometimes they do not hold together at all. Other domestic groupings and configurations exist alongside the traditional family unit, and are accepted as viable. The raising and education of children is seen as a community concern. Indeed, the freeing of children from what Morris considered the tyranny of parents would be among the first beneficial effects of socialism. In Nowhere "domesticity"—that sacred word—has given way to other forms of communal relation. The hearth has been replaced by the common room and the market square: public spaces rather than private.

It is thus appropriate that Guest's final vision of this utopia is of a communal dinner: a feast to celebrate the harvest. Appropriate, too, that the festival occurs on the grounds of a "many-gabled old house" (240)—Morris's own beloved Kelmscott Manor—that is no longer the home of a single family but instead the gathering place for an entire community. As many have noted, Guest's journey up the idyllic Thames is a secular pilgrim's progress, with Kelmscott Manor as Morris's version of the New Jerusalem. Though the house is inevitably associated by readers with Morris's own history, in the novel it is carefully divested of all merely personal significances. It is no longer anyone's home, no longer "property." Guest notices that the interior is neither furnished nor decorated, and he decides that "the house itself and its associations was the ornament of the country life amidst which it had been left stranded from old times" (241-42). It is now itself "a piece of natural beauty" (242) as well as a repository of historical knowledge, what Ellen calls "the gathered crumbs of happiness of the confused and turbulent past" (240). The house has passed out of the hands of any individual to become a visible sign of the new community. Guest (and Morris) can reclaim it precisely because it is "his" no more.

Having reached this point, Guest's journey can go—need go—no further. Embedded in his final contentment, though, is the implicit question that has driven Morris's narrative throughout, and which produces the yearning that even at the end mingles with Guest's joy. How do we get here?

How the Change Came

How do we get there? Is it possible to achieve such a utopia? Another way to ask this is: how does historical change come about? What are its mechanisms? Such questions vexed Morris just as they vexed his contemporaries, and like them he often gave conflicting answers. From early on he was skeptical of models of historical change based on a belief in gradual progress or amelioration. Writing to Georgiana Burne-Jones in 1883, six months before he joined the Social Democratic Federation, Morris confessed that "the hope in me has been that matters would mend gradually." Now, though, "the mixture of tyranny and hypocrisy with which the world is governed" makes him and all "thinking people so sick at heart that [we] are driven from all interest in politics save revolutionary politics" (*Letters*, 2:51).

What Morris meant by "revolutionary politics" is not always clear. In the same letter to Georgiana Burne-Jones he refers vaguely to "the last struggle, which must needs be mingled with violence and madness" but which he hopes "would be so short as scarcely to count" (*Letters*, 2:51). Such optimism came quickly to seem misplaced, yet Morris was unable to give more than intermittent assent to Marx's belief in the inevitability of class warfare. "I have a religious hatred to all war and violence," he wrote to Thomas Coglan Horsfall in February 1883. He has therefore tried, Morris continues, through his socialist work to sow the seeds of "goodwill and justice that *may* make it possible for the next great revolution, which will be a social one, to work itself out without violence being an essential part of it" (*Letters*, 2:157). Eight months later he was writing to Horsfall again, but this time to assert that "the basis of all change must be, as it has always been, the antagonism of classes" and to predict that the coming struggle will have "its terrible side," may even "ruin all civilization for a time" (*Letters*, 2:238). On the whole, Morris's imagination did not run to the apocalyptic, though on occasion he indulged in fantasies of a world wiped clean and begun anew.

"I *know* now [civilization] is doomed to destruction," he wrote to Georgiana Burne-Jones in 1885, "and probably before very long: what a joy it is to think of! and how often it consoles me to think of barbarism once more flooding the world, and real feelings and passions, however rudimentary, taking the place of our wretched hypocrisies" (*Letters*, 2:436).

His experiences in the Social Democratic Federation led Morris to reject the use of "agitation" as a political tool. He considered Hyndman's taunting of the government and his threats of mass uprising to be worse than useless, since they did not correspond to any popular will. "Education & organization ... have been neglected for agitation," Morris complained of Hyndman's tactics, "which in the present state of things is nearly worthless; for when you have agitated miserable & ignorant people, what are you to advise them to do [?]" (*Letters*, 3:372). Morris believed that the successful uprising, when it came, would come spontaneously. It would reflect the coherent and directed will of the masses, who would need no one from outside their ranks to advise them what to do once they recognized their collective interests and how to secure them. "Preaching wont turn men into revolutionists," Morris wrote to J.W. Browne, "but men driven into revolutionary ideas may be educated to look to the right aims instead of wild folly" (*Letters*, 2:402). In effect, the successful revolution in the streets would be the sign of a prior revolution in the minds of working men and women. Then, Morris confided to his "Socialist Diary" of 1887, "riots or shows of force" would be simply the most visible "indications of the rising tide," a tide impossible to turn back.[1]

The futility of premature uprising was confirmed for Morris by the events of "Bloody Sunday," November 13, 1887. On that day some 10,000 demonstrators attempting to march on Trafalgar Square were met and violently dispersed by a large contingent of police and soldiers under the command of the Commissioner of Police, Sir Charles Warren. The conflict had been preparing for several months. Through the summer and fall of 1887

---

[1] *William Morris's Socialist Diary*, ed. Florence S. Boos (London: Journeyman Press, 1985): 32

Trafalgar Square was the site of numerous open air meetings and demonstrations, most relating to the question of unemployment. Official responses to these gatherings grew steadily harsher. The Square was cleared by mounted police on three occasions in October, then three more times in early November. Finally, on November 8, Warren banned all further meetings on the Square "in consequence of the disorderly scenes which have recently occurred" there and on the pretext that the Square was legally the property of the Crown.[1] The ban changed the terms of the conflict, from unemployment to free speech, and it directly provoked the demonstration on the thirteenth. Groups of socialists, radicals, anarchists, Irish nationalists, and others marched towards Trafalgar Square from different quarters of London. Before any of them reached their destination, they were attacked by Warren's forces. After a series of brief but bloody scuffles, the marchers fled in disarray. The brutality of the police response surprised even those who had come expecting a fight. Though no one was killed, several hundred were injured, many seriously. The day itself was an utter defeat for the demonstrators, but "Bloody Sunday" quickly became a rallying cry for the radical-socialist cause, and remained so for several generations.[2]

Morris, who marched with the Clerkenwell branch of the Socialist League, saw the events of November 13 at first-hand, and they made a lasting impression on him. They confirmed his sense that the government, backed by the middle classes, would not hesitate to use violence to protect its interests. Moreover, the immediate collapse of the Bloody Sunday demonstration in the face of such violence strengthened Morris's belief that the conditions for a successful revolution were still well in the future. He took refuge in the hope that the government's recourse to open violence was "distinctly a sign of the recrudescence of the reaction which in its turn is a sign of the advance of the revolution" (*Letters*, 2:724), but it was not a hope he could sustain with much conviction.

The events of Bloody Sunday form a leitmotif that runs throughout *News from Nowhere*. Coming upon the former site of

---

[1] Warren's proclamation was reprinted in the *Times* (London): 9 November 1887, 10.
[2] See Appendix E for accounts of the events of this day.

Trafalgar Square (now an orchard), Guest has a hallucinatory vision of "a sweltering and excited crowd" confronted by "a four-fold line of big men clad in blue" in "the greyness of the chilly November afternoon" (90). In Guest's ensuing conversation with Dick and the old man accompanying them, the history of that day is briefly given. Shortly afterwards, during his talk with old Hammond, Guest hears of three subsequent confrontations that took place on the Square, each of them a repetition of the ur-conflict of Bloody Sunday. But they are repetitions with a difference. In each case the violence of the authorities escalates, but it is matched by the increasing self-consciousness of the demonstrators, a growing awareness of themselves as the vehicles of historical transformation. In Hammond's version of twentieth-century history, the "education and organization" of the working class has been accomplished. Thus, the final confrontation, the "Trafalgar Square Massacre" of 1952, does not, as Guest surmises, "put an end to the whole revolution" (160), as it would have in his time. Instead, Hammond triumphantly informs him, it begins the civil war that eventually leads to the utopia they now inhabit.

What enables this transforming change in consciousness, though, is left unspecified. Hammond says little more than that it arose from "a longing for freedom and equality, akin if you please to the unreasonable passion of the lover" (149), which avoids the question of how such a longing—abundant enough in Morris's own day—came to be translated into coherent and effective social action. Having posited such a change, however, Morris goes on to offer a canny and detailed overview of the course of the revolution itself. *News from Nowhere* is alone among utopian fictions in the attention it gives to the revolutionary period, as well as in its frank acknowledgement of the costs in human terms of radical historical change. In 1884 Morris had written to Robert Thomson of his faith that the "determination [to revolt] once come to by the people its execution will be easy, and the details of it will clear up one after the other" (*Letters*, 2:305). In Hammond's account the execution is neither easy nor clear, an indication of how far Morris's thinking had progressed in the intervening years.

Hammond's two-part narrative—"How the Change Came" followed by "The Beginning of the New Life"—unfolds across the mid-point of Morris's novel. When that narrative is done, we have reached the end of history. The success of the revolution is the end of historical change, the end of the need for change. That is utopia. Having reached Nowhere, we need go nowhere else. Yet even as Morris's narrative moves closer to its final vision of the earthly paradise, here called Kelmscott Manor, it opens up a new space for doubt. Musing on what Guest has told her of past time, Ellen wonders whether people in Nowhere have become

> too careless of the history of the past.... Who knows? happy as we are, times may alter; we may be bitten with some impulse towards change, and many things may seem too wonderful for us to resist, too exciting not to catch at, if we do not know that they are but phases of what has been before; and withal ruinous, deceitful, and sordid. (233)

Earlier in the novel, Guest is told that few now study history since "it is mostly in periods of turmoil and strife and confusion that people much care" about it (79). A few continue to study the records of the past, but the society as a whole exists in a perpetual present. For most, "the last harvest, the last baby, the last knot of carving in the market-place is history enough" (102). The fruit orchard that stands on the site of Trafalgar Square can stand as a symbol for the replacement of history's linear time with the cyclical time of nature. Guest's "phantasmagoria of another day" (90) as he stands on this site—his nightmare vision of a human past which for him overlays Nowhere's timeless present—clearly marks him as an outsider in this world.

The historical innocence of the inhabitants of Nowhere is viewed with decided ambivalence by Guest, and by Morris as well. That ambivalence is palpable at different moments in the text, nowhere more so than during Old Hammond's account of the yearly May Day celebrations:

> "On that occasion the custom is for the prettiest girls to sing some of the old revolutionary songs, and those which were the groans of the discontent, once so hopeless, on the very spots where those terrible crimes of class-murder were

committed day by day for so many years. To a man like me, who has studied the past so diligently, it is a curious and touching sight to see some beautiful girl, daintily clad, and crowned with flowers from the neighbouring meadows, standing amongst the happy people, on some mound where of old time stood the wretched apology for a house, a den in which men and women lived packed amongst the filth like pilchards in a cask; lived in such a way that they could only have endured it, as I said just now, by being degraded out of humanity—to hear the terrible words of threatening and lamentation coming from her sweet and beautiful lips, and she unconscious of their real meaning: to hear her, for instance, singing Hood's Song of the Shirt, and to think that all the time she does not understand what it is all about— a tragedy grown inconceivable to her and her listeners. Think of that, if you can, and of how glorious life is grown!"

"Indeed," said I, "it is difficult for me to think of it" (113–14).

The flat understatement of Guest's response allows us to acknowledge the surpassing glory of a world where historical "remembrance" is so little needed while also giving us a space to feel unease, even dissatisfaction, at this state of affairs. The neglect of history entails dangers, as Ellen suggests. But more than that, for Morris it impoverishes even the present, robs it of a certain richness of texture. It is a sign of his intellectual honesty that, having pursued his vision to its logical ends, Morris did not pretend that even he would be wholly content there. In Morris's view, utopia is not achieved once. It is the object of our continual quest, and for that quest a sharpened historical consciousness is requisite. Even in Nowhere, there is reason to ponder, as Morris's narrator does in *A Dream of John Ball*, "how men fight and lose the battle, and the thing they fought for comes about in spite of their defeat, and when it comes turns out not to be what they meant, and other men have to fight for what they meant under another name."[1]

---

[1] *Collected Works*, 16:231–32.

William Morris: A Brief Chronology

1834   Born March 24 in Walthamstow, third of nine
        surviving children of Emma (Shelton) Morris and
        William Morris, a well-to-do financier in the bill-
        broking business.

1847   William Morris the elder dies.

1853   Enters Exeter College, Oxford, with intention to
        study for the Church. First reads Ruskin's *Stones of
        Venice* and Carlyle's *Past and Present*.

1854   Tours Belgium and northern France.

1855   On his twenty-first birthday, comes into an annual
        income of £900, enough to live comfortably on.
        Makes a second tour of France. Abandons his
        intention to enter the Church in favor of a career as
        an artist. Reads Chaucer, Malory, the Pre-
        Raphaelite poets.

1856   First published poems appear in *The Oxford and
        Cambridge Magazine*, which Morris founded and
        financed. Takes his B.A. degree. Articles himself to the
        Oxford architect G. E. Street and moves to London to
        work in Street's office there. Meets the Pre-
        Raphaelite poet and painter Dante Gabriel Rossetti.
        Before the end of the year Morris leaves Street and
        takes up painting. Continues to write poetry.

1857   Meets Jane Burden.

1858   Publishes his first book of poems, *The Defence of
        Guenevere and Other Poems*. Tours France.

1859   Marries Jane Burden on April 26. Tour of France,
        Belgium, and the Rhineland.

1860   William and Jane move into Red House, Upton,
        Kent, built for them by Morris's friend Philip Webb.

1861   Jane Alice ("Jenny") Morris born January 17. The
        firm of Morris, Marshall, Faulkner, and Co.
        founded; Morris begins to design and sell furniture
        and home decorations. "The Firm," as it was
        known, was reestablished as Morris and Co. in 1875

with Morris as sole owner. It remained in operation under that name until 1940.

1862   Mary ("May") Morris born March 25.

1865   Red House sold. Morris family moves to 26 Queen Square, London, which also houses the offices and shops of The Firm.

1867   Publishes *The Life and Death of Jason*.

1868   The first volume of *The Earthly Paradise* published. Morris meets Eiríkr Magnússon and begins studying Icelandic.

1869   First translations and retellings of Icelandic sagas published. Jane falls ill; Morris accompanies her to the spa at Bad Ems.

1870   The second and third volumes of *The Earthly Paradise* published. Collaborates with Magnússon on translation of the *Völsunga Saga*. Produces his first illuminated manuscript, *A Book of Verse*; over the next several years Morris would produce illuminated versions of portions of *The Aeneid* and the *Rubáiyát of Omar Khayyám*.

1871   In joint tenancy with Rossetti, takes Kelmscott Manor, Gloucestershire. Rossetti, Jane, Jenny, and May take up residence, with Morris dividing time between there and London. In July travels to Iceland.

1872   *Love is Enough* published.

1873   Visits northern Italy in the spring. Second trip to Iceland in the summer.

1874   Rossetti moves out of Kelmscott Manor and gives up his share of the joint tenancy.

1875   Publishes *Three Northern Love Stories* and a translation of *The Aeneid*. Begins working with fabric dyes.

1876   First public involvement in political issues; becomes treasurer of Eastern Question Association. *Sigurd the Volsung* published.

1877   Founds Society for the Protection of Ancient Buildings (familiarly known as "Anti-Scrape"). Delivers first public lecture, on "The Decorative Arts."

1878   Begins tapestry weaving. Tours northern Italy with

Jane and their daughters. Purchases Kelmscott House, Upper Mall, Hammersmith.

1879 Becomes treasurer of National Liberal League. Meets H.M. Hyndman.

1881 Purchases a seven-acre site at Merton Abbey in south London and moves the workshops of Morris and Co. there.

1882 First collection of essays, *Hopes and Fears for Art*, published. Rossetti dies on April 9.

1883 Joins Hyndman's Democratic Federation (renamed the next year the Social Democratic Federation) and announces conversion to socialism. Reads French translation of Marx's *Das Kapital*. Tapestry weaving started at Merton Abbey works.

1884 Writes for (and partially underwrites) *Justice*, the paper of the Social Democratic Federation. Co-authors *A Summary of the Principles of Socialism* with Hyndman. Publishes *Chants for Socialists*. Begins frequent lecturing on socialist topics, which will continue through the early 1890s. Increasing dissension with Hyndman leads Morris to resign from the S.D.F. in December.

1885 Along with other ex-S.D.F. members, establishes the Socialist League. Founds (as well as funds and edits) the League's paper, *Commonweal*. Publishes his long narrative poem on the Paris Commune, *The Pilgrims of Hope*, in *Commonweal*. Arrested in September during a free speech demonstration; charges dismissed within twenty-four hours.

1886 "Black Monday" demonstrations of the unemployed in Trafalgar Square on February 8. Morris publishes *A Dream of John Ball* in *Commonweal*. Co-authors with E. Belfort Bax "Socialism from the Root Up," also in *Commonweal*. With Bax and Victor Dave, writes *A Short History of the Commune of Paris*.

1887 Publishes translation of *The Odyssey*. Writes and acts in *The Tables Turned; or Nupkins Awakened* for the

Socialist League. Takes part in "Bloody Sunday" demonstration in Trafalgar Square on November 13.

1888 Second volume of essays, *Signs of Change*, published, as is the prose romance *The House of the Wolfings*. Lectures on tapestry weaving to Arts and Crafts Exhibition Society. Increasing strains within the Socialist League lead Morris to consider withdrawing.

1889 Attends as a delegate the International Socialist Congress in Paris. Publishes *The Roots of the Mountains*.

1890 Forced out as editor of *Commonweal*. Leaves the Socialist League and founds the Hammersmith Socialist Society. Publishes *News from Nowhere* in *Commonweal*. Studies printing and book design, begins designing type.

1891 *News from Nowhere* published in book form in Boston and London. Morris founds the Kelmscott Press; its first book is his *Story of the Glittering Plain*. Later in the year *Poems by the Way* also published by Kelmscott. Morris falls seriously ill, from a combination of nervous exhaustion and gastrointestinal disease. Over the remaining five years of his life, his energy and overall health decline steadily.

1892 Morris mentioned as possible successor to Tennyson as Poet Laureate, but declines to be considered.

1893 Kelmscott Press edition of *News from Nowhere* published. Co-authors with Bax *Socialism: Its Growth and Outcome*.

1894 Publishes *The Wood Beyond the World*. Morris's mother dies, aged ninety.

1895 Translation of *Beowulf* published.

1896 Kelmscott Press edition of Chaucer published. *The Well at the World's End*, the last of Morris's works to be published during his lifetime, is issued in the spring. Morris travels to Norway in a failed effort to restore his health. Dies October 3 and is buried in Kelmscott churchyard.

1897 *The Water of the Wondrous Isles* and *The Sundering Flood* published posthumously.

A Note on the Text

This edition follows the text of the first edition of *News from Nowhere*, published in London by Reeves and Turner in 1891. *News from Nowhere* initially appeared in weekly installments between January 11 and October 4, 1890 in *Commonweal*, the Socialist League periodical which Morris edited. For the Reeves and Turner edition Morris added significantly to his text. He wrote a new chapter, "The Obstinate Refusers" (Chapter XXVI) and divided the following chapter, "The Upper Waters," in two. He also added substantial material to "Trafalgar Square" (Chapter VII), "How Matters are Managed" (Chapter XIV), and "How the Change Came" (Chapter XVII).

In 1892 Morris published a Kelmscott edition of *News from Nowhere*. He made no substantial changes for this edition. The text is printed in Golden type, a face designed by Morris. Because no italic version of the face existed, italicized words from the first edition (of which there are many) were set in Roman. A smaller, but on the whole more important, limitation of the Golden face was that it did not include the dash—one of Morris's favored punctuation marks in *News from Nowhere*, and one he often uses to great effect. To replace the dash, the Kelmscott edition uses a combination of ellipses, commas, semi-colons, and colons, which somehow fails to reproduce the rhythmical effects Morris achieved with the dash.

For a detailed account of the early textual history of *News from Nowhere*, see Michael Liberman, "Major Textual Changes in William Morris's *News from Nowhere*," *Nineteenth-Century Literature* 41 (1986): 349-56.

Throughout this edition Morris's occasional spelling inconsistencies (e.g. "organise" and "organize") have been silently regularized.

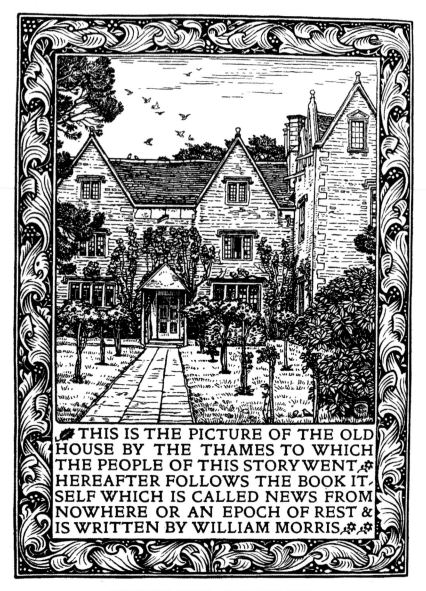

THIS IS THE PICTURE OF THE OLD
HOUSE BY THE THAMES TO WHICH
THE PEOPLE OF THIS STORY WENT
HEREAFTER FOLLOWS THE BOOK IT.
SELF WHICH IS CALLED NEWS FROM
NOWHERE OR AN EPOCH OF REST &
IS WRITTEN BY WILLIAM MORRIS.

KELMSCOTT MANOR, GLOUCESTERSHIRE

Frontispiece of *News From Nowhere* (Kelmscott Press, 1892),
showing east front of Kelmscott Manor

NEWS FROM NOWHERE

or

AN EPOCH OF REST,
BEING SOME CHAPTERS FROM
A UTOPIAN ROMANCE

BY

WILLIAM MORRIS

CHAPTER I

DISCUSSION AND BED

Up at the League,[1] says a friend, there had been one night a brisk conversational discussion, as to what would happen on the Morrow of the Revolution, finally shading off into a vigorous statement by various friends of their views on the future of the fully-developed new society.

Says our friend: Considering the subject, the discussion was good-tempered; for those present being used to public meetings and after-lecture debates, if they did not listen to each other's opinions (which could scarcely be expected of them), at all events did not always attempt to speak all together, as is the custom of people in ordinary polite society when conversing on a subject which interests them. For the rest, there were six persons present, and consequently six sections of the party were represented, four of which had strong but divergent Anarchist opinions. One of the sections, says our friend, a man whom he knows very well indeed, sat almost silent at the beginning of the discussion, but at last got drawn into it, and finished by roaring out very loud, and damning all the rest for fools; after which befel a period of noise, and then a lull, during which the aforesaid section, having said good-night very amicably, took his way home by himself to a western suburb,[2] using the means of trav- *POV* elling which civilization has forced upon us like a habit. As he sat in that vapour-bath of hurried and discontented humanity, a carriage of the underground railway, he, like others, stewed discontentedly, while in self-reproachful mood he turned over

---

[1] For the Socialist League, see Introduction, 18-22.
[2] The western suburb is Hammersmith, where Morris lived from 1878 until his death in 1896. Hammersmith is now a borough of London.

the many excellent and conclusive arguments which, though they lay at his fingers' ends, he had forgotten in the just past discussion. But this frame of mind he was so used to, that it didn't last him long, and after a brief discomfort, caused by disgust with himself for having lost his temper (which he was also well used to), he found himself musing on the subject-matter of discussion, but still discontentedly and unhappily. "If I could but see a day of it," he said to himself; "if I could but see it!"

As he formed the words, the train stopped at his station, five minutes' walk from his own house, which stood on the banks of the Thames, a little way above an ugly suspension bridge.[1] He went out of the station, still discontented and unhappy, muttering "If I could but see it! if I could but see it!" but had not gone many steps towards the river before (says our friend who tells the story) all that discontent and trouble seemed to slip off him.

It was a beautiful night of early winter, the air just sharp enough to be refreshing after the hot room and the stinking railway carriage. The wind, which had lately turned a point or two north of west, had blown the sky clear of all cloud save a light fleck or two which went swiftly down the heavens. There was a young moon halfway up the sky, and as the home-farer caught sight of it, tangled in the branches of a tall old elm, he could scarce bring to his mind the shabby London suburb where he was, and he felt as if he were in a pleasant country place—pleasanter, indeed, than the deep country was as he had known it.

He came right down to the river-side, and lingered a little, looking over the low wall to note the moonlit river, near upon high water, go swirling and glittering up to Chiswick Eyot:[2] as for the ugly bridge below, he did not notice it or think of it, except when for a moment (says our friend) it struck him that he missed the row of lights down stream. Then he turned to his house door and let himself in; and even as he shut the door to, disappeared all remembrance of that brilliant logic and foresight which had so illuminated the recent discussion; and of the discussion itself there remained no trace, save a vague hope, that

---

[1] The Hammersmith suspension bridge, loathed by Morris, opened in 1887.
[2] A small island in the Thames, slightly upriver from Hammersmith.

was now become a pleasure, for days of peace and rest, and cleanness and smiling goodwill.

In this mood he tumbled into bed, and fell asleep after his wont, in two minutes' time; but (contrary to his wont) woke up again not long after in that curiously wide-awake condition which sometimes surprises even good sleepers; a condition under which we feel all our wits preternaturally sharpened, while all the miserable muddles we have ever got into, all the disgraces and losses of our lives, will insist on thrusting themselves forward for the consideration of those sharpened wits.

In this state he lay (says our friend) till he had almost begun to enjoy it: till the tale of his stupidities amused him, and the entanglements before him, which he saw so clearly, began to shape themselves into an amusing story for him.

He heard one o'clock strike, then two and then three; after which he fell asleep again. Our friend says that from that sleep he awoke once more, and afterwards went through such surprising adventures that he thinks that they should be told to our comrades, and indeed the public in general, and therefore proposes to tell them now. But, says he, I think it would be better if I told them in the first person, as if it were myself who had gone through them; which, indeed, will be the easier and more natural to me, since I understand the feelings and desires of the comrade of whom I am telling better than any one else in the world does.

Significance of who tells the story + how

CHAPTER II

A MORNING BATH

Well, I awoke, and found that I had kicked my bedclothes off; and no wonder, for it was hot and the sun shining brightly. I jumped up and washed and hurried on my clothes, but in a hazy and half-awake condition, as if I had slept for a long, long while, and could not shake off the weight of slumber. In fact, I rather took it for granted that I was at home in my own room than saw that it was so.

When I was dressed, I felt the place so hot that I made haste to get out of the room and out of the house; and my first feeling was a delicious relief caused by the fresh air and pleasant breeze; my second, as I began to gather my wits together, mere measureless wonder: for it was winter when I went to bed the last night, and now, by witness of the river-side trees, it was summer, a beautiful bright morning seemingly of early June. However, there was still the Thames sparkling under the sun, and near high water, as last night I had seen it gleaming under the moon.

I had by no means shaken off the feeling of oppression, and wherever I might have been should scarce have been quite conscious of the place; so it was no wonder that I felt rather puzzled in despite of the familiar face of the Thames. Withal I felt dizzy and queer; and remembering that people often got a boat and had a swim in mid-stream, I thought I would do no less. It seems very early, quoth I to myself, but I daresay I shall find someone at Biffin's to take me. However, I didn't get as far as Biffin's, or even turn to my left thitherward, because just then I began to see that there was a landing-stage right before me in front of my house: in fact, on the place where my next-door neighbour had rigged one up, though somehow it didn't look like that either. Down I went on to it, and sure enough among the empty boats moored to it lay a man on his sculls in a solid-looking tub of a boat clearly meant for bathers. He nodded to me, and bade me good-morning as if he expected me, so I jumped in without any words, and he paddled away quietly as I peeled for my swim. As we went, I looked down on the water, and couldn't help saying—

"How clear the water is this morning!"

"Is it?" said he; "I didn't notice it. You know the flood-tide always thickens it a bit."

"H'm," said I, "I have seen it pretty muddy even at half-ebb."

He said nothing in answer, but seemed rather astonished; and as he now lay just stemming the tide, and I had my clothes off, I jumped in without more ado. Of course when I had my head above water again I turned towards the tide, and my eyes naturally sought for the bridge, and so utterly astonished was I by what I saw, that I forgot to strike out, and went spluttering under water again, and when I came up made straight for the boat; for I felt that I must ask some questions of my waterman, so bewildering had been the half-sight I had seen from the face of the river with the water hardly out of my eyes; though by this time I was quit of the slumbrous and dizzy feeling, and was wide-awake and clear-headed.

As I got in up the steps which he had lowered, and he held out his hand to help me, we went drifting speedily up towards Chiswick;[1] but now he caught up the sculls and brought her head round again, and said—

"A short swim, neighbour; but perhaps you find the water cold this morning, after your journey. Shall I put you ashore at once, or would you like to go down to Putney[2] before breakfast?"

He spoke in a way so unlike what I should have expected from a Hammersmith waterman, that I stared at him, as I answered, "Please to hold her a little; I want to look about me a bit."

"All right," he said; "it's no less pretty in its way here than it is off Barn Elms;[3] it's jolly everywhere this time in the morning. I'm glad you got up early; it's barely five o'clock yet."

If I was astonished with my sight of the river banks, I was no less astonished at my waterman, now that I had time to look at him and see him with my head and eyes clear.

He was a handsome young fellow, with a peculiarly pleasant and friendly look about his eyes,—an expression which was quite new to me then, though I soon became familiar with it. For the rest, he was dark-haired and berry-brown of skin, well-knit and strong, and obviously used to exercising his muscles, but with nothing rough or coarse about him, and clean as might be. His dress was not like any modern work-a-day clothes I had seen, but would have served very well as a costume for a picture of fourteenth century life: it was of dark blue cloth, simple enough, but of fine web, and without a stain on it. He had a brown leather belt round

---

1   Like Hammersmith, a former suburb of London, now a borough.
2   A suburb of London (now a borough) east of Hammersmith, on the south bank of the Thames.
3   A sixteenth-century manor house located just west of Putney.

his waist, and I noticed that its clasp was of damascened steel beautifully wrought. In short, he seemed to be like some specially manly and refined young gentleman, playing waterman for a spree, and I concluded that this was the case.

I felt that I must make some conversation; so I pointed to the Surrey bank, where I noticed some light plank stages running down the foreshore, with windlasses at the landward end of them, and said, "What are they doing with those things here? If we were on the Tay,[1] I should have said that they were for drawing the salmon nets; but here—"

"Well," said he, smiling, "of course that is what they *are* for. Where there are salmon, there are likely to be salmon-nets, Tay or Thames; but of course they are not always in use; we don't want salmon *every* day of the season."

I was going to say, "But is this the Thames?" but held my peace in my wonder, and turned my bewildered eyes eastward to look at the bridge again, and thence to the shores of the London river; and surely there was enough to astonish me. For though there was a bridge across the stream and houses on its banks, how all was changed from last night! The soap-works with their smoke-vomiting chimneys were gone; the engineer's works gone; the lead-works gone; and no sound of rivetting and hammering came down the west wind from Thorneycroft's.[2] Then the bridge! I had perhaps dreamed of such a bridge, but never seen such an one out of an illuminated manuscript; for not even the Ponte Vecchio at Florence[3] came anywhere near it. It was of stone arches, splendidly solid, and as graceful as they were strong; high enough also to let ordinary river traffic through easily. Over the parapet showed quaint and fanciful little buildings, which I supposed to be booths or shops, beset with painted and gilded vanes and spirelets. The stone was a little weathered, but showed no marks of the grimy sootiness which I was used to on every London building more than a year old. In short, to me a wonder of a bridge.

---

[1] A river in Scotland famous for its salmon. By the 1890s there was little commercial fishing of any kind in the Thames.

[2] Thorneycroft's factory, upriver from Hammersmith, manufactured marine equipment.

[3] The famous fourteenth-century bridge over the river Arno.

The sculler noted my eager astonished look, and said, as if in answer to my thoughts—

"Yes, it *is* a pretty bridge, isn't it? Even the up-stream bridges, which are so much smaller, are scarcely daintier, and the down-stream ones are scarcely more dignified and stately."

I found myself saying, almost against my will, "How old is it?"

"Oh, not very old," he said; "it was built or at least opened, in 2003.[1] There used to be a rather plain timber bridge before then." The date shut my mouth as if a key had been turned in a padlock fixed to my lips; for I saw that something inexplicable had happened, and that if I said much, I should be mixed up in a game of cross questions and crooked answers. So I tried to look uncon-cerned, and to glance in a matter-of-course way at the banks of the river, though this is what I saw up to the bridge and a little beyond; say as far as the site of the soap-works. Both shores had a line of very pretty houses, low and not large, standing back a little way from the river; they were mostly built of red brick and roofed with tiles, and looked, above all, comfortable, and as if they were, so to say, alive, and sympathetic with the life of the dwellers in them. There was a continuous garden in front of them, going down to the water's edge, in which the flowers were now blooming luxu-riantly, and sending delicious waves of summer scent over the eddy-ing stream. Behind the houses, I could see great trees rising, mostly planes, and looking down the water there were the reaches towards Putney almost as if they were a lake with a forest shore, so thick were the big trees; and I said aloud, but as if to myself—

"Well, I'm glad that they have not built over Barn Elms."

I blushed for my fatuity as the words slipped out of my mouth, and my companion looked at me with a half smile which I thought I understood; so to hide my confusion I said, "Please take me ashore now: I want to get my breakfast."

He nodded, and brought her head round with a sharp stroke, and in a trice we were at the landing-stage again. He jumped out and I followed him; and of course I was not surprised to see him wait, as if for the inevitable after-piece that follows the doing of a service to a fellow-citizen. So I put my hand into my waistcoat-pocket, and

---

[1]   In the *Commonweal* version of the novel, the date given is 1971.

said, "How much?" though still with the uncomfortable feeling that perhaps I was offering money to a gentleman.

He looked puzzled, and said, "How much? I don't quite understand what you are asking about. Do you mean the tide? If so, it is close on the turn now."

I blushed, and said, stammering, "Please don't take it amiss if I ask you; I mean no offence: but what ought I to pay you? You see I am a stranger, and don't know your customs—or your coins."

And therewith I took a handful of money out of my pocket, as one does in a foreign country. And by the way, I saw that the silver had oxydised, and was like a blackleaded stove in colour.

He still seemed puzzled, but not at all offended; and he looked at the coins with some curiosity. I thought, Well after all, he *is* a waterman, and is considering what he may venture to take. He seems such a nice fellow that I'm sure I don't grudge him a little over-payment. I wonder, by the way, whether I couldn't hire him as a guide for a day or two, since he is so intelligent.

Therewith my new friend said thoughtfully:

"I think I know what you mean. You think that I have done you a service; so you feel yourself bound to give me something which I am not to give to a neighbour, unless he has done something special for me. I have heard of this kind of thing; but pardon me for saying, that it seems to us a troublesome and roundabout custom; and we don't know how to manage it. And you see this ferrying and giving people casts about the water is my *business*, which I would do for anybody; so to take gifts in connection with it would look very queer. Besides, if one person gave me something, then another might, and another, and so on; and I hope you won't think me rude if I say that I shouldn't know where to stow away so many mementos of friendship."

And he laughed loud and merrily, as if the idea of being paid for his work was a very funny joke. I confess I began to be afraid that the man was mad, though he looked sane enough; and I was rather glad to think that I was a good swimmer, since we were so close to a deep swift stream. However, he went on by no means like a madman:

"As to your coins, they are curious, but not very old; they seem to be all of the reign of Victoria; you might give them to some scantily-furnished museum. Ours has enough of such coins, besides a fair number of earlier ones, many of which are beautiful, whereas these nineteenth century ones are so beastly ugly, ain't they? We have a piece of Edward III, with the king in a ship, and little leopards and fleurs-de-lys all along the gunwale, so delicately worked. You see," he said, with something of a smirk, "I am fond of working in gold and fine metals; this buckle here is an early piece of mine."

No doubt I looked a little shy of him under the influence of that doubt as to his sanity. So he broke off short, and said in a kind voice:

"But I see that I am boring you, and I ask your pardon. For, not to mince matters, I can tell that you *are* a stranger, and must come from a place very unlike England. But also it is clear that it won't do to overdose you with information about this place, and that you had best suck it in little by little. Further, I should take it as very kind in you if you would allow me to be the showman of our new world to you, since you have stumbled on me first. Though indeed it will be a mere kindness on your part, for almost anybody would make as good a guide, and many much better."

There certainly seemed no flavour in him of Colney Hatch;[1] and besides I thought I could easily shake him off if it turned out that he really was mad; so I said:

"It is a very kind offer, but it is difficult for me to accept it, unless—" I was going to say, Unless you will let me pay you properly; but fearing to stir up Colney Hatch again, I changed the sentence into, "I fear I shall be taking you away from your work—or your amusement."

"O," he said, "don't trouble about that, because it will give me an opportunity of doing a good turn to a friend of mine, who wants to take my work here. He is a weaver from Yorkshire, who has rather overdone himself between his weaving and his mathematics, both indoor work, you see; and being a great friend of mine, he naturally came to me to get him some outdoor work. If you think you can put up with me, pray take me as your guide."

---

[1]   A north London mental hospital, opened in 1851.

He added presently: "It is true that I have promised to go up-stream to some special friends of mine, for the hay-harvest; but they won't be ready for us for more than a week: and besides, you might go with me, you know, and see some very nice people, besides making notes of our ways in Oxfordshire. You could hardly do better if you want to see the country."

I felt myself obliged to thank him, whatever might come of it; and he added eagerly:

"Well, then, that's settled. I will give my friend a call; he is living in the Guest House like you, and if he isn't up yet, he ought to be this fine summer morning."

Therewith he took a little silver bugle-horn from his girdle and blew two or three sharp but agreeable notes on it; and presently from the house which stood on the site of my old dwelling (of which more hereafter) another young man came sauntering towards us. He was not so well-looking or so strongly made as my sculler friend, being sandy-haired, rather pale, and not stout-built; but his face was not wanting in that happy and friendly expression which I had noticed in his friend. As he came up smiling towards us, I saw with pleasure that I must give up the Colney Hatch theory as to the waterman, for no two madmen ever behaved as they did before a sane man. His dress also was of the same cut as the first man's, though somewhat gayer, the surcoat being light green with a golden spray embroidered on the breast, and his belt being of filigree silver-work.

He gave me good-day very civilly, and greeting his friend joyously, said:

"Well, Dick, what is it this morning? Am I to have my work, or rather your work? I dreamed last night that we were off up the river fishing."

"All right, Bob," said my sculler; "you will drop into my place, and if you find it too much, there is George Brightling on the look out for a stroke of work, and he lives close handy to you. But see, here is a stranger who is willing to amuse me to-day by taking me as his guide about our country-side, and you may imagine I don't want to lose the opportunity; so you had better take to the boat at once. But in any case I shouldn't have kept you out of it for long, since I am due in the hayfields in a few days."

The newcomer rubbed his hands with glee, but turning to me, said in a friendly voice:

"Neighbour, both you and friend Dick are lucky, and will have a good time to-day, as indeed I shall too. But you had better come in with me at once and get something to eat, lest you should forget your dinner in your amusement. I suppose you came into the Guest House after I had gone to bed last night?"

I nodded, not caring to enter into a long explanation which would have led to nothing, and which in truth by this time I should have begun to doubt myself. And we all three turned toward the door of the Guest House.

CHAPTER III

THE GUEST HOUSE AND BREAKFAST THEREIN

I lingered a little behind the others to have a stare at this house, which, as I have told you, stood on the site of my old dwelling. *Can't get back to other wold*

It was a longish building with its gable ends turned away from the road, and long traceried windows coming rather low down set in the wall that faced us. It was very handsomely built of red brick with a lead roof; and high up above the windows there ran a frieze of figure subjects in baked clay, very well executed, and designed with a force and directness which I had never noticed in modern work before. The subjects I recognized at once, and indeed was very particularly familiar with them.

However, all this I took in in a minute; for we were presently within doors, and standing in a hall with a floor of marble mosaic and an open timber roof. There were no windows on the side opposite to the river, but arches below, leading into chambers, one of which showed a glimpse of a garden beyond, and above them a long space of wall gaily painted (in fresco, I thought) with similar subjects to those of the frieze outside; everything about the place was handsome and generously solid as to material; and though it was not very large (somewhat smaller than Crosby Hall perhaps),[1] one felt in it that exhilarating sense of space and freedom which satisfactory architecture always gives to the unanxious man who is in the habit of using his eyes.

In this pleasant place, which of course I knew to be the hall of the Guest House, three young women were flitting to and fro. As they were the first of the sex I had seen on this eventful morning, I naturally looked at them very attentively, and found them at least as good as the gardens, the architecture, and the male men. As to their dress, which of course I took note of, I should say that they were decently veiled with drapery, and not bundled up with millinery; that they were clothed like women, not upholstered like arm-chairs, as most women of our time are. In short, their dress was somewhat between that of the ancient classical costume and the simpler forms of the fourteenth century garments, though it was clearly not an imitation of either: the materials were light and gay to suit the season. As to the women themselves, it was pleasant indeed to see them, they were so kind and happy-looking in expression of face, so shapely and wellknit of body, and thoroughly healthy-looking and strong. All were at least comely, and one of them very handsome and regular of feature. They came up to us at once merrily and without the least affectation of shyness, and all three shook hands with me as if I were a friend newly come back from a long journey: though I could not help noticing that they looked askance at my garments; for I had on my clothes of last night, and at the best was never a dressy person.

A word or two from Robert the weaver, and they bustled about on our behoof, and presently came and took us by the hands and led us to a table in the pleasantest corner of the hall, where our breakfast was spread for us; and, as we sat down, one of them hurried out by the chambers aforesaid, and came back again in a little while with a great bunch of roses, very different in size and quality to what Hammersmith had been wont to grow, but very like the produce of an old country garden. She hurried back thence into the buttery, and came back once more

---

[1]   The mid-fifteenth-century London residence of Sir John Crosby, known for its oak roof and oriel windows.

with a delicately made glass, into which she put the flowers and set them down in the midst of our table. One of the others, who had run off also, then came back with a big cabbage-leaf filled with strawberries, some of them barely ripe, and said as she set them on the table, "There, now; I thought of that before I got up this morning; but looking at the stranger here getting into your boat, Dick, put it out of my head; so that I was not before *all* the blackbirds: however, there are a few about as good as you will get them anywhere in Hammersmith this morning."

Robert patted her on the head in a friendly manner; and we fell to on our breakfast, which was simple enough, but most delicately cooked, and set on the table with much daintiness. The bread was particularly good, and was of several different kinds, from the big, rather close, dark-coloured, sweet-tasting farmhouse loaf, which was most to my liking, to the thin pipestems of wheaten crust, such as I have eaten in Turin.

As I was putting the first mouthfuls into my mouth, my eye caught a carved and gilded inscription on the panelling, behind what we should have called the High Table in an Oxford college hall, and a familiar name in it forced me to read it through. Thus it ran:

"Guests and neighbours, on the site of this Guesthall once stood the lecture-room of the Hammersmith Socialists. Drink a glass to the memory! May 1962."[1]

It is difficult to tell you how I felt as I read these words, and I suppose my face showed how much I was moved, for both my friends looked curiously at me, and there was silence between us for a little while.

Presently the weaver, who was scarcely so well mannered a man as the ferryman, said to me rather awkwardly:

"Guest, we don't know what to call you: is there any indiscretion in asking you your name?"

"Well," said I, "I have some doubts about it myself; so suppose

---

[1] The Hammersmith Branch of the Socialist League held their lectures and meetings in a converted coach-house on Morris's property at Kelmscott House.

you call me Guest, which is a family name, you know, and add William to it if you please."

Dick nodded kindly to me; but a shade of anxiousness passed over the weaver's face, and he said—

"I hope you don't mind my asking, but would you tell me where you come from? I am curious about such things for good reasons, literary reasons."

Dick was clearly kicking him underneath the table; but he was not much abashed, and awaited my answer somewhat eagerly. As for me, I was just going to blurt out "Hammersmith," when I bethought me what an entanglement of cross purposes that would lead us into; so I took time to invent a lie with circumstance, guarded by a little truth, and said:

"You see, I have been such a long time away from Europe that things seem strange to me now; but I was born and bred on the edge of Epping Forest; Walthamstow and Woodford, to wit."[1]

"A pretty place, too," broke in Dick; "a very jolly place, now that the trees have had time to grow again since the great clearing of houses in 1955."

Quoth the irrepressible weaver: "Dear neighbour, since you knew the Forest some time ago, could you tell me what truth there is in the rumour that in the nineteenth century the trees were all pollards?"[2]

This was catching me on my archæological natural-history side, and I fell into the trap without any thought of where and when I was; so I began on it, while one of the girls, the handsome one, who had been scattering little twigs of lavender and other sweet-smelling herbs about the floor, came near to listen, and stood behind me with her hand on my shoulder, in which she held some of the plant that I used to call balm: its strong sweet smell brought back to my mind my very early days in the kitchen-garden at Woodford, and the large blue plums which grew on the wall beyond the sweet-herb patch,—a connection of memories which all boys will see at once.

---

[1] Morris was born at Walthamstow, northeast of London.

[2] A pollarded tree has had its top branches cut back to promote the growth of new shoots. Guest's lament over the fate of Epping Forest reflects Morris's own feelings.

I started off: "When I was a boy, and for long after, except for a piece about Queen Elizabeth's Lodge, and for the part about High Beech,[1] the Forest was almost wholly made up of pollard hornbeams mixed with holly thickets. But when the Corporation of London took it over about twenty-five years ago, the topping and lopping, which was a part of the old commoners' rights, came to an end, and the trees were let to grow. But I have not seen the place for many years, except once, when we Leaguers went apleasuring to High Beech. I was very much shocked then to see how it was built-over and altered; and the other day we heard that the philistines were going to landscapegarden it. But what you were saying about the building being stopped and the trees growing is only too good news;—only you know—"

At that point I suddenly remembered Dick's date, and stopped short rather confused. The eager weaver didn't notice my confusion, but said hastily, as if he were almost aware of his breach of good manners, "But, I say, how old are you?"

Dick and the pretty girl both burst out laughing, as if Robert's conduct were excusable on the grounds of eccentricity; and Dick said amidst his laughter:

"Hold hard, Bob; this questioning of guests won't do. Why, much learning is spoiling you. You remind me of the radical cobblers in the silly old novels, who, according to the authors, were prepared to trample down all good manners in the pursuit of utilitarian knowledge.[2] The fact is, I begin to think that you have so muddled your head with mathematics, and with grubbing into those idiotic old books about political economy (he! he!), that you scarcely know how to behave. Really, it is about time for you to take to some open-air work, so that you may clear away the cobwebs from your brain."

The weaver only laughed good-humouredly; and the girl went up to him and patted his cheek and said laughingly, "Poor fellow! he was born so."

---

[1] Queen Elizabeth's Hunting Lodge is situated on the southern edge of Epping Forest. High Beech, within the forest, was known for its abundance of beautiful beech trees.

[2] In the popular imagination, cobblers were considered to be among the most politically radical of artisans.

As for me, I was a little puzzled, but I laughed also, partly for company's sake, and partly with pleasure at their unanxious happiness and good temper; and before Robert could make the excuse to me which he was getting ready, I said:

"But neighbours" (I had caught up that word), "I don't in the least mind answering questions, when I can do so: ask me as many as you please; it's fun for me. I will tell you all about Epping Forest when I was a boy, if you please; and as to my age, I'm not a fine lady, you know, so why shouldn't I tell you? I'm hard on fifty-six."[1]

In spite of the recent lecture on good manners, the weaver could not help giving a long "whew" of astonishment, and the others were so amused by his *naïveté* that the merriment flitted all over their faces, though for courtesy's sake they forbore actual laughter; while I looked from one to the other in a puzzled manner, and at last said:

"Tell me, please, what is amiss: you know I want to learn from you. And please laugh; only tell me."

Well, they *did* laugh, and I joined them again, for the above-stated reasons. But at last the pretty woman said coaxingly—

"Well, well, he *is* rude, poor fellow! but you see I may as well tell you what he is thinking about: he means that you look rather old for your age. But surely there need be no wonder in that, since you have been travelling; and clearly from all you have been saying, in unsocial countries. It has often been said, and no doubt truly, that one ages very quickly if one lives amongst unhappy people. Also they say that southern England is a good place for keeping good looks." She blushed and said: "How old am I, do you think?"

"Well," quoth I, "I have always been told that a woman is as old as she looks, so without offence or flattery, I should say that you were twenty."

She laughed merrily, and said, "I am well served out for fishing for compliments, since I have to tell you the truth, to wit, that I am forty-two."

I stared at her, and drew musical laughter from her again; but I might well stare, for there was not a careful line on her face; her

---

[1] Morris's age in 1890.

skin was as smooth as ivory, her cheeks full and round, her lips as red as the roses she had brought in; her beautiful arms, which she had bared for her work, firm and well-knit from shoulder to wrist. She blushed a little under my gaze, though it was clear that she had taken me for a man of eighty; so to pass it off I said—

"Well, you see, the old saw is proved right again, and I ought not to have let you tempt me into asking you a rude question."

She laughed again, and said: "Well, lads, old and young, I must get to my work now. We shall be rather busy here presently; and I want to clear it off soon, for I began to read a pretty old book yesterday, and I want to get on with it this morning: so good-bye for the present."

She waved a hand to us, and stepped lightly down the hall, taking (as Scott says) at least part of the sun from our table as she went.

When she was gone, Dick said: "Now, guest; won't you ask a question or two of our friend here? It is only fair that you should have your turn."

"I shall be very glad to answer them," said the weaver.

"If I ask you any questions, sir," said I, "they will not be very severe; but since I hear that you are a weaver, I should like to ask you something about that craft, as I am—or was—interested in it."

"Oh," said he, "I shall not be of much use to you there, I'm afraid. I only do the most mechanical kind of weaving, and am in fact but a poor craftsman, unlike Dick here. Then besides the weaving, I do a little with machine printing and composing, though I am little use at the finer kinds of printing; and moreover machine printing is beginning to die out, along with the waning of the plague of book-making; so I have had to turn to other things that I have a taste for, and have taken to mathematics; and also I am writing a sort of antiquarian book about the peaceable and private history, so to say, of the end of the nineteenth century,—more for the sake of giving a picture of the country before the fighting began than for anything else. That was why I asked you those questions about Epping Forest. You have rather puzzled me, I confess, though your information was so interesting. But later on, I hope, we may have some more talk together, when our friend Dick isn't here. I know he thinks me rather a grinder, and despises me for not being very deft with my hands: that's the way nowadays. From what I have read of the nineteenth century literature (and I have read a good deal), it is clear to me that this is a kind of revenge for the stupidity of that day, which despised everybody who *could* use his hands. But, Dick, old fellow, *Ne quid nimis!*[1] Don't overdo it!"

"Come now," said Dick, "am I likely to? Am I not the most tolerant man in the world? Am I not quite contented so long as you don't make me learn mathematics, or go into your new science of æsthetics, and let me do a little practical æsthetics with my gold and steel, and the blowpipe and the nice little hammer? But, hillo! here comes another questioner for you, my poor guest. I say, Bob, you must help me to defend him now."

"Here, Boffin," he cried out, after a pause; "here we are, if you must have it!"

I looked over my shoulder, and saw something flash and gleam in the sunlight that lay across the hall; so I turned round, and at my ease saw a splendid figure slowly sauntering over the pavement; a man whose surcoat was embroidered most copiously as well as elegantly, so that the sun flashed back from him as if he had been clad in golden armour. The man himself was tall, dark-haired, and exceedingly handsome, and though his face was no less kindly in expression than that of the others, he moved with that somewhat haughty mien which great beauty is apt to give to both men and women. He came and sat down at our table with a smiling face, stretching out his long legs and hanging his arm over the chair in the slowly graceful way which tall and well-built people may use without affectation. He was a man in the prime of life, but looked as happy as a child who has just got a new toy. He bowed gracefully to me and said—

"I see clearly that you are the guest, of whom Annie has just told me, who have come from some distant country that does not know of us, or our ways of life. So I daresay you would not mind answering me a few questions; for you see—"

Here Dick broke in: "No, please, Boffin! let it alone for the present. Of course you want the guest to be happy and comfortable; and how can that be if he has to trouble himself with

---

[1] "Nothing in excess."

answering all sorts of questions while he is still confused with the new customs and people about him? No, no: I am going to take him where he can ask questions himself, and have them answered; that is, to my great-grandfather in Bloomsbury: and I am sure you can't have anything to say against that. So instead of bothering, you had much better go out to James Allen's and get a carriage for me, as I shall drive him up myself; and please tell Jim to let me have the old grey, for I can drive a wherry much better than a carriage.[1] Jump up, old fellow, and don't be disappointed; our guest will keep himself for you and your stories."

I stared at Dick; for I wondered at his speaking to such a dignified-looking personage so familiarly, not to say curtly; for I thought that this Mr. Boffin,[2] in spite of his well-known name out of Dickens, must be at least a senator of these strange people. However, he got up and said, "All right, old oar-wearer, whatever you like; this is not one of my busy days; and though" (with a condescending bow to me) "my pleasure of a talk with this learned guest is put off, I admit that he ought to see your worthy kinsman as soon as possible. Besides, perhaps he will be better able to answer *my* questions after his own have been answered."

And therewith he turned and swung himself out of the hall.

When he was well gone, I said: "Is it wrong to ask what Mr. Boffin is? whose name, by the way, reminds me of many pleasant hours passed in reading Dickens." *[handwritten margin note: Overt address of allusion]*

Dick laughed. "Yes, yes," said he, "as it does us. I see you take the allusion. Of course his real name is not Boffin, but Henry Johnson; we only call him Boffin as a joke, partly because he is a dustman, and partly because he will dress so showily, and get as much gold on him as a baron of the Middle Ages. As why should he not if he likes? only we are his special friends, you know, so of course we jest with him."

---

[1] A wherry is a small rowboat. Dick's point is that he is better at rowing a boat than at driving a carriage.

[2] Noddy Boffin, the "Golden Dustman" of Dickens's *Our Mutual Friend* (1864-65), amasses a fortune through collecting and selling refuse. He is essentially good-humored, though Dickens satirizes his efforts to match his style of living to his newly-acquired wealth.

I held my tongue for some time after that; but Dick went on:

"He is a capital fellow, and you can't help liking him; but he has a weakness: he will spend his time in writing reactionary novels, and is very proud of getting the local colour right, as he calls it; and as he thinks you come from some forgotten corner of the earth, where people are unhappy, and consequently interesting to a story-teller, he thinks he might get some information out of you.[1] O, he will be quite straightforward with you, for that matter. Only for your own comfort beware of him!"

"Well, Dick," said the weaver, doggedly, "I think his novels are very good."

"Of course you do," said Dick; "birds of a feather flock together; mathematics and antiquarian novels stand on much the same footing. But here he comes again."

And in effect the Golden Dustman hailed us from the hall-door; so we all got up and went into the porch, before which, with a strong grey horse in the shafts, stood a carriage ready for us which I could not help noticing. It was light and handy, but had none of that sickening vulgarity which I had known as inseparable from the carriages of our time, especially the "elegant" ones, but was a graceful and pleasant as a Wessex wagon. We got in, Dick and I. The girls, who had come into the porch to see us off, waved their hands to us; the weaver nodded kindly; the dustman bowed as gracefully as a troubadour; Dick shook the reins, and we were off.

CHAPTER IV

A MARKET BY THE WAY

We turned away from the river at once, and were soon in the main road that runs through Hammersmith. But I should have had no guess as to where I was, if I had not started from the

---

[1] Dickens's Boffin, far from being a novelist, is in fact illiterate.

waterside; for King Street was gone, and the highway ran through wide sunny meadows and garden-like tillage. The Creek, which we crossed at once, had been rescued from its culvert, and as we went over its pretty bridge we saw its waters, yet swollen with the tide, covered with gay boats of different sizes. There were houses about, some on the road, some amongst the fields with pleasant lanes leading down to them, and each surrounded by a teeming garden. They were all pretty in design, and as solid as might be, but countryfied in appearance, like yeoman's dwellings; some of them of red brick like those by the river, but more of timber and plaster, which were by the necessity of their construction so like mediæval houses of the same materials that I fairly felt as if I were alive in the fourteenth century; a sensation helped out by the costume of the people that we met or passed, in whose dress there was nothing "modern." Almost everybody was gaily dressed, but especially the women, who were so well-looking, or even so handsome, that I could scarcely refrain my tongue from calling my companion's attention to the fact. Some faces I saw that were thoughtful, and in these I noticed great nobility of expression, but none that had a glimmer of unhappiness, and the greater part (we came upon a good many people) were frankly and openly joyous.

I thought I knew the Broadway by the lie of the roads that still met there. On the north side of the road was a range of buildings and courts, low, but very handsomely built and ornamented, and in that way forming a great contrast to the unpretentiousness of the houses round about; while above this lower building rose the steep lead-covered roof and the buttresses and higher part of the wall of a great hall, of a splendid and exuberant style of architecture, of which one can say little more than that it seemed to me to embrace the best qualities of the Gothic of northern Europe with those of the Saracenic and Byzantine, though there was no copying of any one of these styles. On the other, the south side, of the road was an octagonal building with a high roof, not unlike the Baptistry at Florence in outline, except that it was surrounded by a lean-to that clearly made an arcade or cloisters to it: it also was most delicately ornamented.

This whole mass of architecture which we had come upon so suddenly from amidst the pleasant fields was not only exquisitely beautiful in itself, but bore upon it the expression of such generosity and abundance of life that I was exhilarated to a pitch that I had never yet reached. I fairly chuckled for pleasure. My friend seemed to understand it, and sat looking on me with a pleased and affectionate interest. We had pulled up amongst a crowd of carts, wherein sat handsome healthy-looking people, men, women, and children very gaily dressed, and which were clearly market carts, as they were full of very tempting-looking country produce.

I said, "I need not ask if this is a market, for I see clearly that it is; but what market is it that it is so splendid? And what is the glorious hall there, and what is the building on the south side?"

"O," said he, "it is just our Hammersmith market; and I am glad you like it so much, for we are really proud of it. Of course the hall inside is our winter Mote-House; for in summer we mostly meet in the fields down by the river opposite Barn Elms. The building on our right hand is our theatre: I hope you like it."

"I should be a fool if I didn't," said I.

He blushed a little as he said: "I am glad of that, too, because I had a hand in it; I made the great doors, which are of damascened bronze. We will look at them later in the day, perhaps: but we ought to be getting on now. As to the market, this is not one of our busy days; so we shall do better with it another time, because you will see more people."

I thanked him, and said: "Are these the regular country people? What very pretty girls there are amongst them."

As I spoke, my eye caught the face of a beautiful woman, tall, dark-haired, and white-skinned, dressed in a pretty light-green dress in honour of the season and the hot day, who smiled kindly on me, and more kindly still, I thought, on Dick; so I stopped a minute, but presently went on:

"I ask because I do not see any of the country-looking people I should have expected to see at a market—I mean selling things there."

"I don't understand," said he, "what kind of people you would expect to see; nor quite what you mean by 'country' people. These are the neighbours, and that like they run in the Thames valley. There are parts of these islands which are rougher and rainier than we are here, and there people are rougher in their dress; and they themselves are tougher and more hard-bitten than we are to look at. But some people like their looks better than ours; they say they have more character in them—that's the word. Well, it's a matter of taste.—Anyhow, the cross between us and them generally turns out well," added he, thoughtfully.

I heard him, though my eyes were turned away from him, for that pretty girl was just disappearing through the gate with her big basket of early peas, and I felt that disappointed kind of feeling which overtakes one when one has seen an interesting or lovely face in the streets which one is never likely to see again; and I was silent a little. At last I said: "What I mean is, that I haven't seen any poor people about—not one."

He knit his brows, looked puzzled, and said: "No, naturally; if anybody is poorly, he is likely to be within doors, or at best crawling about the garden: but I don't know of anyone sick at present. Why should you expect to see poorly people on the road?"

"No, no," I said; "I don't mean sick people. I mean poor people, you know; rough people."

"No," said he, smiling merrily, "I really do not know. The fact is, you must come along quick to my great-grandfather, who will understand you better than I do. Come on, Greylocks!" Therewith he shook the reins, and we jogged along merrily eastward.

CHAPTER V

CHILDREN ON THE ROAD

Past the Broadway there were fewer houses on either side. We presently crossed a pretty little brook that ran across a piece of land dotted over with trees, and awhile after came to another market and town-hall, as we should call it. Although there was nothing familiar to me in its surroundings, I knew pretty well where we were, and was not surprised when my guide said briefly, "Kensington Market."

Just after this we came into a short street of houses; or rather, one long house on either side of the way, built of timber and plaster, and with a pretty arcade over the footway before it.

Quoth Dick: "This is Kensington proper. People are apt to gather here rather thick, for they like the romance of the wood; and naturalists haunt it, too; for it is a wild spot even here, what there is of it; for it does not go far to the south: it goes from here northward and west right over Paddington and a little way down Notting Hill, and so on; rather a narrow strip of it gets through Kingsland to Stoke-Newington and Clapton, where it spreads out along the heights above the Lea marshes; on the other side of which, as you know, is Epping Forest holding out a hand to it. This part we are just coming to is called Kensington Gardens; though why 'gardens' I don't know."[1]

I rather longed to say, "Well, *I* know"; but there were so many things about me which I did *not* know, in spite of his assumptions, that I thought it better to hold my tongue.

The road plunged at once into a beautiful wood spreading out on either side, but obviously much further on the north side, where even the oaks and sweet chestnuts were of a good growth; while the quicker-growing trees (amongst which I thought the planes and sycamores too numerous) were very big and fine-grown.

It was exceedingly pleasant in the dappled shadow, for the day was growing as hot as need be, and the coolness and shade soothed my excited mind into a condition of dreamy pleasure, so that I felt as if I should like to go on for ever through that balmy freshness. My companion seemed to share in my feelings, and let the horse go slower and slower as he sat inhaling the green forest scents, chief amongst which was the smell of the trodden bracken near the wayside.

Romantic as this Kensington wood was, however, it was not lonely. We came on many groups both coming and going, or wandering in the edges of the wood. Amongst these were many children from six or eight years old up to sixteen or seventeen. They seemed to me to be especially fine specimens of their race,

---

[1]   The sylvan landscape Dick describes here covers what was in 1890 (and is today) among the more densely built and populated areas in and around London.

and were clearly enjoying themselves to the utmost; some of them were hanging about little tents pitched on the greensward, and by some of these fires were burning, with pots hanging over them gipsy fashion. Dick explained to me that there were scattered houses in the forest, and indeed we caught a glimpse of one or two. He said they were mostly quite small, such as used to be called cottages when there were slaves in the land, but they were pleasant enough and fitting for the wood.

"They must be pretty well stocked with children," said I, pointing to the many youngsters about the way.

"O," said he, "these children do not all come from the near houses, the woodland houses, but from the countryside generally. They often make up parties, and come to play in the woods for weeks together in summer-time, living in tents, as you see. We rather encourage them to it; they learn to do things for themselves, and get to notice the wild creatures; and, you see, the less they stew inside houses the better for them. Indeed, I must tell you that many grown people will go to live in the forests through the summer; though they for the most part go to the bigger ones, like Windsor, or the Forest of Dean, or the northern wastes. Apart from the other pleasures of it, it gives them a little rough work, which I am sorry to say is getting somewhat scarce for these last fifty years."

He broke off, and then said, "I tell you all this, because I see that if I talk I must be answering questions, which you are thinking, even if you are not speaking them out; but my kinsman will tell you more about it."

I saw that I was likely to get out of my depth again, and so merely for the sake of tiding over an awkwardness and to say something, I said—

"Well, the youngsters here will be all the fresher for school when the summer gets over and they have to go back again."

"School?" he said; "yes, what do you mean by that word? I don't see how it can have anything to do with children. We talk, indeed, of a school of herring, and a school of painting, and in the former sense we might talk of a school of children—but otherwise," said he, laughing, "I must own myself beaten."

Hang it! thought I, I can't open my mouth without digging

up some new complexity. I wouldn't try to set my friend right in his etymology; and I thought I had best say nothing about the boy-farms which I had been used to call schools, as I saw pretty clearly that they had disappeared; so I said after a little fumbling, "I was using the word in the sense of a system of education."

"Education?" said he, meditatively, "I know enough Latin to know that the word must come from *educere*, to lead out; and I have heard it used; but I have never met anybody who could give me a clear explanation of what it means."

You may imagine how my new friends fell in my esteem when I heard this frank avowal; and I said, rather contemptuously, "Well, education means a system of teaching young people."

"Why not old people also?" said he with a twinkle in his eye. "But," he went on, "I can assure you our children learn, whether they go through a 'system of teaching' or not. Why, you will not find one of these children about here, boy or girl, who cannot swim; and every one of them has been used to tumbling about the little forest ponies—there's one of them now! They all of them know how to cook; the bigger lads can mow; many can thatch and do odd jobs at carpentering; or they know how to keep shop. I can tell you they know plenty of things."

"Yes, but their mental education, the teaching of their minds," said I, kindly translating my phrase.

"Guest," said he, "perhaps you have not learned to do these things I have been speaking about; and if that's the case, don't you run away with the idea that it doesn't take some skill to do them, and doesn't give plenty of work for one's mind: you would change your opinion if you saw a Dorsetshire lad thatching, for instance. But, however, I understand you to be speaking of book-learning; and as to that, it is a simple affair. Most children, seeing books lying about, manage to read by the time they are four years old; though I am told it has not always been so. As to writing, we do not encourage them to scrawl too early (though scrawl a little they will), because it gets them into a habit of ugly writing; and what's the use of a lot of ugly writing being done, when rough printing can be done so easily. You understand that handsome writing we like, and many people will write their books out when they make them, or get them written; I mean books of which only a few copies are needed—poems, and such like, you know. However, I am wandering from my lambs; but you must excuse me, for I am interested in this matter of writing, being myself a fair-writer."

"Well," said I, "about the children; when they know how to read and write, don't they learn something else—languages, for instance?"

"Of course," he said; "sometimes even before they can read, they can talk French, which is the nearest language talked on the other side of the water; and they soon get to know German also, which is talked by a huge number of communes and colleges on the mainland. These are the principle languages we speak in these islands, along with English or Welsh, or Irish, which is another form of Welsh; and children pick them up very quickly, because their elders all know them; and besides our guests from over sea often bring their children with them, and the little ones get together, and rub their speech into one another."

"And the older languages?" said I.

"O, yes," said he, "they mostly learn Latin and Greek along with the modern ones, when they do anything more than merely pick up the latter."

"And history?" said I; "how do you teach history?"

"Well," said he, "when a person can read, of course he reads what he likes to; and he can easily get someone to tell him what are the best books to read on such and such a subject, or to explain what he doesn't understand in the books when he is reading them."

"Well," said I, "what else do they learn? I suppose they don't all learn history?"

"No, no," said he; "some don't care about it; in fact, I don't think many do. I have heard my great-grandfather say that it is mostly in periods of turmoil and strife and confusion that people care much about history; and you know," said my friend, with an amiable smile, "we are not like that now. No; many people study facts about the make of things and the matters of cause and effect, so that knowledge increases on us, if that be good; and some, as you heard about friend Bob yonder, will spend time over mathematics. 'Tis no use forcing people's tastes."

Said I: "But you don't mean that children learn all these things?"

Said he: "That depends on what you mean by children; and also you must remember how much they differ. As a rule, they don't do much reading, except for a few story-books, till they are about fifteen years old; we don't encourage early bookishness: though you will find some children who *will* take to books very early; which perhaps is not good for them; but it's no use thwarting them; and very often it doesn't last long with them, and they find their level before they are twenty years old. You see, children are mostly given to imitating their elders, and when they see most people about them engaged in genuinely amusing work, like house-building and street-paving, and gardening, and the like, that is what they want to be doing; so I don't think we need fear having too many book-learned men."

What could I say? I sat and held my peace, for fear of fresh entanglements. Besides, I was using my eyes with all my might, wondering as the old horse jogged on, when I should come into London proper, and what it would be like now.

But my companion couldn't let his subject quite drop, and went on meditatively:

"After all, I don't know that it does them much harm, even if they do grow up book-students. Such people as that, 'tis a great pleasure seeing them so happy over work which is not much sought for. And besides, these students are generally such pleasant people; so kind and sweet-tempered; so humble, and at the same time so anxious to teach everybody all that they know. Really, I like those that I have met prodigiously."

This seemed to me such *very* queer talk that I was on the point of asking him another question; when just as we came to the top of a rising ground, down a long glade of the wood on my right I caught sight of a stately building whose outline was familiar to me, and I cried out, "Westminster Abbey!"

"Yes," said Dick, "Westminster Abbey—what there is left of it."

"Why, what have you done with it?" quoth I in terror.

"What have *we* done with it?" said he; "nothing much, save clean it. But you know the whole outside was spoiled centuries ago: as to the inside, that remains in its beauty after the great clearance, which took place over a hundred years ago, of the

[handwritten marginal note:] not having to be / Children an / Victorian / gentleman

beastly monuments to fools and knaves, which once blocked it up, as great-grandfather says."[1]

We went on a little further, and I looked to the right again, and said, in rather a doubtful tone of voice, "Why, there are the Houses of Parliament! Do you still use them?"

He burst out laughing, and was some time before he could control himself; then he clapped me on the back and said:

"I take you, neighbour; you may well wonder at our keeping them standing, and I know something about that, and my old kinsman has given me books to read about the strange game that they played there. Use them! Well, yes, they are used for a sort of subsidiary market, and a storage place for manure, and they are handy for that, being on the water-side. I believe it was intended to pull them down quite at the beginning of our days; but there was, I am told, a queer antiquarian society, which had done some service in past times, and which straightway set up its pipe against their destruction, as it has done with many other buildings, which most people looked upon as worthless, and public nuisances; and it was so energetic, and had such good reasons to give, that it generally gained its point;[2] and I must say that when all is said I am glad of it: because you know at the worst these silly old buildings serve as a kind of foil to the beautiful ones which we build now. You will see several others in these parts; the place my great-grandfather lives in, for instance, and a big building called St. Paul's.[3] And you see, in this matter we need not grudge a few poorish buildings standing, because we can always build elsewhere; nor need we be anxious as to the breeding of pleasant work in such matters, for there is always room for more and more work in a new building, even without making

---

[1]   Morris was a member of the Society for the Protection of Ancient Buildings from 1877 onward. Shortly before and during the period in which *News from Nowhere* was being written, the Society was active in trying to save the Abbey from what Morris considered disfiguring "restorations."

[2]   If the "queer antiquarian society" is the Society for the Preservation of Ancient Buildings (see previous note), then Morris is here making a joke at his own expense, since he loathed the sham Gothic architecture of Charles Barry's and A. W. Pugin's Palace of Westminster (home to Britain's Parliament) and would undoubtedly have enjoyed seeing the building pulled down.

3   St. Paul's Cathedral, designed by Sir Christopher Wren and built 1675-1710.

it pretentious. For instance, elbow-room *within* doors is to me so delightful that if I were driven to it I would almost sacrifice outdoor space to it. Then, of course, there is the ornament, which, as we must all allow, may easily be overdone in mere living houses, but can hardly be in mote-halls and markets, and so forth. I must tell you, though, that my great-grandfather sometimes tells me I am a little cracked on this subject of fine building; and indeed I *do* think that the energies of mankind are chiefly of use to them for such work; for in that direction I can see no end to the work, while in many others a limit does seem possible."

CHAPTER VI

A LITTLE SHOPPING

As he spoke, we came suddenly out of the woodland into a short street of handsomely built houses, which my companion named to me at once as Piccadilly: the lower part of these I should have called shops, if it had not been that, as far as I could see, the people were ignorant of the arts of buying and selling. Wares were displayed in their finely designed fronts, as if to tempt people in, and people stood and looked at them, or went in and came out with parcels under their arms, just like the real thing. On each side of the street ran an elegant arcade to protect foot-passengers, as in some of the old Italian cities. About half-way down, a huge building of the kind I was now prepared to expect told me that this also was a centre of some kind, and had its special public buildings.

Said Dick: "Here, you see, is another market on a different plan from most others: the upper stories of these houses are used for guest-houses; for people from all about the country are apt to drift up hither from time to time, as folk are very thick upon the ground, which you will see evidence of presently, and there are people who are fond of crowds, though I can't say that I am."

I couldn't help smiling to see how long a tradition would last. Here was the ghost of London still asserting itself as a centre,—

an intellectual centre, for aught I knew. However, I said nothing, except that I asked him to drive very slowly, as the things in the booths looked exceedingly pretty.

"Yes," said he, "this is a very good market for pretty things, and is mostly kept for the handsomer goods, as the Houses-of-Parliament market, where they set out cabbages and turnips and such like things, along with beer and the rougher kind of wine, is so near."

Then he looked at me curiously, and said, "Perhaps you would like to do a little shopping, as 'tis called."

I looked at what I could see of my rough blue duds, which I had plenty of opportunity of contrasting with the gay attire of the citizens we had come across; and I thought that if, as seemed likely, I should presently be shown about as a curiosity for the amusement of this most unbusinesslike people, I should like to look a little less like a discharged ship's purser. But in spite of all that had happened, my hand went down into my pocket again, where to my dismay it met nothing metallic except two rusty old keys, and I remembered that amidst our talk in the guest-hall at Hammersmith I had taken the cash out of my pocket to show to the pretty Annie, and had left it lying there. My face fell fifty per cent., and Dick, beholding me, said rather sharply—

"Hilloa, Guest! What's the matter now? Is it a wasp?"

"No," said I, "but I've left it behind."

"Well," said he, "whatever you have left behind, you can get in this market again, so don't trouble yourself about it."

I had come to my senses by this time, and remembering the astounding customs of this country, had no mind for another lecture on social economy and the Edwardian coinage;[1] so I said only—

"My clothes—Couldn't I? You see—What do you think could be done about them?"

He didn't seem in the least inclined to laugh, but said quite gravely:

"O don't get new clothes yet. You see, my great-grandfather is an antiquarian, and he will want to see you just as you are. And,

---

[1] Guest is recalling his earlier conversation with Dick about ancient coins (see pp. 60-61).

shifting power dynamic from observer to observed

you know, I mustn't preach to you, but surely it wouldn't be right for you to take away people's pleasure of studying your attire, by just going and making yourself like everybody else. You feel that, don't you?" said he, earnestly.

I did *not* feel it my duty to set myself up for a scarecrow amidst this beauty-loving people, but I saw I had got across some ineradicable prejudice, and that it wouldn't do to quarrel with my new friend. So I merely said, "O certainly, certainly."

"Well," said he, pleasantly, "you may as well see what the inside of these booths is like: think of something you want."

Said I: "Could I get some tobacco and a pipe?"

"Of course," said he; "what was I thinking of, not asking you before? Well, Bob is always telling me that we non-smokers are a selfish lot, and I'm afraid he is right. But come along; here is a place just handy."

Therewith he drew rein and jumped down, and I followed. A very handsome woman, splendidly clad in figured silk, was slowly passing by, looking into the windows as she went. To her quoth Dick: "Maiden, would you kindly hold our horse while we go in for a little?" She nodded to us with a kind smile, and fell to patting the horse with her pretty hand.

"What a beautiful creature!" said I to Dick as we entered.

"What, old Greylocks?" said he, with a sly grin.

"No, no," said I; "Goldylocks,—the lady."

"Well, so she is," said he. "'Tis a good job there are so many of them that every Jack may have his Jill: else I fear that we should get fighting for them. Indeed," said he, becoming very grave, "I don't say that it does not happen even now, sometimes. For you know love is not a very reasonable thing, and perversity and self-will are commoner than some of our moralists think." He added, in a still more sombre tone: "Yes, only a month ago there was a mishap down by us, that in the end cost the lives of two men and a woman, and, as it were, put out the sunlight for us for a while. Don't ask me about it just now; I may tell you about it later on."

By this time we were within the shop or booth, which had a counter, and shelves on the walls, all very neat, though without any pretence of showiness, but otherwise not very different to what I had been used to. Within were a couple of children—a brown-skinned boy of about twelve, who sat reading a book, and a pretty little girl of about a year older, who was sitting also reading behind the counter; they were obviously brother and sister.

"Good morning, little neighbours," said Dick. "My friend here wants tobacco and a pipe; can you help him?"

"O yes, certainly," said the girl with a sort of demure alertness which was somewhat amusing. The boy looked up, and fell to staring at my outlandish attire, but presently reddened and turned his head, as if he knew that he was not behaving prettily.

"Dear neighbour," said the girl, with the most solemn countenance of a child playing at keeping shop, "what tobacco is it you would like?"

"Latakia,"[1] quoth I, feeling as if I were assisting at a child's game, and wondering whether I should get anything but make-believe.

But the girl took a dainty little basket from a shelf beside her, went to a jar, and took out a lot of tobacco and put the filled basket down on the counter before me, where I could both smell and see that it was excellent Latakia.

"But you haven't weighed it," said I, "and—and how much am I to take?"

"Why," she said, "I advise you to cram your bag, because you may be going where you can't get Latakia. Where is your bag?"

I fumbled about, and at last pulled out my piece of cotton print which does duty with me for a tobacco pouch. But the girl looked at it with some disdain, and said—

"Dear neighbour, I can give you something much better than that cotton rag." And she tripped up the shop and came back presently, and as she passed the boy whispered something in his ear, and he nodded and got up and went out. The girl held up in her finger and thumb a red morocco bag, gaily embroidered, and said, "There, I have chosen one for you, and you are to have it: it is pretty, and will hold a lot."

Therewith she fell to cramming it with the tobacco, and laid it down by me and said, "Now for the pipe: that also you must let me choose for you; there are three pretty ones just come in."

---

[1]   A kind of Turkish tobacco.

She disappeared again, and came back with a big-bowled pipe in her hand, carved out of some hard wood very elaborately, and mounted in gold sprinkled with little gems. It was, in short, as pretty and gay a toy as I had ever seen; something like the best kind of Japanese work, but better.

"Dear me!" said I, when I set eyes on it, "this is altogether too grand for me, or for anybody but the Emperor of the World. Besides, I shall lose it—I always lose my pipes."

The child seemed rather dashed, and said, "Don't you like it, neighbour?"

"O yes," I said, "of course I like it."

"Well, then, take it," said she, "and don't trouble about losing it. What will it matter if you do? Somebody is sure to find it, and he will use it, and you can get another."

I took it out of her hand to look at it, and while I did so, forgot my caution, and said, "But however am I to pay for such a thing as this?"

Dick laid his hand on my shoulder as I spoke, and turning I met his eyes with a comical expression in them, which warned me against another exhibition of extinct commercial morality; so I reddened and held my tongue, while the girl simply looked at me with the deepest gravity, as if I were a foreigner blundering in my speech, for she clearly didn't understand me a bit.

"Thank you so very much," I said at last, effusively, as I put the pipe in my pocket, not without a qualm of doubt as to whether I shouldn't find myself before a magistrate presently.

"O, you are so very welcome," said the little lass, with an affectation of grown-up manners at their best which was very quaint. "It is such a pleasure to serve dear old gentlemen like you; especially when one can see at once that you have come from far over sea."

"Yes, my dear," quoth I, "I have been a great traveller."

As I told this lie from pure politeness, in came the lad again, with a tray in his hands, on which I saw a long flask and two beautiful glasses. "Neighbours," said the girl (who did all the talking, her brother being very shy, clearly) "please to drink a glass to us before you go, since we do not have guests like this every day."

Therewith the boy put the tray on the counter and solemnly poured out a straw-coloured wine into the long bowls. Nothing loth, I drank, for I was thirsty with the hot day; and thinks I, I am yet in the world, and the grapes of the Rhine have not yet lost their flavour; for if ever I drank good Steinberg,[1] I drank it that morning; and I made a mental note to ask Dick how they managed to make fine wine when there were no longer labourers compelled to drink rot-gut instead of the fine wine which they themselves made.

"Don't you drink a glass to us, dear little neighbours?" said I.

"I don't drink wine," said the lass; "I like lemonade better: but I wish your health!"

"And I like ginger-beer better," said the little lad.

Well, well, thought I, neither have children's tastes changed much. And therewith we gave them good day and went out of the booth.

To my disappointment, like a change in a dream, a tall old man was holding our horse instead of the beautiful woman. He explained to us that the maiden could not wait, and that he had taken her place; and he winked at us and laughed when he saw how our faces fell, so that we had nothing for it but to laugh also.

"Where are you going?" said he to Dick.

"To Bloomsbury," said Dick.

"If you two don't want to be alone, I'll come with you," said the old man.

"All right," said Dick, "tell me when you want to get down and I'll stop for you. Let's get on."

So we got under way again; and I asked if children generally waited on people in the markets. "Often enough," said he, "when it isn't a matter of dealing with heavy weights, but by no means always. The children like to amuse themselves with it, and it is good for them, because they handle a lot of diverse wares and get to learn about them, how they are made, and where they come from, and so on. Besides, it is such very easy work that anybody can do it. It is said that in the early days of our epoch there were a good many people who were hereditarily afflicted with a disease called Idleness, because they were the direct descendants of those who in the bad times used to force other people to work for them—the people,

---

[1]   One of the finer German white wines.

you know, who are called slave-holders or employers of labour in the history books. Well, these Idleness-stricken people used to serve booths *all* their time, because they were fit for so little. Indeed, I believe that at one time they were actually *compelled* to do some such work, because they, especially the women, got so ugly and produced such ugly children if their disease was not treated sharply, that the neighbours couldn't stand it. However, I'm happy to say that all that is gone by now; the disease is either extinct, or exists in such a mild form that a short course of aperient[1] medicine carries it off. It is sometimes called the Blue-devils now, or the Mulleygrubs.[2] Queer names, ain't they?"

"Yes," said I, pondering much. But the old man broke in:

"Yes, all that is true, neighbour; and I have seen some of those poor women grown old. But my father used to know some of them when they were young; and he said that they were as little like young women as might be: they had hands like bunches of skewers, and wretched little arms like sticks; and waists like hour-glasses, and thin lips and peaked noses and pale cheeks; and they were always pretending to be offended at anything you said or did to them. No wonder they bore ugly children, for no one except men like them could be in love with them—poor things!"

He stopped, and seemed to be musing on his past life, and then said:

"And do you know, neighbours, that once on a time people were still anxious about that disease of Idleness: at one time we gave ourselves a great deal of trouble in trying to cure people of it. Have you not read any of the medical books on the subject?"

"No," said I; for the old man was speaking to me.

"Well," said he, "it was thought at the time that it was the survival of the old mediæval disease of leprosy: it seems it was very catching, for many of the people afflicted by it were much secluded, and were waited upon by a special class of diseased persons queerly dressed up, so that they might be known. They wore amongst other garments, breeches made of worsted velvet, that stuff which used to be called plush some years ago."

---

[1] An aperient is a laxative.
[2] Colloquialisms for low spirits.

All this seemed very interesting to me, and I should like to have made the old man talk more. But Dick got rather restive under so much ancient history: besides, I suspect he wanted to keep me as fresh as he could for his great-grandfather. So he burst out laughing at last, and said: "Excuse me, neighbours, but I can't help it. Fancy people not liking to work!—it's too ridiculous. Why, even you like to work, old fellow—sometimes," said he, affectionately patting the old horse with the whip. "What a queer disease! it may well be called Mulleygrubs!"

And he laughed out again most boisterously; rather too much so, I thought, for his usual good manners; and I laughed with him for company's sake, but from the teeth outward only; for *I* saw nothing funny in people not liking to work, as you may well imagine.

CHAPTER VII

TRAFALGAR SQUARE

And now again I was busy looking about me, for we were quite clear of Piccadilly Market, and were in a region of elegantly-built much ornamented houses, which I should have called villas if they had been ugly and pretentious, which was very far from being the case. Each house stood in a garden carefully cultivated, and running over with flowers. The blackbirds were singing their best amidst the garden-trees, which, except for a bay here and there, and occasional groups of limes, seemed to be all fruit-trees: there were a great many cherry-trees, now all laden with fruit; and several times as we passed by a garden we were offered baskets of fine fruit by children and young girls. Amidst all these gardens and houses it was of course impossible to trace the sites of the old streets: but it seemed to me that the main roadways were the same as of old.

We came presently into a large open space, sloping somewhat toward the south, the sunny site of which had been taken advantage of for planting an orchard, mainly, as I could see, of apricot-trees, in the midst of which was a pretty gay little structure of wood, painted and gilded, that looked like a refreshment-stall. From the southern side of the said orchard ran a long road, chequered over with the shadow of tall old pear trees, at the end of which showed the high tower of the Parliament House, or Dung Market.

A strange sensation came over me; I shut my eyes to keep out the sight of the sun glittering on this fair abode of gardens, and for a moment there passed before them a phantasmagoria of another day. A great space surrounded by tall ugly houses, with an ugly church at the corner and a nondescript ugly cupolaed building at my back; the roadway thronged with a sweltering and excited crowd, dominated by omnibuses crowded with spectators. In the midst a paved be-fountained square, populated only by a few men dressed in blue, and a good many singularly ugly bronze images (one on the top of a tall column). The said square guarded up to the edge of the roadway by a four-fold line of big men clad in blue, and across the southern roadway the helmets of a band of horse-soldiers, dead white in the greyness of the chilly November afternoon—[1]

I opened my eyes to the sunlight again and looked round me, and cried out among the whispering trees and odorous blossoms, "Trafalgar Square!"

"Yes," said Dick, who had drawn rein again, "so it is. I don't wonder at your finding the name ridiculous: but after all, it was nobody's business to alter it, since the name of a dead folly does-n't bite. Yet sometimes I think we might have given it a name which would have commemorated the great battle which was fought on the spot itself in 1952,—*that* was important enough, if the historians don't lie."

"Which they generally do, or at least did," said the old man. "For instance, what can you make of this, neighbours? I have read a muddled account in a book—O a stupid book!—called James' Social Democratic History,[2] of a fight which took place here in

---

[1]   Guest is evoking the atmosphere of Trafalgar Square immediately preceding the Bloody Sunday clashes, November 13, 1887. See Introduction, pp. 40-42, and Appendix E. The "ugly church" is St. Martin's-in-the-Fields, the "ugly cupolaed building" the National Gallery of Art, both of which adjoin Trafalgar Square. At the center of the Square is a 170-foot-tall column topped with a statue in bronze of Lord Nelson, victor over Napoleon at the Battle of Trafalgar.

[2]   If such a book exists, I have been unable to locate it.

or about the year 1887 (I am bad at dates). Some people, says this story, were going to hold a ward-mote[1] here, or some such thing, and the Government of London, or the Council, or the Commission, or what not other barbarous half-hatched body of fools, fell upon these citizens (as they were then called) with the armed hand. That seems too ridiculous to be true; but according to this version of the story, nothing much came of it, which certainly *is* too ridiculous to be true."

"Well," quoth I, "but after all your Mr. James is right so far, and it *is* true; except that there was no fighting, merely unarmed and peaceable people attacked by ruffians armed with bludgeons."

"And they put up with that?" said Dick, with the first unpleasant expression I had seen on his good-tempered face.

Said I, reddening: "We *had* to put up with it; we couldn't help it."

The old man looked at me keenly, and said: "You seem to know a great deal about it, neighbour! And is it really true that nothing came of it?"

"This came of it," said I, "that a good many people were sent to prison because of it."

"What, of the bludgeoners?" said the old man. "Poor devils!"

"No, no," said I, "of the bludgeoned."

Said the old man rather severely: "Friend, I expect that you have been reading some rotten collection of lies, and have been taken in by it too easily."

"I assure you," said I, "what I have been saying is true."

"Well, well, I am sure you think so, neighbour," said the old man, "but I don't see why you should be so cocksure."

As I couldn't explain why, I held my tongue. Meanwhile Dick, who had been sitting with knit brows, cogitating, spoke at last, and said gently and rather sadly:

"How strange to think that there have been men like ourselves, and living in this beautiful and happy country, who I suppose had feelings and affections like ourselves, who could yet do such dreadful things."

"Yes," said I, in a didactic tone; "yet after all, even those days were

---

[1] A mote is a gathering of the citizens in a particular area or region, in this case a city ward. Such gatherings would not have occurred in Victorian London.

a great improvement on the days that had gone before them. Have you not read of the Mediæval period, and the ferocity of its criminal laws; and how in those days men fairly seemed to have enjoyed tormenting their fellow men?—nay, for the matter of that, they made their God a tormentor and a jailer rather than anything else."

"Yes," said Dick, "there are good books on that period also, some of which I have read. But as to the great improvement of the nineteenth century, I don't see it. After all, the Mediæval folk acted after their conscience, as your remark about their God (which is true) shows, and they were ready to bear what they inflicted on others; whereas the nineteenth century ones were hypocrites, and pretended to be humane, and yet went on tormenting those whom they dared to treat so by shutting them up in prison, for no reason at all, except that they were what they themselves, the prison-masters, had forced them to be. O, it's horrible to think of!"

"But perhaps," said I, "they did not know what the prisons were like."

Dick seemed roused, and even angry. "More shame for them," said he, "when you and I know it all these years afterwards. Look you, neighbour, they couldn't fail to know what a disgrace a prison is to the Commonwealth at the best, and that their prisons were a good step on towards being at the worst."

Quoth I: "But have you no prisons at all now?"

As soon as the words were out of my mouth, I felt that I had made a mistake, for Dick flushed red and frowned, and the old man looked surprised and pained; and presently Dick said angrily, yet as if restraining himself somewhat—

"Man alive! how can you ask such a question? Have I not told you that we know what a prison means by the undoubted evidence of really trustworthy books, helped out by our own imaginations? And haven't you specially called me to notice that the people about the roads and streets look happy? and how could they look happy if they knew that their neighbours were shut up in prison, while they bore such things quietly? And if there were people in prison, you couldn't hide it from folk, like you may an occasional man-slaying; because that isn't done of set purpose, with a lot of people backing up the slayer in cold blood, as this prison business is. Prisons, indeed! O no, no, no!"

He stopped, and began to cool down, and said in a kind voice: "But forgive me! I needn't be so hot about it, since there are *not* any prisons: I'm afraid you will think the worse of me for losing my temper. Of course, you, coming from the outlands, cannot be expected to know about these things. And now I'm afraid I have made you feel uncomfortable."

In a way he had; but he was so generous in his heat, that I liked him the better for it, and I said: "No, really 'tis all my fault for being so stupid. Let me change the subject, and ask you what the stately building is on our left just showing at the end of that grove of plane-trees?"

"Ah," he said, "that is an old building built before the middle of the twentieth century, and as you see, in a queer fantastic style not over beautiful; but there are some fine things inside it, too, mostly pictures, some very old. It is called the National Gallery; I have sometimes puzzled as to what the name means: anyhow, nowadays wherever there is a place where pictures are kept as curiosities permanently it is called a National Gallery, perhaps after this one. Of course there are a good many of them up and down the country."

I didn't try to enlighten him, feeling the task too heavy; but I pulled out my magnificent pipe and fell a-smoking, and the old horse jogged on again. As we went, I said:

"This pipe is a very elaborate toy, and you seem so reasonable in this country, and your architecture is so good, that I rather wonder at your turning out such trivialities."

It struck me as I spoke that this was rather ungrateful of me, after having received such a fine present; but Dick didn't seem to notice my bad manners, but said:

"Well, I don't know; it *is* a pretty thing, and since nobody need make such things unless they like, I don't see why they shouldn't make them, *if* they like. Of course, if carvers were scarce they would all be busy on the architecture, as you call it, and then these 'toys' (a good word) would not be made; but since there are plenty of people who can carve—in fact, almost everybody, and as work is somewhat scarce, or we are afraid it may be, folk do not discourage this kind of petty work."

He mused a little, and seemed somewhat perturbed; but

presently his face cleared, and he said: "After all, you must admit that the pipe is a very pretty thing, with the little people under the trees all cut so clean and sweet;—too elaborate for a pipe, perhaps, but—well, it is very pretty."

"Too valuable for its use, perhaps," said I.

"What's that?" said he; "I don't understand."

I was just going in a helpless way to try to make him understand, when we came by the gates of a big rambling building, in which work of some sort seemed going on. "What building is that?" said I, eagerly; for it was a pleasure amidst all these strange things to see something a little like what I was used to: "it seems to be a factory."

"Yes," he said, "I think I know what you mean, and that's what it is; but we don't call them factories now, but Banded-workshops: that is, places where people collect who want to work together."

"I suppose," said I, "power of some sort is used there?"

"No, no," said he. "Why would people collect together to use power, when they can have it at the places where they live, or hard by, any two or three of them; or any one, for the matter of that? No; folk collect in these Banded-workshops to do hand-work in which working together is necessary or convenient; such work is often very pleasant. In there, for instance, they make pottery and glass,—there, you can see the tops of the furnaces. Well, of course it's handy to have fair-sized ovens and kilns and glass-pots, and a good lot of things to use them for: though of course there are a good many such places, as it would be ridiculous if a man had a liking for pot-making or glass-blowing that he should have to live in one place or be obliged to forego the work he liked."

"I see no smoke coming from the furnaces," said I.

"Smoke?" said Dick; "why should you see smoke?"

I held my tongue, and he went on: "It's a nice place inside, though as plain as you see outside. As to the crafts, throwing the clay must be jolly work: the glass-blowing is rather a sweltering job; but some folk like it very much indeed; and I don't much wonder: there is such a sense of power, when you have got deft in it, in dealing with the hot metal. It makes a lot of pleasant work," said he, smiling, "for however much care you take of such goods, break they will, one day or another, so there is always plenty to do."

I held my tongue and pondered.[1]

We came just here on a gang of men road-mending which delayed us a little; but I was not sorry for it; for all I had seen hitherto seemed a mere part of a summer holiday; and I wanted to see how this folk would set to on a piece of real necessary work. They had been resting, and had only just begun work again as we came up; so that the rattle of the picks was what woke me from my musing. There were about a dozen of them, strong young men, looking much like a boating party at Oxford would have looked in the days I remembered, and not more troubled with their work: their outer raiment lay on the road-side in an orderly pile under the guardianship of a six-year-old boy, who had his arm thrown over the neck of a big mastiff, who was as happily lazy as if the summer-day had been made for him alone. As I eyed the pile of clothes, I could see the gleam of gold and silk embroidery on it, and judged that some of these workmen had tastes akin to those of the Golden Dustman of Hammersmith. Beside them lay a good big basket that had hints about it of cold pie and wine: a half dozen of young women stood by watching the work or the workers, both of which were worth watching, for the latter smote great strokes and were very deft in their labour, and as handsome clean-built fellows as you might find a dozen of in a summer day. They were laughing and talking merrily with each other and the women, but presently their foreman looked up and saw our way stopped. So he stayed his pick and sang out, "Spell ho, mates! here are neighbours want to get past." Whereon the others stopped also, and, drawing around us, helped the old horse by easing our wheels over the half undone road, and then, like men with a pleasant task on hand, hurried back to their work, only stopping to give us a smiling good-day; so that the sound of the picks broke out again before Greylocks had taken to his jog-trot. Dick looked back over his shoulder at them and said:

"They are in luck today: it's right down good sport trying how

---

[1]   In *Das Kapital*, Marx dwells on the horrors of working in a nineteenth-century glass factory.

much pick-work one can get into an hour; and I can see those neighbours know their business well. It is not a mere matter of strength getting on quickly with such work; is it, guest?"

"I should think not," said I, "but to tell you the truth, I have never tried my hand at it."

"Really?" said he gravely, "that seems a pity; it is good work for hardening the muscles, and I like it; though I admit it is pleasanter the second week than the first. Not that I am a good hand at it: the fellows used to chaff me at one job where I was working, I remember, and sing out to me, 'Well rowed, stroke!' 'Put your back into it, bow!'"[1]

"Not much of a joke," quoth I.

"Well," said Dick, "everything seems like a joke when we have a pleasant spell of work on, and good fellows merry about us; we feel so happy, you know." Again I pondered silently.

CHAPTER VIII

AN OLD FRIEND

We now turned into a pleasant lane where the branches of great plane-trees nearly met overhead, but behind them lay low houses standing rather close together.

"This is Long Acre,"[2] quoth Dick; "so there must once have been a cornfield here. How curious it is that places change so, and yet keep their old names! Just look how thick the houses stand! and they are still going on building, look you!"

"Yes," said the old man, "but I think the cornfields must have been built over before the middle of the nineteenth century. I have heard that about here was one of the thickest parts of the town. But I must get down here, neighbours; I have got to call

---

[1] Terms from competitive rowing: the bow is the first oarsman, the stroke the oarsman furthest astern.
[2] A London street a few blocks from the British Museum.

on a friend who lives in the gardens behind this Long Acre. Good-bye and good luck, Guest!"

And he jumped down and strode away vigorously, like a young man.

"How old should you say that neighbour will be?" said I to Dick as we lost sight of him; for I saw that he was old, and yet he looked dry and sturdy like a piece of old oak; a type of old man I was not used to seeing.

"O, about ninety, I should say," said Dick.

"How long-lived your people must be!" said I.

"Yes," said Dick, "certainly we have beaten the threescore-and-ten of the old Jewish proverb-book.[1] But then you see that was written of Syria, a hot dry country, where people live faster than in our temperate climate. However, I don't think it matters much, so long as a man is healthy and happy while he *is* alive. But now, Guest, we are so near to my old kinsman's dwelling-place that I think you had better keep all future questions for him."

I nodded a yes; and therewith we turned to the left, and went down a gentle slope through some beautiful rose-gardens, laid out on what I took to be the site of Endell Street. We passed on, and Dick drew rein an instant as we came across a long straightish road with houses scantily scattered up and down it. He waved his hand right and left, and said, "Holborn that side, Oxford Road that. This was once a very important part of the crowded city outside the ancient walls of the Roman and Mediæval burg: many of the feudal lords of the Middle Ages, we are told, had big houses on either side of Holborn. I daresay you remember that the Bishop of Ely's house is mentioned in Shakespeare's play of King Richard III.;[2] and there are some remains of that still left. However, this road is not of the same importance, now that the ancient city is gone, walls and all."

He drove on again, while I smiled faintly to think how the nineteenth century, of which such big words have been said, counted for nothing in the memory of this man, who read Shakespeare and had not forgotten the Middle Ages.

---

[1] See Psalms 90:10.

[2] See *Richard III*, III.iv.33-36, though Dick may be recalling a better-known episode set at the Bishop of Ely's palace in *Richard II*, II.i.

We crossed the road into a short narrow lane between the gardens, and came out again into a wide road, on one side of which was a great and long building, turning its gables away from the highway, which I saw at once was another public group. Opposite to it was a wide space of greenery, without any wall or fence of any kind. I looked through the trees and saw beyond them a pillared portico quite familiar to me—no less old a friend, in fact, than the British Museum. It rather took my breath away, amidst all the strange things I had seen; but I held my tongue and let Dick speak. Said he:

"Yonder is the British Museum, where my great-grandfather mostly lives; so I won't say much about it. The building on the left is the Museum Market, and I think we had better turn in there for a minute or two; for Greylocks will be wanting his rest and his oats; and I suppose you will stay with my kinsman the greater part of the day; and to say the truth, there may be some one there whom I particularly want to see, and perhaps have a long talk with."

He blushed and sighed, not altogether with pleasure, I thought; so of course I said nothing, and he turned the horse under an archway which brought us into a very large paved quadrangle, with a big sycamore tree in each corner and a plashing fountain in the midst. Near the fountain were a few market stalls, with awnings over them of gay striped linen cloth, about which some people, mostly women and children, were moving quietly, looking at the goods exposed there. The ground floor of the building round the quadrangle was occupied by a wide arcade or cloister, whose fanciful but strong architecture I could not enough admire. Here also a few people were sauntering or sitting reading on the benches.

Dick said to me apologetically: "Here as elsewhere there is little doing to-day; on a Friday you would see it thronged, and gay with people, and in the afternoon there is generally music about the fountain. However, I daresay we shall have a pretty good gathering at our mid-day meal."

We drove through the quadrangle and by an archway, into a large handsome stable on the other side, where we speedily stalled the old nag and made him happy with horse-meat, and then turned and walked back again through the market, Dick looking rather thoughtful, as it seemed to me.

I noticed that people couldn't help looking at me rather hard; and considering my clothes and theirs, I didn't wonder; but whenever they caught my eye they made me a very friendly sign of greeting.

We walked straight into the forecourt of the Museum, where, except that the railings were gone, and the whispering boughs of the trees were all about, nothing seemed changed; the very pigeons were wheeling about the building and clinging to the ornaments of the pediment as I had seen them of old.

Dick seemed grown a little absent, but he could not forbear giving me an architectural note, and said:

"It is rather an ugly old building, isn't it? Many people have wanted to pull it down and rebuild it: and perhaps if work does really get scarce we may yet do so. But, as my great-grandfather will tell you, it would not be quite a straightforward job; for there are wonderful collections in there of all kinds of antiquities, besides an enormous library with many exceedingly beautiful books in it, and many most useful ones as genuine records, texts of ancient works and the like; and the worry and anxiety, and even risk, there would be in moving all this has saved the buildings themselves. Besides, as we said before, it is not a bad thing to have some record of what our forefathers thought a handsome building. For there is plenty of labour and material in it."

"I see there is," said I, "and I quite agree with you. But now hadn't we better make haste to see your great-grandfather?"

In fact, I could not help seeing that he was rather dallying with the time. He said, "Yes, we will go into the house in a minute. My kinsman is too old to do much work in the Museum, where he was a custodian of the books for many years; but he still lives here a good deal; indeed I think," said he, smiling, "that he looks upon himself as a part of the books, or the books a part of him, I don't know which."

He hesitated a little longer, then flushing up, took my hand, saying, "Come along, then!" led me toward the door of one of the old official dwellings.

CHAPTER IX

CONCERNING LOVE

"Your kinsman doesn't much care for beautiful building, then," said I, as we entered the rather dreary classical house; which indeed was as bare as need be, except for some big pots of the June flowers which stood about here and there; though it was very clean and nicely whitewashed.

"O, I don't know," said Dick, rather absently. "He is getting old, certainly, for he is over a hundred and five, and no doubt he doesn't care about moving. But of course he could live in a prettier house if he liked: he is not obliged to live in one place any more than any one else. This way, Guest."

And he led the way upstairs, and opening a door we went into a fair-sized room of the old type, as plain as the rest of the house, with a few necessary pieces of furniture, and those very simple and even rude, but solid and with a good deal of carving about them, well designed but rather crudely executed. At the furthest corner of the room, at a desk near the window, sat a little old man in a roomy oak chair, well becushioned. He was dressed in a sort of Norfolk jacket of blue serge worn threadbare, with breeches of the same, and grey worsted stockings. He jumped up from his chair, and cried out in a voice of considerable volume for such an old man, "Welcome, Dick, my lad; Clara is here, and will be more than glad to see you; so keep your heart up."

"Clara here?" quoth Dick; "if I had known, I would not have brought—At least, I mean I would—"

He was stuttering and confused, clearly because he was anxious to say nothing to make me feel one too many. But the old man, who had not seen me at first, helped him out by coming forward and saying to me in a kind tone:

"Pray pardon me, for I did not notice that Dick, who is big enough to hide anybody, you know, had brought a friend with him. A most hearty welcome to you! All the more, as I almost hope that you are going to amuse an old man by giving him news from over sea, for I can see that you are come from over the water and far off countries."

He looked at me thoughtfully, almost anxiously, as he said in a changed voice, "Might I ask you where you come from, as you are so clearly a stranger?"

I said in an absent way: "I used to live in England, and now I am come back again; and I slept last night at the Hammersmith Guest House."

He bowed gravely, but seemed, I thought, a little disappointed with my answer. As for me, I was now looking at him harder than good manners allowed of, perhaps; for in truth his face, dried-apple-like as it was, seemed strangely familiar to me; as if I had seen it before—in a looking-glass, it might be, said I to myself.

"Well," said the old man, "wherever you come from, you are come among friends. And I see my kinsman Richard Hammond has an air about him as if he had brought you here for me to do something for you. Is that so, Dick?"

Dick, who was getting still more absent-minded and kept looking uneasily at the door, managed to say, "Well, yes, kinsman: our guest finds things much altered, and cannot understand it; nor can I; so I thought I would bring him to you, since you know more of all that has happened within the last two hundred years than anybody else does.—What's that?"

And he turned toward the door again. We heard footsteps outside; the door opened, and in came a very beautiful young woman, who stopped short on seeing Dick, and flushed as red as a rose, but faced him nonetheless. Dick looked at her hard, and half-reached out his hand toward her, and his whole face quivered with emotion.

The old man did not leave them long in this shy discomfort, but said, smiling with an old man's mirth: "Dick, my lad, and you, my dear Clara, I rather think that we two oldsters are in your way; for I think you will have plenty to say to each other. You had better go into Nelson's room up above; I know he has gone out; and he has just been covering the walls all over with mediæval books, so it will be pretty enough for you two and your renewed pleasure."

The girl reached out her hand to Dick, and taking his led him out of the room, looking straight before her; but it was easy to see that her blushes came from happiness, not anger; as, indeed, love is far more self-conscious than wrath.

When the door had shut on them the old man turned to me, still smiling, and said:

"Frankly, my dear guest, you will do me a great service if you are come to set my old tongue wagging. My love of talk still abides with me, or rather grows on me; and though it is pleasant enough to see these youngsters moving about and playing together so seriously, as if the whole world depended on their kisses (as indeed it does somewhat), yet I don't think my tales of the past interest them much. The last harvest, the last baby, the last knot of carving in the market-place, is history enough for them. It was different, I think, when I was a lad, when we were not so assured of peace and continuous plenty as we are now—Well, well! Without putting you to the question, let me ask you this: Am I to consider you as an enquirer who knows a little of our modern ways of life, or as one who comes from some place where the very foundations of life are different from ours,—do you know anything or nothing about us?"

He looked at me keenly and with growing wonder in his eyes as he spoke; and I answered in a low voice:

"I know only so much of your modern life as I could gather from using my eyes on the way here from Hammersmith, and from asking some questions of Richard Hammond, most of which he could hardly understand."

The old man smiled at this. "Then," said he, "I am to speak to you as—"

"As if I were a being from another planet," said I.

The old man, whose name, by the bye, like his kinsman's, was Hammond, smiled and nodded, and wheeling his seat round to me, bade me sit in a heavy oak chair, and said, as he saw my eyes fix on its curious carving:

"Yes, I am much tied to the past, *my* past, you understand. These very pieces of furniture belong to a time before my early days; it was my father who got them made; if they had been done within the last fifty years they would have been much cleverer in execution; but I don't think I should have liked them the better. We were almost beginning again in those days: and they were brisk, hot-headed times. But you hear how garrulous I am: ask me questions, ask me questions about anything, dear guest; since I *must* talk, make my talk profitable to you."

I was silent for a minute, and then I said, somewhat nervously: "Excuse me if I am rude: but I am so much interested in Richard, since he has been so kind to me, a perfect stranger, that I should like to ask a question about him."

"Well," said old Hammond, "if he were not 'kind,' as you call it, to a perfect stranger he would be thought a strange person, and people would be apt to shun him. But ask on, ask on! Don't be shy of asking."

Said I : "That beautiful girl, is he going to be married to her?"

"Well," said he, "yes, he is. He has been married to her once already, and now I should say it is pretty clear that he will be married to her again."

"Indeed," quoth I, wondering what that meant.

"Here is the whole tale," said old Hammond; "a short one enough; and now I hope a happy one: they lived together two years the first time; were both very young; and then she got it into her head that she was in love with somebody else. So she left poor Dick; I say *poor* Dick, because he had not found any one else. But it did not last long, only about a year. Then she came to me, as she was in the habit of bringing her troubles to the old carle,[1] and asked me how Dick was, and whether he was happy, and all the rest of it. So I saw how the land lay, and said that he was very unhappy, and not at all well; which last at any rate was a lie. There, you can guess the rest. Clara came to have a long talk with me to-day, but Dick will serve her turn much better. Indeed, if he hadn't chanced in upon me to-day I should have had to have sent for him to-morrow."

"Dear me," said I. "Have they any children?"

"Yes," said he, "two; they are staying with one of my daughters at present, where, indeed, Clara has mostly been. I wouldn't lose sight of her, as I felt sure they would come together again: and Dick, who is the best of good fellows, really took the matter

---

[1]   A rude or base countryman; usually used disparagingly. Old Hammond is being self-deprecating here.

to heart. You see, he had no other love to run to, as she had. So I managed it all; as I have done with such-like matters before."

"Ah," said I, "no doubt you wanted to keep them out of the Divorce Court: but I suppose it often has to settle such matters."

"Then you suppose nonsense," said he. "I know that there used to be such lunatic affairs as divorce-courts: but just consider; all the cases that came into them were matters of property quarrels: and I think, dear guest," said he, smiling, "that though you do come from another planet, you can see from the mere outside look of our world that quarrels about private property could not go on amongst us in our days."

Indeed, my drive from Hammersmith to Bloomsbury, and all the quiet happy life I had seen so many hints of, even apart from my shopping, would have been enough to tell me that "the sacred rights of property," as we used to think of them, were now no more.

So I sat silent while the old man took up the thread of the discourse again, and said:

"Well, then, property quarrels being no longer possible, what remains in these matters that a court of law could deal with? Fancy a court for enforcing a contract of passion or sentiment! If such a thing were needed as a *reductio ad absurdum* of the enforcement of contract, such a folly would do that for us."

He was silent again a little, and then said: "You must understand once for all that we have changed these matters; or rather, that our way of looking at them has changed, as we have changed within the last two hundred years. We do not deceive ourselves, indeed, or believe that we can get rid of all the trouble that besets the dealings between the sexes. We know that we must face the unhappiness that comes of man and woman confusing the relations between natural passion, and sentiment, and the friendship which, when things go well, softens the awakening from passing illusions: but we are not so mad as to pile up degradation on that unhappiness by engaging in sordid squabbles about livelihood and position, and the power of tyrannizing over the children who have been the results of love or lust."

Again he paused awhile, and again went on: "Calf love, mistaken for a heroism that shall be life-long, yet early waning into disappointment; the inexplicable desire that comes on a man of riper years to be the all-in-all to some one woman, whose ordinary human kindness and human beauty he has idealized into superhuman perfection, and made the one object of his desire; or lastly the reasonable longing of a strong and thoughtful man to become the most intimate friend of some beautiful and wise woman, the very type of the beauty and glory of the world which we love so well,—as we exult in all the pleasure and exaltation of spirit which goes with these things, so we set ourselves to bear the sorrow which not unseldom goes with them also; remembering those lines of the ancient poet (I quote roughly from memory one of the many translations of the nineteenth century):

'For this the Gods have fashioned man's grief and evil day
That still for man hereafter might be the tale and the lay.'[1]

Well, well, 'tis little likely anyhow that all tales shall be lacking, or all sorrow cured."

He was silent for some time, and I would not interrupt him. At last he began again: "But you must know that we of these generations are strong and healthy of body, and live easily; we pass our lives in reasonable strife with nature, exercising not one side of ourselves only, but all sides, taking the keenest pleasure in all the life of the world. So it is a point of honour with us not to be self-centred; not to suppose that the world must cease because one man is sorry; therefore we should think it foolish, or if you will, criminal, to exaggerate these matters of sentiment and sensibility: we are no more inclined to eke out our sentimental sorrows than to cherish our bodily pains; and we recognize that there are other pleasures besides love-making. You must remember, also, that we are long-lived, and that therefore beauty both in man and woman is not so fleeting as it was in the days when we were burdened so heavily by self-inflicted diseases. So we shake off these griefs in a way which perhaps the sentimentalists of other times would think contemptible and unheroic, but which we

---

[1] A slight misquotation from Morris's own 1887 translation of Homer's *Odyssey*, Book 8, ll. 579-80.

think necessary and manlike. As on the other hand, therefore, we have ceased to be commercial in our love-matters, so also we have ceased to be *artificially* foolish. The folly which comes by nature, the unwisdom of the immature man, or the older man caught in a trap, we must put up with that, nor are we much ashamed of it; but to be conventionally sensitive or sentimental—my friend, I am old and perhaps disappointed, but at least I think we have cast off *some* of the follies of the older world."

He paused, as if for some words of mine; but I held my peace: then he went on: "At least, if we suffer from the tyranny and fickleness of nature or our own want of experience, we neither grimace about it, nor lie. If there must be sundering betwixt those who meant never to sunder, so it must be: but there need be no pretext of unity when the reality of it is gone: nor do we drive those who well know that they are incapable of it to profess an undying sentiment which they cannot really feel: thus it is that as that monstrosity of venal lust is no longer possible, so also it is no longer needed. Don't misunderstand me. You did not seem shocked when I told you that there were no law-courts to enforce contracts of sentiment or passion; but so curiously are men made, that perhaps you will be shocked when I tell you that there is no code of public opinion which takes the place of such courts, and which might be as tyrannical and unreasonable as they were. I do not say that people don't judge their neighbours' conduct, sometimes, doubtless, unfairly. But I do say that there is no unvarying conventional set of rules by which people are judged; no bed of Procrustes to stretch or cramp their minds and lives;[1] no hypocritical excommunication which people are *forced* to pronounce, either by unconsidered habit, or by the unexpressed threat of the lesser interdict if they are lax in their hypocrisy. Are you shocked now?"

"N-o—no," said I, with some hesitation. "It is all so different."

"At any rate," said he, "one thing I think I can answer for: whatever sentiment there is, it is real—and general; it is not confined

---

[1]   In Greek legend, the robber Procrustes placed his victims upon an iron bed. If they were shorter than the bed, he stretched their legs until they fit; if longer than the bed, he chopped them off.

to people very specially refined. I am also pretty sure, as I hinted to you just now, that there is not by a great way as much suffering involved in these matters either to men or to women as there used to be. But excuse me for being so prolix on this question! You know you asked to be treated like a being from another planet."

"Indeed I thank you very much," said I. "Now may I ask you about the position of women in your society?"

He laughed very heartily for a man of his years, and said: "It is not without reason that I have got a reputation as a careful student of history. I believe I really do understand 'the Emancipation of Women movement' of the nineteenth century. I doubt if any other man now alive does."

"Well?" said I, a little bit nettled by his merriment.

"Well," said he, "of course you will see that all that is a dead controversy now. The men have no longer any opportunity of tyrannizing over the women, or the women over the men; both of which things took place in those old times. The women do what they can do best, and what they like best, and the men are neither jealous of it or injured by it. This is such a commonplace that I am almost ashamed to state it."

I said, "O; and legislation? do they take any part in that?"

Hammond smiled and said: "I think you may wait for an answer to that question till we get on to the subject of legislation. There may be novelties to you in that subject also."

"Very well," I said; "but about this woman question? I saw at the Guest House that the women were waiting on the men: that seems a little like reaction, doesn't it?"

"Does it?" said the old man: "perhaps you think housekeeping an unimportant occupation, not deserving of respect. I believe that was the opinion of the 'advanced' women of the nineteenth century, and their male backers. If it is yours, I recommend to your notice an old Norwegian folk-lore tale called How the Man minded the House, or some such title;[1] the result of which minding was that, after various tribulations, the man and the family cow balanced each other at the end of a rope, the man

---

[1] "The Man Who was to Mind the House," which Morris read in G.W. Dasent's 1858 collection of Norse folk-stories, *Popular Tales from the Norse*.

hanging half-way up the chimney, the cow dangling from the roof, which, after the fashion of the country, was of turf and sloping low down to the ground. Hard on the cow, *I* think. Of course no such mishap could happen to such a superior person as yourself," he added, chuckling.

I sat somewhat uneasy under this dry gibe. Indeed, his manner of treating this latter part of the question seemed to me a little disrespectful.

"Come, now, my friend," quoth he, "don't you know that it is a great pleasure to a clever woman to manage a house skilfully, and to do it so that all the house-mates about her look pleased, and are grateful to her? And then, you know, everybody likes to be ordered about by a pretty woman: why, it is one of the pleasantest forms of flirtation. You are not so old that you cannot remember that. Why, I remember it well."

And the old fellow chuckled again, and at last fairly burst out laughing.

"Excuse me," said he, after a while; "I am not laughing at anything you could be thinking of, but at that silly nineteenth-century fashion, current amongst rich so-called cultivated people, of ignoring all the steps by which their daily dinner was reached, as matters too low for their lofty intelligence. Useless idiots! Come, now, I am a 'literary man,' as we queer animals used to be called, yet I am a pretty good cook myself."

"So am I," said I.

"Well, then," said he, "I really think you can understand me better than you would seem to do, judging by your words and your silence."

Said I: "Perhaps that is so; but people putting in practice commonly this sense of interest in the ordinary occupations of life rather startles me. I will ask you a question or two presently about that. But I want to return to the position of women amongst you. You have studied the 'emancipation of women' business of the nineteenth century: don't you remember that some of the 'superior' women wanted to emancipate the more intelligent part of their sex from the bearing of children?"

The old man grew quite serious again. Said he: "I *do* remember about that strange piece of baseless folly, the result, like all other follies of the period, of the hideous class tyranny which then obtained. What do we think of it now? you would say. My friend, that is a question easy to answer. How could it possibly be but that maternity should be highly honoured amongst us? Surely it is a matter of course that the natural and necessary pains which the mother must go through form a bond of union between man and woman, an extra stimulus to love and affection between them, and that this is universally recognized. For the rest, remember that all the *artificial* burdens of motherhood are now done away with. A mother has no longer any mere sordid anxieties for the future of her children. They may indeed turn out better or worse: they may disappoint her highest hopes; such anxieties as these are a part of the mingled pleasure and pain which goes to make up the life of mankind. But at least she is spared the fear (it was most commonly the certainty) that artificial disabilities would make her children something less than men and women: she knows that they will live and act according to the measure of their own faculties. In times past, it is clear that the 'Society' of the day helped its Judaic god, and the 'Man of Science' of the time, in visiting the sins of the fathers upon the children.[1] How to reverse this process, how to take the sting out of heredity, has for long been one of the most constant cares of the thoughtful men amongst us. So that, you see, the ordinarily healthy woman (and almost all our women are both healthy and at least comely), respected as a child-bearer and rearer of children, desired as a woman, loved as a companion, unanxious for the future of her children, has far more instinct for maternity than the poor drudge and mother of drudges of past days could ever have had; or than her sister of the upper classes, brought up in affected ignorance of natural facts, reared in an atmosphere of mingled prudery and prurience."

"You speak warmly," I said, "but I can see that you are right."

"Yes," he said, "and I will point out to you a token of all the benefits which we have gained by our freedom. What did you think of the looks of the people whom you have come across to-day?"

Said I: "I could hardly have believed that there could be so many good-looking people in any civilized country."

---

[1] See Exodus 20:5.

He crowed a little, like the old bird he was. "What! are we still civilized?" said he. "Well, as to our looks, the English and Jutish blood, which on the whole is predominant here, used not to produce much beauty. But I think we have improved it. I know a man who has a large collection of portraits printed from photographs of the nineteenth century, and going over those and comparing them with the everyday faces in these times, puts the improvements in our good looks beyond a doubt. Now, there are some people who think it not too fantastic to connect this increase of beauty directly with our freedom and good sense in the matters we have been speaking of: they believe that a child born from the natural and healthy love between a man and a woman, even if that be transient, is likely to turn out better in all ways, and especially in bodily beauty, than the birth of the respectable commercial marriage bed, or of the dull despair of the drudge of that system. They say, Pleasure begets pleasure. What do you think?"

"I am much of that mind," said I.

CHAPTER X

QUESTIONS AND ANSWERS

"Well," said the old man, shifting in his chair, "you must get on with your questions, Guest; I have been some time answering this first one."

Said I: "I want an extra word or two about your ideas of education; although I gathered from Dick that you let your children run wild and didn't teach them anything; and in short, that you have so refined your education, that now you have none."

"Then you have gathered left-handed," quoth he. "But of course I understand your point of view about education, which is that of times past, when 'the struggle for life,' as men used to phrase it (*i.e.*, the struggle for a slave's rations on one side, and for a bouncing share of the slaveholders' privilege on the other), pinched 'education' for most people into a niggardly dole of not very accurate information; something to be swallowed by the beginner in the art of living whether he liked it or not, and was hungry for it or not: and which had been chewed and digested over and over again by people who didn't care about it in order to serve it out to other people who didn't care about it."

I stopped the old man's rising wrath by a laugh, and said: "Well, *you* were not taught that way, at any rate, so you may let your anger run off you a little."

"True, true," said he, smiling. "I thank you for correcting my ill-temper: I always fancy myself as living in any period of which we may be speaking. But, however, to put it in a cooler way: you expected to see children thrust into schools when they had reached an age conventionally supposed to be the due age, whatever their varying faculties and dispositions might be, and when there, with like disregard to facts to be subjected to a certain conventional course of 'learning.' My friend, can't you see that such a proceeding means ignoring the fact of *growth*, bodily and mental? No one could come out of such a mill uninjured; and those only would avoid being crushed by it who would have the spirit of rebellion strong in them. Fortunately most children have had that at all times, or I do not know that we should ever have reached our present position. Now you see what it all comes to. In the old times all this was the result of *poverty*. In the nineteenth century, society was so miserably poor, owing to the systematized robbery on which it was founded, that real education was impossible for anybody. The whole theory of their so-called education was that it was necessary to shove a little information into a child, even if it were by means of torture, and accompanied by twaddle which it was well known was of no use, or else he would lack information lifelong: the hurry of poverty forbade anything else. All that is past; we are no longer hurried, and the information lies ready to each one's hand when his own inclinations impel him to seek it. In this as in other matters we have become wealthy: we can afford to give ourselves time to grow."

"Yes," said I, "but suppose the child, youth, man, never wants the information, never grows in the direction you might hope him to: suppose, for instance, he objects to learning arithmetic or mathematics; you can't force him when he *is* grown; can't you force him while he is growing, and oughtn't you to do so?"

"Well," said he, "were you forced to learn arithmetic and mathematics?"

"A little," said I.

"And how old are you now?"

"Say fifty-six," said I.

"And how much arithmetic and mathematics do you know now?" quoth the old man, smiling rather mockingly.

Said I : "None whatever, I am sorry to say."

Hammond laughed quietly, but made no other comment on my admission, and I dropped the subject of education, perceiving him to be hopeless on that side.

I thought a little, and said: "You were speaking just now of households: that sounded to me a little like the customs of past times; I should have thought that you would have lived more in public."

"Phalangsteries, eh?" said he. "Well, we live as we like, and we like to live as a rule with certain house-mates that we have got used to. Remember, again, that poverty is extinct, and that the Fourierist phalangsteries and all their kind, as was but natural at the time, implied nothing but a refuge from mere destitution.[1] Such a way of life as that, could only have been conceived of by people surrounded by the worst form of poverty. But you must understand therewith, that though separate households are the rule amongst us, and though they differ in their habits more or less, yet no door is shut to any good-tempered person who is content to live as the other housemates do: only of course it would be unreasonable for one man to drop into a household and bid the folk of it to alter their habits to please him, since he can go elsewhere and live as he pleases. However, I need not say much about all this, as you are going up the river with Dick, and will find out for yourself by experience how these matters are managed."

---

[1]   The works of François Charles Marie Fourier (1772-1837) influenced socialist thinking throughout the nineteenth century. Believing that modern family structures had been irreparably deformed by modern capitalism, Fourier proposed that in a socialist society people would live communally. The buildings that would house such communities he called *phalanstères*. Morris admired Fourier's writings, but discounted the idea of *phalanstères* as too regimented.

After a pause, I said: "Your big towns, now; how about them? London, which—which I have read about as the modern Babylon of civilization, seems to have disappeared."

"Well, well," said old Hammond, "perhaps after all it is more like ancient Babylon now than the 'modern Babylon' of the nineteenth century was. But let that pass. After all, there is a good deal of population in places between here and Hammersmith; nor have you seen the most populous part of the town yet."

"Tell me, then," said I, "how is it towards the east?"

Said he: "Time was when if you mounted a good horse and rode straight away from my door here at a round trot for an hour and a half you would still be in the thick of London, and the greater part of that would be 'slums,' as they were called; that is to say, places of torture for innocent men and women; or worse, stews for rearing and breeding men and women in such degradation that torture should seem to them mere ordinary and natural life."

Slums

"I know, I know," I said, rather impatiently. "That was what was; tell me something of what is. Is any of that left?"

"Not an inch," said he; "but some memory of it abides with us, and I am glad of it. Once a year, on May-day,[1] we hold a solemn feast in those easterly communes of London to commemorate The Clearing of Misery, as it is called. On that day we have music and dancing, and merry games and happy feasting on the site of some of the worst of the old slums, the traditional memory of which we have kept. On that occasion the custom is for the prettiest girls to sing some of the old revolutionary songs, and those which were the groans of the discontent, once so hopeless, on the very spots where those terrible crimes of class-murder were committed day by day for so many years. To a man like me, who have studied the past so diligently, it is a curious and touching sight to see some beautiful girl, daintily clad, and crowned with flowers from the neighbour-ing meadows, standing amongst the happy people, on some mound where of old time stood the wretched apology for a house, a den in which men and women lived packed amongst the filth like pilchards in a cask;[2] lived in such a way that they could only have

---

[1]   May Day (May 1), which celebrates the labor of workers, was first observed in 1888.
[2]   I.e., sardines in a tin.

endured it, as I said just now, by being degraded out of humanity—to hear the terrible words of threatening and lamentation coming from her sweet and beautiful lips, and she unconscious of their real meaning: to hear her, for instance, singing Hood's Song of the Shirt,[1] and to think that all the time she does not understand what it is all about—a tragedy grown inconceivable to her and her listeners. Think of that, if you can, and of how glorious life is grown!"

"Indeed," said I, "it is difficult for me to think of it."

And I sat watching how his eyes glittered, and how the fresh life seemed to glow in his face, and I wondered how at his age he should think of the happiness of the world, or indeed anything but his coming dinner.

"Tell me in detail," said I, "what lies east of Bloomsbury now?"

Said he: "There are but few houses between this and the outer part of the old city; but in the city we have a thickly-dwelling population. Our forefathers, in the first clearing of the slums, were not in a hurry to pull down the houses in what was called at the end of the nineteenth century the business quarter of the town, and what later got to be known as the Swindling Kens.[2] You see, these houses, though they stood hideously thick on the ground, were roomy and fairly solid in building, and clean, because they were not used for living in, but as mere gambling booths; so the poor people from the cleared slums took them for lodgings and dwelt there, till the folk of those days had time to think of something better for them; so the buildings were pulled down so gradually that people got used to living thicker on the ground there than in most places; therefore it remains the most populous part of London, or perhaps of all these islands. But it is very pleasant there, partly because of the splendour of the architecture, which goes further than what you will see elsewhere. However, this crowding, if it may be called so, does not go further than a street called Aldgate, a name which perhaps you may have heard of. Beyond that the houses are scattered wide about the meadows there, which are very beautiful, especially when you get on to the lovely river Lea (where old Isaak Walton used to

---

[1]   Thomas Hood's "Song of the Shirt" (1843), an impassioned attack on the abuses of sweated labor, became a rallying cry for workers.

[2]   Slang for thieves' den.

fish, you know[1]) about the places called Stratford and Old Ford, names which of course you will not have heard of, though the Romans were busy there once upon a time."

Not heard of them! thought I to myself. How strange! that I who had seen the very last remnant of the pleasantness of the meadows by the Lea destroyed, should have heard them spoken of with pleasantness come back to them in full measure.

Hammond went on: "When you get down to the Thames side you come on the Docks, which are works of the nineteenth century, and are still in use, although not so thronged as they once were, since we discourage centralization all we can, and we have long ago dropped the pretension to be the market of the world. About these Docks are a good few houses, which, however, are not inhabited by many people permanently; I mean, those who use them come and go a good deal, the place being too low and marshy for pleasant dwelling. Past the Docks eastward and landward it is all flat pasture, once marsh, except for a few gardens, and there are very few permanent dwellings there: scarcely anything but a few sheds, and cots for the men who come to look after the great herds of cattle pasturing there. But however, what with the beasts and the men, and the scattered red-tiled roofs and the big hayricks, it does not make a bad holiday to get a quiet pony and ride about there on a sunny afternoon of autumn, and look over the river and the craft passing up and down, and on to Shooters' Hill and the Kentish uplands, and then turn round to the wide green sea of the Essex marsh-land, with the great domed line of the sky, and the sun shining down in one flood of peaceful light over the long distance. There is a place called Canning's Town, and further out, Silvertown, where the pleasant meadows are at their pleasantest: doubtless they were once slums, and wretched enough."

So idyllic

The names grated on my ear, but I could not explain why to him.[2] So I said: "And south of the river, what is it like?"

---

[1] Isaak Walton's *The Compleat Angler, or the Contemplative Man's Recreation* (1653) is a famous celebration of fishing. Morris, who loved fishing, often fished in the Lea, which flowed past Walthamstow, his birthplace. Stratford and Old Ford were heavily industrialized areas in the 1890s.

[2] The names Silvertown and Canning Town grate on Guest's ear because they were, as Hammond surmises, wretched slums in the nineteenth century.

He said: "You would find it much the same as the land about Hammersmith. North, again, the land runs up high, and there is an agreeable and well-built town called Hampstead, which fitly ends London on that side. It looks down on the north-western end of the forest you passed through."

I smiled. "So much for what was once London," said I. "Now tell me about the other towns of the country."

He said: "As to the big murky places which were once, as we know, the centres of manufacture, they have, like the brick and mortar desert of London, disappeared; only, since they were centres of nothing but 'manufacture,' and served no purpose but that of the gambling market, they have left less signs of their existence than London. Of course, the great change in the use of mechanical force made this an easy matter, and some approach to their break-up as centres would probably have taken place, even if we had not changed our habits so much: but they being such as they were, no sacrifice would have seemed too great a price to pay for getting rid of 'manufacturing districts,' as they used to be called. For the rest, whatever coal or mineral we need is brought to grass and sent whither it is needed with as little possible of dirt, confusion, and the distressing of quiet people's lives. One is tempted to believe from what one has read of the condition of those districts in the nineteenth century, that those who had them under their power worried, befouled, and degraded men out of malice prepense:[1] but it was not so; like the mis-education of which we were talking just now, it came of their dreadful poverty. They were obliged to put up with everything, and even pretend that they liked it; whereas we can now deal with things reasonably, and refuse to be saddled with what we do not want."

I confess I was not sorry to cut short with a question his glorifications of the age he lived in. Said I: "How about the smaller towns? I suppose you have swept them away entirely?"

"No, no," said he, "it hasn't gone that way. On the contrary, there has been but little clearance, though much rebuilding, in the smaller towns. Their suburbs, indeed, when they had any, have melted away into the general country, and space and elbow-room has been got

---

[1] "Malice prepense" is premeditated malice: an injury done on purpose.

in their centres: but there are the towns still with their streets and squares and market-places; so that it is by means of these smaller towns that we of to-day can get some kind of idea of what the towns of the older world were like;—I mean to say at their best."

"Take Oxford, for instance," said I.

"Yes," said he, "I suppose Oxford was beautiful even in the nineteenth century. At present it has the great interest of still preserving a great mass of pre-commercial building, and is a very beautiful place, yet there are many towns which have become scarcely less beautiful."

Said I: "In passing, may I ask if it is still a place of learning?"

"Still?" said he, smiling. "Well, it has reverted to some of its best traditions; so you may imagine how far it is from its nineteenth-century position. It is real learning, knowledge cultivated for its own sake—the Art of Knowledge, in short—which is followed there, not the Commercial learning of the past. Though perhaps you do not know that in the nineteenth century Oxford and its less interesting sister Cambridge became definitely commercial. They (and especially Oxford) were the breeding places of a peculiar class of parasites, who called themselves cultivated people; they were indeed cynical enough, as the so-called educated classes of the day generally were; but they affected an exaggeration of cynicism in order that they might be thought knowing and worldly-wise. The rich middle classes (they had no relation with the working classes) treated them with the kind of contemptuous toleration with which a mediæval baron treated his jester; though it must be said that they were by no means so pleasant as the old jesters were, being, in fact, *the* bores of society. They were laughed at, despised—and paid. Which last was what they aimed at."

Dear me! thought I, how apt history is to reverse contemporary judgments. Surely only the worst of them were as bad as that. But I must admit that they were mostly prigs, and that they *were* commercial. I said aloud, though more to myself than to Hammond, "Well, how could they be better than the age that made them?"

"True," he said, "but their pretensions were higher."

"Were they?" said I, smiling.

"You drive me from corner to corner," said he, smiling in

turn. "Let me say at least that they were a poor sequence to the aspirations of Oxford of 'the barbarous Middle Ages.'"

"Yes, that will do," said I.

"Also," said Hammond, "what I have been saying of them is true in the main. But ask on!"

I said: "We have heard about London and the manufacturing districts and the ordinary towns: how about the villages?"

Said Hammond: "You must know that toward the end of the nineteenth century the villages were almost destroyed, unless where they became mere adjuncts to the manufacturing districts, or formed a sort of minor manufacturing district themselves.

"Houses were allowed to fall into decay and actual ruin; trees were cut down for the sake of the few shillings which the poor sticks would fetch; the building became inexpressibly mean and hideous. Labour was scarce; but wages fell nevertheless. All the small country arts of life which once added to the little pleasures of country people were lost. The country produce which passed through the hands of the husbandmen never got so far as their mouths. Incredible shabbiness and niggardly pinching reigned over the fields and acres which, in spite of the rude and careless husbandry of the times, were so kind and bountiful. Had you any inkling of all this?"

"I have heard that it was so," said I; "but what followed?"

"The change," said Hammond, "which in these matters took place very early in our epoch, was most strangely rapid. People flocked into the country villages, and, so to say, flung themselves upon the freed land like a wild beast upon his prey; and in a very little time the villages of England were more populous than they had been since the fourteenth century, and were still growing fast. Of course, this invasion of the country was awkward to deal with, and would have created much misery, if the folk had still been under the bondage of class monopoly. But as it was, things soon righted themselves. People found out what they were fit for, and gave up attempting to push themselves into occupations in which they must needs fail. The town invaded the country; but the invaders, like the warlike invaders of early days, yielded to the influence of their surroundings, and became country people; and in their turn, as they became more numerous than the townsmen, influenced them also; so that the difference between town and country grew less and less; and it was indeed this world of the country vivified by the thought and briskness of town-bred folk which has produced that happy and leisurely but eager life of which you have had a first taste. Again I say, many blunders were made, but we have had time to set them right. Much was left for the men of my earlier life to deal with. The crude ideas of the first half of the twentieth century, when men were still oppressed by the fear of poverty, and did not look enough to the present pleasure of ordinary daily life, spoilt a great deal of what the commercial age had left us of external beauty: and I admit that it was but slowly that men recovered from the injuries that they inflicted on themselves after they became free. But slowly as the recovery came, it *did* come; and the more you see of us, the clearer it will be to you that we are happy. That we live amidst beauty without any fear of becoming effeminate; that we have plenty to do, and on the whole enjoy doing it. What more can we ask of life?"

He paused, as if he were seeking for words with which to express his thought. Then he said:

"This is how we stand. England was once a country of clearings amongst the woods and wastes, with a few towns interspersed, which were fortresses for the feudal army, markets for the folk, gathering places for the craftsmen. It then became a country of huge and foul workshops and fouler gambling-dens, surrounded by an ill-kept, poverty-stricken farm, pillaged by the masters of the workshops. It is now a garden, where nothing is wasted and nothing is spoilt, with the necessary dwellings, sheds, and workshops scattered up and down the country, all trim and neat and pretty. For, indeed, we should be too much ashamed of ourselves if we allowed the making of goods, even on a large scale, to carry with it the appearance, even, of desolation and misery. Why, my friend, those housewives we were talking of just now would teach us better than that."

Said I: "This side of your change is certainly for the better. But though I shall soon see some of these villages, tell me in a word or two what they are like, just to prepare me."

"Perhaps," said he, "you have seen a tolerable picture of these villages as they were before the end of the nineteenth century. Such things exist."

"I have seen several of such pictures," said I.

"Well," said Hammond, "our villages are something like the best of such places, with the church or mote-house of the neighbors for their chief building. Only note that there are no tokens of poverty about them: no tumble-down picturesque; which, to tell you the truth, the artist usually availed himself of to veil his incapacity for drawing architecture. Such things do not please us, even when they indicate no misery. Like the mediævals, we like everything trim and clean, and orderly and bright; as people always do when they have any sense of architectural power; because then they know that they can have what they want, and they won't stand any nonsense from Nature in their dealings with her."

"Besides the villages, are there any scattered country houses?" said I.

"Yes, plenty," said Hammond; "in fact, except in the wastes and forests and amongst the sand-hills (like Hindhead in Surrey), it is not easy to be out of sight of a house; and where the houses are thinly scattered they run large, and are more like the old colleges than ordinary houses as they used to be. That is done for the sake of society, for a good many people can dwell in such houses, as the country dwellers are not necessarily husbandmen; though they almost all help in such work at times. The life that goes on in these big dwellings in the country is very pleasant, especially as some of the most studious men of our time live in them, and altogether there is a great variety of mind and mood to be found in them which brightens and quickens the society there."

"I am rather surprised," said I, "by all this, for it seems to me that after all the country must be tolerably populous."

"Certainly," said he; "the population is pretty much the same as it was at the end of the nineteenth century; we have spread it, that is all. Of course, also, we have helped to populate other countries—where we were wanted and were called for."

Said I: "One thing, it seems to me, does not go with your word of 'garden' for the country. You have spoken of wastes and forests, and I myself have seen the beginning of your Middlesex and Essex forest. Why do you keep such things in a garden? and isn't it very wasteful to do so?"

"My friend," he said, "we like these pieces of wild nature, and can afford them, so we have them; let alone that as to the forests, we need a great deal of timber, and suppose that our sons and sons' sons will do the like. As to the land being a garden, I have heard that they used to have shrubberies and rockeries in gardens once; and though I might not like the artificial ones, I assure you that some of the natural rockeries of our garden are worth seeing. Go north this summer and look at the Cumberland and Westmoreland ones;—where, by the way, you will see some sheep-feeding, so that they are not so wasteful as you think; not so wasteful as forcing-grounds for fruit out of season, I think. Go and have a look at the sheep-walks high up the slopes between Ingleborough and Pen-y-gwent, and tell me if you think we *waste* the land there by not covering it with factories for making things that nobody wants, which was the chief business of the nineteenth century."

"I will try to go there," said I.

"It won't take much trying," said he.

CHAPTER XI

CONCERNING GOVERNMENT

"Now," said I, "I have come to the point of asking questions which I suppose will be dry for you to answer and difficult for you to explain; but I have foreseen for some time past that I must ask them, will I 'nill I. What kind of a government have you? Has republicanism finally triumphed? or have you come to a mere dictatorship, which some persons in the nineteenth century used to prophesy as the ultimate outcome of democracy? Indeed, this last question does not seem so very unreasonable, since you have turned your Parliament House into a dung-market. Or where do you house your present Parliament?"

The old man answered my smile with a hearty laugh, and said: "Well, well, dung is not the worst kind of corruption; fertility may come of that, whereas mere dearth came from the other kind, of which those walls once held the great supporters. Now, dear guest, let me tell you that our present parliament would be hard to house in one place, because the whole people is our parliament."

"I don't understand," said I.

"No, I suppose not," said he. "I must now shock you by telling you that we have no longer anything which you, a native of another planet, would call a government."

"I am not so much shocked as you might think," said I, "as I know something about governments. But tell me, how do you manage, and how have you come to this state of things?"

Said he: "It is true that we have to make some arrangements about our affairs, concerning which you can ask presently; and it is also true that everybody does not always agree with the details of these arrangements; but, further, it is true that a man no more needs an elaborate system of government, with its army, navy, and police, to force him to give way to the will of the majority of his *equals*, than he wants a similar machinery to make him understand that his head and a stone wall cannot occupy the same space at the same moment. Do you want further explanation?"

"Well, yes, I do," quoth I.

Old Hammond settled himself in his chair with a look of enjoyment which rather alarmed me, and made me dread a scientific disquisition: so I sighed and abided. He said:

"I suppose you know pretty well what the process of government was in the bad old times?"

"I am supposed to know," said I.

(Hammond) What was the government of those days ? Was it really the Parliament or any part of it?

(I) No.

(H.) Was not the Parliament on the one side a kind of watch-committee sitting to see that the interests of the Upper Classes took no hurt; and on the other side a sort of blind to delude the people into supposing that they had some share in the management of their own affairs?

(I) History seems to show us this.

(H.) To what extent did the people manage their own affairs?

(I) I judge from what I have heard that sometimes they forced the Parliament to make a law to legalize some alteration which had already taken place.

(H.) Anything else?

(I) I think not. As I am informed, if the people made any attempt to deal with the *cause* of their grievances, the law stepped in and said, this is sedition, revolt, or what not, and slew or tortured the ringleaders of such attempts.

(H.) If Parliament was not the government then, nor the people either, what was the government?

(I) Can you tell me?

(H.) I think we shall not be far wrong if we say that government was the Law-Courts, backed up by the executive, which handled the brute force that the deluded people allowed them to use for their own purposes; I mean the army, navy, and police.

(I) Reasonable men must needs think you are right.

(H.) Now as to those Law-Courts. Were they places of fair dealing according to the ideas of the day? Had a poor man a good chance of defending his property and person in them?

(I) It is a commonplace that even rich men looked upon a law-suit as a dire misfortune, even if they gained the case: and as for a poor one—why, it was considered a miracle of justice and beneficence if a poor man who had once got into the clutches of the law escaped prison or utter ruin.

(H.) It seems, then, my son, that the government by law-courts and police, which was the real government of the nineteenth century, was not a great success even to the people of that day, living under a class system which proclaimed inequality and poverty as the law of God and the bond which held the world together.

(I) So it seems, indeed.

(H.) And now that all this is changed, and the "rights of property," which mean the clenching the fist on a piece of goods and crying out to the neighbours, You shan't have this!—now that all this has disappeared so utterly that it is no longer possible even to jest upon its absurdity, is such a Government possible?

(I) It is impossible.

(H.) Yes, happily. But for what other purpose than the protection of the rich from the poor, the strong from the weak, did this Government exist?

(I) I have heard that it was said that their office was to defend their own citizens against attack from other countries.

(H.) It was said; but was anyone expected to believe this? For instance, did the English Government defend the English citizen against the French?

(I) So it was said.

(H.) Then if the French had invaded England and conquered it, they would not have allowed the English workmen to live well?

(I, laughing) As far as I can make out, the English masters of the English workmen saw to that: they took from their workmen as much of their livelihood as they dared, because they wanted it for themselves.

(H.) But if the French had conquered, would they not have taken more still from the English workmen?

(I) I do not think so; for in that case the English workmen would have died of starvation; and then the French conquest would have ruined the French, just as if the English horses and cattle had died of underfeeding. So that after all, the English *workmen* would have been no worse off for the conquest: their French masters could have got no more from them than their English masters did.

(H.) This is true; and we may admit that the pretensions of the government to defend the poor (*i.e.*, the useful) people against other countries come to nothing. But that is but natural; for we have seen already that it was the function of government to protect the rich against the poor. But did not the government defend its rich men against other nations?

(I) I do not remember to have heard that the rich needed defence; because it is said that even when two nations were at war, the rich men of each nation gambled with each other pretty much as usual, and even sold each other weapons wherewith to kill their own countrymen.

(H.) In short, it comes to this, that whereas the so-called government of protection of property by means of the law-courts meant destruction of wealth, this defence of the citizens of one country against those of another country by means of war or the threat of war meant pretty much the same thing.

(I) I cannot deny it.

(H.) Therefore the government really existed for the destruction of wealth?

(I) So it seems. And yet—

(H.) Yet what?

(I) There were many rich people in those times.

(H.) You see the consequences of that fact?

(I) I think I do. But tell me what they were.

(H.) If the government habitually destroyed wealth, the country must have been poor?

(I) Yes, certainly.

(H.) Yet amidst this poverty the persons for the sake of whom the government existed insisted on being rich whatever might happen?

(I) So it was.

(H.) What *must* happen if in a poor country some people insist on being rich at the expense of the others?

(I) Unutterable poverty for the others. All this misery, then, was caused by the destructive government of which we have been speaking?

(H.) Nay, it would be incorrect to say so. The government itself was but the necessary result of the careless, aimless tyranny of the times; it was but the machinery of tyranny. Now tyranny has come to an end, and we no longer need such machinery; we could not possibly use it since we are free. Therefore in your sense of the word we have no government. Do you understand this now?

(I) Yes, I do. But I will ask you some more questions as to how you as free men manage your affairs.

(H.) With all my heart. Ask away.

CHAPTER XII

CONCERNING THE ARRANGEMENT OF LIFE

"Well," I said, "about those 'arrangements' which you spoke of as taking the place of government, could you give me any account of them?"

"Neighbour," he said, "although we have simplified our lives a great deal from what they were, and have got rid of many conventionalities and many sham wants, which used to give our forefathers much trouble, yet our life is too complex for me to tell you in detail by means of words how it is arranged; you must find that out by living amongst us. It is true that I can better tell you what we don't do, than what we do do."

"Well?" said I.

"This is the way to put it," said he. "We have been living for a hundred and fifty years, at least, more or less in our present manner, and a tradition or habit of life has been growing on us; and that habit has become a habit of acting on the whole for the best. It is easy for us to live without robbing each other. It would be possible for us to contend with and rob each other, but it would be harder for us than refraining from strife and robbery. That is in short the foundation of our life and our happiness."

"Whereas in the old days," said I, "it was very hard to live without strife and robbery. That's what you mean, isn't it, by giving me the negative side of your good conditions?"

"Yes," he said, "it was so hard, that those who habitually acted fairly to their neighbours were celebrated as saints and heroes, and were looked up to with the greatest reverence."

"While they were alive?" said I.

"No," said he, "after they were dead."

"But as to these days," I said; "you don't mean to tell me that no one ever transgresses this habit of good fellowship?"

"Certainly not," said Hammond, "but when the transgressions occur, everybody, transgressors and all, know them for what they are; the errors of friends, not the habitual actions of persons driven into enmity against society."

"I see," said I; "you mean that you have no 'criminal classes.'"

"How could we have them," said he, "since there is no rich class to breed enemies against the state by means of the injustice of the state?"

Said I: "I thought that I understood from something that fell from you a little while ago that you had abolished civil law. Is that so, literally?"

"It abolished itself, my friend," said he. "As I said before, the civil law-courts were upheld for the defence of private property; for nobody ever pretended that it was possible to make people act fairly to each other by means of brute force. Well, private property being abolished, all the laws and all the legal 'crimes' which it had manufactured of course came to an end. Thou shalt not steal, had to be translated into, Thou shalt work in order to live happily. Is there any need to enforce that commandment by violence?"

"Well," said I, "that is understood, and I agree with it; but how about crimes of violence? would not their occurrence (and you admit that they occur) make criminal law necessary?"

Said he: "In your sense of the word, we have no criminal law either. Let us look at the matter closer, and see whence crimes of violence spring. By far the greater part of these in past days were the result of the laws of private property, which forbade the satisfaction of their natural desires to all but a privileged few, and of the general visible coercion which came of those laws. All *that* cause of violent crime is gone. Again, many violent acts came from the artificial perversion of the sexual passions, which caused overweening jealousy and the like miseries. Now, when you look carefully into these, you will find that what lay at the bottom of them was mostly the idea (a law-made idea) of the woman being the property of the man, whether he were husband, father, brother, or what not. *That* idea has of course vanished with private property, as well as certain follies about the 'ruin' of women for following their natural desires in an illegal way, which of course was a convention caused by the laws of private property.

"Another cognate cause of crimes of violence was the family tyranny, which was the subject of so many novels and stories of the past, and which once more was the result of private property. Of course that is all ended, since families are held together by no bond of coercion, legal or social, but by mutual liking and affection, and everybody is free to come or go as he or she pleases. Furthermore, our standards of honour and public estimation are very different from the old ones; success in besting our neighbours is a road to renown now closed, let us hope for ever. Each man is free to exercise his special faculty to the utmost, and every one encourages him in so doing. So that we have got rid of the scowling envy, coupled by the poets with hatred, and surely with good reason; heaps of unhappiness and ill-blood were caused by it, which with irritable and passionate men—*i.e.*, energetic and active, men—often led to violence."

I laughed, and said: "So that you now withdraw your admission, and say that there is no violence amongst you?"

"No," said he, "I withdraw nothing; as I told you, such things will happen. Hot blood will err sometimes. A man may strike another, and the stricken strike back again, and the result be a homicide, to put it at the worst. But what then? Shall we the neighbours make it worse still? Shall we think so poorly of each other as to suppose that the slain man calls on us to revenge him, when we *know* that if he had been maimed, he would, when in cold blood and able to weigh all the circumstances, have forgiven his maimer? Or will the death of the slayer bring the slain man to life again and cure the unhappiness his loss has caused?"

"Yes," I said, "but consider, must not the safety of society be safeguarded by some punishment?"

"There, neighbour!" said the old man, with some exultation. "You have hit the mark. That *punishment* of which men used to talk so wisely and act so foolishly, what was it but the expression of their fear? And they had no need to fear, since *they*—*i.e.*, the rulers of society—were dwelling like an armed band in a hostile country. But we who live amongst our friends need neither fear nor punish. Surely if we, in dread of an occasional rare homicide, an occasional rough blow, were solemnly and legally to commit homicide and violence, we could only be a society of ferocious cowards. Don't you think so, neighbour?"

"Yes, I do, when I come to think of it from that side," said I.

"Yet you must understand," said the old man, "that when any violence is committed, we expect the transgressor to make any atonement possible to him, and he himself expects it. But again, think if the destruction or serious injury of a man momentarily overcome by wrath or folly can be any atonement to the commonwealth? Surely it can only be an additional injury to it."

Said I: "But suppose the man has a habit of violence,—kills a man a year, for instance?"

"Such a thing is unknown," said he. "In a society where there is no punishment to evade, no law to triumph over, remorse will certainly follow transgression."

"And lesser outbreaks of violence," said I, "how do you deal with them? for hitherto we have been talking of great tragedies, I suppose?"

Said Hammond: "If the ill-doer is not sick or mad (in which case he must be restrained till his sickness or madness is cured) it is clear that grief and humiliation must follow the ill-deed; and society in general will make that pretty clear to the ill-doer if he should chance to be dull to it; and again, some kind of atonement will follow,—at the least, an open acknowledgement of the grief and humiliation. Is it so hard to say, I ask your pardon, neighbour?—Well, sometimes it is hard—and let it be."

"You think that enough?" said I.

"Yes," said he, "and moreover it is all that we *can* do. If in addition we torture the man, we turn his grief into anger, and the humiliation he would otherwise feel for *his* wrong-doing is swallowed up by a hope of revenge for *our* wrong-doing to him. He has paid the legal penalty, and can 'go and sin again' with comfort. Shall we commit such a folly, then? Remember Jesus had got the legal penalty remitted before he said 'Go and sin no more.'[1] Let alone that in a society of equals you will not find any one to play the part of torturer or jailer, though many to act as nurse or doctor."

"So," said I, "you consider crime a mere spasmodic disease, which requires no body of criminal law to deal with it?"

"Pretty much so," said he; "and since, as I have told you, we are a healthy people generally, so we are not likely to be much troubled with *this* disease."

"Well, you have no civil law, and no criminal law. But have you no laws of the market, so to say—no regulation for the exchange of wares? for you must exchange, even if you have no property."

Said he: "We have no obvious individual exchange, as you saw this morning when you went a-shopping; but of course there are regulations of the markets, varying according to the circumstances and guided by general custom. But as these are matters of general assent, which nobody dreams of objecting to, so also

---

[1] John 8:11.

we have made no provision for enforcing them: therefore I don't call them laws. In law, whether it be criminal or civil, execution always follows judgment, and someone must suffer. When you see the judge on his bench, you see through him, as clearly as if he were made of glass, the policeman to emprison, and the soldier to slay some actual living person. Such follies would make an agreeable market, wouldn't they?"

"Certainly," said I, "that means turning the market into a mere battle-field, in which many people must suffer as much as in the battle-field of bullet and bayonet. And from what I have seen I should suppose that your marketing, great and little, is carried on in a way that makes it a pleasant occupation."

"You are right, neighbour," said he. "Although there are so many, indeed by far the greater number amongst us, who would be unhappy if they were not engaged in actually making things, and things which turn out beautiful under their hands,—there are many, like the housekeepers I was speaking of, whose delight is in administration and organization, to use long-tailed words; I mean people who like keeping things together, avoiding waste, seeing that nothing sticks fast uselessly. Such people are thoroughly happy in their business, all the more as they are dealing with actual facts, and not merely passing counters round to see what share they shall have in the privileged taxation of useful people, which was the business of the commercial folk in past days. Well, what are you going to ask me next?"

CHAPTER XIII

CONCERNING POLITICS

Said I: "How do you manage with politics?"

Said Hammond, smiling: "I am glad that it is of *me* that you ask that question; I do believe that anybody else would make you explain yourself, or try to do so, till you were sickened of asking questions. Indeed, I believe I am the only man in England who would know what you mean; and since I know, I will answer your question briefly by saying that we are very well off as to politics,—because we have none. If ever you make a book out of this conversation, put this in a chapter by itself, after the model of old Horrebow's Snakes in Iceland."[1]

"I will," said I.

CHAPTER XIV

HOW MATTERS ARE MANAGED

Said I: "How about your relations with foreign nations?"

"I will not affect not to know what you mean," said he, "but I will tell you at once that the whole system of rival and contending nations which played so great a part in the 'government' of the world of civilization has disappeared along with the inequality betwixt man and man in society."

"Does not that make the world duller?" said I.

"Why?" said the old man.

"The obliteration of national variety," said I.

"Nonsense," he said, somewhat snappishly. "Cross the water and see. You will find plenty of variety: the landscape, the building, the diet, the amusements, all various. The men and women varying in looks as well as in habits of thought; the costume far more various than in the commercial period. How should it add to the variety or dispel the dulness, to coerce certain families or tribes, often heterogeneous and jarring with one another, into certain artificial and mechanical groups, and call them nations, and stimulate their patriotism—*i.e.*, their foolish and envious prejudices?"

"Well—I don't know how," said I.

---

[1] Chapter 77 of Niels Horrebow's *Natural History of Iceland* is titled "Concerning Snakes." In its entirety it reads: "No snakes of any kind are to be met with throughout the whole island."

"That's right," said Hammond cheerily; "you can easily understand that now we are freed from this folly it is obvious to us that by means of this very diversity the different strains of blood in the world can be serviceable and pleasant to each other, without in the least wanting to rob each other: we are all bent on the same enterprise, making the most of our lives. And I must tell you whatever quarrels or misunderstandings arise, they very seldom take place between people of different race; and consequently since there is less unreason in them, they are the more readily appeased."

"Good," said I, "but as to those matters of politics; as to general differences of opinion in one and the same community. Do you assert that there are none?"

"No, not at all," said he, somewhat snappishly; "but I do say that differences of opinion about real solid things need not, and with us do not, crystallize people into parties permanently hostile to one another, with different theories as to the build of the universe and the progress of time. Isn't that what politics used to mean?"

"H'm, well," said I, "I am not so sure of that."

Said he: "I take, you, neighbour; they only *pretended* to this serious difference of opinion; for if it had existed they could not have dealt together in the ordinary business of life; couldn't have eaten together, bought and sold together, gambled together, cheated other people together, but must have fought whenever they met: which would not have suited them at all. The game of the masters of politics was to cajole or force the public to pay the expense of a luxurious life and exciting amusement for a few cliques of ambitious persons: and the *pretence* of serious difference of opinion, belied by every action of their lives, was quite good enough for that. What has all that got to do with us?"

Said I : "Why, nothing, I should hope. But I fear—In short, I have been told that political strife was a necessary result of human nature."

"Human nature!" cried the old boy, impetuously; "what human nature? The human nature of paupers, of slaves, of slave-holders, or the human nature of wealthy freemen? Which? Come, tell me that!"

"Well," said I, "I suppose there would be a difference according to circumstances in people's action about these matters."

"I should think so, indeed," said he. "At all events, experience shows that it is so. Amongst us, our differences concern matters of business, and passing events as to them, and could not divide men permanently. As a rule, the immediate outcome shows which opinion on a given subject is the right one; it is a matter of fact, not of speculation. For instance, it is clearly not easy to knock up a political party on the question as to whether haymaking in such and such a country-side shall begin this week or next, when all men agree that it must at latest begin the week after next, and when any man can go down into the fields himself and see whether the seeds are ripe enough for the cutting."

Said I: "And you settle these differences, great and small, by the will of the majority, I suppose?"

"Certainly," said he; "how else could we settle them? You see in matters which are merely personal which do not affect the welfare of the community—how a man shall dress, what he shall eat and drink, what he shall write and read, and so forth—there can be no difference of opinion, and everybody does as he pleases. But when the matter is of common interest to the whole community, and the doing or not doing something affects everybody, the majority must have their way; unless the minority were to take up arms and show by force that they were the effective or real majority; which, however, in a society of men who are free and equal is little likely to happen; because in such a community the majority *is* the real majority, and the others, as I have hinted before, know that too well to obstruct from mere pig-headedness; especially as they have had plenty of opportunity of putting forward their side of the question."

"How is that managed?" said I.

"Well," said he. "Let us take one of our units of management, a commune, or a ward, or a parish (for we have all three names, indicating little real distinction between them now, though time was there was a good deal). In such a district, as you would call it, some neighbours think that something ought to be done or undone: a new town-hall built; a clearance of inconvenient houses; or say a stone bridge substituted for some ugly old iron one,—there you have undoing and doing in one. Well, at the next ordinary meeting of the neighbours, or Mote, as we call it, according to the ancient tongue of the times before bureaucracy, a neighbour proposes the change, and of course, if everybody agrees, there is an end of discussion, except about details. Equally, if no one backs the proposer,—'seconds him,' it used to be called—the matter drops for the time being; a thing not likely to happen amongst reasonable men, however, as the proposer is sure to have talked it over with others before the Mote. But supposing the affair proposed and seconded, if a few of the neighbours disagree to it, if they think that the beastly iron bridge will serve a little longer and they don't want to be bothered with building a new one just then, they don't count heads that time, but put off the formal discussion to the next Mote; and meantime arguments *pro* and *con* are flying about, and some get printed, so that everybody knows what is going on; and when the Mote comes together again there is a regular discussion and at last a vote by show of hands. If the division is a close one, the question is again put off for further discussion; if the division is a wide one, the minority are asked if they will yield to the more general opinion, which they often, nay, most commonly do. If they refuse, the question is debated a third time, when, if the minority has not perceptibly grown, they always give way; though I believe there is some half-forgotten rule by which they might still carry it on further; but I say, what always happens is that they are convinced, not perhaps that their view is the wrong one, but they cannot persuade or force the community to adopt it."

"Very good," said I; "but what happens if the divisions are still narrow?"

Said he: "As a matter of principle and according to the rule of such cases, the question must then lapse, and the majority, if so narrow, has to submit to sitting down under the *status quo*. But I must tell you that in point of fact the minority very seldom enforces this rule, but generally yields in a friendly manner."

"But do you know," said I, "that there is something in all this very like democracy; and I thought that democracy was considered to be in a moribund condition many, many years ago."

The old boy's eyes twinkled. "I grant you that our methods have that drawback. But what is to be done? We can't get *anyone* amongst us to complain of his not always having his own way in the teeth of the community, when it is clear that *everybody* cannot have that indulgence. What *is* to be done?"

"Well," said I, "I don't know."

Said he: "The only alternatives to our method that I can conceive of are these. First, that we should choose out, or breed, a class of superior persons capable of judging on all matters without consulting the neighbours; that, in short, we should get for ourselves what used to be called an aristocracy of intellect; or, secondly, that for the purpose of safe-guarding the freedom of the individual will, we should revert to a system of private property again, and have slaves and slave-holders once more. What do you think of those two expedients?"

"Well," said I, "there is a third possibility—to wit, that every man should be quite independent of every other, and that thus the tyranny of society should be abolished."

He looked hard at me for a second or two, and then burst out laughing very heartily; and I confess that I joined him. When he recovered himself he nodded at me, and said: "Yes, yes, I quite agree with you—and so we all do."

"Yes," I said, "and besides, it does not press hardly on the minority: for, take this matter of the bridge, no man is obliged to work on it if he doesn't agree to its building. At least, I suppose not."

He smiled, and said: "Shrewdly put; and yet from the point of view of the native of another planet. If the man of the minority does find his feelings hurt, doubtless he may relieve them by refusing to help in building the bridge. But, dear neighbour, that is not a very effective salve for the wound caused by the 'tyranny of a majority' in our society; because all work that is done is either beneficial or hurtful to every member of society. The man is benefited by the bridge-building if it turns out a good thing, and hurt by it if it turns out a bad one, whether he puts a hand to it or not; and meanwhile he is benefiting the bridge builders by his work, whatever that may be. In fact, I see no help for him except the pleasure of saying 'I told you so' if the bridge-building turns out to be a mistake and hurts him; if it benefits him he must suffer in silence. A terrible tyranny our Communism, is it not? Folk used often to be warned against this very unhappiness in times past, when for every well-fed, contented person you saw a thousand miserable starvelings. Whereas for us, we grow fat and well-liking on the tyranny; a tyranny, to say the truth, not to be made visible by any microscope I know. Don't be afraid, my friend; we are not going to seek for troubles by calling our peace and plenty and happiness by ill names whose very meaning we have forgotten!"

He sat musing for a little, and then started and said: "Are there any more questions, dear guest? The morning is waning fast amidst my garrulity."

CHAPTER XV

ON THE LACK OF INCENTIVE TO LABOUR IN A COMMUNIST SOCIETY

"Yes," said I. "I was expecting Dick and Clara to make their appearance any moment: but is there time to ask just one or two questions before they come?"

"Try it, dear neighbour—try it," said old Hammond. "For the more you ask me the better I am pleased; and at any rate if they do come and find me in the middle of an answer, they must sit quiet and pretend to listen till I come to an end. It won't hurt them; they will find it quite amusing enough to sit side by side, conscious of their proximity to each other."

I smiled, as I was bound to, and said: "Good; I will go on talking without noticing them when they come in. Now, this is what I want to ask you about—to wit, how you get people to work when there is no reward of labour, and especially how you get them to work strenuously?"

"No reward of labour?" said Hammond, gravely. "The reward of labour is *life*. Is that not enough?"

"But no reward for especially good work," quoth I.

"Plenty of reward," said he—"the reward of creation. The wages which God gets, as people might have said time agone. If you are going to ask to be paid for the pleasure of creation, which is what excellence in work means, the next thing we shall hear of will be a bill sent in for the begetting of children."

"Well, but," said I, "the man of the nineteenth century would say there is a natural desire towards the procreation of children, and a natural desire not to work."

"Yes, yes," said he, "I know the ancient platitude,—wholly untrue; indeed, to us quite meaningless. Fourier, whom all men laughed at, understood the matter better."[1]

"Why is it meaningless to you?" said I.

He said: "Because it implies that all work is suffering, and we are so far from thinking that, that, as you may have noticed, whereas we are not short of wealth, there is a kind of fear growing up amongst us that we shall one day be short of work. It is a pleasure which we are afraid of losing, not a pain."

"Yes," said I, "I have noticed that, and I was going to ask you about that also. But in the meantime, what do you positively mean to assert about the pleasurableness of work amongst you?"

"This, that *all* work is now pleasurable; either because of the hope of gain in honour and wealth with which the work is done, which causes pleasurable excitement, even when the actual work is not pleasant; or else because it has grown into a pleasurable *habit*, as in the case with what you may call mechanical work; and lastly (and most of our work is of this kind) because there is conscious sensuous pleasure in the work itself; it is done, that is, by artists."

"I see," said I. "Can you now tell me how you have come to this happy condition? For, to speak plainly, this change from the conditions of the older world seems to me far greater and more important than all the other changes you have told me about as to crime, politics, property, marriage."

"You are right there," said he. "Indeed, you may say rather that it is this change which makes all the others possible. What is the object of Revolution? Surely to make people happy. Revolution having brought its foredoomed change about, how can you prevent the counter-revolution from setting in except by making

---

[1] For Fourier, see footnote, p. 112. Like Morris, Fourier believed that the basic human desire to work and to find pleasure in work had been crippled by modern social conditions, and that the first goal of a properly ordered society would be to make labor pleasurable again.

people happy? What! shall we expect peace and stability from unhappiness? The gathering of grapes from thorns and figs from thistles[1] is a reasonable expectation compared with that! And happiness without happy daily work is impossible."

"Most obviously true," said I: for I thought the old boy was preaching a little. "But answer my question, as to how you gained this happiness."

"Briefly," said he, "by the absence of artificial coercion, and the freedom for every man to do what he can do best, joined to the knowledge of what productions of labour we really wanted. I must admit that this knowledge we reached slowly and painfully."

"Go on," said I, "give me more detail; explain more fully. For this subject interests me intensely."

"Yes, I will," said he; "but in order to do so I must weary you by talking a little about the past. Contrast is necessary for this explanation. Do you mind?"

"No, no," said I.

Said he, settling himself in his chair again for a long talk: "It is clear from all that we hear and read, that in the last age of civilization men had got into a vicious circle in the matter of production of wares. They had reached a wonderful facility of production, and in order to make the most of that facility they had gradually created (or allowed to grow, rather) a most elaborate system of buying and selling, which has been called the World-Market; and that World-Market, once set a-going, forced them to go on making more and more of these wares, whether they needed them or not. So that while (of course) they could not free themselves from the toil of making real necessaries, they created in a never-ending series sham or artificial necessaries, which became, under the iron rule of the aforesaid World-Market, of equal importance to them with the real necessaries which supported life. By all this they burdened themselves with a prodigious mass of work merely for the sake of keeping their wretched system going."

"Yes—and then?" said I.

"Why, then, since they had forced themselves to stagger along under this horrible burden of unnecessary production, it became

---

[1]   An allusion to Matthew 7:16.

impossible for them to look upon labour and its results from any other point of view than one—to wit, the ceaseless endeavour to expend the least possible amount of labour on any article made, and yet at the same time to make as many articles as possible. To this 'cheapening of production,' as it was called, everything was sacrificed: the happiness of the workman at his work, nay, his most elementary comfort and bare health, his food, his clothes, his dwelling, his leisure, his amusement, his education—his life, in short—did not weigh a grain of sand in the balance against this dire necessity of 'cheap production' of things, a great part of which were not worth producing at all. Nay, we are told, and we must believe it, so overwhelming is the evidence, though many of our people scarcely *can* believe it, that even rich and powerful men, the masters of the poor devils aforesaid, submitted to live amidst sights and sounds and smells which it is in the very nature of man to abhor and flee from, in order that their riches might bolster up this supreme folly. The whole community, in fact, was cast into the jaws of this ravening monster, 'the cheap production' forced upon it by the World-Market."

"Dear me!" said I. "But what happened? Did not their cleverness and facility in production master this chaos of misery at last? Couldn't they catch up with the World-Market, and then set to work to devise means for relieving themselves from this fearful task of extra labour?"

He smiled bitterly. "Did they even try to?" said he. "I am not sure. You know that according to the old saw the beetle gets used to living in dung; and these people, whether they found the dung sweet or not, certainly lived in it."

His estimate of the life of the nineteenth century made me catch my breath a little; and I said feebly, "But the labour-saving machines?"

"Heyday!" quoth he. "What's that you are saying? the labour-saving machines? Yes, they were made to 'save labour' (or, to speak more plainly, the lives of men) on one piece of work in order that it might be expended—I will say wasted—on another, probably useless, piece of work. Friend, all their devices for cheapening labour simply resulted in increasing the burden of labour. The appetite of the World-Market grew with what it fed on: the countries within the ring of 'civilization' (that is, organized misery) were glutted with the abortions of the market, and force and fraud were used unsparingly to 'open up' countries *outside* that pale. This process of 'opening up' is a strange one to those who have read the professions of the men of that period and do not understand their practice; and perhaps shows us at its worst the great vice of the nineteenth century, the use of hypocrisy and cant to evade the responsibility of vicarious ferocity. When the civilized World-Market coveted a country not yet in its clutches, some transparent pretext was found—the suppression of a slavery different from and not so cruel as that of commerce; the pushing of a religion no longer believed in by its promoters; the 'rescue' of some desperado or homicidal madman whose misdeeds had got him into trouble amongst the natives of the 'barbarous' country—any stick, in short, which would beat the dog at all. Then some bold, unprincipled, ignorant adventurer was found (no difficult task in the days of competition), and he was bribed to 'create a market' by breaking up whatever traditional society there might be in the doomed country, and by destroying whatever leisure or pleasure he found there. He forced wares on the natives which they did not want, and took their natural products in 'exchange,' as this form of robbery was called, and thereby he 'created new wants,' to supply which (that is, to be allowed to live by their new masters) the hapless, helpless people had to sell themselves into the slavery of hopeless toil so that they might have something wherewith to purchase the nullities of 'civilization.' Ah," said the old man, pointing to the Museum, "I have read books and papers in there, telling strange stories indeed of the dealings of civilization (or organized misery) with 'non-civilization'; from the time when the British Government deliberately sent blankets infected with small-pox as choice gifts to inconvenient tribes of Red-skins, to the time when Africa was infested by a man named Stanley, who—" [1]

---

[1] After British forts near Detroit were captured in 1763, Lord Jeffrey Amherst distributed linens and blankets infested with small-pox to the conquering Ottawa tribe. Sir Henry Morton Stanley, famous nineteenth-century explorer of Africa, was known for his often ruthless attacks on the native populations he encountered during his travels. Stanley was in London during 1890, and the hero's reception he received rankled Morris.

"Excuse me," said I, "but as you know, time presses; and I want to keep our question on the straightest line possible; and I want at once to ask this about these wares made for the World-Market— how about their quality; these people who were so clever about making goods, I suppose they made them well?"

"Quality!" said the old man crustily, for he was rather peevish at being cut short in his story; "how could they possibly attend to such trifles as the quality of the wares they sold? The best of them were of a lowish average, the worst were transparent make-shifts for the things asked for, which nobody would have put up with if they could have got anything else. It was a current jest of the time that the wares were made to sell and not to use; a jest which you, as coming from another planet, may understand, but which our folk could not."

Said I: "What! did they make nothing well?"

"Why, yes," said he, "there was one class of goods which they did make thoroughly well, and that was the class of machines which were used for making things. These were usually quite perfect pieces of workmanship, admirably adapted to the end in view. So that it may be fairly said that the great achievement of the nineteenth century was the making of machines which were wonders of invention, skill, and patience, and which were used for the production of measureless quantities of worthless make-shifts.

"In truth, the owners of the machines did not consider anything which they made as wares, but simply as means for the enrichment of themselves. Of course the only admitted test of utility in wares was the finding of buyers for them—wise men or fools, as it might chance."

"And people put up with this?" said I.

"For a time," said he.

"And then?"

"And then the overturn," said the old man, smiling, "and the nineteenth century saw itself as a man who has lost his clothes whilst bathing, and has to walk naked through the town."

"You are very bitter about that unlucky nineteenth century," said I.

"Naturally," said he, "since I know so much about it."

He was silent a little, and then said: "There are traditions—

nay, real histories—in our family about it: my grandfather was one of its victims. If you know something about it, you will understand what he suffered when I tell you that he was in those days a genuine artist, a man of genius, and a revolutionist."

"I think I do understand," said I: "but now, as it seems, you have reversed all this?"

"Pretty much so," said he. "The wares which we make are made because they are needed: men make for their neighbours' use as if they were making for themselves, not for a vague market of which they know nothing, and over which they have no control: as there is no buying and selling, it would be mere insanity to make goods on the chance of their being wanted; for there is no longer anyone who can be *compelled* to buy them. So that whatever is made is good, and thoroughly fit for its purpose. Nothing *can* be made except for genuine use; therefore no inferior goods are made. Moreover, as aforesaid, we have now found out what we want, so we make no more than we want; and as we are not driven to make a vast quantity of useless things, we have time and resources enough to consider our pleasure in making them. All work which would be irksome to do by hand is done by immensely improved machinery; and in all work which it is a pleasure to do by hand machinery is done without. There is no difficulty in finding work which suits the special turn of mind of everybody; so that no man is sacrificed to the wants of another. From time to time, when we have found out that some piece of work was too disagreeable or troublesome, we have given it up and done altogether without the thing produced by it. Now, surely you can see that under these circumstances all the work that we do is an exercise of the mind and body more or less pleasant to be done: so that instead of avoiding work everybody seeks it: and, since people have got defter in doing the work generation after generation, it has become so easy to do, that it seems as if there were less done, though probably more is produced. I suppose this explains that fear, which I hinted at just now, of a possible scarcity in work, which perhaps you have already noticed, and which is a feeling on the increase, and has been for a score of years."

"But do you think," said I, "that there is any fear of a work-famine amongst you?"

"No, I do not," said he, "and I will tell why; it is each man's business to make his own work pleasanter and pleasanter, which of course tends towards raising the standard of excellence, as no man enjoys turning out work which is not a credit to him, and also to greater deliberation in turning it out; and there is such a vast number of things which can be treated as works of art, that this alone gives employment to a host of deft people. Again, if art be inexhaustible, so is science also; and though it is no longer the only innocent occupation which is thought worth an intelligent man spending his time upon, as it once was, yet there are, and I suppose will be, many people who are excited by its conquest of difficulties, and care for it more than for anything else. Again, as more and more of pleasure is imported into work, I think we shall take up kinds of work which produce desirable wares, but which we gave up because we could not carry them on pleasantly. Moreover, I think that it is only in parts of Europe which are more advanced than the rest of the world that you will hear this talk of the fear of a work-famine. Those lands which were once the colonies of Great Britain, for instance, and especially America—that part of it, above all, which was once the United States—are now and will be for a long while a great resource to us. For these lands, and, I say, especially the northern parts of America, suffered so terribly from the full force of the last days of civilization, and became such horrible places to live in, that they are now very backward in all that makes life pleasant. Indeed, one may say that for nearly a hundred years the people of the northern parts of America have been engaged in gradually making a dwelling-place out of a stinking dust-heap; and there is still a great deal to do, especially as the country is so big."

"Well," said I, "I am exceedingly glad to think that you have such a prospect of happiness before you. But I should like to ask a few more questions, and then I have done for to-day."

CHAPTER XVI

DINNER IN THE HALL OF THE
BLOOMSBURY MARKET

As I spoke, I heard footsteps near the door; the latch yielded, and in came our two lovers, looking so handsome that one had no feeling of shame in looking on at their little-concealed love-making; for indeed it seemed as if all the world must be in love with them. As for old Hammond, he looked on them like an artist who has just painted a picture nearly as well as he thought he could when he began it, and was perfectly happy. He said:

"Sit down, sit down, young folk, and don't make a noise. Our guest here has still some questions to ask me."

"Well, I should suppose so," said Dick; "you have only been three hours and a half together; and it isn't to be hoped that the history of two centuries could be told in three hours and a half: let alone that, for all I know, you may have been wandering into the realms of geography and craftsmanship."

"As to noise, my dear kinsman," said Clara, "you will very soon be disturbed by the noise of the dinner-bell, which I should think will be very pleasant music to our guest, who breakfasted early, it seems, and probably had a tiring day yesterday."

I said: "Well, since you have spoken the word, I begin to feel that it is so; but I have been feeding myself with wonder this long time past: really, it's quite true," quoth I, as I saw her smile, O so prettily!

But just then from some tower high up in the air came the sound of silvery chimes playing a sweet clear tune, that sounded to my unaccustomed ears like the song of the first blackbird in the spring, and called a rush of memories to my mind, some of bad times, some of good, but all sweetened now into mere pleasure.

"No more questions now before dinner," said Clara; and she took my hand as an affectionate child would, and led me out of the room and down stairs into the forecourt of the Museum, leaving the two Hammonds to follow as they pleased.

We went into the market-place which I had been in before,

a thinnish stream of elegantly[1] dressed people going in along with us. We turned into the cloister and came to a richly moulded and carved doorway, where a very pretty dark-haired young girl gave us each a beautiful bunch of summer flowers, and we entered a hall much bigger than that of the Hammersmith Guest House, more elaborate in its architecture and perhaps more beautiful. I found it difficult to keep my eyes off the wall-pictures (for I thought it bad manners to stare at Clara all the time, though she was quite worth it). I saw at a glance that their subjects were taken from queer old-world myths and imaginations which in yesterday's world only about half a dozen people in the country knew anything about; and when the two Hammonds sat down opposite to us, I said to the old man, pointing to the frieze:

"How strange to see such subjects here!"

"Why?" said he. "I don't see why you should be surprised; everybody knows the tales; and they are graceful and pleasant subjects, not too tragic for a place where people mostly eat and drink and amuse themselves, and yet full of incident."

I smiled, and said: "Well, I scarcely expected to find record of the Seven Swans and the King of the Golden Mountain and Faithful Henry, and such curious pleasant imaginations as Jacob Grimm got together from the childhood of the world, barely lingering even in his time:[2] I should have thought you would have forgotten such childishness by this time."

The old man smiled, and said nothing; but Dick turned rather red, and broke out:

"What *do* you mean, guest? I think them very beautiful, I mean not only the pictures, but the stories; and when we were children we used to imagine them going on in every wood-end, by the bight[3] of every stream: every house in the fields was the Fairyland King's House to us. Don't you remember, Clara?"

---

[1] [Morris's note]: "Elegant," I mean, as a Persian pattern is elegant; not like a rich "elegant" lady out for a morning stroll. I should rather call that *genteel*.

[2] Jacob and Wilhelm Grimm published the folktales Guest refers to in their *Household Tales* (1814): "The Six Swans" (not seven), "The King of the Golden Mountain," and "The Frog-King, or Iron Henry."

[3] A bight is a bend or curve.

"Yes," she said; and it seemed to me as if a slight cloud came over her fair face. I was going to speak to her on the subject, when the pretty waitresses came to us smiling, and chattering sweetly like reed warblers by the river side, and fell to giving us our dinner. As to this, as at our breakfast, everything was cooked and served with a daintiness which showed that those who had prepared it were interested in it; but there was no excess either of quantity or of gourmandise: everything was simple, though so excellent of its kind; and it was made clear to us that this was no feast, only an ordinary meal. The glass, crockery, and plate were very beautiful to my eyes, used to the study of mediæval art; but a nineteenth-century club-haunter would, I daresay, have found them rough and lacking in finish; the crockery being lead-glazed pot-ware, though beautifully ornamented; the only porcelain being here and there a piece of old oriental ware. The glass, again, though elegant and quaint, and very varied in form, was somewhat bubbled and hornier in texture than the commercial articles of the nineteenth century. The furniture and general fittings of the hall were much of a piece with the table-gear, beautiful in form and highly ornamented, but without the commercial 'finish' of the joiners and cabinet-makers of our time. Withal, there was a total absence of what the nineteenth century calls "comfort"—that is, stuffy inconvenience; so that, even apart from the delightful excitement of the day, I had never eaten my dinner so pleasantly before.

When we had done eating, and were sitting a little while, with a bottle of very good Bordeaux wine before us, Clara came back to the question of the subject-matter of the pictures, as though it had troubled her.

She looked up at them, and said: "How is it that though we are so interested with our life for the most part, yet when people take to writing poems or painting pictures they seldom deal with our modern life, or if they do, take good care to make their poems or pictures unlike that life? Are we not good enough to paint ourselves? How is it that we find the dreadful times of the past so interesting to us—in pictures and poetry?"

Old Hammond smiled. "It always was so, and I suppose always will be," said he, "however it may be explained. It is true that in the nineteenth century, when there was so little art and so much talk about it, there was a theory that art and imaginative literature ought to deal with contemporary life; but they never did so; for, if there was any pretence of it, the author always took care (as Clara hinted just now) to disguise, or exaggerate, or idealize, and in some way or another make it strange; so that, for all the verisimilitude there was, he might just as well have dealt with the time of the Pharaohs."

"Well," said Dick, "surely it is but natural to like these things strange; just as when we were children, as I said just now, we used to pretend to be so-and-so in such-and-such a place. That's what these pictures and poems do; and why shouldn't they?"

"Thou hast hit it, Dick," quoth old Hammond; "it is the child-like part of us that produces works of imagination. When we are children time passes so slow with us that we seem to have time for everything."

He sighed, and then smiled and said: "At least let us rejoice that we have got back our childhood again. I drink to the days that are!"

"Second childhood," said I in a low voice, and then blushed at my double rudeness, and hoped that he hadn't heard. But he had, and turned to me smiling, and said: "Yes, why not? And for my part, I hope it may last long; and that the world's next period of wise and unhappy manhood, if that should happen, will speedily lead us to a third childhood: if indeed this age be not our third. Meantime, my friend, you must know that we are too happy, both individually and collectively, to trouble ourselves about what is to come hereafter."

"Well, for my part," said Clara, "I wish we were interesting enough to be written or painted about."

Dick answered her with some lover's speech, impossible to be written down, and then we sat quiet a little.

CHAPTER XVII

HOW THE CHANGE CAME

Dick broke the silence at last, saying: "Guest, forgive us for a little after-dinner dulness. What would you like to do? Shall we have out Greylocks and trot back to Hammersmith? or will you come with us and hear some Welsh folk sing in a hall close by here? or would you like presently to come with me into the City and see some really fine building? Or—what shall it be?"

"Well," said I, "as I am a stranger, I must let you choose for me."

In point of fact, I did not by any means want to be 'amused' just then; and also I rather felt as if the old man, with his knowledge of past times, and even a kind of inverted sympathy for them caused by his active hatred of them, was as it were a blanket for me against the cold of this very new world, where I was, so to say, stripped bare of every habitual thought and way of acting; and I did not want to leave him too soon. He came to my rescue at once, and said—

"Wait a bit, Dick; there is someone else to be consulted besides you and the guest here, and that is I. I am not going to lose the pleasure of his company just now, especially as I know he has something else to ask me. So go to your Welshmen, by all means; but first of all bring us another bottle of wine to this nook, and then be off as you like; and come again and fetch our friend to go westward, but not too soon."

Dick nodded, smilingly, and the old man and I were soon alone in the great hall, the afternoon sun gleaming on the red wine in our tall quaint-shaped glasses. Then said Hammond:

"Does anything especially puzzle you about our way of living, now you have heard a good deal and seen a little of it?"

Said I: "I think what puzzles me most is how it all came about."

"It well may," said he, "so great as the change is. It would be difficult indeed to tell you the whole story, perhaps impossible: knowledge, discontent, treachery, disappointment, ruin, misery, despair—those who worked for the change because they could see further than other people went through all these phases of suffering; and doubtless all the time the most of men looked on, not knowing what was doing, thinking it all a matter of course, like the rising and setting of the sun—and indeed it was so."

"Tell me one thing, if you can," said I. "Did the change, the 'revolution' it used to be called, come peacefully?"

"Peacefully?" said he; "what peace was there amongst those poor confused wretches of the nineteenth century? It was war from beginning to end: bitter war, till hope and pleasure put an end to it."

"Do you mean actual fighting with weapons?" said I, "or the strikes and lock-outs and starvation of which we have heard?"

"Both, both," he said. "As a matter of fact, the history of the terrible period of transition from commercial slavery to freedom may thus be summarized. When the hope of realizing a communal condition of life for all men arose, quite late in the nineteenth century, the power of the middle classes, the then tyrants of society, was so enormous and crushing, that to almost all men, even those who had, you may say despite themselves, despite their reason and judgment, conceived such hopes, it seemed a dream. So much was this the case that some of those more enlightened men who were then called Socialists, although they well knew, and even stated in public, that the only reasonable condition of Society was that of pure Communism (such as you now see around you), yet shrunk from what seemed to them the barren task of preaching the realization of a happy dream. Looking back now, we can see that the great motive power of the change was a longing for freedom and equality, akin if you please to the unreasonable passion of the lover; a sickness of heart that rejected with loathing the aimless solitary life of the well-to-do educated man of that time: phrases, my dear friend, which have lost their meaning to us of the present day; so far removed we are from the dreadful facts which they represent.

"Well, these men, though conscious of this feeling, had no faith in it, as a means of bringing about the change. Nor was that wonderful: for looking around them they saw the huge mass of the oppressed classes too much burdened with the misery of their lives, and too much overwhelmed by the selfishness of misery, to be able to form a conception of any escape from it except by the ordinary way prescribed by the system of slavery under which they lived; which was nothing more than a remote chance of climbing out of the oppressed into the oppressing class.

"Therefore, though they knew that the only reasonable aim for those who would better the world was a condition of equality; in their impatience and despair they managed to convince themselves that if they could by hook or by crook get the machinery of production and the management of property so altered that the 'lower classes' (so the horrible word ran) might have their slavery somewhat ameliorated, they would be ready to fit into this machinery, and would use it for bettering the condition still more and still more, until at last the result would be a practical equality (they were very fond of using the word 'practical'), because 'the rich' would be forced to pay so much for keeping 'the poor' in a tolerable condition that the condition of riches would become no longer valuable and would gradually die out. Do you follow me?"

"Partly," said I. "Go on."

Said old Hammond: "Well, since you follow me, you will see that as a theory this was not altogether unreasonable; but 'practically,' it turned out a failure."

"How so?" said I.

"Well, don't you see," said he, "because it involved the making of a machinery by those who didn't know what they wanted the machines to do. So far as the masses of the oppressed class furthered this scheme of improvement, they did it to get themselves improved slave-rations—as many of them could. And if those classes had really been incapable of being touched by that instinct which produced the passion for freedom and equality aforesaid, what would have happened, I think, would have been this: that a certain part of the working classes would have been so far improved in condition that they would have approached the condition of the middling rich men; but below them would have been a great class of most miserable slaves, whose slavery would have been far more hopeless than the older class-slavery had been."

"What stood in the way of this?" said I.

"Why, of course," said he, "just that instinct for freedom aforesaid. It is true that the slave-class could not conceive the happiness of a free life. Yet they grew to understand (and very speedily too) that they were oppressed by their masters, and they assumed, you see how justly, that they could do without them, though perhaps they scarce knew how; so that it came to this, that though they could not look forward to the happiness or peace of the freeman, they did at least look forward to the war which a vague hope told them would bring that peace about."

"Could you tell me rather more closely what actually took place?" said I; for I thought *him* rather vague here.

"Yes," he said, "I can. That machinery of life for the use of people who didn't know what they wanted of it, and which was known at the time as State Socialism, was partly put in motion, though in a very piecemeal way. But it did not work smoothly; it was, of course, resisted at every turn by the capitalists; and no wonder, for it tended more and more to upset the commercial system I have told you of, without providing anything really effective in its place. The result was growing confusion, great suffering amongst the working classes, and, as a consequence, great discontent. For a long time matters went on like this. The power of the upper classes had lessened, as their command over wealth lessened, and they could not carry things wholly by the high hand as they had been used to in earlier days. So far the State Socialists were justified by the result. On the other hand, the working classes were ill-organized, and growing poorer in reality, in spite of the gains (also real in the long run) which they had forced from the masters. Thus matters hung in the balance; the masters could not reduce their slaves to complete subjection, though they put down some feeble and partial riots easily enough. The workers forced their masters to grant them ameliorations, real or imaginary, of their condition, but could not force freedom from them. At last came a great crash. To explain this you must understand that very great progress had been made amongst the workers, though as before said but little in the direction of improved livelihood."

I played the innocent and said: "In what direction could they improve, if not in livelihood?"

Said he: "In the power to bring about a state of things in which livelihood would be full, and easy to gain. They had at last learned how to combine after a long period of mistakes and disasters. The workmen had now a regular organization in the struggle against their masters, a struggle which for more than half a century had been accepted as an inevitable part of the conditions of the modern system of labour and production. This combination had now taken the form of a federation of all or almost all the recognized wage-paid employments, and it was by its means that those betterments of the conditions of the workmen had been forced from the masters: and though they were not seldom mixed up with the rioting that happened, especially in the earlier days of their organization, it by no means formed an essential part of their tactics; indeed at the time I am now speaking of they had got to be so strong that most commonly the mere threat of a 'strike' was enough to gain any minor point: because they had given up the foolish tactics of the ancient trades unions of calling out of work a part only of the workers of such and such an industry, and supporting them while out of work on the labour of those that remained in. By this time they had a biggish fund of money for the support of strikes, and could stop a certain industry altogether for a time if they so determined."

Said I: "Was there not a serious danger of such moneys being misused—of jobbery, in fact?"

Old Hammond wriggled uneasily on his seat, and said:

"Though all this happened so long ago, I still feel the pain of mere shame when I have to tell you that it was more than a danger: that such rascality often happened; indeed more than once the whole combination seemed dropping to pieces because of it: but at the time of which I am telling, things looked so threatening, and to the workmen at least the necessity of their dealing with the fast-gathering trouble which the labour-struggle had brought about, was so clear, that the conditions of the times had begot a deep seriousness amongst all reasonable people; a determination which put aside all non-essentials, and which to thinking men was ominous of the swiftly-approaching change: such an element was too dangerous for mere traitors and self-seekers, and one by one they were thrust out and mostly joined the declared reactionaries."

"How about those ameliorations," said I; "what were they? or rather of what nature?"

Said he: "Some of them, and these of the most practical importance to the men's livelihood, were yielded by the masters by direct compulsion on the part of the men; the new conditions of labour so gained were indeed only customary, enforced by no law: but, once established, the masters durst not attempt to withdraw them in face of the growing power of the combined workers. Some again were steps on the path of 'State Socialism';

the most important of which can be speedily summed up. At the
end of the nineteenth century the cry arose for compelling the
masters to employ their men a less number of hours in the day:
this cry gathered volume quickly, and the masters had to yield to
it. But it was, of course, clear that unless this meant a higher price
for work per hour, it would be a mere nullity, and that the
masters, unless forced, would reduce it to that. Therefore after a
long struggle another law was passed fixing a minimum price for
labour in the most important industries; which again had to be
supplemented by a law fixing the maximum price on the chief
wares then considered necessary for a workman's life."

"You were getting perilously near to the late Roman poor-
rates,"[1] said I, smiling, "and the doling out of bread to the proletariat."

"So many said at the time," said the old man drily; "and it has
long been a commonplace that that slough awaits State Socialism
in the end, if it gets to the end, which as you know it did not
with us. However it went further than this minimum and maximum business, which by the by we can now see was necessary.
The government now found it imperative on them to meet the
outcry of the master class at the approaching destruction of
commerce (as desirable, had they known it, as the extinction of
the cholera, which has since happily taken place). And they were
forced to meet it by a measure hostile to the masters, the establishment of government factories for the production of necessary wares, and markets for their sale. These measures taken
altogether did do something: they were in fact of the nature of
regulations made by the commander of a beleaguered city. But
of course to the privileged classes it seemed as if the end of the
world were come when such laws were enacted.

"Nor was that altogether without a warrant: the spread of
communistic theories, and the partial practice of State Socialism
had at first disturbed, and at last almost paralyzed the marvellous
system of commerce under which the old world had lived so fever-
ishly, and had produced for some few a life of gambler's pleasure,

---

[1] Poor-rates were taxes paid to provide (the most minimal) food and shelter for the
poor.

and for many, or most, a life of mere misery: over and over again came 'bad times' as they were called, and indeed they were bad enough for the wage-slaves. The year 1952 was one of the worst of these times; the workmen suffered dreadfully: the partial, inefficient government factories, which were terribly jobbed, all but broke down, and a vast part of the population had for the time being to be fed on undisguised 'charity' as it was called.

"The Combined Workers watched the situation with mingled hope and anxiety. They had already formulated their general demands; but now by a solemn and universal vote of the whole of their federated societies, they insisted on the first step being taken toward carrying out their demands: this step would have led directly to handing over the management of the whole natural resources of the country, together with the machinery for using them, into the power of the Combined Workers, and the reduction of the privileged classes into the position of pensioners obviously dependent on the pleasure of the workers. The 'Resolution,' as it was called, which was widely published in the newspapers of the day, was in fact a declaration of war, and was so accepted by the master class. They began henceforward to prepare for a firm stand against the 'brutal and ferocious communism of the day,' as they phrased it. And as they were in many ways still very powerful, or seemed so to be; they still hoped by means of brute force to regain some of what they had lost, and perhaps in the end the whole of it. It was said amongst them on all hands that it had been a great mistake of the various governments not to have resisted sooner; and the liberals and radicals (the name as perhaps you may know of the more democratically inclined part of the ruling classes) were much blamed for having led the world to this pass by their mis-timed pedantry and foolish sentimentality: and one Gladstone, or Gledstein (probably, judging by this name, of Scandinavian descent), a notable politician of the nineteenth century, was especially singled out for reprobation in this respect. I need scarcely point out to you the absurdity of all this. But terrible tragedy lay hidden behind this grinning through a horse-collar of the reactionary party. 'The insatiable greed of the lower classes must be repressed'—'The people must be taught a lesson'—these were the sacramental phrases current amongst the reactionists, and ominous enough they were."

The old man stopped to look keenly at my attentive and wondering face; and then said:

"I know, dear guest, that I have been using words and phrases which few people amongst us could understand without long and laborious explanation; and not even then perhaps. But since you have not yet gone to sleep, and since I am speaking to you as to a being from another planet, I may venture to ask you if you have followed me thus far?"

"O yes," said I, "I quite understand: pray go on; a great deal of what you have been saying was common place with us—when—when—"

"Yes," said he gravely, "when you were dwelling in the other planet. Well, now for the crash aforesaid.

"On some comparatively trifling occasion a great meeting was summoned by the workmen leaders to meet in Trafalgar Square (about the right to meet in which place there had for years and years been bickering). The civic bourgeois guard (called the police) attacked the said meeting with bludgeons, according to their custom; many people were hurt in the *mélée*, of whom five in all died, either trampled to death on the spot, or from the effects of their cudgelling; the meeting was scattered, and some hundred of prisoners cast into gaol. A similar meeting had been treated in the same way a few days before at a place called Manchester, which has now disappeared. Thus the 'lesson' began. The whole country was thrown into a ferment by this; meetings were held which attempted some rough organization for the holding of another meeting to retort on the authorities. A huge crowd assembled in Trafalgar Square and the neighbourhood (then a place of crowded streets), and was too big for the bludgeon-armed police to cope with; there was a good deal of dry-blow fighting;[1] three or four of the people were killed, and half a score of policemen were crushed to death in the throng, and the rest got away as they could. This was a victory for the people as far as it went. The next day all London (remember what it was in those days) was in a state of

---

[1] I.e., fighting with fists and clubs rather than knives and guns.

turmoil. Many of the rich fled into the country; the executive got together soldiery, but did not dare to use them; and the police could not be massed in any one place, because riots or threats of riots were everywhere. But in Manchester, where the people were not so courageous or not so desperate as in London, several of the popular leaders were arrested. In London a convention of leaders was got together from the Federation of Combined Workmen, and sat under the old revolutionary name of the Committee of Public Safety;[1] but as they had no drilled and armed body of men to direct, they attempted no aggressive measures, but only placarded the walls with somewhat vague appeals to the workmen not to allow themselves to be trampled upon. However, they called a meeting in Trafalgar Square for the day fortnight of the last-mentioned skirmish.

"Meantime the town grew no quieter, and business came pretty much to an end. The newspapers—then, as always hitherto, almost entirely in the hands of the masters—clamoured to the Government for repressive measures; the rich citizens were enrolled as an extra body of police, and armed with bludgeons like them; many of these were strong, well-fed, full-blooded young men, and had plenty of stomach for fighting; but the Government did not dare to use them, and contented itself with getting full powers voted to it by the Parliament for suppressing any revolt, and bringing up more and more soldiers to London. Thus passed the week after the great meeting; almost as large a one was held on the Sunday, which went off peaceably on the whole, as no opposition to it was offered, and again the people cried 'victory.' But on the Monday the people woke up to find that they were hungry. During the last few days there had been groups of men parading the streets asking (or, if you please, demanding) money to buy food; and what for goodwill, what for fear, the richer people gave them a good deal. The authorities of the parishes also (I haven't time to explain that phrase at present) gave willy-nilly

---

[1] During the French Revolution a Committee of Public Safety was established in 1793 under Robespierre, though Morris is more likely to be evoking memories of the Paris Commune of 1871, when a Committee of Public Safety was given wide powers in an effort to bolster the crumbling commune.

what provisions they could to wandering people; and the Government, by means of its feeble national workshops, also fed a good number of half-starved folk. But in addition to this, several bakers' shops and other provision stores had been emptied without a great deal of disturbance. So far, so good. But on the Monday in question the Committee of Public Safety, on the one hand afraid of general unorganized pillage, and on the other emboldened by the wavering conduct of the authorities, sent a deputation provided with carts and all necessary gear to clear out two or three big provision stores in the centre of the town, leaving papers with the shop managers promising to pay the price of them: and also in the part of the town where they were strongest they took possession of several bakers' shops and set men at work in them for the benefit of the people;—all of which was done with little or no disturbance, the police assisting in keeping order at the sack of the stores, as they would have done at a big fire.

"But at this last stroke the reactionaries were so alarmed, that they were determined to force the executive into action. The newspapers next day all blazed into the fury of frightened people, and threatened the people, the Government, and everybody they could think of, unless 'order were at once restored.' A deputation of leading commercial people waited on the Government and told them that if they did not at once arrest the Committee of Public Safety, they themselves would gather a body of men, arm them, and fall on 'the incendiaries,' as they called them.

"They, together with a number of the newspaper editors, had a long interview with the heads of the Government and two or three military men, the deftest in their art that the country could furnish. The deputation came away from that interview, says a contemporary eye-witness, smiling and satisfied, and said no more about raising an anti-popular army, but that afternoon left London with their families for their country seats or elsewhere.

"The next morning the Government proclaimed a state of siege in London,—a thing common enough amongst the absolutist governments on the Continent, but unheard-of in England in those days. They appointed the youngest and cleverest of their generals to command the proclaimed district; a man who had won a certain sort of reputation in the disgraceful wars in which the country had been long engaged from time to time. The newspapers were in ecstacies, and all the most fervent of the reactionaries now came to the front; men who in ordinary times were forced to keep their opinions to themselves or their immediate circle, but who began to look forward to crushing once for all the Socialist, and even democratic tendencies, which, said they, had been treated with such foolish indulgence for the last sixty years.

"But the clever general took no visible action; and yet only a few of the minor newspapers abused him; thoughtful men gathered from this that a plot was hatching. As for the Committee of Public Safety, whatever they thought of their position, they had now gone too far to draw back; and many of them, it seems, thought that the government would not act. They went on quietly organizing their food supply, which was a miserable driblet when all is said; and also as a retort to the state of siege, they armed as many men as they could in the quarter where they were strongest, but did not attempt to drill or organize them, thinking, perhaps, that they could not at the best turn them into trained soldiers till they had some breathing space. The clever general, his soldiers, and the police did not meddle with all this in the least in the world; and things were quieter in London that week-end; though there were riots in many places of the provinces, which were quelled by the authorities without much trouble. The most serious of these were at Glasgow and Bristol.

"Well, the Sunday of the meeting came, and great crowds came to Trafalgar Square in procession, the greater part of the Committee amongst them, surrounded by their band of men armed somehow or other. The streets were quite peaceful and quiet, though there were many spectators to see the procession pass. Trafalgar Square had no body of police in it; the people took quiet possession of it, and the meeting began. The armed men stood round the principal platform, and there were a few others armed amidst the general crowd; but by far the greater part were unarmed.

"Most people thought the meeting would go off peaceably; but the members of the Committee had heard from various quarters that something would be attempted against them; but these rumours were vague, and they had no idea of what threatened. They soon found out.

"For before the streets about the Square were filled, a body of soldiers poured into it from the north-west corner and took up their places by the houses that stood on the west side. The people growled at the sight of the red-coats; the armed men of the Committee stood undecided, not knowing what to do; and indeed this new influx so jammed the crowd together that, unorganized as they were, they had little chance of working through it. They had scarcely grasped the fact of their enemies being there, when another column of soldiers, pouring out of the streets which led into the great southern road going down to the Parliament House (still existing, and called the Dung Market), and also from the embankment by the side of the Thames, marched up, pushing the crowd into a denser and denser mass, and formed along the south side of the Square. Then any of those who could see what was going on, knew at once that they were in a trap, and could only wonder what would be done with them.

"The closely-packed crowd would not or could not budge, except under the influence of the height of terror, which was soon to be supplied to them. A few of the armed men struggled to the front, or climbed up to the base of the monument which then stood there, that they might face the wall of hidden fire before them; and to most men (there were many women amongst them) it seemed as if the end of the world had come, and to-day seemed strangely different from yesterday. No sooner were the soldiers drawn up as aforesaid than, says an eye-witness, 'a glittering officer on horseback came prancing out from the ranks on the south, and read something from a paper which he held in his hand;[1] which something, very few heard; but I was told afterwards that it was an order for us to disperse, and a warning that he had legal right to fire on the crowd else, and that he would do so. The crowd took it as a challenge of some sort, and a hoarse threatening roar went up from them; and after that there was comparative silence for a little, till the officer had got back into the ranks. I was near the edge of the crowd, towards the soldiers,' says this eye-witness, 'and I saw three little machines

---

[1] Presumably the Riot Act (1715) is being read. Having read the act aloud, the officer would now be authorized to have arrested everyone who did not immediately disperse.

being wheeled out in front of the ranks, which I knew for mechanical guns. I cried out, "Throw yourselves down! they are going to fire!" But no one scarcely could throw himself down, so tight as the crowd were packed. I heard a sharp order given, and wondered where I should be the next minute; and then— It was as if the earth had opened, and hell had come up bodily amidst us. It is no use trying to describe the scene that followed. Deep lanes were mowed amidst the thick crowd; the dead and dying covered the ground, and the shrieks and wails and cries of horror filled all the air, till it seemed as if there were nothing else in the world but murder and death. Those of our armed men who were still unhurt cheered wildly and opened a scattering fire on the soldiers. One or two soldiers fell; and I saw the officers going up and down the ranks urging the men to fire again; but they received the orders in sullen silence, and let the butts of their guns fall. Only one sergeant ran to a machine-gun and began to set it going; but a tall young man, an officer too, ran out of the ranks and dragged him back by the collar; and the soldiers stood there motionless while the horror-stricken crowd, nearly wholly unarmed (for most of the armed men had fallen in that first discharge), drifted out of the Square. I was told afterwards that the soldiers on the west side had fired also, and done their part of the slaughter. How I got out of the Square I scarcely know: I went, not feeling the ground under me, what with rage and terror and despair.'

"So says our eye-witness. The number of the slain on the side of the people in that shooting during a minute was prodigious: but it was not easy to come at the truth about it; it was probably between one and two thousand. Of the soldiers, six were killed outright, and about a dozen wounded."

I listened, trembling with excitement. The old man's eyes glittered and his face flushed as he spoke, and told the tale of what I had often thought might happen. Yet I wondered that he should have got so elated about a mere massacre, and I said:

"How fearful! And I suppose that this massacre put an end to the whole revolution for that time?"

"No, no," cried old Hammond; "it began it!"

He filled his glass and mine, and stood up and cried out,

"Drink this glass to the memory of those who died there, for indeed it would be a long tale to tell how much we owe them."

I drank, and he sat down again and went on.

"That massacre of Trafalgar Square began the civil war, though, like all such events, it gathered head slowly, and people scarcely knew what a crisis they were acting in.

"Terrible as the massacre was, and hideous and overpowering as the first terror had been, when the people had time to think about it, their feeling was one of anger rather than fear; although the military organization of the state of siege was now carried out without shrinking by the clever young general. For though the ruling-classes when the news spread next morning felt one gasp of horror and even dread, yet the Government and their immediate backers felt that now the wine was drawn and must be drunk. However, even the most reactionary of the capitalist papers, with two exceptions, stunned by the tremendous news, simply gave an account of what had taken place, without making any comment on it. The exceptions were one, a so-called 'liberal' paper (the Government of the day was of that complexion), which, after a preamble which declared its undeviating sympathy with the cause of labour, proceeded to point out that in times of revolutionary disturbance it behoved the Government to be just but firm, and that by far the most merciful way of dealing with the poor madmen who were attacking the very foundations of society (which had made them mad and poor) was to shoot them at once, so as to stop others from drifting into a position in which they would run a chance of being shot. In short, it praised the determined action of the Government as the *acmé* of human wisdom and mercy, and exulted in the inauguration of an epoch of reasonable democracy free from the tyrannical fads of Socialism.

"The other exception was a paper thought to be one of the most violent opponents of democracy, and so it was; but the editor of it found his manhood, and spoke for himself and not for his paper. In a few simple, indignant words he asked people to consider what a society was worth which had to be defended by the massacre of unarmed citizens, and called on the Government to withdraw their state of siege and put the general and his officers who fired on the people on their trial for murder. He went further, and declared that whatever his opinion might be as to the doctrines of the Socialists, he for one should throw in his lot with the people, until the Government atoned for their atrocity by showing that they were prepared to listen to the demands of men who knew what they wanted, and whom the decrepitude of society forced into pushing their demands in some way or other.

"Of course, this editor was immediately arrested by the military power; but his bold words were already in the hands of the public, and produced a great effect: so great an effect that the Government, after some vacillation, withdrew the state of siege; though at the same time it strengthened the military organization and made it more stringent. Three of the Committee of Public Safety had been slain in Trafalgar Square: of the rest, the greater part went back to their old place of meeting, and there awaited the event calmly. They were arrested there on the Monday morning, and would have been shot at once by the general, who was a mere military machine, if the Government had not shrunk before the responsibility of killing men without any trial. There was at first a talk of trying them by a special commission of judges, as it was called—*i.e.*, before a set of men bound to find them guilty, and whose business it was to do so. But with the Government the cold fit had succeeded to the hot one; and the prisoners were brought before a jury at the assizes. There, a fresh blow awaited the Government; for in spite of the judge's charge, which distinctly instructed the jury to find the prisoners guilty, they were acquitted, and the jury added to their verdict a presentment, in which they condemned the action of the soldiery, in the queer phraseology of the day, as 'rash, unfortunate, and unnecessary.' The Committee of Public Safety renewed its sittings, and from thenceforth was a popular rallying-point in opposition to the Parliament. The Government now gave way on all sides, and made a show of yielding to the demands of the people, though there was a widespread plot for effecting a *coup d'état* set on foot between the leaders of the two so-called opposing parties in the parliamentary faction fight. The well-meaning part of the public was overjoyed, and thought that all danger of a civil war was over. The victory of the people was celebrated by huge meetings held in the parks and elsewhere, in memory of the victims of the great massacre.

"But the measures passed for the relief of the workers, though to the upper classes they seemed ruinously revolutionary, were not thorough enough to give the people food and a decent life, and they had to be supplemented by unwritten enactments without legality to back them. Although the Government and Parliament had the law-courts, the army, and 'society' at their backs, the Committee of Public Safety began to be a force in the country, and really represented the producing classes. It began to improve immensely in the days which followed on the acquittal of its members. Its old members had little administrative capacity, though with the exception of a few self-seekers and traitors, they were honest, courageous men, and many of them were endowed with considerable talent of other kinds. But now that the times called for immediate action, came forward the men capable of setting it on foot; and a new network of workmen's associations grew up very speedily, whose avowed single object was the tiding over of the ship of the community into a simple condition of Communism; and as they practically undertook also the manage-ment of the ordinary labour-war, they soon became the mouth-piece and intermediary of the whole of the working classes; and the manufacturing profit-grinders, now found themselves power-less before this combination; unless *their* committee, Parliament, plucked up courage to begin the civil war again, and to shoot right and left, they were bound to yield to the demands of the men whom they employed, and pay higher and higher wages for shorter and shorter day's work. Yet one ally they had, and that was the rapidly approaching breakdown of the whole system founded on the World-Market and its supply; which now became so clear to all people, that the middle classes, shocked for the moment into condemnation of the Government for the great massacre, turned round nearly in a mass, and called on the Government to look to matters, and put an end to the tyranny of the Socialist leaders.

"Thus stimulated, the reactionist plot exploded probably before it was ripe; but this time the people and their leaders were forewarned, and, before the reactionaries could get under way, had taken the steps they thought necessary.

"The Liberal Government (clearly by collusion) was beaten by the Conservatives, though the latter were nominally much in the minority. The popular representatives in the House understood pretty well what this meant, and after an attempt to fight the matter out by divisions in the House of Commons, they made a protest, left the House, and came in a body to the Committee of Public Safety: and the civil war began again in good earnest.

"Yet its first act was not one of mere fighting. The new Tory Government determined to act, yet durst not re-enact the state of siege, but it sent a body of soldiers and police to arrest the Committee of Public Safety in the lump. They made no resistance, though they might have done so, as they had now a considerable body of men who were quite prepared for extremities. But they were determined to try first a weapon which they thought stronger than street fighting.

"The members of the Committee went off quietly to prison; but they had left their soul and their organization behind them. For they depended not on a carefully arranged centre with all kinds of checks and counter-checks about it, but on a huge mass of people in thorough sympathy with the movement, bound together by a great number of links of small centres with very simple instructions. These instructions were now carried out.

"The next morning, when the leaders of the reaction were chuckling at the effect which the report in the newspapers of their stroke would have upon the public—no newspapers appeared; and it was only towards noon that a few straggling sheets, about the size of the gazettes of the seventeenth century, worked by policemen, soldiers, managers, and press-writers, were dribbled through the streets. They were greedily seized on and read; but by this time the serious part of their news was stale, and people did not need to be told that the GENERAL STRIKE had begun. The railways did not run, the telegraph-wires were unserved; flesh, fish, and green stuff brought to market was allowed to lie there still packed and perishing; the thousands of middle-class families, who were utterly dependent for the next meal on the workers, made frantic efforts through their more energetic members to cater for the needs of the day, and amongst those of them who could throw off the fear of what was to follow, there was, I am told, a certain enjoyment of this unexpected picnic—a forecast of the days to come, in which all labour grew pleasant.

"So passed the first day, and towards evening the Government grew quite distracted. They had but one resource for putting down any popular movement—to wit, mere brute-force; but there was nothing for them against which to use their army and police: no armed bodies appeared in the streets; the offices of the Federated Workmen were now, in appearance, at least, turned into places for the relief of people thrown out of work, and under the circumstances, they durst not arrest the men engaged in such business, all the more, as even that night many quite respectable people applied at these offices for relief, and swallowed down the charity of the revolutionists along with their supper. So the Government massed soldiers and police here and there—and sat still for that night, fully expecting on the morrow some manifesto from 'the rebels,' as they now began to be called, which would give them an opportunity of acting in some way or another. They were disappointed. The ordinary newspapers gave up the struggle that morning, and only one very violent reactionary paper (called the *Daily Telegraph*[1]) attempted an appearance, and rated 'the rebels' in good set terms for their folly and ingratitude in tearing out the bowels of their 'common mother,' the English Nation, for the benefit of a few greedy paid agitators, and the fools whom they were deluding. On the other hand, the Socialist papers (of which three only, representing somewhat different schools, were published in London[2]) came out full to the throat of well-printed matter. They were greedily bought by the whole public, who, of course, like the Government, expected a manifesto in them. But they found no word of reference to the great subject. It seemed as if their editors had ransacked their drawers for articles which would have been in place forty years before, under the technical name of educational articles. Most of these were admirable and straightforward expositions of the doctrines and practice of Socialism, free from haste and spite and hard words, and came upon the public with a kind of May-day freshness, amidst the worry and terror of the moment;

---

[1] Nominally liberal until the mid-1880s, the *Daily Telegraph* had by 1890 become associated with considerably more conservative positions.

[2] In 1890 there were in fact three such papers: the Socialist League's *Commonweal* (in which *News from Nowhere* was serialized), *Freedom*, the organ of the anarchists, and *Justice*, journal of the Socialist Democratic Foundation.

and though the knowing well understood that the meaning of this move in the game was mere defiance, and a token of irreconcilable hostility to the then rulers of society, and though, also, they were meant for nothing else by 'the rebels,' yet they really had their effect as 'educational articles.' However, 'education' of another kind was acting upon the public with irresistible power, and probably cleared their heads a little.

"As to the Government, they were absolutely terrified by this act of 'boycotting'[1] (the slang word then current for such acts of abstention). Their counsels became wild and vacillating to the last degree: one hour they were for giving way for the present till they could hatch another plot; the next they all but sent an order for the arrest in the lump of all the workmen's committees; the next they were on the point of ordering their brisk young general to take any excuse that offered for another massacre. But when they called to mind that the soldiery in that 'Battle' of Trafalgar Square were so daunted by the slaughter which they had made, that they could not be got to fire a second volley, they shrank back again from the dreadful courage necessary for carrying out another massacre. Meantime the prisoners, brought the second time before the magistrates under a strong escort of soldiers, were the second time remanded.

"The strike went on this day also. The workmen's committees were extended, and gave relief to great numbers of people, for they had organized a considerable amount of production of food by men whom they could depend upon. Quite a number of well-to-do people were now compelled to seek relief of them. But another curious thing happened: a band of young men of the upper classes armed themselves, and coolly went marauding in the streets, taking what suited them of such eatables and portables that they came across in the shops which had ventured to open. This operation they carried out in Oxford Street, then a great street of shops of all kinds. The Government, being at that hour in one of their yielding moods, thought this a fine opportunity for showing their impartiality in the maintenance of 'order,' and sent to arrest these hungry rich youths; who,

---

[1] A new coinage from the 1880s.

however, surprised the police by a valiant resistance, so that all but three escaped. The Government did not gain the reputation for impartiality which they expected from this move; for they forgot that there were no evening papers; and the account of the skirmish spread wide indeed, but in a distorted form; for it was mostly told simply as an exploit of the starving people from the East-end; and everybody thought it was but natural for the Government to put them down when and where they could.

"That evening the rebel prisoners were visited in their cells by *very* polite and sympathetic persons, who pointed out to them what a suicidal course they were following, and how dangerous these extreme courses were for the popular cause. Says one of the prisoners:'It was great sport comparing notes when we came out anent the attempt of the Government to "get at" us separately in prison, and how we answered the blandishments of the highly "intelligent and refined" persons set on to pump us. One laughed; another told extravagant long-bow stories to the envoy; a third held a sulky silence; a fourth damned the polite spy and bade him hold his jaw—and that was all they got out of us.'

"So passed the second day of the great strike. It was clear to all thinking people that the third day would bring on the crisis; for the present suspense and ill-concealed terror was unendurable. The ruling classes, and the middle-class non-politicians who had been their real strength and support, were as sheep lacking a shepherd; they literally did not know what to do.

"One thing they found they had to do: try to get the 'rebels' to do something. So the next morning, the morning of the third day of the strike, when the members of the Committee of Public Safety appeared again before the magistrate, they found themselves treated with the greatest possible courtesy—in fact, rather as envoys and ambassadors than prisoners. In short, the magistrate had received his orders; and with no more to do than might come of a long stupid speech, which might have been written by Dickens in mockery, he discharged the prisoners, who went back to their meeting-place and at once began a due sitting. It was high time. For this third day the mass was fermenting indeed. There was, of course, a vast number of working people who were not organized in the least in the world; men who had been used to act as their masters drove them, or rather as the system drove, of which their masters were a part. That system was now falling to pieces, and the old pressure of the master having been taken off these poor men, it seemed likely that nothing but the mere animal necessities and passions of men would have any hold on them, and that mere general overturn would be the result. Doubtless this would have happened if it had not been that the huge mass had been leavened by Socialist opinion in the first place, and in the second by actual contact with declared Socialists, many or indeed most of whom were members of those bodies of workmen above said.

"If anything of this kind had happened some years before, when the masters of labour were still looked upon as the natural rulers of the people, and even the poorest and most ignorant man leaned upon them for support, while they submitted to their fleecing, the entire break-up of all society would have followed. But the long series of years during which the workmen had learned to despise their rulers, had done away with their dependence upon them, and they were now beginning to trust (somewhat dangerously, as events proved) in the non-legal leaders whom events had thrust forward; and though most of these were now become mere figure-heads, their names and reputations were useful in this crisis as a stop-gap.

"The effect of the news, therefore, of the release of the Committee gave the Government some breathing time: for it was received with the greatest joy by the workers, and even the well-to-do saw in it a respite from the mere destruction which they had begun to dread, and the fear of which most of them attributed to the weakness of the Government. As far as the passing hour went, perhaps they were right in this."

"How do you mean?" said I. "What could the Government have done? I often used to think that they would be helpless in such a crisis."

Said old Hammond: "Of course I don't doubt that in the long run matters would have come about as they did. But if the Government could have treated their army as a real army, and used them strategically as a general would have done, looking on the people as a mere open enemy to be shot at and dispersed wherever they turned up, they would probably have gained the victory at the time."

"But would the soldiers have acted against the people in this way?" said I.

Said he: "I think from all I have heard that they would have done so if they had met bodies of men armed however badly, and however badly they had been organized. It seems also as if before the Trafalgar Square massacre they might as a whole have been depended upon to fire upon an unarmed crowd, though they were much honeycombed by Socialism. The reason for this was that they dreaded the use by apparently unarmed men of an explosive called dynamite, of which many loud boasts were made by the workers on the eve of these events; although it turned out to be of little use as a material for war in the way that was expected. Of course the officers of the soldiery fanned this fear to the utmost, so that the rank and file probably thought on that occasion that they were being led into a desperate battle with men who were really armed, and whose weapon was the more dreadful, because it was concealed. After that massacre, however, it was at all times doubtful if the regular soldiers would fire upon an unarmed or half-armed crowd."

Said I: "The regular soldiers? Then there were other combatants against the people?"

"Yes," said he, "we shall come to that presently."

"Certainly," I said, " you had better go on straight with your story. I see that time is wearing."

Said Hammond: "The Government lost no time in coming to terms with the Committee of Public Safety; for indeed they could think of nothing else than the danger of the moment. They sent a duly accredited envoy to treat with these men, who somehow had obtained dominion over people's minds, while the formal rulers had no hold except over their bodies. There is no need at present to go into the details of the truce (for such it was) between these high contracting parties, the Government of the empire of Great Britain and a handful of working-men (as they were called in scorn in those days), amongst whom, indeed, were some very capable and 'square-headed' persons, though, as aforesaid, the abler men were not then the recognized leaders. The upshot of it was that all the definite claims of the people had to be granted. We can now see that most of these claims were of themselves not worth either demanding or resisting; but they were looked on at that time as most important, and they were at least tokens of revolt against the miserable system of life which was then beginning to tumble to pieces. One claim, however, was of the utmost immediate importance, and this the Government tried hard to evade; but as they were not dealing with fools, they had to yield at last. This was the claim of recognition and formal status for the Committee of Public Safety, and all the associations which it fostered under its wing. This it is clear meant two things: first, amnesty for 'the rebels,' great and small, who, without a distinct act of civil war, could no longer be attacked; and next, a continuance of the organized revolution. Only one point the Government could gain, and that was a name. The dreadful revolutionary title was dropped, and the body, with its branches, acted under the respectable name of the 'Board of Conciliation and its local offices.' Carrying this name, it became the leader of the people in the civil war which soon followed."

"O," said I, somewhat startled, "so the civil war went on, in spite of all that had happened?"

"So it was," said he. "In fact, it was this very legal recognition which made the civil war possible in the ordinary sense of war; it took the struggle out of the element of mere massacres on one side, and endurance plus strikes on the other."

"And can you tell me in what kind of way the war was carried on?" said I.

"Yes," he said; "we have records and to spare of all that; and the essence of them I can give you in a few words. As I told you, the rank and file of the army was not to be trusted by the reactionists; but the officers generally were prepared for anything, for they were mostly the very stupidest men in the country. Whatever the Government might do, a great part of the upper and middle classes were determined to set on foot a counter revolution; for the Communism which now loomed ahead seemed quite unendurable to them. Bands of young men, like the marauders in the great strike of whom I told you just now, armed themselves and drilled, and began on any opportunity or pretence to skirmish with the people in the streets. The Government neither helped them nor put them down, but stood by, hoping that something might come of it. These 'Friends of Order,'[1] as they were called, had some successes at first, and grew bolder; they got many officers of the regular army to help them, and by their means laid hold of munitions of war of all kinds. One part of their tactics consisted in their guarding and even garrisoning the big factories of the period: they held at one time, for instance, the whole of that place called Manchester which I spoke of just now. A sort of irregular war was carried on with varied success all over the country; and at last the Government, which at first pretended to ignore the struggle, or treat it as mere rioting, definitely declared for 'the Friends of Order,' and joined to their bands whatsoever of the regular army they could get together, and made a desperate effort to overcome 'the rebels,' as they were now once more called, and as indeed they called themselves.

"It was too late. All ideas of peace on a basis of compromise had disappeared on either side. The end, it was seen clearly, must be either absolute slavery for all but the privileged, or a system of life founded on equality and Communism. The sloth, the hopelessness, and if I may say so, the cowardice of the last century, had given place to the eager, restless heroism of a declared revolutionary period. I will not say that the people of that time foresaw the life we are leading now, but there was a general instinct amongst them towards the essential part of that life, and many men saw clearly beyond the desperate struggle of the day into the peace which it was to bring about. The men of that day who were on the side of freedom were not unhappy, I think, though they were harassed by hopes and fears, and sometimes torn by doubts, and the conflict of duties hard to reconcile."

"But how did the people, the revolutionists, carry on the war? What were the elements of success on their side?"

I put this question, because I wanted to bring the old man back to the definite history, and take him out of the musing mood so natural to an old man.

---

[1]   In 1871 the conservative "Friends of Order" was organized in an attempt to suppress the newly-established Commune in Paris.

He answered: "Well, they did not lack organizers; for the very conflict itself, in the days when, as I told you, men of any strength of mind cast away all consideration for the ordinary business of life, developed the necessary talent amongst them. Indeed, from all I have read and heard, I much doubt whether, without this seemingly dreadful civil war, the due talent for administration would have been developed amongst the working men. Anyhow, it was there, and they soon got leaders far more than equal to the best men amongst the reactionaries. For the rest, they had no difficulty about the material of their army; for that revolutionary instinct so acted on the ordinary soldier in the ranks that the greater part, certainly the best part, of the soldiers joined the side of the people. But the main element of their success was this, that wherever the working people were not coerced, they worked, not for the reactionists, but for 'the rebels.' The reactionists could get no work done for them outside the districts where they were all-powerful: and even in those districts they were harassed by continual risings; and in all cases and everywhere got nothing done without obstruction and black looks and sulkiness; so that not only were their armies quite worn out with the difficulties which they had to meet, but the non-combatants who were on their side were so worried and beset with hatred and a thousand little troubles and annoyances that life became almost unendurable to them on those terms. Not a few of them actually died of the worry; many committed suicide. Of course, a vast number of them joined actively in the cause of reaction, and found some solace to their misery in the eagerness of conflict. Lastly, many thousands gave way and submitted to 'the rebels'; and as the number of these latter increased, it at last became clear to all men that the cause which was once hopeless, was now triumphant, and that the hopeless cause was that of slavery and privilege."

CHAPTER XVIII

THE BEGINNING OF THE NEW LIFE

"Well," said I, "so you got clear out of all your trouble. Were people satisfied with the new order of things when it came?"

"People?" he said. "Well, surely all must have been glad of peace when it came; especially when they found, as they must have found, that after all, they—even the once rich—were not living very badly. As to those who had been poor, all through the war, which lasted about two years, their condition had been bettering, in spite of the struggle; and when peace came at last, in a very short time they made great strides towards a decent life. The great difficulty was that the once-poor had such a feeble conception of the real pleasure of life: so to say, they did not ask enough, did not know how to ask enough, from the new state of things. It was perhaps rather a good than an evil thing that the necessity for restoring the wealth destroyed during the war forced them into working at first almost as hard as they had been used to before the Revolution. For all historians are agreed that there never was a war in which there was so much destruction of wares, and instruments for making them as in this civil war."

"I am rather surprised at that," said I.

"Are you? I don't see why," said Hammond.

"Why," I said, "because the party of order would surely look upon the wealth as their own property, no share of which, if they could help it, should go to their slaves, supposing they conquered. And on the other hand, it was just for the possession of that wealth that 'the rebels' were fighting, and I should have thought, especially when they saw that they were winning, that they would have been careful to destroy as little as possible of what was so soon to be their own."

"It was as I have told you, however," said he. "The party of order, when they recovered from their first cowardice of surprise—or, if you please, when they fairly saw that, whatever happened, they would be ruined, fought with great bitterness, and cared little what they did, so long as they injured the enemies who had destroyed the sweets of life for them. As to 'the rebels,' I have told you that the outbreak of actual war made them careless of trying to save the wretched scraps of wealth that they had. It was a common saying amongst them, Let the country be cleared of everything except valiant living men, rather than that we fall into slavery again!"

He sat silently thinking a little while, and then said:

"When the conflict was once really begun, it was seen how little of any value there was in the old world of slavery and inequality. Don't you see what it means? In the times which you are thinking of, and of which you seem to know so much, there was no hope; nothing but the dull jog of the mill-horse under compulsion of collar and whip; but in that fighting-time that followed, all was hope: 'the rebels' at least felt themselves strong enough to build up the world again from its dry bones,—and they did it, too!" said the old man, his eyes glittering under his beetling brows. He went on: "And their opponents at least and at last learned something about the reality of life, and its sorrows, which they—their class, I mean—had once known nothing of. In short, the two combatants, the workman and the gentleman, between them—"

"Between them," said I, quickly, "they destroyed commercialism!"

"Yes, yes, YES," said he; "that is it. Nor could it have been destroyed otherwise; except, perhaps, by the whole of society gradually falling into lower depths, till it should at last reach a condition as rude as barbarism, but lacking both the hope and the pleasures of barbarism. Surely the sharper, shorter remedy was the happiest."

"Most surely," said I.

"Yes," said the old man, "the world was being brought to its second birth; how could that take place without a tragedy? Moreover, think of it. The spirit of the new days, of our days, was to be delight in the life of the world; intense and overweening love of the very skin and surface of the earth on which man dwells, such as a lover has in the fair flesh of the woman he loves; this, I say, was to be the new spirit of the time. All other moods save this had been exhausted: the unceasing criticism, the boundless curiosity in the ways and thoughts of man, which was the mood of the ancient Greek, to whom these things were not so much a means, as an end, was gone past recovery; nor had there been really any shadow of it in the so-called science of the nineteenth century, which, as you must know, was in the main an appendage to the commercial system; nay, not seldom an appendage to the police of that system. In spite of appearances, it was limited and cowardly, because it did not really believe in itself. It was the outcome, as it was the sole relief, of the unhappiness of the period which made life so bitter even to the rich, and which, as you may see with your bodily eyes, the great change has swept away. More akin to our way of looking at life was the spirit of the Middle Ages, to whom heaven and the life of the next world was such a reality, that it became to them a part of the life upon the earth; which accordingly they loved and adorned, in spite of the ascetic doctrines of their formal creed, which bade them contemn it.

"But that also, with its assured belief in heaven and hell as two countries in which to live, has gone, and now we do, both in word and in deed, believe in the continuous life of the world of men, and as it were, add every day of that common life to the little stock of days which our own mere individual experience wins for us: and consequently we are happy. Do you wonder at it? In times past, indeed, men were told to love their kind, to believe in the religion of humanity, and so forth. But look you, just in the degree that a man had elevation of mind and refinement enough to be able to value this idea, was he repelled by the obvious aspect of the individuals composing the mass which he was to worship; and he could only evade that repulsion by making a conventional abstraction of mankind that had little actual or historical relation to the race; which to his eyes was divided into blind tyrants on the one hand and apathetic degraded slaves on the other. But now, where is the difficulty in accepting the religion of humanity, when the men and women who go to make up humanity are free, happy, and energetic at least, and most commonly beautiful of body also, and surrounded by beautiful things of their own fashioning, and a nature bettered and not worsened by contact with mankind? This is what this age of the world has reserved for us."

"It seems true," said I, "or ought to be, if what my eyes have seen is a token of the general life you lead. Can you now tell me anything of your progress after the years of the struggle?"

Said he: "I could easily tell you more than you have time to listen to; but I can at least hint at one of the chief difficulties which had to be met: and that was, that when men began to settle down after the war, and their labour had pretty much filled up the gap in wealth caused by the destruction of that war, a kind of disappointment seemed coming over us, and the prophecies of some of the reactionists of past times seemed as if they would come true, and a dull level of utilitarian comfort be the end for a while of our aspirations and success. The loss of the competitive spur to exertion had not, indeed, done anything to interfere with the necessary production of the community, but how if it should make men dull by giving them too much time for thought or idle musing? But, after all, this dull thunder-cloud only threatened us, and then passed over. Probably, from what I have told you before, you will have a guess at the remedy for such a disaster; remembering always that many of the things which used to be produced—slave-wares for the poor and mere wealth-wasting wares for the rich—ceased to be made. That remedy was, in short, the production of what used to be called art, but which has no name amongst us now, because it has become a necessary part of the labour of every man who produces."

Said I: "What! had men any time or opportunity for cultivating the fine arts amidst the desperate struggle for life and freedom that you have told me of?"

Said Hammond: "You must not suppose that the new form of art was founded chiefly on the memory of the art of the past; although, strange to say, the civil war was much less destructive of art than of other things, and though what of art existed under the old forms, revived in a wonderful way during the latter part of the struggle, especially as regards music and poetry. The art or work-pleasure, as one ought to call it, of which I am now speaking, sprung up almost spontaneously, it seems, from a kind of instinct amongst people, no longer driven desperately to painful and terrible over-work, to do the best they could with the work in hand—to make it excellent of its kind; and when that had gone on for a little, a craving for beauty seemed to awaken in men's minds, and they began rudely and awkwardly to ornament the wares which they made; and when they had once set to work at that, it soon began to grow. All this was much helped by the abolition of the squalor which our immediate ancestors put up with so coolly; and by the leisurely, but not stupid, country-life which now grew (as I told you before) to be common amongst us. Thus at last and by slow degrees we got pleasure into our work; then we became conscious of that pleasure, and cultivated it, and took care that we had our fill of it; and then all was gained, and we were happy. So may it be for ages and ages!"

The old man fell into a reverie, not altogether without melancholy I thought; but I would not break it. Suddenly he started, and said: "Well, dear guest, here are come Dick and Clara to fetch you away, and there is an end of my talk; which I daresay you will not be sorry for; the long day is coming to an end, and you will have a pleasant ride back to Hammersmith."

CHAPTER XIX

THE DRIVE BACK TO HAMMERSMITH

I said nothing, for I was not inclined for mere politeness to him after such very serious talk; but in fact I should liked to have gone on talking with the older man, who could understand something at least of my wonted ways of looking at life, whereas, with the younger people, in spite of all their kindness, I really was a being from another planet. However, I made the best of it, and smiled as amiably as I could on the young couple; and Dick returned the smile by saying, "Well, guest, I am glad to have you again, and to find that you and my kinsman have not quite talked yourselves into another world; I was half suspecting as I was listening to the Welshmen yonder that you would presently be vanishing away from us, and began to picture my kinsman sitting in the hall staring at nothing and finding that he had been talking a while past to nobody."

I felt rather uncomfortable at this speech, for suddenly the picture of the sordid squabble, the dirty and miserable tragedy of the life I had left for a while, came before my eyes; and I had, as it were, a vision of all my longings for rest and peace in the past, and I loathed the idea of going back to it again. But the old man chuckled and said:

"Don't be afraid, Dick. In any case, I have not been talking to thin air; nor, indeed to this new friend of ours only. Who knows but I may not have been talking to many people? For perhaps our guest may some day go back to the people he has come from, and may take a message from us which may bear fruit for them, and consequently for us."

Dick looked puzzled, and said: "Well, gaffer, I do not quite understand what you mean. All I can say is, that I hope he will not leave us: for don't you see, he is another kind of man to what we are used to, and somehow he makes us think of all kind of things; and already I feel as if I could understand Dickens the better for having talked with him."

"Yes," said Clara, "and I think in a few months we shall make him look younger; and I should like to see what he was like with the wrinkles smoothed out of his face. Don't you think he will look younger after a little time with us?"

The old man shook his head, and looked earnestly at me, but did not answer her, and for a moment or two we were all silent. Then Clara broke out:

"Kinsman, I don't like this: something or another troubles me, and I feel as if something untoward were going to happen. You have been talking of past miseries to the guest, and have been living in past unhappy times, and it is in the air all round us, and makes us feel as if we were longing for something that we cannot have."

The old man smiled on her kindly, and said: "Well, my child, if that be so, go and live in the present, and you will soon shake it off." Then he turned to me, and said: "Do you remember anything like that, guest, in the country from which you come?"

The lovers had turned aside now, and were talking together softly, and not heeding us; so I said, but in a low voice: "Yes, when

I was a happy child on a sunny holiday, and had everything that I could think of."

"So it is," said he. "You remember just now you twitted me with living in the second childhood of the world. You will find it a happy world to live in; you will be happy there—for a while."

Again I did not like his scarcely veiled threat, and was beginning to trouble myself with trying to remember how I had got amongst this curious people, when the old man called out in a cheery voice: "Now, my children, take your guest away, and make much of him; for it is your business to make him sleek of skin and peaceful of mind: he has by no means been as lucky as you have. Farewell, guest!" and he grasped my hand warmly.

"Good-bye," said I, "and thank you very much for all that you have told me. I will come and see you as soon as I come back to London. May I?"

"Yes," he said, "come by all means—if you can."

"It won't be for some time yet," quoth Dick, in his cheery voice; "for when the hay is in up the river, I shall be for taking him a round through the country between hay and wheat harvest, to see how our friends live in the north country. Then in the wheat harvest we shall do a good stroke of work, I should hope,—in Wiltshire by preference; for he will be getting a little hard with all the open-air living, and I shall be as tough as nails."

"But you will take me along, won't you, Dick?" said Clara, laying her pretty hand on his shoulder.

"Will I not?" said Dick, somewhat boisterously. "And we will manage to send you to bed pretty tired every night; and you will look so beautiful with your neck all brown, and your hands too, and you under your gown as white as privet,[1] that you will get some of those strange discontented whims out of your head, my dear. However, our week's haymaking will do all that for you."

The girl reddened very prettily, and not for shame but for pleasure; and the old man laughed, and said:

"Guest, I see that you will be as comfortable as need be; for you need not fear that those two will be too officious with you: they will be so busy with each other, that they will leave you a

---

[1] Dick is thinking of the small white flowers of the privet shrub.

good deal to yourself, I am sure, and that is a real kindness to a guest, after all. O, you need not be afraid of being one too many, either: it is just what these birds in a nest like, to have a good convenient friend to turn to, so that they may relieve the ecstasies of love with the solid commonplace of friendship. Besides, Dick, and much more Clara, likes a little talking at times; and you know lovers do not talk unless they get into trouble, they only prattle. Good-bye, guest; may you be happy!"

Clara went up to old Hammond, threw her arms about his neck and kissed him heartily, and said: "You are a dear old man, and may have your jest about me as much as you please; and it won't be long before we see you again; and you may be sure we shall make our guest happy; though, mind you, there is some truth in what you say."

Then I shook hands again, and we went out of the hall and into the cloisters, and so in the street found Greylocks in the shafts waiting for us. He was well looked after; for a little lad of about seven years old had his hand on the rein and was solemnly looking up into his face; on his back, withal, was a girl of fourteen, holding a three-year old sister on before her; while another girl, about a year older than the boy, hung on behind. The three were occupied partly with eating cherries, partly with patting and punching Greylocks, who took all their caresses in good part, but pricked up his ears when Dick made his appearance. The girls got off quietly, and going up to Clara, made much of her and snuggled up to her. And then we got into the carriage, Dick shook the reins, and we got under way at once, Greylocks trotting soberly between the lovely trees of the London streets, that were sending floods of fragrance into the cool evening air; for it was now getting toward sunset.

We could hardly go but fair and softly all the way, as there were a great many people abroad in that cool hour. Seeing so many people made me notice their looks the more; and I must say, my taste, cultivated in the sombre greyness, or rather brownness, of the nineteenth century, was rather apt to condemn the gaiety and brightness of the raiment; and I even ventured to say as much to Clara. She seemed rather surprised, and even slightly indignant, and said: "Well, well, what's the matter? They are not about any dirty work; they are only amusing themselves in the fine evening, there is nothing to foul their clothes. Come, doesn't it all look very pretty? It isn't gaudy, you know."

Indeed that was true; for many of the people were clad in colours that were sober enough, though beautiful, and the harmony of the colours was perfect and most delightful.

I said, "Yes, that is so; but how can everybody afford such costly garments? Look! there goes a middle-aged man in a sober grey dress; but I can see from here that it is made of very fine woollen stuff, and is covered with silk embroidery."

Said Clara: "He could wear shabby clothes if he pleased,—that is, if he didn't think he would hurt people's feelings by doing so."

"But please tell me," said I, "how can they afford it?"

As soon as I had spoken I perceived that I had got back to my old blunder; for I saw Dick's shoulders shaking with laughter; but he wouldn't say a word, but handed me over to the tender mercies of Clara, who said—

"Why, I don't know what you mean. Of course we can afford it, or else we shouldn't do it. It would be easy enough for us to say, we will only spend our labour on making our clothes comfortable: but we don't choose to stop there. Why do you find fault with us? Does it seem to you as if we starved ourselves of food in order to make ourselves fine clothes? or do you think there is anything wrong in liking to see the coverings of our bodies beautiful like our bodies are?—just as a deer's or an otter's skin has been made beautiful from the first? Come, what is wrong with you?"

I bowed before the storm, and mumbled out some excuse or other. I must say, I might have known that people who were so fond of architecture generally, would not be backward in ornamenting themselves: all the more as the shape of their raiment, apart from its colour, was both beautiful and reasonable—veiling the form, without either muffling or caricaturing it.

Clara was soon mollified; and as we drove along toward the wood before mentioned, she said to Dick—

"I tell you what, Dick: now that kinsman Hammond the Elder has seen our guest in his queer clothes, I think we ought to find him something decent to put on for our journey to-morrow:

especially since, if we do not, we shall have to answer all sorts of questions as to his clothes and where they came from. Besides," she said slily, "when he is clad in handsome garments he will not be so quick to blame us for our childishness in wasting our time in making ourselves look pleasant to each other."

"All right, Clara," said Dick; "he shall have everything that you—that he wants to have. I will look something out for him before he gets up to-morrow."

CHAPTER XX

THE HAMMERSMITH
GUEST-HOUSE AGAIN

Amidst such talk, driving quietly through the balmy evening, we came to Hammersmith, and were well received by our friends there. Boffin, in a fresh suit of clothes, welcomed me back with stately courtesy; the weaver wanted to button-hole me and get out of me what old Hammond had said, but was very friendly and cheerful when Dick warned him off; Annie shook hands with me, and hoped I had had a pleasant day—so kindly, that I felt a slight pang as our hands parted; for to say the truth, I liked her better than Clara, who seemed to be always a little on the defensive, whereas Annie was as frank as could be, and seemed to get honest pleasure from everything and everybody about her without the least effort.

We had quite a little feast that evening, partly in my honour, and partly, I suspect, though nothing was said about it, in honour of Dick and Clara coming together again. The wine was of the best; the hall was redolent of rich summer flowers; and after supper we not only had music (Annie, to my mind, surpassing all the others for sweetness and clearness of voice, as well as for feeling and meaning), but at last we even got to telling stories, and sat there listening, with no other light but that of the summer moon streaming through the beautiful traceries of the windows, as if we had belonged to time long passed, when books were scarce and the art of reading somewhat rare. Indeed, I may say here, that, though, as you will have noted, my friends had mostly something to say about books, yet they were not great readers, considering the refinement of their manners and the great amount of leisure which they obviously had. In fact, when Dick, especially, mentioned a book, he did so with an air of a man who has accomplished an achievement; as much as to say, "There, you see, I have actually read that!"

The evening passed all too quickly for me; since that day, for the first time in my life, I was having my fill of the pleasure of the eyes without any of that sense of incongruity, that dread of approaching ruin, which had always beset me hitherto when I had been amongst the beautiful works of art of the past, mingled with the lovely nature of the present; both of them, in fact, the result of the long centuries of tradition, which had compelled men to produce the art, and compelled nature to run into the mould of the ages. Here I could enjoy everything without an afterthought of the injustice and miserable toil which made my leisure; the ignorance and dulness of life which went to make my keen appreciation of history; the tyranny and the struggle full of fear and mishap which went to make my romance. The only weight I had upon my heart was a vague fear as it drew toward bed-time concerning the place wherein I should wake on the morrow: but I choked that down, and went to bed happy, and in a very few moments was in a dreamless sleep.

CHAPTER XXI

GOING UP THE RIVER

When I did wake, to a beautiful sunny morning, I leapt out of bed with my over-night apprehension still clinging to me, which vanished delightfully however in a moment as I looked around my little sleeping chamber and saw the pale but pure-coloured figures painted on the plaster of the wall, with verses written underneath them which I knew somewhat over well. I dressed speedily, in a suit of blue laid ready for me, so handsome that I quite blushed when I had got into it, feeling as I did so that excited pleasure of anticipation of a holiday, which, well remembered as it was, I had not felt since I was a boy, new come home for the summer holidays.

It seemed quite early in the morning, and I expected to have the hall to myself when I came into it out of the corridor wherein was my sleeping chamber; but I met Annie at once, who let fall her broom and gave me a kiss, quite meaningless I fear, except as betokening friendship, though she reddened as she did it, not from shyness, but from friendly pleasure, and then stood and picked up her broom again, and went on with her sweeping, nodding to me as if to bid me stand out of the way and look on; which, to say the truth, I thought amusing enough, as there were five other girls helping her, and their graceful figures engaged in the leisurely work were worth going a long way to see, and their merry talk and laughing as they swept in quite a scientific manner was worth going a long way to hear. But Annie presently threw me back a word or two as she went on to the other end of the hall: "Guest," she said, "I am glad that you are up early, though we wouldn't disturb you; for our Thames is a lovely river at half-past six on a June morning: and as it would be a pity for you to lose it, I am told just to give you a cup of milk and a bit of bread outside there, and put you into the boat: for Dick and Clara are all ready now. Wait half a minute till I have swept down this row."

So presently she let her broom drop again, and came and took me by the hand and led me out on to the terrace above the river, to a little table under the boughs, where my bread and milk took the form of as dainty a breakfast as any one could desire, and then sat by me as I ate. And in a minute or two Dick and Clara came to me, the latter looking most fresh and beautiful in a light silk embroidered gown, which to my unused eyes was extravagantly gay and bright; while Dick was also handsomely dressed in white flannel prettily embroidered. Clara raised her gown in her hands as she gave me the morning greeting, and said laughingly: "Look, guest! you see we are at least as fine as any of the people you felt inclined to scold last night; you see we are not going to make the bright day and the flowers feel ashamed of themselves. Now scold me!"

Quoth I: "No, indeed; the pair of you seem as if you were born out of the summer day itself; and I will scold you when I scold it."

"Well, you know," said Dick, "this is a special day—all these days are, I mean. The hay-harvest is in some ways better than corn-harvest because of the beautiful weather; and really, unless you had worked in the hayfield in fine weather, you couldn't tell what pleasant work it is. The women look so pretty at it, too," he said, shyly; "so all things considered, I think we are right to adorn it in a simple manner."

"Do the women work at it in silk dresses?" said I, smiling.

Dick was going to answer me soberly; but Clara put her hand over his mouth, and said, "No, no, Dick; not too much information for him, or I shall think that you are your old kinsman again. Let him find out for himself: he will not have long to wait."

"Yes," quoth Annie, "don't make your description of the picture too fine, or else he will be disappointed when the curtain is drawn. I don't want him to be disappointed. But now it's time for you to be gone, if you are to have the best of the tide, and also of the sunny morning. Good-bye, guest."

She kissed me in her frank friendly way, and almost took away from me my desire for the expedition thereby; but I had to get over that, as it was clear that so delightful a woman would hardly be without a due lover of her own age. We went down the steps of the landing stage, and got into a pretty boat, not too light to hold us and our belongings comfortably, and handsomely ornamented; and just as we got in, down came Boffin and the weaver to see us off. The former had now veiled his splendour in a due suit of working clothes, crowned with a fantail hat, which he took off, however, to wave us farewell with his grave old-Spanish-like courtesy. Then Dick pushed off into the stream, and bent vigorously to his sculls, and Hammersmith, with its noble trees and beautiful water-side houses, began to slip away from us.

As we went, I could not help putting beside his promised picture of the hay-field as it was then the picture of it as I remembered it, and especially the images of the women engaged in the work rose up before me: the row of gaunt figures, lean, flat-breasted, ugly, without a grace of form or face about them; dressed in wretched skimpy print gowns, and hideous flapping sun-bonnets, moving their rakes in a listless mechanical way. How often had that marred the loveliness of the June day to me; how often had I longed to see the hay-fields peopled with men and women worthy of the sweet abundance of midsummer, of its endless wealth of beautiful sights, and delicious sounds and scents. And now, the world had grown old and wiser, and I was to see my hope realized at last!

CHAPTER XXII

HAMPTON COURT. AND A PRAISER OF PAST TIMES

So on we went, Dick rowing in an easy tireless way, and Clara sitting by my side admiring his manly beauty and heartily good-natured face, and thinking, I fancy, of nothing else. As we went higher up the river, there was less difference between the Thames of that day and Thames as I remembered it; for setting aside the hideous vulgarity of the cockney[1] villas of the well-to-do, stock-brokers and other such, which in older time marred the beauty of the bough-hung banks, even this beginning of the country Thames was always beautiful; and as we slipped between the lovely summer greenery, I almost felt my youth come back to me, and as if I were on one of those water excursions which I used to enjoy so much in days when I was too happy to think that there could be much amiss anywhere.

At last we came to a reach of the river where on the left hand a very pretty little village with some old houses in it came down to the edge of the water, over which was a ferry; and beyond these houses the elm-beset meadows ended in a fringe of tall

---

[1] For Morris, "cockney" is always a synonym for "vulgar" or "philistine."

willows, while on the right hand went the tow-path and a clear space before a row of trees, which rose up behind huge and ancient, the ornaments of a great park: but these drew back still further from the river at the end of the reach to make way for a little town of quaint and pretty houses, some new, some old, dominated by the long walls and sharp gables of a great red-brick pile of building, partly of the latest Gothic, partly of the court-style of Dutch William, but so blended together by the bright sun and beautiful surroundings, including the bright blue river, which it looked down upon, that even amidst the beautiful buildings of that new happy time it had a strange charm about it. A great wave of fragrance, amidst which the lime-tree blossom was clearly to be distinguished, came down to us from its unseen gardens, as Clara sat up in her place, and said:

"O Dick, dear, couldn't we stop at Hampton Court[1] for to-day, and take the guest about the park a little, and show him those sweet old buildings? Somehow, I suppose because you have lived so near it, you have seldom taken me to Hampton Court."

Dick rested on his oars a little, and said: "Well, well, Clara, you are lazy to-day. I didn't feel like stopping short of Shepperton for the night; suppose we just go and have our dinner at the Court, and go on again about five o'clock?"

"Well," she said, "so be it; but I should like the guest to have spent an hour or two in the Park."

"The Park!" said Dick; "why, the whole Thames-side is a park this time of the year; and for my part, I had rather lie under an elm-tree on the borders of a wheat-field, with the bees humming about me and the corn-crake crying from furrow to furrow, than in any park in England. Besides—"

"Besides," said she, "You want to get on to your dearly-loved upper Thames, and show your prowess down the heavy swathes of the mowing grass."

She looked at him fondly, and I could tell that she was seeing him in her mind's eye showing his splendid form at its best amidst the rhymed strokes of the scythes; and she looked down at her own

---

[1]   The royal palace at Hampton Court, built in the sixteenth century for Henry VIII, was a popular destination for a day-outing, as it is today.

pretty feet with a half sigh, as though she were contrasting her slight woman's beauty with his man's beauty; as women will when they are really in love, and are not spoiled with conventional sentiment.

As for Dick, he looked at her admiringly a while, and then said at last: "Well, Clara, I do wish we were there! But, hilloa! we are getting back way." And he set to work sculling again, and in two minutes we were all standing on the gravelly strand below the bridge, which, as you may imagine, was no longer the old hideous iron abortion, but a handsome piece of very solid oak framing.[1]

We went into the Court and straight into the great hall, so well remembered, where there were tables spread for dinner, and everything arranged much as in Hammersmith Guest-Hall. Dinner over, we sauntered through the ancient rooms, where the pictures and tapestry were still preserved, and nothing was much changed, except that the people whom we met there had an indefinable kind of look of being at home and at ease, which communicated itself to me, so that I felt that the beautiful old place was mine in the best sense of the word; and my pleasure of past days seemed to add itself to that of to-day, and filled my whole soul with content.

Dick (who, in spite of Clara's gibe, knew the place very well) told me that the beautiful old Tudor rooms, which I remembered had been the dwellings of the lesser fry of Court flunkies, were now much used by people coming and going; for, beautiful as architecture had now become, and although the whole face of the country had quite recovered its beauty, there was still a sort of tradition of pleasure and beauty which clung to that group of buildings, and people thought going to Hampton Court a necessary summer outing, as they did in the days when London was so grimy and miserable. We went into some of the rooms looking into the old garden, and were well received by the people in them, who got speedily into talk with us, and looked with politely half-concealed wonder at my strange face. Besides these birds of passage, and a few regular dwellers in the place, we saw out in the meadows near the garden, down "the Long Water,"[2] as it used to be called, many gay tents with men, women, and

---

[1] The iron bridge at Hampton Court was completed in 1876. It replaced a wooden one.
[2] A 150-foot-long canal dating from the mid-seventeenth century.

children round about them. As it seemed, this pleasure-loving people were fond of tent-life, with all its inconveniences, which, indeed, they turned into pleasure also.

We left this old friend by the time appointed, and I made some feeble show of taking the sculls; but Dick repulsed me, not much to my grief, I must say, as I found I had quite enough to do between the enjoyment of the beautiful time and my own lazily blended thoughts.

As to Dick, it was quite right to let him pull, for he was as strong as a horse, and had the greatest delight in bodily exercise, whatever it was. We really had some difficulty in getting him to stop when it was getting rather more than dusk, and the moon was brightening just as we were off Runnymede. We landed there, and were looking about for a place whereon to pitch our tents (for we had brought two with us), when an old man came up to us, bade us good evening, and asked if we were housed for that night; and finding that we were not, bade us home to his house. Nothing loth, we went with him, and Clara took his hand in a coaxing way which I noticed she used with old men; and as we went on our way, made some commonplace remark about the beauty of the day. The old man stopped short, and looked at her and said: "You really like it then?"

"Yes," she said, looking very much astonished, "Don't you?"

"Well," said he, "perhaps I do. I did, at any rate, when I was younger; but now I think I should like it cooler."

She said nothing, and went on, the night growing about as dark as it would be; till just at the rise of the hill we came to a hedge with a gate in it, which the old man unlatched and led us into a garden, at the end of which we could see a little house, one of whose little windows was already yellow with candle-light. We could see even under the doubtful light of the moon and the last of the western glow that the garden was stuffed full of flowers; and the fragrance it gave out in the gathering cool-ness was so wonderfully sweet, that it seemed the very heart of the delight of the June dusk; so that we three stopped instinc-tively, and Clara gave forth a little sweet "O," like a bird begin-ning to sing.

"What's the matter?" said the old man, a little testily, and pulling at her hand. "There's no dog; or have you trodden on a thorn and hurt your foot?"

"No, no, neighbour," she said; "but how sweet, how sweet it is!"

"Of course it is," said he, "but do you care so much for that?"

She laughed out musically, and we followed suit in our gruffer voices; and then she said: "Of course I do, neighbour; don't you?"

"Well, I don't know," quoth the old fellow; then he added, as if somewhat ashamed of himself: "Besides, you know, when the waters are out and all Runnymede is flooded, it's none so pleasant."

"*I* should like it," quoth Dick. "What a jolly sail one would get about here on the floods on a frosty January morning!"

"*Would* you like it?" said our host. "Well, I won't argue with you, neighbour; it isn't worth while. Come in and have some supper."

We went up a paved path between the roses, and straight into a very pretty room, panelled and carved and as clean as a new pin; but the chief ornament of which was a young woman, light-haired and grey-eyed, but with her face and hands and bare feet tanned quite brown with the sun. Though she was very lightly clad, that was clearly from choice, not from poverty, though these were the first cottage-dwellers I had come across; for her gown was of silk, and on her wrists were bracelets that seemed to me of great value. She was lying on a sheep-skin near the window, but jumped up as soon as we entered, and when she saw the guests behind the old man, she clapped her hands and cried out with pleasure, and when she got us into the middle of the room, fairly danced round us in delight of our company.

"What!" said the old man, "you are pleased, are you, Ellen?"

The girl danced up to him and threw her arms round him, and said: "Yes I am, and so ought you to be grandfather."

"Well, well, I am," said he, "as much as I can be pleased. Guests, please be seated."

This seemed rather strange to us; stranger, I suspect, to my friends than to me; but Dick took the opportunity of both the host and his grand-daughter being out of the room to say to me, softly. "A grumbler: there are a few of them still. Once upon a time, I am told, they were quite a nuisance."

The old man came in as he spoke and sat down beside us with a sigh, which, indeed, seemed fetched up as if he wanted us to take notice of it; but just then the girl came in with the victuals, and the carle[1] missed his mark, what between our hunger generally and that I was pretty busy watching the grand-daughter moving about as beautiful as a picture.

Everything to eat and drink, though it was somewhat different to what we had had in London, was better than good, but the old man eyed rather sulkily the chief dish on the table, on which lay a leash[2] of fine perch, and said:

"H'm, perch! I am sorry we can't do better for you, guests. The time was when we might have had a good piece of salmon up from London for you; but the times have grown mean and petty."

"Yes, but you might have had it now," said the girl, giggling, "if you had known that they were coming."

"It's our fault for not bringing it with us, neighbours," said Dick, good-humouredly. "But if the times have grown petty, at any rate the perch haven't; that fellow in the middle there must have weighed a good two pounds when he was showing his dark stripes and red fins to the minnows yonder. And as to the salmon, why, neighbour, my friend here, who comes from the outlands, was quite surprised yesterday morning when I told him we had plenty of salmon at Hammersmith. I am sure I have heard nothing of the times worsening."

He looked a little uncomfortable. And the old man, turning to me, said very courteously:

"Well, sir, I am happy to see a man from over the water; but I really must appeal to you to say whether on the whole you are not better off in your country; where I suppose, from what our guest says, you are brisker and more alive, because you have not wholly got rid of competition. You see, I have read not a few books of the past days, and certainly *they* are much more alive than those which are written now; and good sound unlimited competition was the condition under which they were written,—if we didn't know that from the record of history, we should know it from the books themselves. There is a spirit of adventure in them, and signs of a capacity to extract good out of evil which our literature quite lacks

---

[1] A carle is an old man.
[2] A leash is a set of three.

now; and I cannot help thinking that our moralists and historians exaggerate hugely the unhappiness of the past days, in which such splendid works of imagination and intellect were produced."

Clara listened to him with restless eyes, as if she were excited and pleased; Dick knitted his brow and looked still more uncomfortable, but said nothing. Indeed, the old man gradually, as he warmed to his subject, dropped his sneering manner, and both spoke and looked very seriously. But the girl broke out before I could deliver myself of the answer I was framing:

"Books, books! always books, grandfather! When will you understand that after all it is the world we live in which interests us; the world of which we are a part, and which we can never love too much? Look!" she said, throwing open the casement wider and showing us the white light sparkling between the black shadows of the moonlit garden, through which ran a little shiver of the summer night-wind, "look! these are our books in these days!—and these," she said, stepping lightly up to the two lovers and laying a hand on each of their shoulders; "and the guest there, with his over-sea knowledge and experience; yes, and even you, grandfather" (a smile ran over her face as she spoke), "with all your grumbling and wishing yourself back again in the good old days,—in which, as far as I can make out, a harmless and lazy old man like you would either have pretty nearly starved, or have had to pay soldiers and people to take the folk's victuals and clothes and houses away from them by force. Yes, these are our books; and if we want more, can we not find work to do in the beautiful buildings that we raise up all over the country (and I know there was nothing like them in past times), wherein a man can put forth whatever is in him, and make his hands set forth his mind and his soul."

She paused a little, and I for my part could not help staring at her, and thinking that if she were a book, the pictures in it were most lovely. The colour mantled in her delicate sunburnt cheeks; her grey eyes, light amidst the tan of her face, kindly looked on us all as she spoke. She paused, and said again:

"As for your books, they were well enough for times when intelligent people had but little else in which they could take pleasure, and when they must needs supplement the sordid miseries of their own lives with imaginations of the lives of other people. But I say flatly that in spite of all their cleverness and vigour, and capacity for story-telling, there is something loathsome about them. Some of them, indeed, do here and there show some feeling for those whom the history-books call 'poor,' and of the misery of whose lives we have some inkling; but presently they give it up, and towards the end of the story we must be contented to see the hero and heroine living happily in an island of bliss on other people's troubles; and that after a long series of sham troubles (or mostly sham) of their own making, illustrated by dreary introspective nonsense about their feelings and aspirations, and all the rest of it; while the world must even then have gone on its way, and dug and sewed and baked and built and carpentered round about these useless—animals."

"There!" said the old man, reverting to his dry sulky manner again. "There's eloquence! I suppose you like it?"

"Yes," said I, very emphatically.

"Well," said he, "now the storm of eloquence has lulled for a little, suppose you answer my question?—that is, if you like, you know," quoth he, with a sudden access of courtesy.

"What question?" said I. For I must confess that Ellen's strange and almost wild beauty had put it out of my head.

Said he: "First of all (excuse my catechising), is there competition in life, after the old kind, in the country whence you come?"

"Yes," said I, "it is the rule there." And I wondered as I spoke what fresh complications I should get into as a result of this answer.

"Question two," said the carle: "Are you not on the whole much freer, more energetic—in a word, healthier and happier—for it?"

I smiled. "You wouldn't talk so if you had any idea of our life. To me you seem here as if you were living in heaven compared with us of the country from which I came."

"Heaven?" said he: "you like heaven, do you?"

"Yes," said I—snappishly, I am afraid; for I was beginning rather to resent his formula.

"Well, I am far from sure that I do," quoth he. "I think one may do more with one's life than sitting on a damp cloud and singing hymns."

I was rather nettled by this inconsequence, and said: "Well, neighbour, to be short, and without using metaphors, in the land whence I come, where the competition which produced those literary works which you admire so much is still the rule, most people are thoroughly unhappy; here, to me at least, most people seem thoroughly happy."

"No offence, guest—no offence," said he; "but let me ask you; you like that, do you?"

His formula, put with such obstinate persistence, made us all laugh heartily; and even the old man joined in the laughter on the sly. However, he was by no means beaten, and said presently:

"From all I can hear, I should judge that a young woman so beautiful as my dear Ellen yonder would have been a lady, as they called it in the old time, and wouldn't have had to wear a few rags of silk as she does now, or to have browned herself in the sun as she has to do now. What do you say to that, eh?"

Here Clara, who had been pretty much silent hitherto, struck in, and said: "Well, really, I don't think that you would have mended matters, or that they want mending. Don't you see that she is dressed deliciously for this beautiful weather? And as for the sun-burning of your hayfields, why, I hope to pick up some of that for myself when we get a little higher up the river. Look if I don't need a little sun on my pasty white skin!"

And she stripped up the sleeve from her arm and laid it beside Ellen's who was now sitting next her. To say the truth, it was rather amusing to me to see Clara putting herself forward as a town-bred fine lady, for she was as well-knit and clean-skinned a girl as might be met with anywhere at the best. Dick stroked the beautiful arm rather shyly, and pulled down the sleeve again, while she blushed at his touch; and the old man said laughingly: "Well, I suppose you *do* like that; don't you?"

Ellen kissed her new friend, and we all sat silent for a little, till she broke out into a sweet shrill song, and held us all entranced with the wonder of her clear voice; and the old grumbler sat looking at her lovingly. The other young people sang also in due time; and then Ellen showed us to our beds in small cottage chambers, fragrant and clean as the ideal of the old pastoral poets; and the pleasure of the evening quite extinguished my fear of the last night, that I should wake up in the old miserable world of worn-out pleasures, and hopes that were half fears.

CHAPTER XXIII

AN EARLY MORNING BY RUNNYMEDE

Though there were no rough noises to wake me, I could not lie long abed the next morning, where the world seemed so well awake, and, despite the old grumbler, so happy; so I got up, and found that, early as it was, someone had been stirring, since all was trim and in its place in the little parlour, and the table laid for the morning meal. Nobody was afoot in the house as then, however, so I went out a-doors, and after a turn or two round the super-abundant garden, I wandered down over the meadow to the river-side, where lay our boat, looking quite familiar and friendly to me. I walked up stream a little, watching the light mist curling up from the river till the sun gained power to draw it all away; saw the bleak speckling the water under the willow boughs, whence the tiny flies they fed on were falling in myriads; heard the great chub splashing here and there at some belated moth or other, and felt almost back again in my boyhood. Then I went back again to the boat, and loitered there a minute or two, and then walked slowly up the meadow towards the little house. I noted now that there were four more houses of about the same size on the slope away from the river. The meadow in which I was going was not up for hay; but a row of flake-hurdles[1] ran up the slope not far from me on each side, and in the field so parted off from ours on the left they were making hay busily by now, in the simple fashion of the days when I was a boy. My feet turned that way instinctively, as I wanted to see how haymakers looked in these new and better times, and also I rather expected to see Ellen there. I came to the hurdles and stood looking over into the hayfield, and was close to the end of the long line of haymakers who were spreading the low ridges to dry off the night dew. The majority of these were young women clad much like Ellen last night, though not mostly in silk, but in light woollen

---

[1]　A kind of frame on which to dry, in this case, hay.

most gaily embroidered; the men being all clad in white flannel embroidered in bright colours. The meadow looked like a gigantic tulip-bed because of them. All hands were working deliberately but well and steadily, though they were as noisy with merry talk as a grove of autumn starlings. Half a dozen of them, men and women, came up to me and shook hands, gave me the sele[1] of the morning, and asked a few questions as to whence and whither, and wishing me good luck, went back to their work. Ellen, to my disappointment, was not amongst them, but presently I saw a light figure come out of the hayfield higher up the slope, and make for our house; and that was Ellen, holding a basket in her hand. But before she had come to the garden gate, out came Dick and Clara, who, after a minute's pause, came down to meet me, leaving Ellen in the garden; then we three went down to the boat, talking mere morning prattle. We stayed there a little, Dick arranging some of the matters in her, for we had only taken up to the house such things as we thought the dew might damage; and then we went toward the house again; but when we came near the garden, Dick stopped us by laying a hand on my arm and said,—

"Just look a moment."

I looked, and over the low hedge saw Ellen, shading her eyes against the sun as she looked toward the hayfield, a light wind stirring in her tawny hair, her eyes like light jewels amidst her sunburnt face, which looked as if the warmth of the sun were yet in it.

"Look, guest," said Dick; "doesn't it all look like one of those very stories out of Grimm that we were talking about up in Bloomsbury? Here are we two lovers wandering about the world, and we have come to a fairy garden, and there is the very fairy herself amidst of it: I wonder what she will do for us."

Said Clara demurely, but not stiffly: "Is she a good fairy, Dick?"

"O, yes," said he; "and according to the card, she would do better, if it were not for the gnome or woodspirit, our grumbling friend of last night."

We laughed at this; and I said, "I hope you see that you have left me out of the tale."

---

[1]   Happiness or good fortune.

"Well," said he, "that's true. You had better consider that you have got the cap of darkness, and are seeing everything, yourself invisible."

That touched me on my weak side of not feeling sure of my position in this beautiful new country; so in order not to make matters worse, I held my tongue, and we all went into the garden and up to the house together. I noticed by the way that Clara must really rather have felt the contrast between herself as a town madam and this piece of the summer country that we all admired so, for she had rather dressed after Ellen that morning as to thinness and scantiness, and went barefoot also, except for light sandals.

The old man greeted us kindly in the parlour, and said: "Well, guests, so you have been looking about to search into the nakedness of the land: I suppose your illusions of last night have given way a bit before the morning light? Do you still like it, eh?"

"Very much," said I, doggedly; "it is one of the prettiest places on the lower Thames."

"Oho!" said he; "so you know the Thames, do you?"

I reddened, for I saw Dick and Clara looking at me, and scarcely knew what to say. However, since I had said in our early intercourse with my Hammersmith friends that I had known Epping Forest, I thought a hasty generalization might be better in avoiding complications than a downright lie; so I said—

"I have been in this country before; and I have been on the Thames in those days."

"O," said the old man, eagerly, "so you have been in this country before. Now really, don't you *find* it (apart from all theory, you know) much changed for the worse?"

"No, not at all," said I; "I find it much changed for the better."

"Ah," quoth he, "I fear that you have been prejudiced by some theory or another. However, of course the time when you were here before must have been so near our own days that the deterioration might not be very great: as then we were, of course, still living under the same customs as we are now. I was thinking of earlier days than that."

"In short," said Clara, "you have *theories* about the change which has taken place."

"I have facts as well," said he. "Look here! from this hill you can see just four little houses, including this one. Well, I know for certain that in old times, even in the summer, when the leaves were thickest, you could see from the same place six quite big and fine houses; and higher up the water, garden joined garden right up to Windsor; and there were big houses in all the gardens. Ah! England was an important place in those days."

I was getting nettled, and said: "What you mean is that you de-cockneyized the place, and sent the damned flunkies packing, and that everybody can live comfortably and happily, and not a few damned thieves only, who were centres of vulgarity and corruption wherever they were, and who, as to this lovely river, destroyed its beauty morally, and had almost destroyed it physically, when they were thrown out of it."

There was silence after this outburst, which for the life of me I could not help, remembering how I had suffered from cockneyism and its cause on those same waters of old time. But at last the old man said, quite coolly:

"My dear guest, I really don't know what you mean by either cockneys, or flunkies, or thieves, or damned; or how only a few people could live happily and comfortably in a wealthy country. All I can see is that you are angry, and I fear with me: so if you like we will change the subject."

I thought this kind and hospitable in him, considering his obstinacy about his theory; and hastened to say that I did not mean to be angry, only emphatic. He bowed gravely, and I thought the storm was over, when suddenly Ellen broke in:

"Grandfather, our guest is reticent from courtesy; but really what he has in his mind to say to you ought to be said; so as I know pretty well what it is, I will say it for him: for as you know, I have been taught these things by people who—"

"Yes," said the old man, "by the sage of Bloomsbury, and others."

"O," said Dick, "so you know my old kinsman Hammond?"

"Yes," said she, "and other people too, as my grandfather says, and they have taught me things: and this is the upshot of it. We live in a little house now, not because we have nothing grander to do than working in the fields, but because we please; for if we liked, we could go and live in a big house amongst pleasant companions."

Grumbled the old man: "Just so! As if I would live amongst those conceited fellows; all of them looking down upon me!"

She smiled on him kindly, but went on as if he had not spoken. "In the past times, when those big houses of which grandfather speaks were so plenty, we must have lived in a cottage whether we had liked it or not; and the said cottage, instead of having in it everything we want, would have been bare and empty. We should not have got enough to eat; our clothes would have been ugly to look at, dirty and frowsy. You, grandfather, have done no hard work for years now, but wander about and read your books and have nothing to worry you; and as for me, I work hard when I like it, because I like it, and think it does me good, and knits up my muscles, and makes me prettier to look at, and healthier and happier. But in those past days you, grandfather, would have had to work hard after you were old; and would have been always afraid of having to be shut up in a kind of prison along with other old men, half-starved and without amusement. And as for me, I am twenty years old. In those days my middle age would be beginning now, and in a few years I should be pinched, thin, and haggard, beset with troubles and miseries, so that no one could have guessed that I was once a beautiful girl.

"Is this what you have had in your mind, guest?" said she, the tears in her eyes at the thought of the past miseries of people like herself.

"Yes," said I, much moved; "that and more. Often—in my country I have seen that wretched change you have spoken of, from the fresh handsome country lass to the poor draggle-tailed country woman."

The old man sat silent for a little, but presently recovered himself and took comfort in his old phrase of "Well, you like it so, do you?"

"Yes," said Ellen, "I love life better than death."

"O, you do, do you?" said he. "Well, for my part I like reading a good old book with plenty of fun in it, like Thackeray's 'Vanity Fair.'[1] Why don't you write books like that now? Ask that question of your Bloomsbury sage."

---

[1] William Thackeray's comic novel *Vanity Fair* (1847-48) has "plenty of fun in it," but it is also witheringly critical of mid-Victorian hypocrisies and inequalities.

Seeing Dick's cheeks reddening a little at this sally, and noting that silence followed, I thought I had better do something. So I said: "I am only the guest, friends; but I know you want to show me your river at its best, so don't you think we had better be moving presently, as it is certainly going to be a hot day?"

CHAPTER XXIV

UP THE THAMES: THE SECOND DAY

They were not slow to take my hint; and indeed, as to the mere time of day, it was best for us to be off, as it was past seven o'clock, and the day promised to be very hot. So we got up and went down to our boat—Ellen thoughtful and abstracted; the old man very kind and courteous, as if to make up for his crabbedness of opinion. Clara was cheerful and natural, but a little subdued, I thought; and she at least was not sorry to be gone, and often looked shyly and timidly at Ellen and her strange wild beauty. So we got into the boat, Dick saying as he took his place, "Well, it *is* a fine day!" and the old man answering "What! you like that, do you?" once more; and presently Dick was sending the bows swiftly through the slow weed-checked stream. I turned round as we got into mid-stream, and waving my hand to our hosts, saw Ellen leaning on the old man's shoulder, and caressing his healthy apple-red cheek, and quite a keen pang smote me as I thought how I should never see the beautiful girl again. Presently I insisted on taking the sculls, and I rowed a good deal that day which no doubt accounts for the fact that we got very late to the place which Dick had aimed at. Clara was particularly affectionate to Dick, as I noticed from the rowing thwart: but as for him, he was as frankly kind and merry as ever; and I was glad to see it, as a man of his temperament could not have taken her caresses cheerfully and without embarrassment if he had been at all entangled by the fairy of our last night's abode.

I need say little about the lovely reaches of the river here. I duly noted that absence of cockney villas which the old man had lamented; and I saw with pleasure that my old enemies the "Gothic" cast-iron bridges had been replaced by handsome oak and stone ones. Also the banks of the forest that we passed through had lost their courtly game-keeperish trimness, and were as wild and beautiful as need be, though the trees were clearly well seen to. I thought it best, in order to get the most direct information, to play the innocent about Eton and Windsor;[1] but Dick volunteered his knowledge to me as we lay in Datchet lock about the first. Quoth he:

"Up yonder are some beautiful old buildings, which were built for a great college or teaching-place by one of the mediæval kings—Edward the Sixth, I think" (I smiled to myself at his rather natural blunder).[2] "He meant poor people's sons to be taught there what knowledge was going in his days; but it was a matter of course that in the times of which you seem to know so much they spoilt whatever good there was in the founder's intentions. My old kinsman says that they treated them in a very simple way, and instead of teaching poor men's sons to know something, they taught rich men's sons to know nothing. It seems from what he says that it was a place for the 'aristocracy' (if you know what that word means; I have been told its meaning) to get rid of the company of their male children for a great part of the year. I daresay old Hammond would give you plenty of information in detail about it."

"What is it used for now?" said I.

"Well," said he, "the buildings were a good deal spoilt by the last few generations of aristocrats, who seem to have had a great hatred against beautiful old buildings, and indeed all records of past history; but it is still a delightful place. Of course, we cannot use it quite as the founder intended, since our ideas about teaching young people are so changed from the ideas of his time; so it is used now as a dwelling for people engaged in learning; and

---

[1] Eton is a famous public school; Windsor Castle is one of the official residences of the British monarch.

[2] Though Edward VI (who does not qualify as a medieval king) endowed a number of schools in the sixteenth century, Eton was founded not by him but by Henry VI in 1440.

folk from round about come and get taught things that they want to learn; and there is a great library there of the best books. So that I don't think that the old dead king would be much hurt if he were to come to life and see what we are doing there."

"Well," said Clara, laughing, "I think he would miss the boys."

"Not always, my dear," said Dick, "for there are often plenty of boys there, who come to get taught; and also," said he, smiling, "to learn boating and swimming. I wish we could stop there: but perhaps we had better do that coming down the water."

The lock-gates opened as he spoke, and out we went, and on. And as for Windsor, he said nothing till I lay on my oars (for I was sculling then) in Clewer reach, and looking up, said, "What is all that building up there?"

Said he: "There, I thought I would wait till you asked, yourself. That is Windsor Castle: that also I thought I would keep for you till we come down the water. It looks fine from here, doesn't it? But a great deal of it has been built or skinned in the time of the Degradation, and we wouldn't pull the buildings down, since they were there; just as with the buildings of the Dung-Market. You know, of course, that it was the palace of our old mediæval kings, and was used later on for the same purpose by the parliamentary commercial sham-kings, as my old kinsman calls them."

"Yes," said I, "I know all that. What is it used for now?"

"A great many people live there," said he, "as, with all drawbacks, it is a pleasant place; there is also a well-arranged store of antiquities of various kinds that have seemed worth keeping—a museum, it would have been called in the times you understand so well."

I drew my sculls through the water at that last word, and pulled as if I were fleeing from those times which I understood so well; and we were soon going up the once sorely be-cockneyed reaches of the river about Maidenhead, which now looked as pleasant and enjoyable as the up-river reaches.

The morning was now getting on, the morning of a jewel of a summer day; one of those days which, if they were commoner in these islands, would make our climate the best of all climates, without dispute. A light wind blew from the west; the little clouds that had arisen at about our breakfast time had seemed to get higher and higher in the heavens; and in spite of the burning sun we no more longed for rain than we feared it. Burning as the sun was, there was a fresh feeling in the air that almost set us a-longing for the rest of the hot afternoon, and the stretch of blossoming wheat seen from the shadow of the boughs. No one unburdened with very heavy anxieties could have felt otherwise than happy that morning: and it must be said that whatever anxieties might lie beneath the surface of things, we didn't seem to come across any of them.

We passed by several fields where haymaking was going on, but Dick, and especially Clara, were so jealous of our up-river festival that they would not allow me to have much to say to them. I could only notice that the people in the fields looked strong and handsome, both men and women, and that so far from there being any appearance of sordidness about their attire, they seemed to be dressing specially for the occasion,—lightly, of course, but gaily and with plenty of adornment.

Both on this day as well as yesterday we had, as you may think, met and passed and been passed by many craft of one kind and another. The most part of these were being rowed like ourselves, or were sailing, in the sort of way that sailing is managed on the upper reaches of the river; but every now and then we came on barges, laden with hay or other country produce, or carrying bricks, lime, timber, and the like, and these were going on their way without any means of propulsion visible to me—just a man at the tiller, with often a friend or two laughing and talking with him. Dick, seeing on one occasion this day, that I was looking rather hard on one of these, said: "That is one of our force-barges; it is quite easy to work vehicles by force by water as by land."

I understood pretty well that these "force vehicles" had taken the place of our old steam-power carrying; but I took good care not to ask any questions about them, as I knew well enough both that I should never be able to understand how they were worked, and that in attempting to do so I should betray myself, or get into some complication impossible to explain; so I merely said, "Yes, of course, I understand."

We went ashore at Bisham, where the remains of the old

Abbey and the Elizabethan house[1] that had been added to them yet remained, none the worse for many years of careful and appreciative habitation. The folk of the place, however, were mostly in the fields that day, both men and women; so we met only two old men there, and a younger one who had stayed at home to get on with some literary work, which I imagine we considerably interrupted. Yet I also think that the hard-working man who received us was not very sorry for the interruption. Anyhow, he kept on pressing us to stay over and over again, till at last we did not get away till the cool of the evening.

However, that mattered little to us; the nights were light, for the moon was shining in her third quarter, and it was all one to Dick whether he sculled or sat quiet in the boat: so we went away a great pace. The evening sun shone bright on the remains of the old buildings at Medmenham;[2] close beside which arose an irregular pile of building which Dick told us was a very pleasant house; and there were plenty of houses visible on the wide meadows opposite, under the hill; for, as it seems that the beauty of Hurley had compelled people to build and live there a good deal. The sun very low down showed us Henley little altered in outward aspect from what I remembered it. Actual daylight failed us as we passed through the lovely reaches of Wargrave and Shiplake; but the moon rose behind us presently. I should like to have seen with my eyes what success the new order of things had had in getting rid of the sprawling mess with which commercialism had littered the banks of the wide stream about Reading and Caversham: certainly everything smelt too deliciously in the early night for there to be any of the old careless sordidness of so-called manufacture; and in answer to my question as to what sort of a place Reading was, Dick answered:

"O, a nice town enough in its way; mostly rebuilt within the last hundred years; and there are a good many houses, as you can see by the lights just down under the hills yonder. In fact, it is one of the most populous places on the Thames round about here. Keep up your spirits, guest! we are close to our journey's end for

---

[1]   The remains of the fourteenth-century Bisham Abbey were incorporated into the present manor house when it was built in the late sixteenth century.

[2]   Ruins of a Cistercian abbey founded in 1220.

the night. I ought to ask your pardon for not stopping at one of the houses here or higher up; but a friend, who is living in a very pleasant house in the Maple-Durham meads, particularly wanted me and Clara to come and see him on our way up the Thames; and I thought you wouldn't mind this bit of night travelling."

He need not have adjured me to keep up my spirits, which were as high as possible; though the strangeness and excitement of the happy and quiet life which I saw everywhere around me was, it is true, a little wearing off, yet a deep content, as different as possible from languid acquiescence, was taking its place, and I was, as it were, really new-born.

We landed presently just where I remembered the river making an elbow to the north towards the ancient house of the Blunts;[1] with the wide meadows spreading on the right-hand side, and on the left the long line of beautiful old trees over-hanging the water. As we got out of the boat, I said to Dick—

"Is it the old house we are going to?"

"No," he said, "though that is standing still in green old age, and is well inhabited. I see, by the way, that you know your Thames well. But my friend Walter Allen, who asked me to stop here, lives in a house, not very big, which has been built here lately, because these meadows are so much liked, especially in the summer, that there was getting to be rather too much of tenting on the open field; so the parishes here about, who rather objected to that, built three houses between this and Caversham, and quite a large one at Basildon, a little higher up. Look, yonder are the lights of Walter Allen's house!"

So we walked over the grass of the meadows under a flood of moonlight, and soon came to the house, which was low and built round a quadrangle big enough to get plenty of sunshine in it. Walter Allen, Dick's friend, was leaning against the jamb of the doorway waiting for us, and took us into the hall without over-plus of words. There were not many people in it, as some of the dwellers there were away at the haymaking in the neighbourhood, and some, as Walter told us, were wandering about the meadow enjoying the beautiful moonlit night. Dick's friend looked to be a man of about forty; tall, black-haired, very kind-looking and

---

[1]   Mapledurham House was built in the late sixteenth century by Sir Richard Blount.

thoughtful; but rather to my surprise there was a shade of melancholy on his face, and he seemed a little distracted and inattentive to our chat, in spite of obvious efforts to listen.

Dick looked on him from time to time, and seemed troubled; and at last he said: "I say, old fellow, if there is anything the matter which we didn't know of when you wrote to me, don't you think you had better tell us about it at once? or else we shall think we have come here at an unlucky time, and are not quite wanted."

Walter turned red, and seemed to have some difficulty in restraining his tears, but said at last: "Of course everybody here is very glad to see you, Dick, and your friends; but it is true that we are not at our best, in spite of the fine weather and the glorious hay-crop. We have had a death here."

Said Dick: "Well, you should get over that, neighbour: such things must be."

"Yes," Walter said, "but this was a death by violence, and it seems likely to lead to at least one more: and somehow it makes us feel rather shy of one another; and to say the truth, that is one reason why there are so few of us present to-night."

"Tell us the story, Walter," said Dick; "perhaps telling it will help you to shake off your sadness."

Said Walter: "Well, I will; and I will make it short enough, though I daresay it might be spun out into a long one, as used to be done with such subjects in the old novels. There is a very charming girl here whom we all like, and whom some of us do more than like; and she very naturally liked one of us better than anybody else. And another of us (I won't name him) got fairly bitten with love-madness, and used to go about making himself as unpleasant as he could—not of malice prepense, of course; so that the girl, who liked him well enough at first, began fairly to dislike him. Of course, those of us who knew him best—myself amongst others—advised him to go away, as he was making matters worse for himself every day. Well, he wouldn't take our advice (that also, I suppose, was a matter of course), so we had to tell him that he *must* go, or the inevitable sending to Coventry would follow;[1] for

---

[1]   To be "sent to Coventry" is to be ostracized. During the English Civil War Royalist prisoners of war were quartered in Coventry.

his individual trouble had so overmastered him that we felt that *we* must go if he did not.

"He took that better than we expected, when something or other—an interview with the girl, I think, and some hot words with the successful lover following close upon it, threw him quite off his balance; and he got hold of an axe and fell upon his rival when there was no one by; and in the struggle that followed the man attacked, hit him an unlucky blow and killed him. And the slayer in his turn is so upset that he is like to kill himself; and if he does, the girl will do as much, I fear. And all this we could no more help than the earthquake of the year before last."

"It is very unhappy," said Dick; "but since the man is dead, and cannot be brought to life again, and since the slayer had no malice in him, I cannot for the life of me see why he shouldn't get over it before long. Besides, it was the right man that was killed and not the wrong. Why should a man brood over a mere accident for ever? And the girl?"

"As to her," said Walter, "the whole thing seems to have inspired her with terror rather than grief. What you say about the man is true, or should be; but then, you see, the excitement and jealousy that was the prelude to this tragedy had made an evil and feverish element round about him, from which he does not seem to be able to escape. However, we have advised him to go away—in fact, to cross the seas; but he is in such a state that I do not think he *can* go unless someone *takes* him, and I think it will fall to my lot to do so; which is scarcely a cheerful outlook for me."

"O, you will find a certain interest in it," said Dick. "And of course he *must* soon look upon the affair from a reasonable point of view sooner or later."

"Well, at any rate," quoth Walter, "now that I have eased my mind by making you uncomfortable, let us have an end of the subject for the present. Are you going to take your guest to Oxford?"

"Why, of course we must pass through it," said Dick, smiling, "as we are going into the upper waters: but I thought that we wouldn't stop there, or we shall be belated as to the haymaking up our way. So Oxford and my learned lecture on it, all got at second-hand from my old kinsman, must wait till we come down the water a fortnight hence."

I listened to this story with much surprise, and could not help wondering at first that the man who had slain the other had not been put in custody till it could be proved that he killed his rival in self-defense only. However, the more I thought of it, the plainer it grew to me that no amount of examination of witnesses, who had witnessed nothing but the ill-blood between the two rivals, would have done anything to clear up the case. I could not help thinking, also, that the remorse of this homicide gave point to what old Hammond had said to me about the way in which this strange people dealt with what I had been used to hear called crimes. Truly, the remorse was exaggerated; but it was quite clear that the slayer took the whole consequences of the act upon himself, and did not expect society to whitewash him by punishing him. I had no fear any longer that "the sacredness of human life" was likely to suffer amongst my friends from the absence of gallows and prison.

CHAPTER XXV

THE THIRD DAY ON THE THAMES

As we went down to the boat next morning, Walter could not quite keep off the subject of last night, though he was more hopeful than he had been then, and seemed to think that if the unlikely homicide could not be got to go over-sea, he might at any rate go and live somewhere in the neighbourhood pretty much by himself; at any rate, that was what he himself had proposed. To Dick, and I must say to me also, this seemed a strange remedy; and Dick said as much. Quoth he:

"Friend Walter, don't set the man brooding on the tragedy by letting him live alone. That will only strengthen his idea that he has committed a crime, and you will have him killing himself in good earnest."

Said Clara: "I don't know. If I may say what I think of it, it is that he had better have his fill of gloom now, and, so to say, wake up presently to see how little need there has been for it; and then he will live happily afterwards. As for his killing himself, you need not be afraid of that; for, from all you tell me, he is really very much in love with the woman; and to speak plainly, until his love is satisfied, he will not only stick to life as tightly as he can, but will also make the most of every event of his life—will, so to say, hug himself up in it; and I think that this is the real explanation of his taking the whole matter with such an excess of tragedy."

Walter looked thoughtful, and said: "Well, you may be right; and perhaps we should have treated it all more lightly: but you see, guest" (turning to me), "such things happen so seldom, that when they do happen, we cannot help being much taken up with it. For the rest, we are all inclined to excuse our poor friend for making us so unhappy, on the ground that he does it out of an exaggerated respect for human life and its happiness. Well, I will say no more about it; only this: will you give me a cast up stream, as I want to look after a lonely habitation for the poor fellow, since he will have it so, and I hear that there is one which would suit us very well on the downs beyond Streatley; so if you will put me ashore there I will walk up the hill and look to it."

"Is the house in question empty?" said I.

"No," said Walter, "but the man who lives there will go out of it, of course, when he hears that we want it. You see, we think that the fresh air of the downs and the very emptiness of the landscape will do our friend good."

"Yes," said Clara, smiling, "and he will not be so far from his beloved that they cannot easily meet if they have a mind to—as they certainly will."

This talk had brought us down to the boat, and we were presently afloat on the beautiful broad stream, Dick driving the prow swiftly through the windless water of the early summer morning, for it was not yet six o'clock. We were at the lock in a very little time; and as we lay rising and rising on the in-coming water, I could not help wondering that my old friend the pound-lock, and that of the very simplest and most rural kind, should hold its place there; so I said:

"I have been wondering, as we passed lock after lock, that you people, so prosperous as you are, and especially since you are so anxious for pleasant work to do, have not invented something which would get rid of this clumsy business of going up-stairs by means of these rude contrivances."

Dick laughed. "My dear friend," said he, "as long as water has the clumsy habit of running down hill, I fear we must humour it by going up-stairs when we have our faces turned from the sea. And really I don't see why you should fall foul of Maple-Durham lock, which I think a very pretty place."

There was no doubt about the latter assertion, I thought, as I looked up at the overhanging boughs of the great trees, with the sun coming glittering through the leaves, and listened to the song of the summer blackbirds as it mingled with the sound of the backwater near us. So not being able to say why I wanted the locks away—which, indeed, I didn't do at all—I held my peace. But Walter said—

"You see, guest, this is not an age of inventions. The last epoch did all that for us, and we are now content to use such of its inventions as we find handy, and leaving those alone which we don't want. I believe, as a matter of fact, that some time ago (I can't give you a date) some elaborate machinery was used for the locks, though people did not go so far as try to make the water run up hill. However, it was troublesome, I suppose, and the simple hatches, and the gates, with a big counterpoising beam, were found to answer every purpose, and were easily mended when wanted with material always to hand: so here they are, as you see."

"Besides," said Dick, "this kind of lock is pretty, as you can see; and I can't help thinking that your machine-lock, winding up like a watch, would have been ugly and would have spoiled the look of the river: and that is surely reason enough for keeping such locks as these. Good-bye, old fellow!" said he to the lock, as he pushed us out through the now open gates by a vigorous stroke of the boat-hook. "May you live long, and have your green old age renewed for ever."

On we went; and the water had the familiar aspect to me of the days before Pangbourne had been thoroughly cocknified, as I have seen it. It (Pangbourne) was distinctly a village still—*i.e.*, a definite group of houses, and as pretty as might be. The beech-woods still covered the hill that rose above Basildon; but the flat fields beneath them were much more populous than I remembered them, as there were five large houses in sight, very carefully designed so as not to hurt the character of the country. Down on the green lip of the river, just where the water turns toward the Goring and Streatley reaches, were half a dozen girls playing about on the grass. They hailed us as we were about passing them, as they noted that we were travellers, and we stopped a minute to talk with them. They had been bathing, and were light clad and bare-footed, and were bound for the meadows on the Berkshire side, where the haymaking had begun, and were passing the time merrily enough till the Berkshire folk came in their punt to fetch them. At first nothing would content them but we must go with them into the hayfield, and breakfast with them; but Dick put forward his theory of beginning the hay-harvest higher up the water, and not spoiling my pleasure therein by giving me a taste of it elsewhere, and they gave way, though unwillingly. In revenge they asked me a great many questions about the country I came from and the manners of life there, which I found rather puzzling to answer; and doubtless what answers I did give were puzzling enough to them. I noticed both with these pretty girls and with everybody else we met, that in default of serious news, such as we had heard at Maple-Durham, they were eager to discuss all the little details of life: the weather, the hay-crop, the last new house, the plenty or lack of such and such birds, and so on; and they talked of these things not in a fatuous and conventional way, but as taking, I say, real interest in them. Moreover, I found that the women knew as much about all these things as the men: could name a flower, and knew its qualities; could tell you the habitat of such and such birds and fish, and the like.

It is almost strange what a difference this intelligence made in my estimate of the country life of that day; for it used to be said in past times, and on the whole truly, that outside their daily work country people knew little of the country, and at least could tell you nothing about it; while here were these people as eager about all the goings on in the fields and woods and downs as if they had been Cockneys newly escaped from the tyranny of bricks and mortar.

I may mention as a detail worth noticing that not only did there seem to be a great many more birds about of the non-predatory kinds, but their enemies the birds of prey were also commoner. A kite hung above our heads as we passed Medmenham yesterday; magpies were quite common in the hedgerows; I saw several sparrow-hawks, and I think a merlin; and now just as we were passing the pretty bridge which had taken the place of Basildon railway-bridge, a couple of ravens croaked above our boat, as they sailed off to the higher ground of the downs. I concluded from all this that the days of the gamekeeper were over, and did not even need to ask Dick a question about it.

CHAPTER XXVI

THE OBSTINATE REFUSERS

Before we parted from these girls we saw two sturdy young men and a woman putting off from the Berkshire shore, and then Dick bethought him of a little banter of the girls, and asked them how it was that there was nobody of the male kind to go with them across the water, and where the boats were gone to. Said one, the youngest of the party: "O, they have got the big punt to lead stone from up the water."

"Who do you mean by 'they,' dear child?" said Dick.

Said an older girl, laughing: "You had better go and see them. Look there," and she pointed northwest, "don't you see building going on there?"

"Yes," said Dick, "and I am rather surprised at this time of the year; why are they not haymaking with you?"

The girls all laughed at this, and before their laugh was over, the Berkshire boat had run on to the grass and the girls stepped in lightly, still sniggering, while the new comers gave us the sele of the day. But before they were under way again, the tall girl said: "Excuse us for laughing, dear neighbours, but we have had some friendly bickering with the builders up yonder, and as we have no time to tell you the story, you had better go and ask them: they will be glad to see you—if you don't hinder their work."

They all laughed again at that, and waved us a pretty farewell as the punters set them over toward the other shore, and left us standing on the bank beside our boat.

"Let us go and see them," said Clara; "that is, if you are not in a hurry to get to Streatley, Walter?"

"O no," said Walter, "I shall be glad of the excuse to have a little more of your company."

So we left the boat moored there, and went on up the slow slope of the hill; but I said to Dick on the way, being somewhat mystified: "What was all that laughing about? what was the joke?"

"I can guess pretty well," said Dick; "some of them up there have got a piece of work which interests them, and they won't go to the haymaking, which doesn't matter at all, because there are plenty of people to do such easy-hard work as that; only, since haymaking is a regular festival, the neighbours find it amusing to jeer good-humouredly at them."

"I see," said I, "much as if in Dickens's time some young people were so wrapped up in their work that they wouldn't keep Christmas."

"Just so," said Dick, "only these people need not be young either."

"But what did you mean by easy-hard work?" said I.

Quoth Dick: "Did I say that? I mean work that tries the muscles and hardens them and sends you pleasantly weary to bed, but which isn't trying in other ways: doesn't harass you in short. Such work is always pleasant if you don't overdo it. Only, mind you, good mowing requires some little skill. I'm a pretty good mower."

This talk brought us up to the house that was a-building, not a large one, which stood at the end of a beautiful orchard surrounded by an old stone wall. "O yes, I see," said Dick; "I remember, a beautiful place for a house: but a starveling of a nineteenth century house stood there: I am glad they are rebuilding: it's all stone, too, though it need not have been in this part of the country: my word, though, they are making a neat job of it: but I wouldn't have made it all ashlar."[1]

---

[1] Ashlar is masonry made of square-cut stones.

Walter and Clara were already talking to a tall man clad in his mason's blouse, who looked about forty, but was I daresay older, who had his mallet and chisel in hand; there were at work in the shed and on the scaffold about half a dozen men and two women, blouse-clad like the carles, while a very pretty woman who was not in the work but was dressed in an elegant suit of blue linen came sauntering up to us with her knitting in her hand. She welcomed us and said, smiling: "So you are come up from the water to see the Obstinate Refusers: where are you going haymaking, neighbours?"

"O, right up above Oxford," said Dick; "it is rather a late country. But what share have you got with the Refusers, pretty neighbour?"

Said she, with a laugh: "O, I am the lucky one who doesn't want to work; though sometimes I get it, for I serve as model to Mistress Philippa there when she wants one: she is our head carver; come and see her."

She led us up to the door of the unfinished house, where a rather little woman was working with mallet and chisel on the wall near by. She seemed very intent on what she was doing, and did not turn round when we came up; but a taller woman, quite a girl she seemed, who was at work near by, had already knocked off, and was standing looking from Clara to Dick with delighted eyes. None of the others paid much heed to us.

The blue-clad girl laid her hand on the carver's shoulder and said: "Now Philippa, if you gobble up your work like that, you will soon have none to do; and what will become of you then?"

The carver turned round hurriedly and showed us the face of a woman of forty (or so she seemed), and said rather pettishly, but in a sweet voice:

"Don't talk nonsense, Kate, and don't interrupt me if you can help it." She stopped short when she saw us, then went on with the kind smile of welcome which never failed us. "Thank you for coming to see us, neighbours; but I am sure that you won't think me unkind if I go on with my work, especially when I tell you that I was ill and unable to do anything all through April and May; and this open-air and the sun and the work together, and my feeling well again too, make a mere delight of every hour to me; and excuse me, I must go on."

She fell to work accordingly on a carving in low relief of flowers and figures, but talked on amidst her mallet strokes: "You see, we all think this the prettiest place for a house up and down these reaches; and the site has been so long encumbered with an unworthy one, that we masons were determined to pay off fate and destiny for once, and build the prettiest house we could compass here—and so—and so—"

Here she lapsed into mere carving, but the tall foreman came up and said: "Yes, neighbours, that is it: so it is going to be all ashlar because we want to carve a kind of a wreath of flowers and figures all round it; and we have been much hindered by one thing or other—Philippa's illness amongst others,—and though we could have managed our wreath without her—"

"Could you, though?" grumbled the last-named from the face of the wall.

"Well, at any rate, she is our best carver, and it would not have been kind to begin the carving without her. So you see," said he, looking at Dick and me, "we really couldn't go haymaking, could we, neighbours? But you see, we are getting on so fast now with this splendid weather, that I think we may well spare a week or ten days at wheat-harvest; and won't we go at *that* work then! Come down then to the acres that lie north and by west here at our backs and you shall see good harvesters, neighbours."

"Hurrah, for a good brag!" called a voice from the scaffold above us; "our foreman thinks that an easier job than putting one stone on another!"

There was a general laugh at this sally, in which the tall foreman joined; and with that we saw a lad bringing out a little table into the shadow of the stone-shed, which he set down there, and then going back, came out again with the inevitable big wickered flask and tall glasses, whereon the foreman led us up to due seats on blocks of stone, and said:

"Well, neighbours, drink to my brag coming true, or I shall think you don't believe me! Up there!" said he, hailing the scaffold, "are you coming down for a glass?" Three of the workmen came running down the ladder as men with "building legs" will do; but the others didn't answer, except the joker (if he must be so called), who called out without turning round: "Excuse me, neighbours, for not getting down. I must get on: my work is not superintending, like the gaffer's yonder; but, you fellows, send us up a glass to drink the haymakers' health." Of course, Philippa would not turn away from her beloved work; but the other woman carver came; she turned out to be Philippa's daughter, but was a tall strong girl, black-haired and gipsey-like of face and curiously solemn of manner. The rest gathered round us and clinked glasses, and the men on the scaffold turned about and drank to our healths; but the busy little woman by the door would have none of it all, but only shrugged her shoulders when her daughter came up to her and touched her.

So we shook hands and turned our backs on the Obstinate Refusers, went down the slope to our boat, and before we had gone many steps heard the full tune of tinkling trowels mingle with the humming of the bees and the singing of the larks above the little plain of Basildon.

CHAPTER XXVII

THE UPPER WATERS

We set Walter ashore on the Berkshire side, amidst all the beauties of Streatley, and so went our ways into what once would have been the deeper country under the foot-hills of the White Horse;[1] and though the contrast between half-cocknified and wholly unsophisticated country existed no longer, a feeling of exultation rose within me (as it used to do) at sight of the familiar and still unchanged hills of the Berkshire range.

We stopped at Wallingford for our mid-day meal; of course, all signs of squalor and poverty had disappeared from the streets of the ancient town, and many ugly houses had been taken down and many pretty new ones built, but I thought it curious, that

---

[1] A 374-foot-long figure of a horse cut into the chalk of a hill near Abingdon; its origin is uncertain.

the town still looked like the old place I remembered so well; for indeed it looked like that ought to have looked.

At dinner we fell in with an old, but very bright and intelligent man, who seemed in a country way to be another edition of old Hammond. He had an extraordinary detailed knowledge of the ancient history of the countryside from the time of Alfred to the days of the Parliamentary Wars,[1] many events of which, as you may know, were enacted around Wallingford. But, what was more interesting to us, he had a detailed record of the period of the change to the present state of things, and told us a great deal about it, and especially of that exodus of the people from the town to the country, and the gradual recovery by the town-bred people on one side, and the country-bred people on the other, of those arts of life which they had each lost; which loss, as he told us, had at one time gone so far that not only was it impossible to find a carpenter or a smith in a village or small country town, but that people in such places had even forgotten how to bake bread, and that at Wallingford, for instance, the bread came down with the newspapers by an early train from London, worked in some way, the explanation of which I could not understand. He told us also that the townspeople who came into the country used to pick up the agricultural arts by carefully watching the way in which the machines worked, gathering an idea of handicraft from machinery; because at that time almost everything in and about the fields was done by elaborate machines used quite unintelligently by the labourers. On the other hand, the old men amongst the labourers managed to teach the younger ones gradually a little artisanship, such as the use of the saw and the plane, the work of the smithy, and so forth; for once more, by that time it was as much as—or rather, more than—a man could do to fix an ash pole to a rake by handiwork; so that it would take a machine worth a thousand pounds, a group of workmen, and half a day's travelling, to do five shillings' worth of work. He showed us, among other things, an account of a certain village council who were working hard at all this business; and the record of their intense earnestness in getting to the

---

[1] Roughly, from the late ninth century through the middle of the seventeenth century.

bottom of some matter which in time past would have been thought quite trivial, as, for example, the due proportions of alkali and oil for soap-making for the village wash, or the exact heat of the water into which a leg of mutton should be plunged for boiling—all this joined to the utter absence of anything like party feeling, which even in a village assembly would certainly have made its appearance in an earlier epoch, was very amusing, and at the same time instructive.

This old man, whose name was Henry Morsom, took us, after our meal and a rest, into a biggish hall which contained a large collection of articles of manufacture and art from the last days of the machine period to that day; and he went over them with us, and explained them with great care. They also were very interesting, showing the transition from the makeshift work of the machines (which was at about its worst a little after the Civil War before told of) into the first years of the new handicraft period. Of course, there was much overlapping of the periods: and at first the new handwork came in very slowly.

"You must remember," said the old antiquary, "that the handicraft was not the result of what used to be called material necessity: on the contrary, by that time the machines had been so much improved that almost all necessary work might have been done by them: and indeed many people at that time, and before it, used to think that machinery would entirely supersede handicraft; which certainly, on the face of it, seemed more than likely. But there was another opinion, far less logical, prevalent amongst the rich people before the days of freedom, which did not die out at once after that epoch had begun. This opinion, which from all I can learn seemed as natural then, as it seems absurd now, was, that while the ordinary daily work of the world would be done entirely by automatic machinery, the energies of the more intelligent part of mankind would be set free to follow the higher forms of the arts, as well as science and the study of history. It was strange, was it not, that they should thus ignore that aspiration after complete equality which we now recognize as the bond of all happy human society?"

I did not answer, but thought the more. Dick looked thoughtful, and said:

"Strange, neighbour? Well, I don't know. I have often heard my old kinsman say the one aim of all people before our time was to avoid work, or at least they thought it was; so of course the work which their daily life *forced* them to do, seemed more like work than that which they *seemed* to choose for themselves."

"True enough," said Morsom. "Anyhow, they soon began to find out their mistake, and that only slaves and slaveholders could live solely by setting machines going."

Clara broke in here, flushing a little as she spoke: "Was not their mistake once more bred of the life of slavery that they had been living?—a life which was always looking upon everything, except mankind, animate and inanimate—'nature,' as people used to call it—as one thing, and mankind as another. It was natural to people thinking in this way, that they should try to make 'nature' their slave, since they thought 'nature' was something outside them."

"Surely," said Morsom; "and they were puzzled as to what to do, till they found the feeling against a mechanical life, which had begun before the Great Change amongst people who had leisure to think of such things, was spreading insensibly; till at last under the guise of pleasure that was not supposed to be work, work that was pleasure began to push out the mechanical toil, which they had once hoped at the best to reduce to narrow limits indeed, but never to get rid of; and which, moreover, they found they could not limit as they had hoped to do."

"When did this new revolution gather head?" said I.

"In the half-century that followed the Great Change," said Morsom, "it began to be noteworthy; machine after machine was quietly dropped under the excuse that the machines could not produce works of art, and that works of art were more and more called for. Look here," he said, "here are some of the works of that time—rough and unskilful in handiwork, but solid and showing some sense of pleasure in the making."

"They are very curious," said I, taking up a piece of pottery from amongst the specimens which the antiquary was showing us; "not a bit like the work of either savages or barbarians, and yet with what would once have been called a hatred of civilization impressed upon them."

"Yes," said Morsom, "you must not look for delicacy there: in that period you could only have got that from a man who was practically a slave. But now, you see," said he, leading me on a little, "we have learned the trick of handicraft, and have added the utmost refinement of workmanship to the freedom of fancy and imagination."

I looked, and wondered indeed at the deftness and abundance of beauty of the work of men who had at last learned to accept life itself as a pleasure, and the satisfaction of the common needs of mankind and the preparation for them, as work fit for the best of the race. I mused silently; but at last I said—

"What is to come after this?"

The old man laughed. "I don't know," said he; "we will meet it when it comes."

"Meanwhile," quoth Dick, "we have got to meet the rest of our day's journey; so out into the street and down to the strand! Will you come a turn with us, neighbour? Our friend is greedy of your stories."

"I will go as far as Oxford with you," said he; "I want a book or two out of the Bodleian Library.[1] I suppose you will sleep in the old city?"

"No," said Dick, "we are going higher up; the hay is waiting us there, you know."

Morsom nodded, and we all went into the street together, and got into the boat a little above the town bridge. But just as Dick was getting the sculls into the rowlocks, the bows of another boat came thrusting through the low arch. Even at first sight it was a gay little craft indeed—bright green, and painted over with elegantly drawn flowers. As it cleared the arch, a figure as bright and gay-clad as the boat rose up in it; a slim girl dressed in light blue silk that fluttered in the draughty wind of the bridge. I thought I knew the figure, and sure enough, as she turned her head to us, and showed her beautiful face, I saw with joy that it was none other than the fairy godmother from the abundant garden on Runnymede—Ellen, to wit.

---

[1]   The Bodleian Library at Oxford University houses one of the world's greatest collections. In 1890 access to its collections would have been extremely difficult to someone like Dick or Henry Morsom.

We all stopped to receive her. Dick rose in the boat and cried out a genial good morrow; I tried to be as genial as Dick, but failed; Clara waved a delicate hand to her; and Morsom nodded and looked on with interest. As to Ellen, the beautiful brown of her face was deepened by a flush, as she brought the gunwale of her boat alongside ours, and said:

"You see, neighbours, I had some doubt if you would all three come back past Runnymede, or if you did, whether you would stop there; and besides, I am not sure whether we—my father[1] and I—shall not be away in a week or two, for he wants to see a brother of his in the north country, and I should not like him to go without me. So I thought I might never see you again, and that seemed uncomfortable to me, and—and so I came after you."

"Well," said Dick, "I am sure we are all very glad of that; although you may be sure that as for Clara and me, we should have made a point of coming to see you, and of coming the second time, if we had found you away the first. But, dear neighbour, there you are alone in the boat, and you have been sculling pretty hard, I should think, and might find a little quiet sitting pleasant; so we had better part our company into two."

"Yes," said Ellen, "I thought you would do that, so I have brought a rudder for my boat: will you help me to ship it, please?"

And she went aft in her boat and pushed along our side till she had brought the stern close to Dick's hand. He knelt down in our boat and she in hers, and the usual fumbling took place over hanging the rudder on its hooks; for, as you may imagine, no change had taken place in the arrangement of such an unimportant matter as the rudder of a pleasure-boat. As the two beautiful young faces bent over the rudder, they seemed to me to be very close together, and though it only lasted a moment, a sort of pang shot through me as I looked on. Clara sat in her place and did not look round, but presently she said, with just the least stiffness in her tone:

"How shall we divide? Won't you go into Ellen's boat, Dick, since, without offence to our guest, you are the better sculler?"

Dick stood up and laid his hand on her shoulder, and said: "No,

---

[1]   Earlier the "old grumbler" is identified as Ellen's grandfather.

no; let Guest try what he can do—he ought to be getting into training now. Besides, we are in no hurry: we are not going far above Oxford; and even if we are benighted, we shall have the moon, which will give us nothing worse of a night than a greyer day."

"Besides," said I, "I may manage to do a little more with my sculling than merely keeping the boat from drifting down stream."

They all laughed at this, as if it had been a very good joke; and I thought that Ellen's laugh, even amongst the others, was one of the pleasantest sounds I had ever heard.

To be short, I got into the new-come boat, not a little elated, and taking the sculls, set to work to show off a little. For—must I say it?—I felt as if even that happy world were made the happier for my being so near this strange girl; although I must say that of all the persons I had seen in that world renewed, she was the most unfamiliar to me, the most unlike what I could have thought of. Clara, for instance, beautiful and bright as she was, was not unlike a *very* pleasant and unaffected young lady; and the other girls also seemed nothing more than specimens of very much improved types which I had known in other times. But this girl was not only beautiful with a beauty quite different from that of "a young lady," but was in all ways so strangely interesting; so that I kept wondering what she would say or do next to surprise and please me. Not, indeed, that there was anything startling in what she actually said or did; but it was all done in a new way, and always with that indefinable interest and pleasure of life, which I had noticed more or less in everybody, but which in her was more marked and more charming than in anyone else that I had seen.

We were soon under way and going at a fair pace through the beautiful reaches of the river, between Bensington and Dorchester. It was now about the middle of the afternoon, warm rather than hot, and quite windless; the clouds high up and light, pearly white, and gleaming, softened the sun's burning, but did not hide the pale blue in most places, though they seemed to give it height and consistency; the sky, in short, looked really like a vault, as poets have sometimes called it, and not like mere limitless air, but a vault so vast and full of light that it did not in any way oppress the spirits. It was the sort of afternoon that Tennyson must have been thinking about, when he said of the Lotos-Eaters' land that it was a land where it was always afternoon.[1]

Ellen leaned back in the stern and seemed to enjoy herself thoroughly. I could see that she was really looking at things and let nothing escape her, and as I watched her, an uncomfortable feeling that she had been a little touched by love of the deft, ready, and handsome Dick, and that she had been constrained to follow us because of it, faded out of my mind; since if it had been so, she surely could not have been so excitedly pleased, even with the beautiful scenes we were passing through. For some time she did not say much, but at last, as we had passed under Shillingford Bridge (new built, but somewhat on its old lines[2]), she bade me hold the boat while she had a good look at the landscape through the graceful arch. Then she turned about to me and said:

"I do not know whether to be sorry or glad that this is the first time that I have been in these reaches. It is true that it is a great pleasure to see all this for the first time; but if I had had a year or two of memory of it, how sweetly it would all have mingled with my life, waking or dreaming! I am so glad Dick has been pulling slowly, so as to linger out the time here. How do you feel about your first visit to these waters?"

I do not suppose she meant a trap for me, but anyhow I fell into it, and said: "My first visit! It is not my first visit by many a time. I know these reaches well; indeed, I may say that I know every yard of the Thames from Hammersmith to Cricklade."

I saw the complications that might follow, as her eyes fixed mine with a curious look in them, that I had seen before at Runnymede, when I had said something which made it difficult for others to understand my present position amongst these people. I reddened, and said, in order to cover my mistake: "I wonder you have never been up so high as this, since you live on the Thames, and moreover row so well that it would be no great labour to you. Let alone," quoth I, insinuatingly, "that anybody would be glad to row you."

---

[1] "In the afternoon they came unto a land/In which it seemèd always afternoon" ("The Lotos-Eaters" [1832], ll. 3-4).

[2] Unlike all the bridges mentioned to this point in the story, Shillingford Bridge was admired by Morris. Built of stone, it was opened in 1829.

She laughed, clearly not at my compliment (as I am sure she need not have done, since it was a very commonplace fact), but at something which was stirring in her mind; and she still looked at me kindly, but with the above-said keen look in her eyes, and then she said:

"Well, perhaps it is strange, though I have a good deal to do at home, what with looking after my father, and dealing with two or three young men who have taken a special liking to me, and all of whom I cannot please at once. But you, dear neighbour; it seems to me stranger that you should know the upper river, than that I should not know it; for, as I understand, you have only been in England a few days. But perhaps you mean that you have read about it in books, and seen pictures of it?— though that does not come to much, either."

"Truly," said I. "Besides, I have not read any books about the Thames: it was one of the minor stupidities of our time that no one thought fit to write a decent book about what may fairly be called our only English river."

The words were no sooner out of my mouth than I saw that I had made another mistake; and I felt really annoyed with myself, as I did not want to go into a long explanation just then, or begin another series of Odyssean lies. Somehow, Ellen seemed to see this, and she took no advantage of my slip; her piercing look changed into one of mere frank kindness, and she said:

"Well, anyhow I am glad that I am travelling these waters with you, since you know our river so well, and I know little of it past Pangbourne, for you can tell me all I want to know about it." She paused a minute, and then said: "Yet you must understand that the part I do know, I know as thoroughly as you do. I should be sorry for you to think that I am careless of a thing so beautiful and interesting as the Thames."

She said this quite earnestly, and with an air of affectionate appeal to me which pleased me very much; but I could see that she was only keeping her doubts about me for another time.

Presently we came to Day's Lock, where Dick and his two sitters had waited for us. He would have me go ashore, as if to show me something which I had never seen before; and nothing loth I followed him, Ellen by my side, to the well-remembered

Dykes, and the long church beyond them, which was still used for various purposes by the good folk of Dorchester:[1] where, by the way, the village guest-house still had the sign of the Fleur-de-luce which it used to bear in the days when hospitality had to be bought and sold. This time, however, I made no sign of all this being familiar to me: though as we sat for a while on the mound of the Dykes looking up at Sinodun and its clear-cut trench, and its sister *mamelon*[2] of Whittenham, I felt somewhat uncomfortable under Ellen's serious attentive look, which almost drew from me the cry, "How little anything is changed here!"

We stopped again at Abingdon, which, like Wallingford, was in a way both old and new to me, since it had been lifted out of its nineteenth-century degradation, and otherwise was as little altered as might be.

Sunset was in the sky as we skirted Oxford by Oseney; we stopped a minute or two hard by the ancient castle to put Henry Morsom ashore. It was a matter of course that so far as they could be seen from the river, I missed none of the towers and spires of that once don-beridden city; but the meadows all round, which, when I had last passed through them, were getting daily more and more squalid, more and more impressed with the seal of the "stir and intellectual life of the nineteenth century," were no longer intellectual, but had once again become as beautiful as they should be, and the little hill of Hinksey, with two or three very pretty stone houses new-grown on it (I use the word advisedly; for they seemed to belong to it) looked down happily on the full streams and waving grass, grey now, but for the sunset, with its fast-ripening seeds.

The railway having disappeared, and therewith the various level bridges over the streams of Thames, we were soon through Medley Lock and in the wide water that washes Port Meadow, with its numerous population of geese nowise diminished; and I thought with interest how its name and use had survived from the older imperfect communal period, through the time of the

---

[1] The Abbey Church at Dorchester is primarily Norman in construction, with Gothic additions dating from the late thirteenth century.

[2] A small rounded hill.

confused struggle and tyranny of the rights of property, into the present rest and happiness of complete Communism.

I was taken ashore again at Godstow, to see the remains of the old nunnery, pretty nearly in the same condition as I had remembered them;[1] and from the high bridge over the cut close by, I could see, even in the twilight, how beautiful the little village with its grey stone houses had become; for we had now come into the stone-country, in which every house must be either built, walls and roof, of grey stone or be a blot on the landscape.

We still rowed on after this, Ellen taking the sculls in my boat; we passed a weir[2] a little higher up, and about three miles beyond it came by moonlight again to a little town, where we slept at a house thinly inhabited, as its folk were mostly tented in the hay-fields.

CHAPTER XXVIII

THE LITTLE RIVER

We started before six o'clock the next morning, as we were still twenty-five miles from our resting place, and Dick wanted to be there before dusk. The journey was pleasant, though to those who do not know the upper Thames, there is little to say about it. Ellen and I were once more together in her boat, though Dick, for fairness' sake, was for having me in his, and letting the two women scull the green toy. Ellen, however, would not allow this, but claimed me as the interesting person of the company. "After having come so far," said she, "I will not be put off with a companion who will be always thinking of somebody else than me: the guest is the only person who can amuse me properly. I mean that really," said she, turning to me, "and have not said it merely as a pretty saying."

---

[1]   The ruins of a twelfth-century nunnery stand in Godstow.
[2]   A weir is an enclosure of stakes set in a river to trap or keep fish.

Clara blushed and looked very happy at all thi.
to this time she had been rather frightened of Elle
felt young again, and strange hopes of my youth w
with the pleasure of the present; almost destroying it,
ening it into something like pain.

As we passed through the short and winding reach.
now quickly lessening stream, Ellen said: "How pleasant ι
river is to me, who am used to a great wide wash of w
almost seems as if we shall have to stop at every reach-ι
expect before I get home this evening I shall have realized ν
a little country England is, since we can so soon get to the ι
of its biggest river."

"It is not big," said I, "but it is pretty."

"Yes," she said, "and don't you find it difficult to imagine the
times when this little pretty country was treated by its folk as if it
had been an ugly characterless waste, with no delicate beauty to be
guarded, with no heed taken of the ever fresh pleasure of the recurring seasons, and changeful weather, and diverse quality of the soil,
and so forth? How could people be so cruel to themselves?"

"And to each other," said I. Then a sudden resolution took hold
of me, and I said: "Dear neighbour, I may as well tell you at once
that I find it easier to imagine all that ugly past than you do, because
I myself have been part of it. I see both that you have divined something of this in me; and also I think you will believe me when I tell
you of it, so that I am going to hide nothing from you at all."

She was silent a little, and then she said: "My friend, you have
guessed right about me; and to tell you the truth I have followed
you up from Runnymede in order that I might ask you many
questions, and because I saw that you were not one of us; and
that interested and pleased me, and I wanted to make you as
happy as you could be. To say the truth, there was a risk in it,"
said she, blushing—"I mean as to Dick and Clara; for I must tell
you, since we are going to be such close friends, that even
amongst us, where there are so many beautiful women, I have
often troubled men's minds disastrously. That is one reason why
I was living alone with my father in the cottage at Runnymede.
But it did not answer on that score; for of course people came
there, as the place is not a desert, and they seemed to find me all

the more interesting for living alone like that, and fell to making stories of me to themselves—like I know you did, my friend. Well, let that pass. This evening, or to-morrow morning, I shall make a proposal to you to do something which would please me very much, and I think would not hurt you."

I broke in eagerly, saying that I would do anything in the world for her; for indeed, in spite of my years and the too obvious signs of them (though that feeling of renewed youth was not a mere passing sensation, I think)—in spite of my years, I say, I felt altogether too happy in the company of this delightful girl, and was prepared to take her confidences for more than they meant perhaps.

She laughed now, but looked very kindly on me. "Well," she said, "meantime for the present we will let it be; for I must look at this new country that we are passing through. See how the river has changed character again: it is broad now, and the reaches are long and very slow-running. And look, there is a ferry!"

I told her the name of it, as I slowed off to put the ferry-chain over our heads; and on we went passing by a bank clad with oak trees on our left hand, till the stream narrowed again and deepened, and we rowed on between walls of tall reeds, whose population of reed sparrows and warblers were delightfully restless, twittering and chuckling as the wash of the boats stirred the reeds from the water upwards in the still, hot morning.

She smiled with pleasure, and her lazy enjoyment of the new scene seemed to bring out her beauty doubly as she leaned back amidst the cushions, though she was far from languid; her idleness being the idleness of a person, strong and well-knit both in body and mind, deliberately resting.

"Look!" she said, springing up suddenly from her place without any obvious effort, and balancing herself with exquisite grace and ease; "look at the beautiful old bridge ahead!"

"I need scarcely look at that," said I, not turning my head away from her beauty. "I know what it is; though" (with a smile) "we used not to call it the Old Bridge time agone."[1]

---

1   New Bridge, opened around 1250, was even in Morris's time the oldest bridge over the Thames.

She looked down upon me kindly, and said, "How well we get on now you are no longer on your guard against me!"

And she stood looking thoughtfully at me still, till she had to sit down as we passed under the middle one of the row of little pointed arches of the oldest bridge across the Thames.

"O the beautiful fields!" she said; "I had no idea of the charm of a very small river like this. The smallness of the scale of everything, the short reaches, and the speedy change of the banks, give one a feeling of going somewhere, of coming to something strange, a feeling of adventure which I have not felt in bigger waters."

I looked up at her delightedly; for her voice, saying the very thing which I was thinking, was like a caress to me. She caught my eye and her cheeks reddened under their tan, and she said simply:

"I must tell you, my friend, that when my father leaves the Thames this summer he will take me away to a place near the Roman wall[1] in Cumberland; so that this voyage of mine is farewell to the south; of course with my goodwill in a way; and yet I am sorry for it. I hadn't the heart to tell Dick yesterday that we were as good as gone from the Thames-side; but somehow to you I must needs tell it."

She stopped and seemed very thoughtful for awhile, and then said smiling:

"I must say that I don't like moving about from one home to another; one gets so pleasantly used to all the detail of the life about one; it fits so harmoniously and happily into one's own life, that beginning again, even in a small way, is a kind of pain. But I daresay in the country which you come from, you would think this petty and unadventurous, and would think the worse of me for it."

She smiled at me caressingly as she spoke, and I made haste to answer: "O, no, indeed; again you echo my very thoughts. But I hardly expected to hear you speak so. I gathered from all I have heard that there was a great deal of changing of abode amongst you in this country."

"Well," she said, "of course people are free to move about; but except for pleasure-parties, especially in harvest and hay-time,

---

[1]   The seventy-mile-long stone wall built in the second century under the Roman Emperor Hadrian.

like this of ours, I don't think they do so much. I admit that I also have other moods than that of stay-at-home, as I hinted just now, and I should like to go with you all through the west-country—thinking of nothing," concluded she smiling.

"I should have plenty to think of," said I.

CHAPTER XXIX

A RESTING-PLACE ON THE UPPER THAMES

Presently at a place where the river flowed round a headland of the meadows, we stopped a while for rest and victuals, and settled ourselves on a beautiful bank which almost reached the dignity of a hill-side: the wide meadows spread before us, and already the scythe was busy amidst the hay. One change I noticed amidst the quiet beauty of the fields—to wit, that they were planted with trees here and there, often fruit-trees, and that there was none of the niggardly begrudging of space to a handsome tree which I remembered too well; and though the willows were often polled (or shrowded, as they call it in that country-side), this was done with some regard to beauty: I mean that there was no polling of rows on rows so as to destroy the pleasantness of half a mile of country, but a thoughtful sequence in the cutting, that prevented a sudden bareness anywhere. To be short, the fields were everywhere treated as a garden made for the pleasure as well as the livelihood of all, as old Hammond told me was the case.

On this bank or bent of the hill, then, we had our mid-day meal; somewhat early for dinner, if that mattered, but we had been stirring early: the slender stream of the Thames winding below us between the garden of a country I have been telling of; a furlong from us was a beautiful little islet begrown with graceful trees; on the slopes westward of us was a wood of varied growth overhanging the narrow meadow on the south side of the river; while to the north was a wide stretch of mead rising very gradually from the river's edge. A delicate spire of an ancient building rose up from out of the trees in the middle distance, with a few grey houses clustered about it; while nearer to us, in fact not half a furlong from the water, was a quite modern stone house—a wide quadrangle of one story, the buildings that made it being quite low. There was no garden between it and the river, nothing but a row of pear-trees still quite young and slender; and though there did not seem to be much ornament about it, it had a sort of natural elegance, like that of the trees themselves.

As we sat looking down on all this in the sweet June day, rather happy than merry, Ellen, who sat next me, her hand clasped about one knee, leaned sideways to me, and said in a low voice which Dick and Clara might have noted if they had not been busy in happy wordless love-making: "Friend, in your country were the houses of your field-labourers anything like that?"

I said: "Well, at any rate the houses of our rich men were not; they were mere blots upon the face of the land."

"I find that hard to understand," she said. "I can see why the workmen, who were so oppressed, should not have been able to live in beautiful houses; for it takes time and leisure, and minds not over-burdened with care, to make beautiful dwellings; and I quite understand that these poor people were not allowed to live in such a way as to have these (to us) necessary good things. But why the rich men, who had the time and the leisure and the materials for building, as it would be in this case, should not have housed themselves well, I do not understand as yet. I know what you are meaning to say to me," she said, looking me full in the eyes and blushing, "to wit that their houses and all belonging to them were generally ugly and base, unless they chanced to be ancient like yonder remnant of our forefathers' work" (pointing to the spire); "that they were—let me see; what is the word?"

"Vulgar," said I. "We used to say," said I, "that the ugliness and vulgarity of the rich men's dwellings was a necessary reflection from the sordidness and bareness of life which they forced upon the poor people."

She knit her brows as in thought; then turned a brightened face on me, as if she had caught the idea, and said: "Yes, friend, I see what you mean. We have sometimes—those of us who look into these things—talked this very matter over; because, to say the truth, we have plenty of record of the so-called arts of the time before Equality of Life; and there are not wanting people who say that the state of that society was not the cause of all that ugliness; that they were ugly in their life because they liked to be, and could have had beautiful things about them if they had chosen; just as a man or body of men now may, if they please, make things more or less beautiful—Stop! I know what you are going to say."

"Do you?" said I, smiling, yet with a beating heart.

"Yes," she said; "you are answering me, teaching me, in some way or another, although you have not spoken the words aloud. You were going to say that in times of inequality it was an essential condition of the life of these rich men that they should not themselves make what they wanted for the adornment of their lives, but should force those to make them whom they forced to live pinched and sordid lives; and that as a necessary consequence the sordidness and pinching, the ugly barrenness of those ruined lives, were worked up into the adornment of the lives of the rich, and art died out amongst men? Was that what you would say, my friend?"

"Yes, yes," I said, looking at her eagerly; for she had risen and was standing on the edge of the bent, the light wind stirring her dainty raiment, one hand laid on her bosom, the other arm stretched downward and clenched in her earnestness.

"It is true," she said, "it is true! We have proved it true!"

I think amidst my—something more than interest in her, and admiration for her, I was beginning to wonder how it would all end. I had a glimmering of fear of what might follow; of anxiety as to the remedy which this new age might offer for the missing of something one might set one's heart on. But now Dick rose to his feet and cried out in his hearty manner: "Neighbour Ellen, are you quarrelling with the guest, or are you worrying him to tell you things which he cannot properly explain to our ignorance?"

"Neither, dear neighbour," she said. "I was so far from quarrelling with him that I think I have been making him good friends both with himself and me. Is it so, dear guest?" she said, looking down at me with a delightful smile of confidence in being understood.

"Indeed it is," said I.

"Well, moreover," she said, "I must say for him that he has explained himself to me very well indeed, so that I quite understand him."

"All right," quoth Dick. "When I first set eyes on you at Runnymede I knew that there was something wonderful in your keenness of wits. I don't say that as a mere pretty speech to please you," said he quickly, "but because it is true; and it made me want to see more of you. But, come, we ought to be going; for we are not half way, and we ought to be in well before sunset."

And therewith he took Clara's hand, and led her down the bent. But Ellen stood thoughtfully looking down for a little, and as I took her hand to follow Dick, she turned round to me and said:

"You might tell me a great deal and make many things clear to me, if you would."

"Yes," said I, "I am pretty well fit for that,—and for nothing else—an old man like me."

She did not notice the bitterness which, whether I liked it or not, was in my voice as I spoke, but went on: "It is not so much for myself; I should be quite content to dream about past times, and if I could not idealize them, yet at least idealize some of the people who lived in them. But I think sometimes people are too careless of the history of the past—too apt to leave it in the hands of old learned men like Hammond. Who knows? happy as we are, times may alter; we may be bitten with some impulse towards change, and many things may seem too wonderful for us to resist, too exciting not to catch at, if we do not know that they are but phases of what has been before; and withal ruinous, deceitful, and sordid."

As we went slowly down toward the boats she said again: "Not for myself alone, dear friend; I shall have children; perhaps before the end a good many;—I hope so. And though of course I cannot force any special kind of knowledge upon them, yet, my friend, I cannot help thinking that just as they might be like me in body, so I might impress upon them some part of my ways of thinking; that is, indeed, some of the essential part of myself; that part which was not mere moods, created by the matters and events round about me. What do you think?"

Of one thing I was sure, that her beauty and kindness and eagerness combined, forced me to think as she did, when she was not earnestly laying herself open to receive my thoughts. I said, what at the time was true, that I thought it most important; and presently stood entranced by the wonder of her grace as she stepped into the light boat, and held out her hand to me. And so on we went up the Thames still—or whither?

CHAPTER XXX

THE JOURNEY'S END

On we went. In spite of my new-born excitement about Ellen, and my gathering fear of where it would land me, I could not help taking abundant interest in the condition of the river and its banks; all the more as she never seemed weary of the changing picture, but looked at every yard of flowery bank and gurgling eddy with the same kind of affectionate interest which I myself once had so fully, as I used to think, and perhaps had not altogether lost even in this strangely changed society with all its wonders. Ellen seemed delighted with my pleasure at this, that, or the other piece of carefulness in dealing with the river: the nursing of pretty corners; the ingenuity in dealing with difficulties of water-engineering, so that the most obviously useful works looked beautiful and natural also. All this, I say, pleased me hugely, and she was pleased at my pleasure—but rather puzzled too.

"You seem astonished," she said, just after we had passed a mill[1] which spanned all the stream save the water-way for traffic, but which was as beautiful in its way as a Gothic cathedral—"You seem astonished at this being so pleasant to look at."

---

[1] [Morris's note]: I should have said that all along the Thames there were abundance of mills used for various purposes; none of which were in my degree unsightly, and many strikingly beautiful and the gardens about them marvels of loveliness.

"Yes," I said, "in a way I am; though I don't see why it should not be."

"Ah!" she said, looking at me admiringly, yet with a lurking smile in her face, "you know all about the history of the past. Were they not always careful about this little stream which now adds so much pleasantness to the country side? It would always be easy to manage this little river. Ah! I forgot, though," she said, as her eye caught mine, "in the days we are thinking of pleasure was wholly neglected in such matters. But how did they manage the river in the days that you—" Lived in she was going to say; but correcting herself, said—"in the days of which you have record?"

"They *mis*managed it," quoth I. "Up to the first half of the nineteenth century, when it was still more or less of a highway for the country people, some care was taken of the river and its banks; and though I don't suppose anyone troubled himself about its aspect, yet it was trim and beautiful. But when the railways—of which no doubt you have heard—came into power, they would not allow the people of the country to use either the natural or artificial waterways, of which latter there were a great many. I suppose when we get higher up we shall see one of these; a very important one, which one of these rail-ways entirely closed to the public so that they might force people to send their goods by their private road, and so tax them as heavily as they could."[1]

Ellen laughed heartily. "Well," she said, "that is not stated clearly enough in our history-books, and it is worth knowing. But certainly the people of those days must have been a curiously lazy set. We are not either fidgety or quarrelsome now, but if any one tried such a piece of folly on us, we should use the said water-ways, whoever gainsaid us: surely that would be simple enough. However, I remember other cases of this stupidity: when I was on the Rhine two years ago, I remember they showed us ruins of old castles, which, according to what we heard, must have been made

---

[1] Guest is probably referring to the fate of the Thames and Severn canal. Once a primary route for barge traffic, the canal fell into disuse with the coming of the railways. During the time Morris was writing *News from Nowhere* the Great Western Railway was attempting to purchase the canal in order to close it, which is what happened in 1893.

for pretty much the same purpose as the railways were. But I am interrupting your history of the river: pray go on."

"It is both short and stupid enough," said I. "The river having lost its practical or commercial value—that is, being of no use to make money of—"

She nodded. "I understand what that queer phrase means," said she. "Go on!"

"Well, it was utterly neglected, till at last it became a nuisance—"

"Yes," quoth Ellen, "I understand: like the railways and the robber knights. Yes?"

"So then they turned the makeshift business on to it, and handed it over to a body up in London,[1] who from time to time, in order to show that they had something to do, did some damage here and there,—cut down trees, destroying the banks thereby; dredged the river (where it was not needed always), and threw the dredgings on the fields so as to spoil them; and so forth. But for the most part they practised 'masterly inactivity,' as it was then called—that is, they drew their salaries, and let things alone."

"Drew their salaries," she said. "I know that means that they were allowed to take an extra lot of other people's goods for doing nothing. And if that had been all, it really might have been worth while to let them do so, if you couldn't find any other way of keeping them quiet; but it seems to me that being so paid, they could not help doing something, and that something was bound to be mischief,—because," said she, kindling with sudden anger, "the whole business was founded on lies and false pretensions. I don't mean only these river-guardians, but all these master-people I have read of."

"Yes," said I, "how happy you are to have got out of the parsimony of oppression!"

"Why do you sigh?" she said, kindly and somewhat anxiously. "You seem to think that it will not last?"

"It will last for you," quoth I.

"But why not for you?" said she. "Surely it is for all the world; and if your country is somewhat backward, it will come into line

---

[1] The Thames Conservancy Authority, established in 1866.

before long. Or," she said quickly, "are you thinking that you must soon go back again? I will make my proposal which I told you of at once, and so perhaps put an end to your anxiety. I was going to propose that you should live with us where we are going. I feel quite old friends with you, and should be sorry to lose you." Then she smiled on me, and said: "Do you know, I begin to suspect you of wanting to nurse a sham sorrow, like the ridiculous characters in some of those queer old novels that I have come across now and then."

I really had almost begun to suspect it myself, but I refused to admit so much; so I sighed no more, but fell to giving my delightful companion what little pieces of history I knew about the river and its borderlands; and the time passed pleasantly enough; and between the two of us (she was a better sculler than I was, and seemed quite tireless) we kept up fairly well with Dick, hot as the afternoon was, and swallowed up the way at a great rate. At last we passed under another ancient bridge;[1] and through meadows bordered at first with huge elm-trees mingled with sweet chestnut of younger but very elegant growth; and the meadows widened out so much that it seemed as if the trees must now be on the bents only, or about the houses, except for the growth of willows on the immediate banks; so that the wide stretch of grass was little broken here. Dick got very much excited now, and often stood up in the boat to cry out to us that this was such and such a field, and so forth; and we caught fire at his enthusiasm for the hayfield and its harvest, and pulled our best.

At last as we were passing through a reach of the river where on the side of the towing-path was a highish bank with a thick whispering bed of reeds before it, and on the other side a higher bank, clothed with willows that dipped into the stream and crowned by ancient elm-trees, we saw bright figures coming along close to the bank, as if they were looking for something; as, indeed, they were, and we—that is, Dick and his company— were what they were looking for. Dick lay on his oars, and we followed his example. He gave a joyous shout to the people on the bank, which was echoed back from it in many voices, deep

---

[1] Radcot Bridge, which like New Bridge dates from the thirteenth century.

and sweetly shrill; for there were above a dozen persons, both men, women, and children. A tall handsome woman, with black wavy hair and deep-set grey eyes, came forward on the bank and waved her hand gracefully to us, and said:

"Dick, my friend, we have almost had to wait for you! What excuse have you to make for your slavish punctuality? Why didn't you take us by surprise, and come yesterday?"

"O," said Dick, with an almost imperceptible jerk of his head toward our boat, "we didn't want to come too quick up the water; there is so much to see for those who have not been up here before."

"True, true," said the stately lady, for stately is the word that must be used for her; "and we want them to get to know the wet way from the east thoroughly well, since they must often use it now. But come ashore at once, Dick, and you, dear neighbours; there is a break in the reeds and a good landing-place just round the corner. We can carry up your things, or send some of the lads after them."

"No, no," said Dick; "it is easier going by water, though it is but a step. Besides, I want to bring my friend here to the proper place. We will go on to the Ford; and you can talk to us from the bank as we paddle along."

He pulled his sculls through the water, and on we went, turning a sharp angle and going north a little. Presently we saw before us a bank of elm-trees, which told us of a house amidst them, though I looked in vain for the grey walls that I expected to see there. As we went, the folk on the bank talked indeed, mingling their kind voices with the cuckoo's song, the sweet strong whistle of the blackbirds, and the ceaseless note of the corn-crake as he crept through the long grass of the mowing-field; whence came waves of fragrance from the flowering clover amidst of the ripe grass.

In a few minutes we had passed through a deep eddying pool into the sharp stream that ran from the ford, and beached our craft on a tiny strand of limestone-gravel, and stepped ashore into the arms of our up-river friends, our journey done.

I disentangled myself from the merry throng, and mounting on the cart-road that ran along the river some feet above the water, I looked round about me. The river came down through a wide meadow on my left, which was grey now with the ripened seeding grasses; the gleaming water was lost presently by a turn of the bank, but over the meadow I could see the mingled gables of a building where I knew the lock must be, and which now seemed to combine a mill with it. A low wooded ridge bounded the river-plain to the south and south-east, whence we had come, and a few low houses lay about its feet and up its slope. I turned a little to my right, and through the hawthorn sprays and long shoots of the wild roses could see the flat country spreading out far away under the sun of the calm evening, till something that might be called hills with a look of sheep-pastures about them bounded it with a soft blue line. Before me, the elm-boughs still hid most of what houses there might be in this river-side dwelling of men; but to the right of the cart-road a few grey buildings of the simplest kind showed here and there.

There I stood in a dreamy mood, and rubbed my eyes as if I were not wholly awake, and half expected to see the gay-clad company of beautiful men and women change to two or three spindle-legged backbowed men and haggard, hollow-eyed, ill-favoured women, who once wore down the soil of this land with their heavy hopeless feet, from day to day, and season to season, and year to year. But no change came as yet, and my heart swelled with joy as I thought of all the beautiful grey villages, from the river to the plain and the plain to the uplands, which I could picture to myself so well, all peopled now with this happy and lovely folk, who had cast away riches and attained to wealth.

CHAPTER XXXI

AN OLD HOUSE AMONGST NEW FOLK

As I stood there Ellen detached herself from our happy friends who still stood on the little strand and came up to me. She took me by the hand, and said softly, "Take me on to the house; we need not wait for the others: I had rather not."

I had a mind to say that I did not know the way thither, and that the river-side dwellers should lead; but almost without my will my feet moved on along the road they knew. The raised way led us into a little field bounded by a backwater of the river on one side; on the right hand we could see a cluster of small houses and barns, new and old, and before us a grey stone barn and a wall partly overgrown with ivy, over which a few grey gables showed. The village road ended in the shallow of the aforesaid backwater. We crossed the road, and again almost without my will my hand raised the latch of a door in the wall, and we stood presently on a stone path which led up to the old house to which fate in the shape of Dick had so strangely brought me in this new world of men.[1] My companion gave a sigh of pleased surprise and enjoyment; nor did I wonder, for the garden between the wall and the house was redolent of the June flowers, and the roses were rolling over one another with that delicious superabundance of small well-tended gardens which at first sight takes away all thought from the beholder save that of beauty. The blackbirds were singing their loudest, the doves were cooing on the roof-ridge, the rooks in the high elm-trees beyond were garrulous among the young leaves, and the swifts wheeled whining about the gables. And the house itself was a fit guardian for all the beauty of this heart of summer.

Once again Ellen echoed my thoughts as she said: "Yes, friend, this is what I came out for to see; this many-gabled old house built by the simple country-folk of the long-past times, regardless of all the turmoil that was going on in cities and courts, is lovely still amidst all the beauty which these latter days have created; and I do not wonder at our friends tending it carefully and making much of it. It seems to me as if it had waited for these happy days, and held in it the gathered crumbs of happiness of the confused and turbulent past."

She led me up close to the house, and laid her shapely sun-browned hand and arm on the lichened wall as if to embrace it,

---

[1]   Kelmscott Manor, in which Morris held a joint tenancy from 1871 until his death. The house dates from the later sixteenth century, with numerous additions and alterations over the succeeding centuries.

and cried out, "O me! O me! How I love the earth, and the seasons, and weather, and all things that deal with it, and all that grows out of it,—as this has done!"

I could not answer her, or say a word. Her exultation and pleasure were so keen and exquisite, and her beauty, so delicate, yet so interfused with energy, expressed it so fully, that any added word would have been commonplace and futile. I dreaded lest the others should come in suddenly and break the spell she had cast about me; but we stood there a while by the corner of the big gable of the house, and no one came. I heard the merry voices some way off presently, and knew that they were going along the river to the great meadow on the other side of the house and garden.

We drew back a little, and looked up at the house: the door and the windows were open to the fragrant sun-cured air; from the upper window-sills hung festoons of flowers in honour of the festival, as if the others shared in the love for the old house.

"Come in," said Ellen. "I hope nothing will spoil it inside; but I don't think it will. Come! we must go back presently to the others. They have gone on to the tents; for surely they must have tents pitched for the haymakers—the house would not hold a tithe of the folk, I am sure."

She led me on to the door, murmuring a little above her breath as she did so, "The earth and the growth of it and the life of it! If I could but say or show how I love it!"

We went in, and found no soul in any room as we wandered from room to room,—from the rose-covered porch to the strange and quaint garrets amongst the great timbers of the roof, where of old time the tillers and herdsmen of the manor slept, but which a-nights seemed now, by the small size of the beds, and the litter of useless and disregarded matters—bunches of dying flowers, feathers of birds, shells of starling's eggs, caddis worms in mugs, and the like—seemed to be inhabited for the time by children.

Everywhere there was but little furniture, and that only the most necessary, and of the simplest forms. The extravagant love of ornament which I had noted in this people elsewhere seemed here to have given place to the feeling that the house itself and its associations was the ornament of the country life amidst which it had been left stranded from old times, and that to re-ornament it would but take away its use as a piece of natural beauty.

We sat down at last in a room over the wall which Ellen had caressed, and which was still hung with old tapestry, originally of no artistic value, but now faded into pleasant grey tones which harmonized thoroughly well with the quiet of the place, and which would have been ill supplanted by brighter and more striking decoration.

I asked a few random questions of Ellen as we sat there, but scarcely listened to her answers, and presently became silent, and then scarce conscious of anything, but that I was there in that old room, the doves crooning from the roofs of the barn and dove-cote beyond the window opposite to me.

My thought returned to me after what I think was but a minute or two, but which, as in a vivid dream, seemed as if it had lasted a long time, when I saw Ellen sitting, looking all the fuller of life and pleasure and desire from the contrast with the grey faded tapestry with its futile design, which was now only bearable because it had grown so faint and feeble.

She looked at me kindly, but as if she read me through and through. She said: "You have begun again your never-ending contrast between the past and this present. Is it not so?"

"True," said I. "I was thinking of what you, with your capacity and intelligence, joined to your love of pleasure, and your impatience of unreasonable restraint—of what you would have been in that past. And even now, when all is won and has been for a long time, my heart is sickened with thinking of all the waste of life that has gone on for so many years."

"So many centuries," she said, "so many ages!"

"True," I said; "too true," and sat silent again.

She rose up and said: "Come, I must not let you go off into a dream again so soon. If we must lose you, I want you to see all that you can see first before you go back again."

"Lose me?" I said—"go back again? Am I not to go up to the North with you? What do you mean?"

She smiled somewhat sadly, and said: "Not yet; we will not talk of that yet. Only, what were you thinking of just now?"

I said falteringly: "I was saying to myself, The past, the present?

Should she not have said the contrast of the present with the future: of blind despair with hope?"

"I knew it," she said. Then she caught my hand and said excitedly, "Come, while there is yet time! Come!" And she led me out of the room; and as we were going downstairs and out of the house into the garden by a little side door which opened out of a curious lobby, she said in a calm voice, as if she wished me to forget her sudden nervousness: "Come! we ought to join the others before they come here looking for us. And let me tell you, my friend, that I can see you are too apt to fall into mere dreamy musing: no doubt because you are not yet used to our life of repose amidst energy; of work which is pleasure and pleasure which is work."

She paused a little, and as we came out into the lovely garden again, she said: "My friend, you were saying that you wondered what I should have been if I had lived in those past days of turmoil and oppression. Well, I think I have studied the history of them to know pretty well. I should have been one of the poor, for my father when he was working was a mere tiller of the soil. Well, I could not have borne that; therefore my beauty and cleverness and brightness" (she spoke with no blush or simper of false shame) "would have been sold to rich men, and my life would have been wasted indeed; for I know enough of that to know that I should have had no choice, no power of will over my life; and that I should never have bought pleasure from the rich men, or even opportunity of action, whereby I might have won some true excitement. I should have been wrecked and wasted in one way or another, either by penury or by luxury. Is it not so?"

"Indeed it is," said I.

She was going to say something else, when a little gate in the fence, which led into a small elm-shaded field, was opened, and Dick came with hasty cheerfulness up the garden path, and was presently standing between us, a hand laid on the shoulder of each. He said: "Well, neighbours, I thought you two would like to see the old house quietly without a crowd in it. Isn't it a jewel of a house after its kind? Well, come along, for it is getting towards dinner-time. Perhaps you, guest, would like a swim before we sit down to what I fancy will be a pretty long feast?"

"Yes," I said, "I should like that."

"Well, good-bye for the present, neighbour Ellen," said Dick. "Here comes Clara to take care of you, as I fancy she is more at home amongst our friends here."

Clara came out of the fields as he spoke; and with one look at Ellen I turned and went with Dick, doubting, if I must say the truth, whether I should see her again.

CHAPTER XXXII

THE FEAST'S BEGINNING—THE END

Dick brought me at once into the little field which, as I had seen from the garden, was covered with gaily-coloured tents arranged in orderly lanes, about which were sitting and lying on the grass some fifty or sixty men, women, and children, all of them in the height of good temper and enjoyment—with their holiday mood on, so to say.

"You are thinking that we don't make a great show as to numbers," said Dick; "but you must remember that we shall have more to-morrow; because in this haymaking work there is room for a great many people who are not over-skilled in country matters: and there are many who lead sedentary lives, whom it would be unkind to deprive of their pleasure in the hayfield—scientific men and close students generally: so that the skilled workmen, outside those who are wanted as mowers, and foremen of the haymaking, stand aside, and take a little downright rest, which you know is good for them, whether they like it or not: or else they go to other countrysides, as I am doing here. You see, the scientific men and historians, and students generally, will not be wanted till we are fairly in the midst of the tedding,[1] which of course will not be till the day after to-morrow." With that he brought me out of the little field on to a kind of causeway above

---

[1] Spreading newly-mown grass in the sun to be dried.

the riverside meadow, and thence turning to the left on to a path through the mowing grass, which was thick and very tall, led on till we came to the river above the weir and its mill. There we had a delightful swim in the broad piece of water above the lock, where the river looked much bigger than its natural size from its being dammed up by the weir.

"Now we are in a fit mood for dinner," said Dick, when we had dressed and were going through the grass again; "and certainly of all the cheerful meals in the year, this one of haysel[1] is the cheerfullest, not even excepting the corn-harvest feast; for then the year is beginning to fail, and one cannot help having a feeling behind all the gaiety, of the coming of the dark days, and the shorn fields and empty gardens; and the spring is almost too far off to look forward to. It is, then, in the autumn, when one almost believes in death."

"How strangely you talk," said I, "of such a constantly recurring and consequently commonplace matter as the sequence of the seasons." And indeed these people were like children about such things, and had what seemed to me a quite exaggerated interest in the weather, a fine day, a dark night, or a brilliant one, and the like.

"Strangely?" said he. "Is it strange to sympathize with the year and its gains and losses?"

"At any rate," said I, "if you look upon the course of the year as a beautiful and interesting drama, which is what I think you do, you should be as much pleased and interested with the winter and its trouble and pain as with this wonderful summer luxury."

"And am I not?" said Dick, rather warmly; "only I can't look upon it as if I were sitting in a theatre seeing the play going on before me, myself taking no part of it. It is difficult," said he, smiling good-humouredly, "for a non-literary man like me to explain myself properly, like that dear girl Ellen would; but I mean that I am part of it all, and feel the pain as well as the pleasure in my own person. It is not done for me by somebody else, merely that I may eat and drink and sleep; but I myself do my share of it."

In his way also, as Ellen in hers, I could see that Dick had that passionate love of the earth which was common to but few people,

---

[1]   Hay season.

at least, in the days I knew; in which the prevailing feeling amongst intellectual persons was a kind of sour distaste for the changing drama of the year, for the life of earth and its dealings with men. Indeed, in those days it was thought poetic and imaginative to look upon life as a thing to be borne, rather than enjoyed.

So I mused till Dick's laugh brought me back into the Oxfordshire hayfields. "One thing seems strange to me," said he—"that I must needs trouble myself about the winter and its scantiness, in the midst of the summer abundance. If it hadn't happened to me before, I should have thought it was your doing, guest; that you had thrown a kind of evil charm over me. Now, you know," said he, suddenly, "that's only a joke, so you mustn't take it to heart."

"All right," said I; "I don't." Yet I did feel somewhat uneasy at his words, after all.

We crossed the causeway this time, and did not turn back to the house, but went along a path beside a field of wheat now almost ready to blossom. I said: "We do not dine in the house or garden, then?—as indeed I did not expect to do. Where do we meet, then? for I can see that the houses are mostly very small."

"Yes," said Dick, "you are right, they are small in this country-side: there are so many good old houses left, that people dwell a good deal in such small detached houses. As to our dinner, we are going to have our feast in the church. I wish, for your sake, it were as big and handsome as that of the old Roman town to the west, or the forest town to the north;[1] but, however, it will hold us all; and though it is a little thing, it is beautiful in its way."

This was somewhat new to me, this dinner in a church, and I thought of the church-ales[2] of the Middle Ages; but I said nothing, and presently we came out into the road which ran through the village. Dick looked up and down it, and seeing only two straggling groups before us, said: "It seems as if we must be somewhat late; they are all gone on; and they will be sure to make a point of waiting for you, as the guest of guests, since you come from so far."

He hastened as he spoke, and I kept up with him, and

---

[1] [Morris's note]: Cirencester and Burford he must have meant.
[2] A festive gathering held in a church, not necessarily associated with a liturgical feast-day.

presently we came to a little avenue of lime-trees which led us straight to the church porch, from whose open door came the sound of cheerful voices and laughter, and varied merriment.

"Yes," said Dick, "it's the coolest place for one thing, this hot evening. Come along; they will be glad to see you."

Indeed, in spite of my bath, I felt the weather more sultry and oppressive than on any day of our journey yet.

We went into the church, which was a simple little building with one little aisle divided from the nave by three round arches, a chancel, and a rather roomy transept for so small a building, the windows mostly of the graceful Oxfordshire fourteenth century type. There was no modern architectural decoration in it; it looked, indeed, as if none had been attempted since the Puritans whitewashed the medieval saints and histories on the wall. It was, however, gaily dressed up for this latter-day festival, with festoons of flowers from arch to arch, and great pitchers of flowers standing about on the floor; while under the west window hung two cross scythes, their blades polished white, and gleaming from out of the flowers that wreathed them. But its best ornament was the crowd of handsome, happy-looking men and women that were set down to table, and who, with their bright faces and rich hair over their gay holiday raiment, looked, as the Persian poet puts it, like a bed of tulips in the sun.[1] Though the church was a small one, there was plenty of room; for a small church makes a biggish house; and on this evening there was no need to set cross tables along the transepts; though doubtless these would be wanted next day, when the learned men of whom Dick has been speaking should be come to take their more humble part in the haymaking.

I stood on the threshold with the expectant smile on my face of a man who is going to take part in a festivity which he is really prepared to enjoy. Dick, standing by me, was looking round the company with an air of proprietorship in them, I thought. Opposite me sat Clara and Ellen, with Dick's place open

[1] An allusion to the *Shahnameh*, an eleventh-century epic poem of some 60,000 couplets. A portion of verse 387 describes a bridal procession in which the row of escorts looks as if "heaven has planted tulips in the earth." Morris, who read the poem in 1883 in a French translation, for a time considered producing his own English translation. (See *Collected Works*, 17:xxii-iii.)

between them: they were smiling, but their beautiful faces were each turned towards the neighbours on either side, who were talking to them, and they did not seem to see me. I turned to Dick, expecting him to lead me forward, and he turned his face to me; but strange to say, though it was as smiling and cheerful as ever, it made no response to my glance—nay, he seemed to take no heed at all of my presence, and I noticed that none of the company looked at me. A pang shot through me, as of some disaster long expected and suddenly realized. Dick moved on a little without a word to me. I was not three yards from the two women who, though they had been my companions for such a short time, had really, as I thought, become my friends. Clara's face was turned full upon me now, but she also did not seem to see me, though I know I was trying to catch her eye with an appealing look. I turned to Ellen, and she *did* seem to recognize me for an instant; but her bright face turned sad directly, and she shook her head with a mournful look, and the next moment all consciousness of my presence had faded from her face.

I felt lonely and sick at heart past the power of words to describe. I hung about a minute longer, and then turned and went out of the porch again and through the lime-avenue into the road, while the blackbirds sang their strongest from the bushes about me in the hot June evening.

Once more without any conscious effort of will I set my face toward the old house by the ford, but as I turned round the corner which led to the remains of the village cross, I came upon a figure strangely contrasting with the joyous, beautiful people I had left behind in the church. It was a man who looked old, but whom I knew from habit, now half forgotten, was really not much more than fifty. His face was rugged, and grimed rather than dirty; his eyes dull and bleared; his body bent, his calves thin and spindly, his feet dragging and limping. His clothing was a mixture of dirt and rags long over-familiar to me. As I passed him he touched his hat with some real good-will and courtesy, and much servility.

Inexpressibly shocked, I hurried past him and hastened along the road that led to the river and the lower end of the village; but suddenly I saw as it were a black cloud rolling along to meet me, like a nightmare of my childish days; and for a while I was conscious of nothing else than being in the dark, and whether I was walking, or sitting, or lying down, I could not tell.

★   ★   ★   ★   ★   ★

I lay in my bed in my house at dingy Hammersmith thinking about it all; and trying to consider if I was overwhelmed with despair at finding I had been dreaming a dream; and strange to say, I found that I was not so despairing.

Or indeed *was* it a dream? If so, why was I so conscious all along that I was really seeing all that new life from the outside, still wrapped up in the prejudices, the anxieties, the distrust of this time of doubt and struggle?

All along, though those friends were so real to me, I had been feeling as if I had no business amongst them: as though the time would come when they would reject me, and say, as Ellen's last mournful look seemed to say, "No, it will not do; you cannot be of us; you belong so entirely to the unhappiness of the past that our happiness even would weary you. Go back again, now you have seen us, and your outward eyes have learned that in spite of all the infallible maxims of your day there is yet a time of rest in store for the world, when mastery has changed into fellowship—but not before. Go back again, then, and while you live you will see all round you people engaged in making others live lives which are not their own, while they themselves care nothing for their own real lives—men who hate life though they fear death. Go back and be the happier for having seen us, for having added a little hope to your struggle. Go on living while you may, striving, with whatsoever pain and labour needs must be, to build up little by little the new day of fellowship, and rest, and happiness."

Yes, surely! and if others can see it as I have seen it, then it may be called a vision rather than a dream.

THE END

KELMSCOTT MANOR, OXFORDSHIRE.
East Front.
Summer home of William Morris.

Appendix A: Morris on the Platform

[*"Our immediate aim should be chiefly educational,"* Morris wrote of the socialist movement in 1884, "to teach ourselves and others what the due social claims of labour are, and how they can be advanced and sustained.... In short, to make Socialists however slowly for the permeation of the society in which we live" *(Letters,* 2:364). To that end Morris travelled widely and spoke often on behalf of socialist organizations. During the peak years of his involvement, 1884-1889, he delivered over 450 public lectures. In this section are gathered substantial excerpts from three representative lectures.]

1. From "Art and Socialism" (1884)

[Morris first delivered this address in January 1884 to the Secular Society of Leicester. It was published as a separate pamphlet later that year.]

My friends, I want you to look into the relation of Art to Commerce, using the latter word to express what is generally meant by it; namely, that system of competition in the market which is indeed the only form which most people now-a-days suppose that Commerce can take. Now whereas there have been times in the world's history when Art held the supremacy over Commerce; when Art was a good deal, and Commerce, as we understand the word, was a very little; so now on the contrary it will be admitted by all, I fancy, that Commerce has become of very great importance and Art of very little. I say this will be generally admitted, but different persons will hold very different opinions not only as to whether this is well or ill, but even as to what it really means when we say that Commerce has become of supreme importance and that Art has sunk into an unimportant matter.

Allow me to give you my opinion of the meaning of it: which will lead me on to ask you to consider what remedies should be applied for curing the evils that exist in the relations between Art and Commerce. Now to speak plainly it seems to me that the supremacy of Commerce (as we understand the word) is an evil, and a very serious one; and I should call it an unmixed evil, but for the strange continuity of life which runs through all historical events, and by means of which the very evils of such and such a period tend to abolish themselves. For to my mind it means this: that the world of modern civilization in its haste to gain a very inequitably divided material prosperity has entirely suppressed popular Art; or in other words that the greater part of the people have no share in Art, which as things now are must be kept in the hands of a few rich or well-to-do people, who we may fairly say need it less and not more than the laborious workers. Nor is that all the evil, nor the worst of it; for the cause of this famine of Art is that whilst people work throughout the civilized world as laboriously as ever they did, they have lost, in losing an Art which was done by and for the people, the natural solace of that labour; a solace which they once had, and always should have, the opportunity of express-ing their own thoughts to their fellows by means of that very labour, by means of that daily work which nature or long custom, a second nature, does indeed require of them, but without meaning that it should be an unrewarded and repulsive burden. But, through a strange blindness and error in the civilization of these latter days, the world's work, almost all of it, the work some share of which should have been the helpful companion of every man, has become even such a burden, which every man, if he could, would shake off. I have said that people work no less laboriously than they ever did; but I should have said that they work more laboriously. The wonderful machines which in the hands of just and foreseeing men would have been used to minimize repulsive labour and to give pleasure, or in other words added life, to the human race, have been so used on the contrary that they have driven all men into mere frantic haste and hurry, thereby destroying pleasure, that is life, on all hands: they have, instead of lightening the labour of the work-men, intensified it, and thereby added more weariness yet to the burden which the poor have to carry. Nor can it be pleaded for the system of modern civilization that the mere material or bodily gains of it balance the loss of pleasure which it has brought upon the world; for as I hinted before those gains have been so unfairly divided that the contrast between rich and poor has been fearfully intensified, so that in all civilized countries, but most of all in England, the terrible spectacle is exhibited of two peoples, living street by street, and door by door, people of the same blood, the same tongue, and at least nominally living under the same laws, but yet one civilized and the other uncivilized. All this I say is the result of the system that has trampled down Art, and exalted Commerce into a sacred religion....

And now in the teeth of this stupid tyranny I put forward a claim on behalf of labour enslaved by Commerce, which I know no thinking man can deny is reasonable, but which if acted on would involve such a change as would defeat Commerce; that is, would put Association instead of Competition, Social Order instead of Individualist Anarchy. Yet I have looked at this claim by the light of history and my own conscience, and it seems to me so looked at to be a most just claim, and that resistance to it means nothing short of a denial of the hope of civilization. This then is the claim: *It is right and necessary that all men should have work to do which shall be worth doing, and be of itself pleasant to do; and which should be done under such conditions as would make it neither over-wearisome nor over-anxious.* Turn that claim about as I may, think of it as long as I can, I cannot find that it is an exorbitant claim; yet again I say if Society would or could admit it, the face of the world would be changed; discontent and strife and dishonesty would be ended. To feel that we were doing work useful to others and pleasant to ourselves, and that such work and its due reward could not fail us! What serious harm could happen to us then? And the price to be paid for so making the world happy is Revolution: Socialism instead of Laissez faire.

How can we of the middle classes help to bring such a state of things about: a state of things as nearly as possible the reverse of the present state of things? The reverse; no less than that. For first, THE WORK MUST BE WORTH DOING: think what a change that would make in the world! I tell you I feel dazed at the thought of the immensity of work which is undergone for the making of useless things. It would be an instructive day's work for any one of us who is strong enough to walk through two or three of the principal streets of London on a week-day, and take accurate note of everything in the shop windows which is embarrassing or superfluous to the daily life of a serious man. Nay, the most of these things no one, serious or unserious, wants at all; only a foolish habit makes even the lightest-minded of us suppose that he wants them, and to many people even of those who buy them they are obvious encumbrances to real work, thought, and pleasure. But I beg you to think of the enormous mass of men who are occupied with this miserable trumpery, from the engineers who have had to make the machines for making them, down to the hapless clerks who sit daylong year after year in the horrible dens wherein the wholesale exchange of them is transacted, and the shopmen, who not daring to call their souls their own, retail them amidst numberless insults which they must not resent, to the idle public which doesn't want them but buys them to be bored by them and sick to death of them. I am talking of the merely useless things; but there are other matters not merely useless, but actively destructive and poisonous which command a good price in the market; for instance, adulterated food and drink. Vast is the number of slaves whom competitive Commerce employs in turning out infamies such as these. But quite apart from them there is an enormous mass of labour which is just merely wasted; many thousands of men and women making Nothing with terrible and inhuman toil which deadens the soul and shortens mere animal life itself.

All these are the slaves of what is called luxury, which in the modern sense of the word comprises a mass of sham wealth, the invention of competitive Commerce, and enslaves not only the poor people who are compelled to work at its production, but also the foolish and not over happy people who buy it to harass themselves with its encumbrance. Now if we are to have popular Art, or indeed Art of any kind, we must at once and for all be done with this luxury: it is the supplanter, the changeling of Art; so much so that by those who know of nothing better it has even been taken for Art, the divine solace of human labour, the romance of each day's hard practice of the difficult art of living. But I say Art cannot live beside it, nor self-respect in any class of life. Effeminacy and brutality are its companions on the right hand and the left. This, first of all, we of the well-to-do classes must get rid of if we are serious in desiring the new birth of Art: and if not, then corruption is digging a terrible pit of perdition for society, from which indeed the new birth may come, but surely from amidst of terror, violence, and misery....

Here then is one thing for us of the middle-classes to do before we can clear the ground for the new birth of Art, before we can clear our own consciences of the guilt of enslaving men by their labour. One thing; and if we could do it perhaps that one thing would be enough, and all other healthy changes would follow it: but can we do it? Can we escape from the corruption of Society which threatens us? Can the middle-classes regenerate themselves? At first sight one would say that a body of people so powerful, who have built up the gigantic edifice of modern Commerce, whose science, invention and energy have subdued the forces of nature to serve their everyday purposes, and who guide the organization that keeps these natural powers in subjection in a way almost miraculous; at first sight one would say surely such a mighty mass of wealthy men could do anything they please. And yet I doubt it: their own creation, the Commerce they are so proud of, has become their master; and all we of the well-to-do classes, some of us with triumphant glee, some with dull satisfaction, and some with sadness of heart, are compelled to admit not that Commerce was made for man, but that man was made for Commerce.

On all sides we are forced to admit it. There are of the English middle-class to-day, for instance, men of the highest aspirations towards Art, and of the strongest will; men who are most deeply convinced of the necessity to civilization of surrounding men's lives with beauty; and many lesser men, thousands for what I know, refined and cultivated, follow them and praise their opinions. But both the leaders and the led are incapable of saving so much as half a dozen commons from the grasp of inexorable Commerce: they are as helpless in spite of their culture and their genius as if they were just so many over-worked shoemakers. Less lucky than King Midas, our green fields and clear waters, nay the very air we breathe, are turned not to gold (which might please some of us for an hour may be) but to dirt; and to speak plainly we know full well that under the present gospel of Capital not only there is no hope of bettering it, but that things grow worse year by year, day by day. Let us eat and drink, for to-morrow we die, choked by filth....

Surely there are some of you who long to be free; who have been educated and refined, and had your perceptions of beauty and order quickened only that they might be shocked and wounded at every turn by the brutalities of competitive Commerce; who have been so hunted and driven by it that, though you are well-to-do, rich even maybe, you have now nothing to lose from social revolution: love of Art, that is to say of the true pleasure of life, has brought you to this, that you must throw in your lot with that of the wage-slave of competitive Commerce; you and he must help each other and have one hope in common, or you at any rate will live and die hopeless and unhelped. You who long to be set free from the oppression of the money grubbers, hope for the day when you will be compelled to be free!

Meanwhile, if otherwise that oppression has left us scarce any work to do worth doing, one thing at least is left us to strive for, the raising of the standard of life where it is lowest, where it is low: that will put a spoke in the wheel of the triumphant car of competitive Commerce. Nor can I conceive of anything more likely to raise the standard of life than the convincing some thousands of those who live by labour of the necessity of their supporting the second part of the claim I have made for Labour; namely, THAT THEIR WORK SHOULD BE OF ITSELF PLEASANT TO DO. If we could but convince them that such a strange revolution in Labour as this would be of infinite benefit not to them only, but to all men; and that it is so right and natural that for the reverse to be the case, that most men's work should be grievous to them, is a mere monstrosity of these latter days, which must in the long run bring ruin and confusion on the Society that allows it—If we could but convince them, then indeed there would be a chance of the phrase Art of the People being something more than a mere word. At first sight, indeed, it would seem impossible to make men born under the present system of Commerce understand that labour may be a blessing to them: not in the sense in which the phrase is sometimes preached to them by those whose labour is light and easily evaded: not as a necessary task laid by nature on the poor for the benefit of the rich: not as an opiate to dull their sense of right and wrong, to make them sit down quietly under their burdens to the end of time, blessing the squire and his relations: all this they could understand our saying to them easily enough, and sometimes would listen to it I fear with at least a show of complacency, if they thought there were anything to be made out of us thereby. But the true doctrine that labour should be a real tangible blessing in itself to the working man, a pleasure even as sleep and strong drink are to him now: this one might think it hard indeed for him to understand, so different as it is to anything which he has found labour to be.

Nevertheless, though most men's work is only borne as a necessary evil like sickness, my experience as far as it goes is, that whether it be from a certain sacredness in handiwork which does cleave to it even under the worst circumstances, or whether it be that the poor man who is driven by necessity to deal with things which are terribly real, when he thinks at all on such matters, thinks less conventionally than the rich; whatever it may be, my experience so far is that the working man finds it easier to understand the doctrine of the claim of Labour to pleasure in the work itself than the rich or well-to-do man does. Apart from any trivial words of my own, I have been surprised to find, for instance, such a hearty feeling toward John Ruskin among working-class audiences: they can see the prophet in him rather than the fantastic rhetorician, as more superfine audiences do. That is a good omen, I think, for the education of times to come. But we who somehow are so tainted by cynicism, because of our helplessness in the ugly world which surrounds and presses on us, cannot we somehow raise our own hopes at least to the point of thinking that what hope glimmers on the millions of the slaves of Commerce is something better than a mere delusion, the false dawn of a cloudy midnight with which 'tis only the moon that struggles? Let us call to mind that there yet remain monuments in the world which show us that all human labour was not always a grief and a burden to men. Let us think of the mighty and lovely architecture, for instance, of mediæval Europe: of the buildings raised before Commerce had put the coping stone on the edifice of tyranny by the discovery that fancy, imagination, sentiment, the joy of creation, and the hope of fair fame are marketable articles too precious to be allowed to men who have not the money to buy them, to mere handicraftsmen and day labourers. Let us remember there was a time when men had pleasure in their daily work, but yet as to other matters hoped for light and freedom even as they do now: their dim hope grew brighter, and they watched its seeming fulfilment drawing nearer and nearer, and gazed so eagerly on it that they did not note how the ever watchful foe, oppression, had changed his shape and was stealing from them what they had already gained in the days when the light of their new hope was but a feeble glimmer; so they lost the old gain, and for lack of it the new gain was changed and spoiled for them into something not much better than loss.

Betwixt the days in which we now live and the end of the middle ages, Europe has gained freedom of thought, increase of knowledge, and huge talent for dealing with the material forces of nature; comparative political freedom withal and respect for the lives of civilized men, and other gains that go with these things: nevertheless I say deliberately that if the present state of society is to endure, she has bought these gains at too high a price in the loss of the pleasure in daily work which once did certainly solace the mass of men for their fears and oppressions: the death of Art was too high a price to pay for the material prosperity of the middle classes. Grievous indeed it was, that we could not keep both our hands full, that we were forced to spill from one while we gathered with the other: yet to my mind it is more grievous still to be unconscious of the loss; or being dimly conscious of it to have to force ourselves to forget it and to cry out that all is well. For, though all is not well, I know that men's natures are not so changed in three centuries, that we can say to all the thousands of years which went before them: You were wrong to cherish Art, and now we have found out that all men need is food and raiment and shelter, with a smattering of knowledge of the material fashion of the universe. Creation is no longer a need of man's soul, his right hand may forget its cunning, and he be none the worse for it.

Three hundred years, a day in the lapse of ages, has not changed man's nature thus utterly, be sure of that: one day we shall win back Art, that is to say the pleasure of life; win back Art again to our daily labour....

There is our hope, I say. If the bargain had been really fair, complete all round, then were there nought else to do but to bury Art, and forget the beauty of life: but now the cause of Art has something else to appeal to: no less than the hope of the people for the happy life which has not yet been granted to them. There is our hope: the cause of Art is the cause of the people....

[Source: *The Collected Works of William Morris*, ed. May Morris, 24 vols. (London: Longmans, Green and Co., 1910-1915), 23:192-96, 198-204.]

2. From "How We Live and How We Might Live" (1884)

[Morris gave this lecture approximately a dozen times between 1884 and 1887. First published in *Commonweal* in June and July of the latter year, it was reprinted by Morris as the opening essay in *Signs of Change* (1888).]

For what I want you to understand is this: that in every civilized country at least there is plenty for all—is, or at any rate might be. Even with labour so misdirected as it is at present, an equitable distribution of the wealth we have would make all people comparatively comfortable; but that is nothing to the wealth we might have if labour were not misdirected.

Observe, in the early days of the history of man he was the slave of his most immediate necessities; Nature was mighty and he was feeble, and he had to wage constant war with her for his daily food and such shelter as he could get. His life was bound down and limited by this constant struggle; all his morals, laws, religion, are in fact the outcome and the reflection of this ceaseless toil of earning his livelihood. Time passed, and little by little, step by step, he grew stronger, till now after all these ages he has completely conquered Nature, and one would think should now have leisure to turn his thoughts towards higher things than procuring to-morrow's dinner. But, alas! his progress has been broken and halting; and though he has indeed conquered Nature and has her forces under his control to do what he will with, he still has himself to conquer, he still has to think how he will best use those forces which he has mastered. At present he uses them blindly, foolishly, as one driven by mere fate. It would almost seem as if some phantom of the ceaseless pursuit of food which was once the master of the savage was still hunting the civilized man; who toils in a dream, as it were, haunted by mere dim unreal hopes, borne of vague recollections of the days gone by. Out of that dream he must wake, and face things as they really are. The conquest of Nature is complete, may we not say? and now our business is and has for long been the organization of man, who wields the forces of Nature. Nor till this is attempted at least shall we ever be free of that terrible phantom of fear of starvation which, with its brother devil, desire of domination, drives us into injustice, cruelty, and dastardliness of all kinds: to cease to fear our fellows and learn to depend on them, to do away with competition and build up co-operation, is our one necessity.

Now, to get closer to details; you probably know that every man in civilization is worth, so to say, more than his skin; working, as he must work, socially, he can produce more than will keep himself alive and in fair condition; and this has been so for many centuries, from the time, in fact, when warring tribes began to make their conquered enemies slaves instead of killing them; and of course his capacity of producing these extras has gone on increasing faster and faster, till to-day one man will weave, for instance, as much cloth in a week as will clothe a whole village for years; and the real question of civilization has always been what are we to do with this extra produce of labour—a question which the phantom, fear of starvation, and its fellow, desire of domination, has driven men to answer pretty badly always, and worst of all perhaps in these present days, when the extra produce has grown with such prodigious speed. The practical answer has always been for man to struggle with his fellow for private possession of undue shares of these extras, and all kinds of devices have been employed by those who found themselves in possession of the power of taking them from others to keep those whom they had robbed in perpetual subjection; and these latter, as I have already hinted, had no chance of resisting this fleecing as long as they were few and scattered, and consequently could have little sense of their common oppression. But now that, owing to the very pursuit of these undue shares of profits, or extra earnings, men have become more dependent on each other for production, and have been driven, as I said before, to combine together for that end more completely, the power of the workers—that is to say, of the robbed or fleeced class—has enormously increased, and it only remains for them to understand that they have this power. When they do that they will be able to give the right answer to the question what is to be done with the extra products of labour over and above what will keep the labourer alive to labour: which answer is, that the worker will have all that he produces, and not be fleeced at all: and remember that he produces collectively, and therefore he will do effectively what work is required of him according to his capacity, and of the produce of that work he will have what he needs; because, you see, he cannot *use* more than he needs—he can only *waste* it.

If this arrangement seems to you preposterously ideal, as it well may, looking at our present condition, I must back it up by saying that when men are organized so that their labour is not wasted, they will be relieved from the fear of starvation and the desire of domination, and will have freedom and leisure to look round and see what they really do need.

Now something of that I can conceive for my own self, and I will lay my ideas before you, so that you may compare them with your own, asking you always to remember that the very differences in men's capacities and desires, after the common need of food and shelter is satisfied, will make it easier to deal with their desires in a communal state of things.

What is it that I need, therefore, which my surrounding circumstances can give me—my dealings with my fellow-men—setting aside inevitable accidents which co-operation and forethought cannot control, if there be such?

Well, first of all I claim good health; and I say that a vast proportion of people in civilization scarcely even know what that means. To feel mere life a pleasure; to enjoy the moving one's limbs and exercising one's bodily powers; to play, as it were, with sun and wind and rain; to rejoice in satisfying the due bodily appetites of a human animal without fear of degradation or sense of wrong-doing: yes, and therewithal to be well-formed, straight-limbed, strongly knit, expressive of countenance—to be, in a word, beautiful—that also I claim. If we cannot have this claim satisfied, we are but poor creatures after all; and I claim it in the teeth of those terrible doctrines of asceticism, which, born of the despair of the oppressed and degraded, have been for so many ages used as instruments for the continuance of that oppression and degradation.

And I believe that this claim for a healthy body for all of us carries with it all other due claims: for who knows where the seeds of disease which even rich people suffer from were first sown: from the luxury of an ancestor, perhaps; yet often, I suspect, from his poverty. And for the poor: a distinguished physicist has said that the poor suffer always from one disease—hunger; and at least I know this, that if a man is overworked in any degree he cannot enjoy the sort of health I am speaking of; nor can he if he is continually chained to one dull round of mechanical work, with no hope at the other end of it; nor if he lives in continual sordid anxiety for his livelihood, nor if he is ill-housed, nor if he is deprived of all enjoyment of the natural beauty of the world, nor if he has no amusement to quicken the flow of his spirits from time to time: all these things, which touch more or less directly on his bodily condition, are born of the claim I make to live in good health; indeed, I suspect that these good conditions must have been in force for several generations before a population in general will be really healthy, as I have hinted above; but also I doubt not that in the course of time they would, joined to other conditions, of which more hereafter, gradually breed such a population, living in enjoyment of animal life at least, happy therefore, and beautiful according to the beauty of their race. On this point I may note that the very variations in the races of men are caused by the conditions under which they live, and though in these rougher parts of the world we lack some of the advantages of climate and surroundings, yet, if we were working for livelihood and not for profit, we might easily neutralize many of the disadvantages of our climate, at least enough to give due scope to the full development of our race.

Now the next thing I claim is education. And you must not say that every English child is educated now; that sort of education will not answer my claim, though I cheerfully admit it is something: something, and yet after all only class education. What I claim is liberal education; opportunity, that is, to have my share of whatever knowledge there is in the world according to my capacity or bent of mind, historical or scientific; and also to have my share of skill of hand which is about in the world, either in the industrial handicrafts or in the fine arts; picture-painting, sculpture, music, acting, or the like: I claim to be taught, if I can be taught, more than one craft to exercise for the benefit of the community. You may think this a large claim, but I am clear it is not too large a claim if the community is to have any gain out of my special capacities, if we are not all to be beaten down to a dull level of mediocrity as we are now, all but the very strongest and toughest of us.

But I also know that this claim for education involves one for public advantages in the shape of public libraries, schools, and the like, such as no private person, not even the richest, could command: but these I claim very confidently, being sure that no reasonable community could bear to be without such helps to a decent life.

Again, the claim for education involves a claim for abundant leisure, which once more I make with confidence; because when once we have shaken off the slavery of profit, labour would be organized so unwastefully that no heavy burden would be laid on the individual citizens; every one of whom as a matter of course would have to pay his toll of some obviously useful work. At present you must note that all the amazing machinery which we have invented has served only to increase the amount of profit-bearing wares; in other words, to increase the amount of profit pouched by individuals for their own advantage, part of which profit they use as capital for the production of more profit, with ever the same waste attached to it; and part as private riches or means for luxurious living, which again is sheer waste—is in fact to be looked on as a kind of bonfire on which rich men burn up the product of the labour they have fleeced from the workers beyond what they themselves can use. So I say that, in spite of our inventions, no worker works under the present system an hour the less on account of those labour-saving machines, so-called. But under a happier state of things they would be used simply for saving labour, with the result of a vast amount of leisure gained for the community to be added to that gained by the avoidance of the waste of useless luxury, and the abolition of the service of commercial war.

And I may say that as to that leisure, as I should in no case do any harm to any one with it, so I should often do some direct good to the community with it, by practising arts or occupations for my hands or brain which would give pleasure to many of the citizens; in other words, a great deal of the best work done would be done in the leisure time of men relieved from any anxiety as to their livelihood, and eager to exercise their special talent, as all men, nay, all animals are.

Now, again, this leisure would enable me to please myself and expand my mind by travelling if I had a mind to it: because, say, for instance, that I were a shoemaker; if due social order were established, it by no means follows that I should always be obliged to make shoes in one place; a due amount of easily conceivable arrangement would enable me to make shoes in Rome, say, for three months, and to come back with new ideas of building, gathered from the sight of the works of past ages, amongst other things which would perhaps be of service in London.

But now, in order that my leisure might not degenerate into idleness and aimlessness, I must set up a claim for due work to do. Nothing to my mind is more important than this demand, and I must ask your leave to say something about it. I have mentioned that I should probably use my leisure for doing a good deal of what is now called work; but it is clear that if I am a member of a Socialist Community I must do my due share of rougher work than this— my due share of what my capacity enables me to do, that is; no fitting of me to a Procrustean bed;[1] but even that share of work necessary to the existence of the simplest social life must, in the first place, whatever else it is, be reasonable work; that is, it must be such work as a good citizen can see the necessity for; as a member of the community, I must have agreed to do it.

To take two strong instances of the contrary, I won't submit to be dressed up in red and marched off to shoot at my French or German or Arab friend in a quarrel that I don't understand; I will rebel sooner than do that.

---

[1]   In Greek legend, the robber Procrustes placed his victims on a bed. He cut off the feet of those who were too long for the bed and stretched the legs of those who were too short.

Nor will I submit to waste my time and energies in making some trifling toy which I know only a fool can desire; I will rebel sooner than do that.

However, you may be sure that in a state of social order I shall have no need to rebel against any such pieces of unreason; only I am forced to speak from the way we live to the way we might live....

The last claim I make for my work is that the places I worked in, factories or workshops, should be pleasant, just as the fields where our most necessary work is done are pleasant. Believe me there is nothing in the world to prevent this being done, save the necessity of making profits on all wares; in other words, the wares are cheapened at the expense of people being forced to work in crowded, unwholesome, squalid, noisy dens: that is to say, they are cheapened at the expense of the workman's life.

Well, so much for my claims as to my *necessary* work, my tribute to the community. I believe people would find, as they advanced in their capacity for carrying on social order, that life so lived was much less expensive than we now can have any idea of, and that, after a little, people would rather be anxious to seek work than to avoid it; that our working hours would rather be merry parties of men and maids, young men and old enjoying themselves over their work, than the grumpy weariness it mostly is now. Then would come the time for the new birth of art, so much talked of, so long deferred; people could not help showing their mirth and pleasure in their work, and would be always wishing to express it in a tangible and more or less enduring form, and the workshop would once more be a school of art, whose influence no one could escape from.

And, again, that word art leads me to my last claim, which is that the material surroundings of my life should be pleasant, generous, and beautiful; that I know is a large claim, but this I will say about it, that if it cannot be satisfied, if every civilized community cannot provide such surroundings for all its members, I do not want the world to go on; it is a mere misery that man has ever existed. I do not think it possible under the present circumstances to speak too strongly on this point. I feel sure that the time will come when people will find it difficult to believe that a rich community such as ours, having such command over external Nature, could have submitted to live such a mean, shabby, dirty life as we do.

[Source: *The Collected Works of William Morris*, ed. May Morris, 24 vols. (London: Longmans, Green and Co., 1910-1915), 23:14-22.]

3. From "The Society of the Future" (1887)

[May Morris thought this lecture "deserving of special consideration" among her father's works. "Written almost at the climax of his work as a leader, it represents his views over the whole field of his teaching ... explaining why he was a Socialist and what he hoped for from the future" (*Artist, Writer, Socialist* 2:367).]

In making our claims for the changes in Society which we believe would set labour free and thus bring about a new Society, we Socialists are satisfied with demanding what we think necessary for that Society to form itself, which we are sure it is getting ready to do; this we think better than putting forward elaborate utopian schemes for the future. We assert that monopoly must come to an end, and that those who can use the means of the production of wealth should have all opportunity of doing so, without being forced to surrender a great part of the wealth which they have created to an irresponsible owner of the necessaries to production; and we have faith in the regenerative qualities of this elementary piece of honesty, and believe that the world thus set free will enter on a new cycle of progress. We are prepared to face whatever drawbacks may accompany this new development with equanimity, being convinced that it will at any rate be a great gain to have got rid of a system which has at last become nearly all drawbacks. The extinction of the disabilities of an effete system of production will not, we are convinced, destroy the gains which the world has already won, but will, on the contrary, make those gains available to the whole population instead of confining their enjoyment to a few. In short, considering the present condition of the world, we have come to the conclusion that the function of the reformers now alive is not so much prophecy as action. It is our business to use the means ready to our hands to remedy the immediate evils which oppress us; to the coming generations we must leave the task of safeguarding and of using the freedom which our efforts shall have won them.

Nevertheless, we do partly know the direction which the development of the world will take in the immediate future; the evolution of past history teaches us that. We know that the world cannot go back on its footsteps, and that men will develop swiftly both bodily and mentally in the new Society; we know that men in general will feel the obligations of Society much more than the latter generations have done, that the necessity for co-operation in production and life in general will be more consciously felt than it has been; that the comparative ease of life which the freeing of labour will bring about will give all men more leisure and time for thought; that crime will be rarer because there will not be the same temptation to it; that increased ease of life and education combined will tend to free us from disease of body and mind. In short, that the world cannot take a step forward in justice, honesty and kindliness, without a corresponding gain in all the material conditions of life.

And besides what we know, a knowledge without which we should not take the trouble to agitate for a change in the basis of Society, we cannot help guessing at a great deal which we cannot know; and again, this guessing, these hopes, or if you will, these dreams for the future, make many a man a Socialist whom sober reason deduced from science and political economy and the selection of the fittest would not move at all. They put a man in a fit frame of mind to study the reasons for his hope; give him courage to wade through studies, which, as the Arab king said of arithmetic, would otherwise be too dull for the mind of man to think of.

There are, in fact, two groups of mind with whom Social Revolutionists like other people have to deal, the analytical and the constructive. Belonging to the latter group myself, I am fully conscious of the dangers which we incur, and still more perhaps of the pleasures which we lose, and am, I hope, duly grateful to the more analytical minds for their setting of us straight when our yearning for action leads us astray, and I am also, I confess, somewhat envious of the beatitude of their dreamy contemplation of the perfection of some favourite theory; a happiness which we who use our eyes more than our reasoning powers for noting what is going on in the world, seldom or never enjoy.

However, as they would and do call our instinctive vision dreaming, and as they almost always, at least in their own estimation, have the better of us in argument when we meet in friendly battle, I must be careful what I say of them, and so will for the present at least only deal with the visionaries or *practical people*. And one thing I must confess from the beginning, which is that the visions of us visionary or practical people differ largely from each other, and that we are not much interested in each others' visions; whereas the theories of the analysts differ little from each other, and they are hugely interested in each others' theories—in the way that a butcher is interested in an ox—to wit, for cutting up.

So I will not attempt to compare my visions with those of other Socialists, but will simply talk to you of some of my own, and let you make the comparison yourselves, those of you who are visionaries, or let you unassisted by me criticize them, those of you who are analytically given. In short, I am going to give you a chapter of confessions. I want to tell you what it is I desire of the Society of the Future, just as if I were going to be reborn into it; I daresay that you will find some of my visions strange enough.

One reason which will make some of you think them strange is a sad and shameful one. I have always belonged to the well-to-do classes, and was born into luxury, so that necessarily I ask much more of the future than many of you do; and the first of all my visions, and that which colours all my others, is of a day when that misunderstanding will no longer be possible; when the words poor and rich, though they will still be found in our dictionaries, will have lost their old meaning; which will have to be explained with care by great men of the analytical kind, spending much time and many words over the job, and not succeeding in the end in making people do more than pretend to understand them.

Well now, to begin with, I am bound to suppose that the realization of Socialism will tend to make men happy. What is it then makes people happy? Free and full life and the consciousness of life. Or, if you will, the pleasurable exercise of our energies, and the enjoyment of the rest which that exercise or expenditure of energy makes necessary to us. I think that is happiness for all, and covers all difference of capacity and temperament from the most energetic to the laziest.

Now, whatever interferes with that freedom and fulness of life, under whatever specious guise it may come, is an evil; is something to be got rid of as speedily as possible. It ought not to be endured by reasonable men, who naturally wish to be happy.

Here you see is an admission on my part which I suspect indicates the unscientific mind. It proposes the exercise of free will on the part of men, which the latest scientists deny the possibility of, I believe; but don't be afraid, I am not going into argument on the matter of free will and predestination; I am only going to assert that if individual men are the creatures of their surrounding conditions, as indeed I think they are, it must be the business of man as a social animal, or of Society, if you will, to make the surroundings which make the individual man what he is. Man must and does create the conditions under which he lives; let him be conscious of that, and create them wisely.

Has he done so hitherto? He has tried to do so, I think, but with only moderate success, at any rate at times. However, the results of that moderate success he is proud of, and he calls it *civilization*. Now, there has been amongst people of different minds abundant discussion as to whether civilization is a good thing or an evil. Our friend Bax[1] in his very able article on the subject, did, I think, really put the matter on its true footing when he pointed out that as a step to something better, civilization was a good, but as an achievement it was an evil. In that sense I declare myself an enemy of civilization; nay, since this is to be a chapter of confessions, I must tell you that my *special* leading motive as a Socialist is hatred of civilization; my ideal of the new Society would not be satisfied unless that Society destroyed civilization.

For if happiness be the pleasurable exercise of our energies and the enjoyment of necessary rest, it seems to me that civilization looked at from the static point of view, as Bax phrases it, tends to deny us both these good things, and thereby tends to reduce man to a machine without a will; to deprive him gradually of all the functions of an animal and the pleasure of fulfilling them, except the most elementary ones. The scientific ideal of the future of man would appear to be an intellectual paunch, nourished by circumstances over which he has no control, and without the faculty of communicating the results of his intelligence to his brother-paunches.

Therefore my ideal of the Society of the future is first of all the freedom and cultivation of the individual will, which civilization ignores, or even denies the existence of; the shaking off the slavish dependence, not on other men, but on artificial systems made to save men manly trouble and responsibility: and in order that this will may be vigorous in us, I demand a free and unfettered animal life for man first of all: I demand the utter extinction of all asceticism. If we feel the least degradation in being amorous, or merry, or hungry, or sleepy, we are so far bad animals, and therefore miserable men. And you know civilization *does* bid us to be ashamed of all

---

[1] For E. Belfort Bax, see headnote to Appendix D. 5.

these moods and deeds, and as far as she can, begs us to conceal them, and where possible to get other people to do them for us. In fact, it seems to me that civilization may almost be defined as a system arranged for ensuring the vicarious exercise of human energies for a minority of privileged persons.

Well, but this demand for the extinction of asceticism bears with it another demand: for the extinction of luxury. Does that seem a paradox to you? It ought not to do so. What brings about luxury but a sickly discontent with the simple joys of the lovely earth? What is it but a warping of the natural beauty of things into a perverse ugliness to satisfy the jaded appetite of a man who is ceasing to be a man—a man who will not work, and cannot rest? Shall I tell you what luxury has done for you in modern Europe? It has covered the merry green fields with the hovels of slaves, and blighted the flowers and trees with poisonous gases, and turned the rivers into sewers; till over many parts of Britain the common people have forgotten what a field or a flower is like, and their idea of beauty is a gas-poisoned gin-palace or a tawdry theatre. And civilization thinks that is all right, and it doesn't heed it; and the rich man practically thinks, 'Tis all right, the common people are used to it now, and so long as they can fill their bellies with the husks that the swine do eat, it is enough. And all for what? To have fine pictures painted, beautiful buildings built, good poems written? O no: those are the deeds of the ages before luxury, before civilization. Luxury rather builds clubs in Pall Mall, and upholsters them as though for delicate invalid ladies, for the behoof of big whiskered men, that they may lounge there amidst such preposterous effeminacy that the very plushed-breeched flunkies that wait upon the loungers are better men than they are. I needn't go further than that: a grand club is the very representative of luxury.

Well, you see I dwell upon that matter of luxury, which is really the sworn foe of pleasure, because I don't want workmen even temporarily to look upon a swell club as a desirable thing. I know how difficult it is for them to look from out of their poverty and squalor to a life of real and manly pleasure; but I ask them to think that the good life of the future will be as little like the life of the present rich as may be: that life of the rich is only the wrong side of their own misery; and surely since it is the cause of the misery, there can be nothing enviable or desirable in it. When our opponents say, as they sometimes do, How should we be able to procure the luxuries of life in a Socialist society? answer boldly, We could not do so, and we don't care, for we don't want them and won't have them; and indeed, I feel sure that we cannot if we are all free men together. Free men, I am sure, must lead simple lives and have simple pleasures: and if we shudder away from that necessity now, it is because we are not free men, and have in consequence wrapped up our lives in such a complexity of dependence that we have grown feeble and helpless....

So, then, my ideal is first unconstrained life, and next simple and natural life. First you must be free; and next you must learn to take pleasure in all the details of life: which, indeed, will be necessary for you, because, since others will be free, you will have to do your own work. That is in direct opposition to civilization, which says, Avoid trouble, which you can only do by making other people live your life for you. I say, Socialists ought to say, Take trouble, and turn your trouble into pleasure: that I shall always hold is the key to a happy life.

Now let us try to use that key to unlock a few of the closed doors of the future: and you must remember, of course, in speaking of the Society of the future, I am taking the indulgence of passing over the transitional period—whatever that may be—that will divide the present from the ideal; which, after all, we must all of us more or less form in our minds when we have once fixed our belief in the regeneration of the world. And first as to the form of the position of people in the new Society—their political position, so to say. Political society as we know it will have come to an end: the relations between man and man will no longer be that of status or of property. It will no longer be the hierarchical position, the office of the man, that will be considered, as in the Middle Ages, nor his property as now, but his person. Contract enforced by the State will have vanished into the same limbo as the holiness of the nobility of blood. So we shall at one stroke get rid of all that side of artificiality which bids us sacrifice each our own life to the supposed necessity of an institution which is to take care of the troubles of people which may never happen: every case of clashing rights and desires will be dealt with on its own merits—that is, really, and not legally. Private property of course will not exist as a right: there will be such an abundance of all ordinary necessaries that between private persons there will be no obvious and immediate exchange necessary; though no one will want to meddle with matters that have as it were grown to such and such an individual—which have become part of his habits, so to say.

Now, as to occupations, we shall clearly not be able to have the same division of labour in them as now: vicarious servanting, sewer-emptying, butchering, letter-carrying, boot-blacking, hair-dressing, and the rest of it, will have come to an end: we shall either make all these occupations agreeable to ourselves in some mood or to some minds, who will take to them voluntarily, or we shall have to let them lapse altogether. A great many fidgety occupations will come to an end: we shan't put a pattern on a cloth or a twiddle on a jug-handle to sell it, but to make it prettier and to amuse ourselves and others. Whatever rough or inferior wares we make, will be made rough and inferior to perform certain functions of use, and not to sell: as there will be no slaves, there will be no use for wares which none but slaves would need. Machinery will probably to a great extent have served its purpose in allowing the workers to shake off privilege, and will I believe be much curtailed. Possibly the few more important machines will be very much improved, and the host of unimportant ones fall into disuse; and as to many or most of them, people will be able to use them or not as they feel inclined—as, e.g., if we want to go a journey we shall not be compelled to go by railway as we are now, in the interests of property, but may indulge our personal inclinations and travel in a tilted waggon or on the hindquarters of a donkey.

Again, the aggregation of the population having served its purpose of giving people opportunities of inter-communication and of making the workers feel their solidarity, will also come to an end; and the huge manufacturing districts will be broken up, and nature heal the horrible scars that man's heedless greed and stupid terror have made: for it will no longer be a matter of dire necessity that cotton cloth should be made a fraction of a farthing cheaper this year than last. It will be in our own choice whether we will work an extra half-hour a-day more to obtain a clean home and green fields; nor will the starvation or misery of thousands follow some slight caprice in the market for wares not worth making at all. Of course (as I ought to have said before) there are many ornamental matters which will be made privately in people's leisure hours, as they could easily be: since it is not the making of a real work of art that takes so much ingenuity as the making of a machine for the making of a makeshift. And of course mere cheating and flunky centres like the horrible muck-heap in which we dwell (London, to wit) could be got rid of easier still; and a few pleasant villages on the side of the Thames might mark the place of that preposterous piece of folly once called London.

Now let us use the key to unlock the door of the education of the future. Our present education is purely commercial and political: we are none of us educated to be men, but some to be property-owners, and others to be property servers. Again I demand the due results of revolution on the basis of non-ascetic simplicity of life. I think here also we must get rid of the fatal division-of-labour system. All people should learn how to swim, and to ride, and to sail a boat on sea or river; such things are not arts, they are merely bodily exercises, and should become habitual in the race; and also one or two elementary arts of life, as carpentry or smithying; and most should know how to shoe a horse and shear a sheep and reap a field and plough it (we should soon drop machinery in agriculture I believe when we were free). Then again there are things like cooking and baking, sewing, and the like, which can be taught to every sensible person in a few hours, and which everybody ought to have at his fingers' ends. All these elementary arts would be once again habitual, as also I suppose would be the arts of reading and writing; as also I suspect would the art of thinking, at present not taught in any school or university that I know of.

Well, armed with these habits and arts, life would lie before the citizen for him to enjoy; for whatever line he might like to take up for the exercise of his energies, he would find the community ready to help him with teaching, opportunities, and material. Nor for my part would I prescribe for him what he should do, being persuaded that the habits which would have given him the capacities of a man would stimulate him to use them; and that the process of the enjoyment of his life would be carried out, not at the expense of his fellow-citizens, but for their benefit. At present, you know, the gains held out as a stimulus to exertion, to all those who are not stimulated by the whip or the threat of death by starvation, are narrow, and are mainly the hope that the successfully energetic man shall be placed in a position where he shall not have to exercise his energies: the boredom of satiety, in short, is the crown of valiant exertion in civilization. But in a social condition of things, the gains that would lie before the exercise of one's energies would be various and wide indeed; nor do I in the least in the world believe that the possibility of mere personal use would, or indeed could, limit people's endeavour after them; since men would at last have recognized that it was their business to live, and would at once come to the conclusion that life without endeavour is *dull*. Now what direction that endeavour would take, of course I cannot tell you; I can only say that it would be set free from the sordid necessity to work at what doesn't please us, which is the besetting curse of civilization. The suggestion of a hope I may, however, make, which is of course personal—which is that perhaps mankind will regain their eyesight, which they have at present lost to a great extent. I am not here alluding to what I believe is also a fact, that the number of people of imperfect mechanical sight is increasing, but to what I suppose is connected with that fact, namely, that people have largely ceased to take in mental impressions through the eyes; whereas in times past the eyes were the great feeders of the fancy and imagination....

Now I have dwelt at some length on this matter of the eyesight, because to my mind it is the most obvious sign of the march of civilization towards the intellectual-paunch stage of existence which I have deprecated already; and also because I feel sure that no special claim need be made for the art and literature of the future: healthy bodily conditions, a sound and all round development of the senses, joined to the due social ethics which the destruction of all slavery will give us, will, I am convinced, as a matter of course give us the due art and literature, whatever that due may turn out to be. Only if I may prophesy ever so little, I should say that both art and literature, and especially art, will appeal to the senses directly, just as the art of the past has done. You see you will no longer be able to have novels relating the troubles of a middle-class couple in their struggle towards social uselessness, because the material for such literary treasures will have passed way. On the other hand the genuine tales of history will still be with us, and will, one might well hope, then be told in a cheerfuller strain than is now possible. Nor for my part can I doubt that art will appeal to the senses of men now grown healthy; which means that architecture and the kindred arts will again flourish amongst us as in the days before civilization. Civilization renders these arts impossible, because its politics and ethics force us to live in a grimy disorderly uncomfortable world, a world that offends the senses at every turn: that necessity reacts on the senses again, and forces us unconsciously to blunt their keenness. A man who notices the external forms of things much nowadays must suffer in South Lancashire or London, must live in a state of perpetual combat and anger; and he really must try to blunt his sensibility, or he will go mad, or kill some obnoxious person and be hanged for it; and this of course means that people will gradually get to be born without this inconvenient sensibility. On the other hand, let this irrational compulsion be removed from us, and the senses will grow again to their due and normal fulness and demand expression of the pleasure which their exercise gives us, which in short means art and literature at once sensuous and human.

[Source: *William Morris: Artist, Writer, Socialist*, ed. May Morris, 2 vols. (Oxford: Basil Blackwell, 1936): 2:453-63, 465-66.]

Appendix B: Art, Work, and Society

1. Robert Owen, from *Report to the County of Lanark* (1820)

[Cotton manufacturer and social reformer Robert Owen (1771–1858) influenced radical thinking in Great Britain well into the twentieth century. He is best known for his factory and village at New Lanark in the Scottish borders, where he sought to put into practice his ideal of the "co-operative society." Morris admired Owen's emphasis on education and housing reform, though he dismissed the co-operative movement as "incomplete" socialism (see for instance *Letters* 2:687-88 and 858).]

It has been, and still is, a received opinion among theorists in political economy, that man can provide better for himself, and more advantageously for the public, when left to his own individual exertions, opposed to, and in competition with his fellows, than when aided by any social arrangement, which shall unite his interests individually and generally with society. This principle of individual interest, opposed, as it is perpetually, to the public good, is considered, by the most celebrated political economists, to be the corner stone of the social system, and without which, society could not subsist. Yet when they shall know themselves, and discover the wonderful effects, which combination and union can produce, they will acknowledge that the present arrangement of society is the most antisocial, impolitic, and irrational, that can be devised; that under its influence, all the superior and valuable qualities of human nature are repressed from infancy, and that the most unnatural means are used to bring out the most injurious propensities; in short, that the utmost pains are taken to make that which by nature is the most delightful compound for producing excellence and happiness, absurd, imbecile, and wretched.... In short, if there be one closet doctrine more contrary to truth than another, it is the notion that individual interest, as that term is now understood, is a more advantageous principle on which to found the social system, for the benefit of all, or of any, than the principle of union and mutual co-operation. The former acts like an immense weight to repress the most valuable faculties and dispositions, and to give a wrong direction to all human powers. It is one of those magnificent errors (if the expression may be allowed), that when enforced in practice, brings ten thousand evils in its train. The principle on which these economists proceed, instead of adding to the wealth of nations or of individuals, is itself the sole cause of poverty; and but for its operation, wealth would long ago have ceased to be a subject of contention in any part of the world. If, it may be asked, experience has proved that union, combination, and extensive arrangement among mankind, are a thousand times more powerful to *destroy*, than the efforts of an unconnected multitude, where each acts individually for himself,—would not a similar increased effect be produced by union, combination, and extensive arrangement, to *create and conserve*? Why should not the result be the same in the one case as in the other? But it is well known that a combination of men and of interests, can effect that which it would be futile to attempt, and impossible to accomplish, by individual exertions and separate interests....

Are not the mental energies of the world at this moment in a state of high effervescence?

Is not society at a stand, incompetent to proceed at its present course?, and do not all men cry out that "something must be done?" That "something," to produce the effect desired, must be a complete renovation of the whole social compact; one not forced on prematurely, by confusion and violence; not one to be brought about by the futile measures of the Radicals, Whigs, or Tories, of Britain,— the Liberals or Royalists of France—the Illuminati of Germany,[1] or the mere party proceedings of any little local portion of human beings, trained as they have hitherto been in almost every kind of error, and without any true knowledge of themselves. No! The change sought for, must be preceded by the clear development of a great and universal principle which shall unite in one, all the petty jarring interests, by which, till now, human nature has been made a most inveterate enemy to itself. No! Extensive, nay, rather, universal, as the re-arrangement of society must be, to relieve it from the difficulties with which it is now overwhelmed, it will be effected in peace and quietness, with the good will and hearty concurrence of all parties, and of every people. It will necessarily commence by

---

[1] The Illuminati were liberal Freemasons who were politically active in Bavaria especially during the last quarter of the eighteenth century.

common consent, on account of its advantage, almost simultaneously among all civilized nations; and, once begun, will daily
advance with an accelerating ratio, unopposed, and bearing down
before it the existing systems of the world. The only astonishment
then will be that such systems could so long have existed.

[Source: Robert Owen, *Report to the County of Lanark, of a Plan for
Relieving Public Distress, and Removing Discontent, by Giving Permanent,
Productive Employment, to the Poor and Working Classes; Under
Arrangements which Will Essentially Improve their Character, and
Ameliorate their Condition; Diminish the Expenses of Production and
Consumption, and Create Markets Co-extensive with Production*
(Glasgow: Wardlaw and Cunninghame, 1820): 28-31.]

2. John Ruskin, from "The Nature of Gothic" (1852)

[Morris's intellectual debt to John Ruskin (1819-1900) would be
hard to overestimate. In his introduction to the 1892 Kelmscott
Press edition of "The Nature of Gothic" Morris predicted that
"in future days [Ruskin's essay] will be considered as one of the
very few necessary and inevitable utterances of the century. To
some of us when we first read it, now many years ago, it seemed
to point out a new road on which the world should travel."]

[A]bove all, in our dealings with the souls of other men, we are to
take care how we check, by severe requirement or narrow caution,
efforts which might otherwise lead to a noble issue; and, still more,
how we withhold our admiration from great excellences, because
they are mingled with rough faults. Now, in the make and nature of
every man, however rude or simple, whom we employ in manual
labour, there are some powers for better things; some tardy imagination, torpid capacity of emotion, tottering steps of thought, there
are, even at the worst; and in most cases it is all our own fault that
they *are* tardy or torpid. But they cannot be strengthened, unless we
are content to take them in their feebleness, and unless we prize and
honour them in their imperfection above the best and most perfect
manual skill. And this is what we have to do with all our labourers;
to look for the *thoughtful* part of them, and get that out of them,
whatever we lose for it, whatever faults and errors we are obliged to

take with it. For the best that is in them cannot manifest itself, but in company with much error. Understand this clearly: You can teach a man to draw a straight line, and to cut one; to strike a curved line, and to carve it; and to copy and carve any number of given lines and forms, with admirable speed and perfect precision; and you find his work perfect of its kind: but if you ask him to think about any of those forms, to consider if he cannot find any better in his own head, he stops; his execution becomes hesitating; he thinks, and ten to one he thinks wrong; ten to one he makes a mistake in the first touch he gives to his work as a thinking being. But you have made a man of him for all that. He was only a machine before, an animated tool.

And observe, you are put to stern choice in this matter. You must either make a tool of the creature, or a man of him. You cannot make both. Men were not intended to work with the accuracy of tools, to be precise and perfect in all their actions. If you will have that degree of precision out of them, and make their fingers measure degrees like cog-wheels, and their arms strike curves like compasses, you must unhumanize them. All the energy of their spirits must be given to make cogs and compasses of themselves.... On the other hand, if you will make a man of the working creature, you cannot make him a tool. Let him but begin to imagine, to think, to try to do anything worth doing; and the engine-turned precision is lost at once. Out come all his roughness, all his dulness, all his incapability; shame upon shame, failure upon failure, pause after pause: but out comes the whole majesty of him also; and we know the height of it only when we see the clouds settling upon him. And, whether the clouds be bright or dark, there will be transfiguration behind and within them.

And now, reader, look round this English room of yours, about which you have been proud so often, because the work of it was so good and strong, and the ornaments of it so finished. Examine again all those accurate mouldings, and perfect polishings, and unerring adjustments of the seasoned wood and tempered steel. Many a time you have exulted over them, and thought how great England was, because her slightest work was done so thoroughly. Alas! if read rightly, these perfectnesses are signs of a slavery in our England a thousand times more bitter and more degrading than that of the scourged African, or helot Greek. Men may be beaten, chained, tormented, yoked like cattle, slaughtered like summer flies, and yet remain in one sense, and the best sense, free. But to smother their souls with them, to blight and hew into rotting pollards the suckling branches of their human intelligence, to make the flesh and skin which, after the worm's work on it, is to see God,[1] into leathern thongs to yoke machinery with,—this is to be slave-masters indeed; and there might be more freedom in England, though her feudal lords' lightest words were worth men's lives, and though the blood of vexed husbandman dropped in the furrows of her fields, than there is while the animation of her multitudes is sent like fuel to feed the factory smoke, and the strength of them is given daily to be wasted into the fineness of a web, or racked into the exactness of a line.

And, on the other hand, go forth again to gaze upon the old cathedral front, where you have smiled so often at the fantastic ignorance of the old sculptors: examine once more those ugly goblins, and formless monsters, and stern statues, anatomiless and rigid, but do not mock at them, for they are signs of the life and liberty of every workman who struck the stone; a freedom of thought, and rank in scale of being, such as no laws, no charters, no charities can secure; but which it must be the first aim of all Europe at this day to regain for her children.

Let me not be thought to speak wildly or extravagantly. It is verily this degradation of the operative into a machine, which, more than any other evil of the times, is leading the mass of the nations everywhere into vain, incoherent, destructive struggling for a freedom of which they cannot explain the nature to themselves. Their universal outcry against wealth, and against nobility, is not forced from them either by the pressure of famine, or the sting of mortified pride. These do much, and have done much in all ages; but the foundations of society were never yet shaken as they are at this day. It is not that men are ill fed, but that they have no pleasure in the work by which they make their bread, and therefore look to wealth as the only means of pleasure.

It is not that men are pained by the scorn of the upper classes, but they cannot endure their own; for they feel that the kind of labour to which they are condemned is verily a degrading one, and makes them less than men....

We have much studied, and much perfected, of late, the great civilized invention of the division of labour; only we give it a false name. It is not, truly speaking, the labour that is divided; but the men:— Divided into mere segments of men—broken into small fragments

---

[1] An allusion to Job 19.26: "And though after my skin, worms destroy this body, yet in my flesh shall I see God."

and crumbs of life; so that all the little piece of intelligence that is left in a man is not enough to make a pin, or a nail, but exhausts itself in making the point of a pin or the head of a nail. Now it is a good and desirable thing, truly, to make many pins in a day; but if we could only see with what crystal sand their points were polished,—sand of human soul, much to be magnified before it can be discerned for what it is—we should think there might be some loss in it also. And the great cry that rises from all our manufacturing cities, louder than their furnace blast, is all in very deed for this,—that we manufacture everything there except men; we blanch cotton, and strengthen steel, and refine sugar, and shape pottery; but to brighten, to strengthen, to refine, or to form a single living spirit, never enters into our estimate of advantages. And all the evil to which that cry is urging our myriads can be met only in one way: not by teaching nor preaching, for to teach them is but to show them their misery, and to preach to them, if we do nothing more than preach, is to mock at it. It can be met only by a right understanding, on the part of all classes, of what kinds of labour are good for men, raising them, and making them happy; by a determined sacrifice of such convenience, or beauty, or cheapness as is to be got only by the degradation of the workman; and by equally determined demand for the products and results of healthy and ennobling labour.

And how, it will be asked, are these products to be recognized, and this demand to be regulated? Easily: by the observance of three broad and simple rules:

1. Never encourage the manufacture of any article not absolutely necessary, in the production of which *Invention* has no share.

2. Never demand an exact finish for its own sake, but only for some practical or noble end.

3. Never encourage imitation or copying of any kind, except for the sake of preserving records of great works.

[Source: *"The Nature of Gothic," by John Ruskin, printed by William Morris at the Kelmscott Press, Hammersmith, and published by George Allen, 8, Bell Yard, Temple Bar, and Sunnyside, Orpington* (1892): 16-20, 22-24.]

3. Karl Marx, from *Das Kapital* (1867)

[Morris read *Das Kapital* in French translation in 1883. (The first English translation of Volume I, from which the following extract is taken, did not appear until 1887.) Though he sometimes claimed to find Marx's theories unintelligible, Morris's views on alienated labor, the historical development of capitalism, and the inevitability of class warfare all draw heavily on his reading of *Das Kapital*. The passage below appears in Marx's discussion of "The Factory" in Volume I, Part IV of that work. Marx's own quite extensive footnotes are omitted.]

To work at a machine, the workman should be taught from childhood, in order that he may learn to adapt his own movements to the uniform and unceasing motion of an automaton. When the machinery, as a whole, forms a system of manifold machines, working simultaneously and in concert, the co-operation based upon it, requires the distribution of various groups of workmen among the different kinds of machines. But the employment of machinery does away with the necessity of crystallizing this distribution after the manner of Manufacture, by the constant annexation of a particular man to a particular function.[1] Since the motion of the whole system does not proceed from the workman, but from the machinery, a change of persons can take place at any time without an interruption of the work.... [T]he quickness with which machine work is learnt by young people, does away with the necessity of bringing up for exclusive employment by machinery, a special class of operatives. With regard to the work of the mere attendants, it can, to some extent, be replaced in the mill by machines, and owing to its extreme simplicity, it allows of a rapid and constant change of the individuals burdened with this drudgery.

Although then, technically speaking, the old system of division of labour is thrown overboard by machinery, it hangs on in the factory, as a traditional habit handed down from Manufacture, and is afterwards systematically re-moulded and established in a more hideous form by capital, as a mean of exploiting labour-power. The life-long specialty of handling one and the same tool, now becomes the life-long specialty of serving one and the same machine.

---

[1] According to Marx, the stage of Manufacture is an early episode in the development of Capitalism. During this stage the division of labor is intensified but, unlike in the modern factory system, workers are not yet interchangeable, since each needs to hone certain skills in the overall process. With the advent of machines, any worker can do any job, even women and children.

Machinery is put to a wrong use, with the object of transforming the workman, from his very childhood, into a part of a detail-machine. In this way, not only are the expenses of his reproduction considerably lessened,[1] but at the same time his helpless dependence upon the factory as a whole, and therefore upon the capitalist, is rendered complete. Here as everywhere else, we must distinguish between the increased productiveness due to the development of the social processes of production, and that due to the capitalist exploitation of that process. In handicraft and manufacture, the workman makes use of a tool, in the factory, the machine makes use of him. There the movements of the instrument of labour proceed from him, here it is the movements of the machine that he must follow. In manufacture the workmen are parts of a living mechanism. In the factory we have a lifeless mechanism independent of the workman, who becomes its mere living appendage. "The miserable routine of endless drudgery and toil in which the same mechanical process is gone through over and over again, is like the labour of Sisyphus. The burden of labour, like the rock, keeps ever falling back on the worn-out labourer."[2] At the same time that factory work exhausts the nervous system to the uttermost, it does away with the many-sided play of the muscles, and confiscates every atom of freedom, both in bodily and intellectual activity. The lightening of the labour, even, becomes a sort of torture, since the machine does not free the labourer from work, but deprives the work of all interest.... The special skill of each individual insignificant factory operative vanishes as an infinitesimal quantity before the science, the gigantic physical forces, and the mass of labour that are embodied in the factory mechanism and, together with that mechanism, constitute the power of the "master." ...

We shall here merely allude to the material conditions under which factory labour is carried on. Every organ of sense is injured in an equal degree by artificial elevation of the temperature, by the dust-laden atmosphere, by the deafening noise, not to mention danger to life and limb among the thickly crowded machinery, which, with the regularity of the seasons, issues its list of the killed and wounded in

---

[1] I.e., what it costs the employer to replace him.

[2] From Friedrich Engels, *The Condition of the Working Class in England in 1844* (1845). In Greek mythology, Sisyphus was condemned in Hades to the endless labor of pushing a large stone up a hill; the stone would always roll down the hill just before he reached the summit.

the industrial battle. Economy of the social means of production, matured and forced as in a hothouse by the factory system, is turned, in the hands of capital, into systematic robbery of what is necessary for the life of the workman while he is at work, robbery of space, light, air, and of protection to his person against the dangerous and unwholesome accompaniments of the productive process, not to mention the robbery of appliances for the comfort of the workman.

[Source: Karl Marx, *Capital: A Critical Analysis of Capitalist Production*, translated from the third German edition by Samuel Moore and Edward Aveling, and edited by Friedrich Engels (London: Swan Sonnenschein, Lowrey, & Co., 1887): 420-26.]

4. Henry George, from *Progress and Poverty* (1879)

[With *Progress and Poverty*, the American economist Henry George (1839-1897) achieved that most unlikely of successes for a political economist, a best seller. George's advocacy of land nationalization and a single tax at first found a ready audience among British radicals, who received him enthusiastically during an 1882 lecture tour through England and Ireland. Morris praised *Progress and Poverty* when he read it that same year, though he soon came to view George's position as simply a way-station on the road to genuine socialism.]

Where the conditions to which material progress everywhere tends are most fully realized—that is to say, where population is densest, wealth greatest, and the machinery of production and exchange most highly developed—we find the deepest poverty, the sharpest struggle for existence, and the most enforced idleness.

It is to the newer countries—that is, to the countries where material progress is yet in its earlier stages—that laborers emigrate in search of higher wages, and capital flows in search of higher interest. It is in the older countries—that is to say, the countries where material progress has reached later stages—that widespread destitution is found in the midst of the greatest abundance. Go into one of the new communities where Anglo-Saxon vigor is just beginning the race of progress; where the machinery of production and exchange is yet rude and inefficient; where the increment of wealth is not yet great enough to enable any class to live in ease and luxury; where the best house is but a cabin of logs or a cloth and paper shanty, and the richest man is forced to daily work—and though you will find an absence of wealth and all its concomitants, you will find no beggars. There is no luxury, but there is no destitution. No one makes an easy living, nor a very good living; but every one *can* make a living, and no one able and willing to work is oppressed by the fear of want.

But just as a community realizes the conditions which all civilized communities are striving for, and advances in the scale of material progress—just as closer settlement and a more intimate connection with the rest of the world, and greater utilization of labor-saving machinery, make possible greater economies in production and exchange, and wealth in consequence increases, not merely in the aggregate, but in proportion to population—so does poverty take a darker aspect. Some get an infinitely better and easier living, but others find it hard to get a living at all. The "tramp" comes with the locomotive, and alms-houses and prisons are as surely the marks of "material progress" as are costly dwellings, rich warehouses, and magnificent churches. Upon streets lighted with gas and patrolled by uniformed policemen, beggars wait for the passer-by, and in the shadow of college, and library, and museum, are gathering the more hideous Huns and fiercer Vandals of whom Macaulay prophesied.[1]

This fact—the great fact that poverty and all its concomitants show themselves in communities just as they develop into the conditions towards which material progress tends—proves that the social difficulties existing wherever a certain stage of progress has been reached, do not arise from local circumstances, but are, in some way or another, engendered by progress itself.

And, unpleasant as it may be to admit it, it is at last becoming evident that the enormous increase in productive power which has

---

[1] In an 1857 letter to Henry Stephens Randall, the American biographer of Thomas Jefferson, English writer and politician Thomas Babington Macaulay (1800-1859) argued that Jeffersonian democracy would lead inevitably either to despotism or to anarchy. "Either some Caesar or Napoleon will seize the reins of government with a strong hand; or your republic will be as fearfully plundered and laid waste by barbarians in the twentieth Century as the Roman Empire was in the fifth;—with this difference, that the Huns and Vandals who ravaged the Roman Empire came from without, and that your Huns and Vandals will have been engendered within your own country by your own institutions." The letter was first published in full in *Harper's Magazine* in February 1877, shortly before Henry George began to write *Progress and Poverty*. Thanks to William McKelvy for his assistance in identifying this passage.

marked the present century and is still going on with accelerating ratio, has no tendency to extirpate poverty or to lighten the burdens of those compelled to toil. It simply widens the gulf between Dives and Lazarus,[1] and makes the struggle for existence more intense. The march of invention has clothed mankind with powers of which a century ago the boldest imagination could not have dreamed. But in factories where labor-saving machinery has reached its most wonderful development, little children are at work; wherever the new forces are anything like fully utilized, large classes are maintained by charity or live on the verge of recourse to it; amid the greatest accumulations of wealth, men die of starvation, and puny infants suckle dry breasts; while everywhere the greed of gain, the worship of wealth, shows the force of the fear of want. The promised land flies before us like the mirage. The fruits of the tree of knowledge turn as we grasp them to apples of Sodom that crumble at the touch.[2]

[Source: Henry George, *Progress and Poverty: An Inquiry into the Cause of Industrial Depressions, and of Increase of Want with Increase of Wealth. The Remedy.* 4th ed. (New York: Appleton, 1882): 6-8.]

5. James MacNeill Whistler, from "Mr. Whistler's Ten O'Clock" (1885)

[James MacNeill Whistler (1834-1903), ex-patriate American painter, bohemian, aesthete, and self-styled scourge of the middle classes, first delivered his "Ten O'Clock" lecture (so-called because it started at the unheard-of hour of 10 p.m.) in evening dress to a select audience in February 1885. Despite the self-conscious eccentricities of its style, Whistler's lecture presents some commonly-held late-Victorian views on the relation of art to work, education, history, and popular culture, views that diverge from those of Morris in just about every conceivable way.]

---

[1] Jesus's parable about the rich man, Dives, and the poor man, Lazarus, is recounted in Luke 16: 19-31.

[2] An odd yoking of allusions. The wanderings of the Israelites under Moses in search of the promised land is recounted primarily in Exodus 19-34 and Numbers 14. God's prohibition against eating the fruit of the tree of knowledge is found in Genesis 2:15-17. The apple of Sodom, first mentioned in Tacitus, was supposedly beautiful on the outside but ashes within; it is thus a proverbial figure for disillusionment.

So Art has become foolishly confounded with education—that all should be equally qualified.

Whereas, while polish, refinement, culture, and breeding are in no way, arguments for artistic result, it is also no reproach to the most finished scholar or greatest gentleman in the land that he be absolutely without eye for painting or ear for music—that in his heart he prefer the popular print to the scratch of Rembrandt's needle—or the songs of the hall[1] to Beethoven's "C minor Symphony."

Let him have but the wit to say so, and not feel the admission a proof of inferiority.

Art happens—no hovel is safe from it, no Prince may depend upon it, the vastest intelligence cannot bring it about, and puny efforts to make it universal end in quaint comedy, and coarse farce.

This is as it should be—and all attempts to make it otherwise are due to the eloquence of the ignorant, the zeal of the conceited.

The boundary line is clear. Far from me to propose to bridge it over—that the pestered people be pushed across. No! I would save them from further fatigue. I would come to their relief, and would lift from their shoulders this incubus of Art.

Why, after centuries of freedom from it, and indifference to it, should it now be thrust upon them by the blind—until wearied and puzzled, they know no longer how they shall eat or drink—how they shall sit or stand—or wherewithal they shall clothe them-selves—without afflicting Art....

Why this lifting of the brow in deprecation of the present—this pathos in reference to the past?

If Art be rare to-day, it was seldom heretofore.

It is false, this teaching of decay.

The master stands in no relation to the moment at which he occurs—a monument of isolation—hinting at sadness—having no part in the progress of his fellow men.

He is also no more the product of civilization than is the scientific truth asserted dependent upon the wisdom of a period. The assertion itself requires the *man* to make it. The truth was from the beginning....

False again, the fabled link between the grandeur of Art and the glories and virtues of the State, for art feeds not upon nations, and peoples may be wiped from the face of the Earth, but Art *is*.

---

[1]   I.e., the music hall.

It is indeed high time that we cast aside the weary weight of responsibility and co-partnership, and know that, in no way, do our virtues minister to its worth, in no way do our vices impede its triumph.

How irksome! how hopeless! how superhuman the self-imposed task of the nation! How sublimely vain the belief that it shall live nobly or art perish.

Let us reassure ourselves, at our own option is our virtue. Art, we in no way affect.

A whimsical goddess, and a capricious, her strong sense of joy tolerates no dulness, and, live we never so spotlessly, still may she turn her back upon us.

[Source: James MacNeill Whistler, *The Gentle Art of Making Enemies, as Pleasingly Exemplified in Many Instances, Wherein the Serious Ones of this Earth, Carefully Exasperated, Have Been Prettily Spurred in to Unseemliness and Indiscretion, While Overcome by an Undue Sense of Right* (London: William Heinemann, 1890): 150-51, 154-56.]

6. Eleanor Marx-Aveling and Edward Aveling, from "The Woman Question" (1886)

[Eleanor Marx-Aveling (1855-1898), the youngest daughter of Karl Marx, was a noted translator (of Ibsen and Flaubert among others) and editor (most notably of her father's works) in addition to being a prolific lecturer and essayist on socialist issues. She also co-authored a number of works with her common-law husband, Edward Aveling, including *The Factory Hell* (1885) and *Shelley's Socialism* (1888). While workers' rights and women's rights were often linked rhetorically by radical writers, Marx-Aveling was among the very few to insist both on the specific forms of women's oppression and on the economic basis of that oppression.]

Society is ... in a condition of unrest, of fermentation. The unrest is that of a mass of rottenness; the fermentation that of putrefaction. The death of the capitalist method of production, and therefore of the society based on it, is, as we think, within a distance measureable in terms of years rather than of centuries. And that death means the re-solution of society into simpler forms, even into elements, that re-combining will produce a new and better order of things. Society is morally bankrupt, and in nothing does this gruesome moral bankruptcy come out with a more hideous distinctness than in the relation between men and women. Efforts to postpone the crash by drawing bills upon the imagination are useless. The facts have to be faced.

One of these facts of the most fundamental importance is not, and never has been, fairly confronted by the average man or woman in considering these relations.... This fundamental fact is, that the question is one of economics. The position of women rests, as everything in our complex modern society rests, on an economic basis.... [T]hose who attack the present treatment of women without seeking for the cause of this in the economics of our latter-day society are like doctors who treat a local affection without inquiring into the general bodily health.

This criticism applies not alone to the commonplace person who makes a jest of any discussion into which the element of sex enters. It applies to those higher natures, in many cases earnest and thoughtful, who see that women are in a parlous state, and are anxious that something should be done to better their condition. These are the excellent and hard-working folk who agitate for that perfectly just aim, woman suffrage;[1] for the repeal of the Contagious Diseases Act, a monstrosity begotten of male cowardice and brutality;[2] for the higher education of women; for the opening to them of universities,[3] the learned professions, and all callings, from that of teacher to that of bagman....

The truth, not fully recognized even by those anxious to do good to woman, is that she, like the labour-classes, is in an oppressed condition; that her position, like theirs, is one of merciless degradation. Women are the creatures of an organized tyranny of men, as the workers are the creatures of an organized tyranny of idlers. Even

---

[1] The last quarter of the century saw a number of vigorous campaigns for full woman's suffrage; success, however, did not arrive until after World War I.

[2] Under the Contagious Diseases Acts of 1864, 1866, and 1869, compulsory genital inspections of suspected prostitutes were mandated in areas near military garrisons and ports. The goal was to curb the spread of venereal disease. The soldiers and sailors themselves, however, were exempted from inspection. Calls to repeal the acts continued through the 1870s and 1880s; they were finally repealed in 1886.

[3] Women's colleges were established at both Oxford and Cambridge during the 1870s, though neither university awarded fully accredited degrees to women until well into the twentieth century.

where this much is grasped, we must never be weary of insisting on the non-understanding that for women, as for the labouring classes, no solution of the difficulties and problems that present themselves is really possible in the present condition of society. All that is done, heralded by with no matter what flourish of trumpets, is palliative, not remedial. Both the oppressed classes, women and the immediate producers, must understand that their emancipation will come from themselves. Women will find allies in the better sort of men, as the labourers are finding allies among the philosophers, artists, and poets. But the one has nothing to hope from man as a whole, and the other has nothing to hope from the middle-class as a whole.

[Source: Eleanor Marx-Aveling and Edward Aveling, "The Woman Question: A Socialist Point of View," *Westminster Review* 125 (January 1886): 209-11.]

7. Mona Caird, from "The Emancipation of the Family" (1890)

[Mona Caird (1854-1932) achieved notoriety in 1888 with an essay in the *Westminster Review*, titled simply "Marriage," which argued that for women marriage was disastrous. When the *Daily Telegraph* responded by asking its readers "Is Marriage a Failure?" the paper received over 27,000 letters in less than two months, most of them excoriating Caird. Caird refused to back down, instead publishing over the next decade a series of essays which detailed the moral and social shortcomings of the modern institutions of marriage, motherhood, and the family. In "The Emancipation of the Family" she traces the historical development of the family, arguing that our present arrangement is an ossified holdover from more "barbarous" times. She also argues for dissolving current marriage laws in favor of contractual arrangements between consenting partners.]

If we could only realize how fundamental, in our ideas of family and social life, is the old patriarchal feeling, how strong it still is in all our laws, we should then more clearly see that marriage, with its one-sided obligations, is not a thought-out, rational system of sex-relationship, but a lineal descendent of crystallized barbarian usages, cruel and absurd even when the warlike conditions of society gave them some color of reason; revolting now to all ideas of human justice and of dignity. While society, in other directions, has been moving and changing, ideas on this subject have remained stagnant. This is the last citadel of the less intelligent kind of conservatism, and it has been defended with the ferocity and jealousy with which one instinctively fights for a last hope. History and science are rapidly undermining it; removing those imaginary foundations in the "will of God" or the "ordinance of nature" on which so many happy theories have been built. Under the new light of knowledge, the favorite satires of men against women lose their brilliancy; they sound stupid and ungenerous, like the taunts of gaolers against their half-starved prisoners.

To bring the institution of marriage up to date is among the next great tasks of progressive civilization. So far has it lagged behind that this proposal sounds like a proposal to break up society altogether. So much the worse for society....

That marriage in its present form and the subjection of women are interdependent will surely not be denied by any thinker. If women had shared with men the privilege of making the laws, it is clear that marriage would not have bound the two sexes unequally; and it seems very unlikely, if both law and opinion had insisted on men really submitting to the conditions of this institution, that they would have made it so inflexible and so irrationally harsh in its demands. They would then have seen the incongruity of the ideas of "sanctity" and enforced union, and the cruelty of ruining so many lives in the supposed interests of society, which the marriage law does its best to fill with miserable homes....

I firmly believe that the condition of children under a freer, more developed social life would be infinitely happier and better, even when their parents were divorced, than are the children of average undivorced parents who live undissentingly under the present marriage system. In the shelter of "happy homes," under the care of ignorant nurses or overworked mothers, deprived, through lack of knowledge, of physical advantages often of the simplest kind, of reasonable training, healthful interests and recreation, the unlucky children, for whose fate under a freer system so much anxiety is expressed, are now enduring a thousand wrongs, and suffering in a thousand unnecessary ways, because on this subject the majority of parents still cling to the superstitions of great-grandmothers, whose words of wisdom are handed down, pure and unadulterated, from mother to daughter, assisted, generation after generation, by such lore of old nurses as may happen to attach to them *en route*.

Any change bestowing greater freedom, increasing the sense of responsibility, and extirpating the enchained ideas that marriage necessarily implies children, and motherhood the power of rearing and training them, would be the beginning of a happier future for the ill-used little beings, whom we make serve as apologies for the old established tyranny which we have not yet rebelled against in our domestic institutions.

[Source: Mona Caird, "The Emancipation of the Family," *North American Review* 151 (July 1890): 33-36.]

8. Peter Kropotkin, from *The Conquest of Bread* (1892)

[Prince Peter Kropotkin (1842-1921) was the period's leading theoretician of anarchism. After enduring terms of imprisonment both in his native Russia and in France, he settled in exile in Great Britain in 1886. Despite Morris's rejection of anarchism as a viable social program, he held Kropotkin himself in high regard. Though *The Conquest of Bread* was published after *News from Nowhere*, Morris would have been thoroughly familiar with the ideas expressed in the work, both by way of Kropotkin's numerous periodical writings during the 1880s and through personal conversation.]

Every society, on abolishing private property will be forced, we maintain, to organize itself on the lines of Communistic Anarchy. Anarchy leads to Communism, and Communism to Anarchy, both alike being expressions of the predominant tendency in modern societies, the pursuit of equality.

Time was when a peasant family could consider the corn it sowed and reaped, or the woollen garments woven in the cottage, as the products of its own toil. But even then this way of looking at things was not quite correct. There were the roads and bridges made in common, the swamps drained by common toil, the communal pastures enclosed by hedges which were kept in repair by each and all. If the looms for weaving or the dyes for colouring fabrics were improved by somebody, all profited; and even in those days a peasant family could not live alone, but was dependent in a thousand ways on the village or the commune.

But nowadays, in the present state of industry, when everything is interdependent, when each branch of production is knit up with all the rest, the attempt to claim an individualist origin for the products of industry is absolutely untenable. The astonishing perfection attained by the textile or mining industries in civilized countries is due to the simultaneous development of a thousand other industries, great and small, to the extension of the railroad system, to inter-oceanic navigation, to the manual skill of thousands of workers, to a certain standard of culture reached by the working classes as a whole—to the labours, in short, of men in every corner of the globe.

The Italians who died of cholera while making the Suez Canal, or of anchylosis in the St. Gothard Tunnel, and the Americans mowed down by shot and shell while fighting for the abolition of slavery, have helped to develop the cotton industry in France and England, as well as the work-girls who languish in the factories of Manchester and Rouen, and the inventor who (following the suggestion of some worker) succeeds in improving the looms.[1]

How, then, shall we estimate the share of each in the riches which ALL contribute to amass? ...

As soon as the communes of the tenth, eleventh, and twelfth centuries had succeeded in emancipating themselves from their lords, ecclesiastical or lay, their communal labour and communal consumption began to extend and develop rapidly. The township—and not private persons—freighted ships and equipped expeditions, for the export of their manufacture, and the benefit arising from the foreign trade did not accrue to individuals, but was shared by all. At the outset, the townships also bought provisions for all their citizens. Traces of these institutions have lingered on into the nineteenth century, and the people piously cherish the memory of them in their legends.

---

[1] The construction of the Suez Canal (1858-69) connecting the Mediterranean Sea to the Gulf of Suez and of the St. Gothard's rail tunnel through the Alps (1872-80) made trade routes from the Middle East and India to western Europe more efficient. English and French textile mills, whose cotton supplies from the American South had been disrupted by the Civil War, were by the 1890s importing most of their cotton from India and Egypt. Kropotkin's general point is that global capitalism is only made possible through the interlocking interests (or, as he ironically implies, the "co-operation") of economic, commercial, industrial, and political systems at both the national and international levels.

All that has disappeared. But the rural township still struggles to preserve the last traces of this communism, and it succeeds—except when the state throws its heavy sword into the balance.

Meanwhile new organizations, based on the same principle—*to every man according to his needs*—spring up under a thousand different forms; for without a certain leaven of Communism the present societies could not exist. In spite of the narrowly egoistic turn given to men's minds by the commercial system, the tendency towards Communism is constantly appearing, and it influences our activities in a variety of ways.

The bridges, for the use of which a toll was levied in the old days, have become public property and are free to all; so are the high roads.... Museums, free libraries, free schools, free meals for children, parks and gardens open to all; streets paved and lighted, free to all; water supplied to every house without measure or stint—all such arrangements are founded on the principle: "Take what you need." ...

Moreover, there is a tendency, though still a feeble one, to consider the needs of the individual, irrespective of his past or possible services to the community. We are beginning to think of society as a whole, each part of which is so intimately bound up with the others that a service rendered to one is a service rendered to all.

When you go into a public library ... the librarian does not ask what services you have rendered to society before giving you the book, or the fifty books, which you require; he even comes to your assistance if you do not know how to manage the catalog....

In the same way, those who man the lifeboat do not ask credentials from the crew of a sinking ship; they launch their boat, risk their lives in the raging waves, and sometimes perish, all to save men whom they do not even know. And what need to know them? "They are human beings, and they need our aid—that is enough, that establishes their right—To the rescue!"

Thus we find a tendency, eminently communistic, springing up on all sides, and in various guises, in the very heart of theoretically individualist societies.

[Source: Peter Kropotkin, *The Conquest of Bread*, rev. ed. (New York: Benjamin Blom, 1913): 32-33, 35-38.]

Appendix C: Utopia/Dystopia

1. Sir Thomas More, from *Utopia* (1516)

[In *Utopia* Sir Thomas More (1477?-1535) offers a complex, open-ended inquiry into the nature of the ideal commonwealth. A Kelmscott Press edition of More's book was published in 1893. In his Foreword, Morris called it "a necessary part of a Socialist's library," since it forms "a link between the surviving Communism of the Middle Ages (become hopeless in More's time, and doomed to be soon effaced by the advancing wave of Commercial Bureaucracy), and the hopeful and practical progressive movement of to-day." The extract below is from the section titled "Of Sciences, Craftes, and Ocupations."]

Husbandrie[1] is a Science common to them all ingenerall, bothe men and women, wherein they be all experte and cunning. In this they be all instructe[d] even from their youth: partlie in their scholes with traditions and preceptes, and partlie in the countrey nighe the citie, brought up as it were in playinge, not onely beholding the use of it, but by occasion of exercising their bodies practising it also. Besides husbandrie, whiche (as I saide) is common to them all, everye one of them learnethe one or other several and particular science, as his owne proper crafte.[2] That is most commonly either clothworking in wol or flax, or masonrie, or the smithes craft, or the carpenters science.... Yea, and if anye person, when he hath learned one crafte, be desierous to learne also another, he is likewyse suffred and permitted.

When he hath learned bothe, he occupieth whether he wyll: onelesse the citie have more neade of the one, then of the other. The chiefe and almooste the onelye offyce of the Syphograuntes[3] is, to see and take hede, that no manne sit idle: but that everye one applye

---

1 Farming.
2 I.e., each person learns a particular trade or craft.
3 More's made-up title for the lowest level of administrator in Utopia. Once a year every group of thirty households elects a Syphograunte. Presiding over every ten Syphograuntes is a Tranibore. The two hundred Syphograuntes in Utopia are responsible for electing a prince, who holds that office for life unless convicted of tyranny.

his owne craft with earnest diligence. And yet for all that, not to be wearied from earlie in the morninge, to late in the evenninge, with continuall worke, like labouringe and toylinge beastes. For this is worse then the miserable and wretched condition of bondemen.[1] Whiche nevertheles is almooste everye where the lyfe of workemen and artificers,[2] saving in Utopia. For they dividynge the daye and the nyghte into xxiiii juste houres, appointe and assigne onelye sixe of those houres to woorke, before noone, upon the whiche they go streighte to diner: and after diner, when they have rested two houres, then they worke iii houres and upon that they go to supper. About eyghte of the cloke in the eveninge ... they go to bedde: eyght houres they geve to slepe. All the voide time, that is betwene the houres of worke, slepe, and meate, that they suffered to bestowe, every man as he liketh best him selfe.[3] Not to thintent[4] that they shold mispend this time in riote, or slouthfulnes: but beynge then licensed from the laboure of their owne occupations, to bestow the time well and thriftelye upon some other science, as shall please them.... Howbeit a greate multitude of every sort of people, both men and women go to heare lectures, some one and some an other, as everye mans nature is inclined. Yet, this notwithstanding, if any man had rather bestowe this time upon his owne occupation, (as it chaunceth in manye, whose mindes rise not in the contemplation of any science liberall) he is not letted, nor prohibited, but is also praysed and commended, as profitable to the common wealthe. After supper they bestowe one houre in playe: in summer in their gardens: in winter in their commen halles: where they dine and suppe. There they exercise themselves in musike, or els in honest and wholsome communication.... [S]einge they bestowe but vi houres in woorke, perchaunce you maye thinke that the lacke of some necessarye thinges hereof maye ensewe. But this is nothinge so. For that smal time is not only enough but also to muche for the stoore and abundaunce of all thinges, that be requisite, either for the necessitie, or commoditie of life. The which thinge you also shall perceave, if you weye and consider with your selfes how great a parte of the people in other contreis lyveth ydle.... Nowe consyder with youre selfe, of these fewe

---

[1] Slaves.
[2] Craftsmen.
[3] I.e., leisure time is spent as each person sees fit.
[4] "To thintent": i.e., with the intent

that doe woorke, how fewe be occupied, in necessarye woorkes. For where money beareth all the swinge,[1] there many vayne and super-fluous occupations must nedes be used, to serve only for ryotous superfluite, and unhonest pleasure.... But yf all these, that be nowe busied about unprofitable occupations, with all the whole flocke of them lyve ydellye and slouthfullye ... were sette to profytable occu-patyons: you easelye perceave how lytle tyme would be enoughe, yea and to muche to stoore us with all thinges that maye be requisite either for necessitie, or for commoditye, yea or for pleasure, so that the same pleasure be trewe and natural. And this in Utopia the thinge it selfe makethe manifeste and playne.... Wherefore, seinge they be all exercysed in profitable occupations, and that fewe artificers in the same craftes be sufficiente, this is the cause that plentye of all thinges beinge among them, they doo sometymes bringe forthe an innu-merable companye of people to amend the hyghe wayes, yf anye be broken. Many times also, when they have no suche woorke to be occupied aboute, an open proclamation is made, that they shall bestowe fewer houres in worke. For the magistrates doe not exercise theire citizens againste theire willes in unneadefull laboures. For while in the institution of that weale publique, this ende is onelye and chiefely pretended and mynded, that what time maye possibly be spared from the necessarye occupacions and affayres of the commen wealth, all that the citizeins shoulde withdrawe from the bodely service to the free libertye of the minde, and garnisshinge of the same. For herein they suppose the felicitye of this liffe to consiste.

[Source: Sir Thomas More, *Utopia* (Reading (England): Golden Cockerel Press, 1929): 62-67.]

2. Samuel Butler, from *Erewhon; or, Over the Range* (1872)

[Morris admired Samuel Butler's (1835-1902) often viciously satirical fantasy about a land over the mountains in which illness is treated as a crime, crime is regarded as a form of disease, the development of machines is viewed from a Darwinian perspec-tive, and education is based on the virtues of unreason. In this extract from Chapter XX, "The Colleges of Unreason," Butler's narrator describes the Erewhonian educational system.]

---

[1] I.e., is the standard of all things.

The main feature in their system is the prominence which they give to a study which I can only translate by the word "hypothetics." They argue thus—that to teach a boy merely the nature of the things which exist in the world around him, and about which he will have to be conversant during his whole life, would be giving him but a narrow and shallow conception of the universe, which it is urged might contain all manner of things which are not now to be found therein. To open his eyes to these possibilities, and so to prepare him for all sorts of emergencies, is the object of this system of hypothetics. To imagine a set of utterly strange and impossible contingencies, and require the youths to give intelligent answers to the questions that arise therefrom, is reckoned the fittest conceivable way of preparing them for the actual conduct of their affairs in after life....

The arguments in favour of the deliberate development of the unreasoning faculties were much more cogent. But here they depart from the principles on which they justify their study of hypothetics; for they base the importance which they assign to hypothetics upon the fact of their being a preparation for the extraordinary, while their study of Unreason rests upon its developing those faculties which are required for the daily conduct of affairs. Hence their professorships of Inconsistency and Evasion, in both of which studies the youths are most carefully examined before being allowed to proceed to their degree in hypothetics. The more "earnest" and "conscientious" students attain to a proficiency in these subjects which is quite surprising; there is hardly any inconsistency so glaring but they soon learn to defend it, or injunction so clear that they cannot find some pretext for disregarding it. I saw the lecture-rooms of both these professors. Over the door of one was written, "Consistency is a vice which degrades human nature and levels man with the brute"; over the other, "It is the glory of the parliament to make a law—it is the glory of the minister to evade it."

Life, they urge, would be intolerable if men were to be guided in all they did by reason and reason only. Reason betrays men into the drawing of hard and fast lines, and to the defining by language—language being like the sun, which reareth and then scorcheth.[1] Extremes are alone logical, but they are almost invariably absurd; the mean is illogical or unreasonable, but it is better than the purely

---

[1]   An allusion to the parable of the sower and the seeds, recounted in Matt. 13:1-9. The seeds that fall on stony ground spring up quickly, but "when the sunne was up, they were scorched: and because they had no root, they withered away."

reasonable; in fact there are no follies and no unreasonablenesses so great as those which can apparently be irrefragably defended by reason itself. There is hardly an error into which men might not easily be led if they based their conduct upon reason only....

I sometimes wondered how it was that the mischief done [by training youth in hypothetics and unreason] was not more clearly perceptible, and that the young men and women grew up as sensible and goodly as they did, in spite of the attempts almost deliberately made to warp and stunt their growth. Many doubtless received irreparable damage, from which they suffered to their life's end; but many seemed little or none the worse, and some almost the better. The reason would seem to be that the natural instinct of the lads in most cases so absolutely rebelled against their training, that do what the teachers might they could never get them to pay serious heed to it. The consequence was the boys only lost their time, and not so much of this as might have been expected, for in their hours of leisure they were actively engaged in exercises and sports which developed their physical nature, and made them at any rate strong and healthy; also, being keen and intelligent they kept their eyes and ears constantly open to everything which interested them, and so picked up all manner of really useful knowledge unconsciously. Moreover those who had any special tastes could not be restrained from developing them: they would learn what they wanted to learn and liked, in spite of obstacles which seemed rather to urge them on than to discourage them, while for those who had no special capacity, the loss of time was of comparatively little moment; but in spite of these alleviations of the mischief, I am sure that infinite damage was done to the children of the sub-wealthy classes. Souls destroyed, and lives blighted in vain! The poorer children suffered far less; destruction and death say that they have heard the sound of wisdom with their ears;[1] in many respects poverty has done so also.

[Source: Samuel Butler, *Erewhon; or, Over the Range*, 2nd ed. (London: Trüber & Co., 1872): 180-82, 184-85.]

---

[1]   Perhaps an allusion to Acts 17:19-20. The Athenians ask Paul: "May we know what this new doctrine whereof thou speakest, is: for thou bringeth certain strange things to our eares: we would know therefore what these things mean."

3. Richard Jefferies, from *After London; or, Wild England* (1885)

[Richard Jefferies (1848-1887), best known for his children's books and his numerous essays on rural life, produced a sensation with his apocalyptic novel, *After London*. The story tells of an England returned to a pre-civilized state following an unspecified catastrophe. According to his first biographer, J. W. Mackail, Morris "was never weary of praising" this book.[1] To Georgiana Burne-Jones he confided that "absurd hopes curled round" his heart as he contemplated Jefferies's vision of a world wiped clean of all civilization and returned to a vigorous barbarism (*Letters* 2:426). The first extract below, from Chapter 5 ("The Lake"), describes a two-hundred-mile long lake situated in what used to be the Thames Valley.]

At the eastern extremity the Lake narrows, and finally is lost in the vast marshes which cover the site of the ancient London. Through these, no doubt, in the days of the old world there flowed the river Thames. By changes of the sea level and the sand that was brought up there must have grown great banks, which obstructed the stream. I have formerly mentioned the vast quantities of timber, the wreckage of towns and bridges which was carried down by the various rivers, and by none more so than by the Thames. These added to the accumulation, which increased the faster because the foundations of the ancient bridges held it like piles driven in for the purpose. And before this the river had become partially choked from the cloacæ of the ancient city which poured into it through enormous subterranean aqueducts and drains.

After a time all these shallows and banks became well matted together by the growth of weeds, of willows, and flags, while the tide, ebbing lower at each drawing back, left still more mud and sand. Now it is believed that when this had gone on for a time, the waters of the river, unable to find a channel, began to overflow up into the deserted streets, and especially to fill the underground passages and drains, of which the number and extent was beyond all the power of words to describe. These, by the force of the water, were burst up, and the houses fell in.

---

[1] J. W. Mackail, *The Life of William Morris*, 2 vols. (London: Longmans, Green 1899) 2:144.

For this marvellous city, of which such legends are related, was after all only of brick, and when the ivy grew over and trees and shrubs sprang up, and, lastly, the waters underneath burst in, this huge metropolis was soon overthrown. At this day all those parts which were built upon low ground are marshes and swamps. Those houses that were upon high ground were, of course, like the other towns, ransacked of all they contained by the remnant that was left; the iron, too, was extracted. Trees growing up by them in time cracked the walls, and they fell in. Trees and bushes covered them; ivy and nettles concealed the crumbling masses of brick....

Thus the low-lying parts of the mighty city of London became swamps, and the higher grounds were clad with bushes. The very largest of the buildings fell in, and there was nothing visible but trees and hawthorns on the upper lands, and willows, flags, reeds, and rushes on the lower. These crumbling ruins still more choked the stream, and almost, if not quite, turned it back. If any water ooze past, it is not perceptible, and there is no channel through to the salt ocean. It is a vast stagnant swamp, which no man dare enter, since death would be his inevitable fate.

There exhales from this oozy mass so fatal a vapour that no animal can endure it. The black water bears a greenish-brown floating scum, which for ever bubbles up from the putrid mud of the bottom. When the wind collects the miasma, and, as it were, presses it together, it becomes visible as a low cloud which hangs over the place. The cloud does not advance beyond the limit of the marsh, seeming to stay there by some constant attraction; and well it is for us that it does not, since at such times when the vapour is thickest, the very wildfowl leave the reeds, and fly from the poison. There are no fishes, neither can eels exist in the mud, nor even newts. It is dead.

The flags and reeds are coated with slime and noisome to the touch; there is one place where even these do not grow, and where there is nothing but an oily liquid, green and rank. It is plain there are no fishes in the water, for herons do not go thither, nor the king-fishers, not one of which approaches the spot. They say the sun is sometimes hidden by the vapour when it is thickest, but I do not see how any can tell this, since they could not enter the cloud, as to breathe it when collected by the wind is immediately fatal. For all the rottenness of a thousand years and of many hundred millions of human beings is there festering under the stagnant water, which has sunk down into and penetrated the earth, and floated up to the surface the contents of the buried cloacæ.

[The passage below is from Chapter 23, "Strange Things," in which Jefferies's protagonist, Felix Aquila, enters what remains of London.]

Presently a white object appeared ahead; and on coming to it, he found it was a wall, white as snow, with some kind of crystal. He touched it, when the wall fell immediately with a crushing sound as if pulverized, and disappeared in a vast cavern at his feet. Beyond this chasm he came to more walls like those of houses, such as would be left if the roofs fell in. He carefully avoided touching them, for they seemed as brittle as glass, and merely a white powder having no consistency at all. As he advanced these remnants of buildings increased in number, so that he had to wind in and out round them. In some places the crystallized wall had fallen of itself, and he could see down into the cavern; for the house had either been built partly underground, or, which was more probable, the ground had risen. Whether the walls had been of bricks or stone or other material he could not tell; they were now like salt.

Soon wearying of winding round these walls, Felix returned and retraced his steps till he was outside the place, and then went on towards the left. Not long after, as he still walked in a dream and without feeling his feet, he descended a slight slope and found the ground change in colour from black to a dull red. In his dazed state he had taken several steps out into this red before he noticed that it was liquid, unctuous and slimy, like a thick oil. It deepened rapidly and was already over his shoes; he returned to the black shore and stood looking out over the water, if such it could be called....

He had penetrated into the midst of that dreadful place, of which he had heard many a tradition: how the earth was poison, the water poison, the air poison, the very light of heaven, falling through such an atmosphere, poison. There were said to be places where the earth was on fire and belched forth sulphurous fumes, supposed to be from the combustion of the enormous stores of strange and unknown chemicals collected by the wonderful people of those times. Upon the surface of the water there was a greenish-yellow oil, to touch which was death to any creature; it was the very essence of corruption.... The earth on which he walked, the black earth, leaving phosphoric foot-prints behind him, was composed of the mouldered bodies of millions of men who had passed away in the centuries during which the city existed. He shuddered as he moved; he hastened, yet could not go fast, his numbed limbs would not permit him.

[Source: Richard Jefferies, *After London; or, Wild England* (New York: Cassell and Co., 1885): 65-69, 375-76, 378-80.]

4. Jane Hume Clapperton, from *Margaret Dunmore; or, A Socialist Home* (1888)

[This novel by feminist-socialist Jane Hume Clapperton (1832-1914), set only two years into the future, details the founding and eventual success of the communitarian "socialist home" estab-lished by the title character. In Clapperton's view, the transfor-mation of modern society into a socialist utopia could occur gradually, with "homes" like Margaret Dunmore's providing models of new forms of family life, work, and education that would eventually disseminate into the larger culture. In the passage below, Dunmore describes some of the goals and ideals of the newly-established socialist home.]

"The public spirit of our Unitary Home (it was finally settled) must extend to the uttermost limits of the earth.

"It is nothing less than the Happiness of all Mankind we desire, and shall strive in some small measure to promote. To this end we purpose, first, to show by our life and conduct, in what true happi-ness consists.

"It does not consist in wealth, luxury, idleness; therefore, we eschew all these. Our home must never be wealthy, never luxuri-ous, never the abode of idleness.

"Within its walls abundant comfort, with simplicity, must be main-tained; elegance and refinement, without show or glitter. And whoever departs from this principle, in opinion or action, will be liable to crit-icism in open council, or free to withdraw from the Commune.

"Our second method of promoting General Happiness is, by direct action upon the young; and here we aspire to extension of the action beyond the children of our Unitary Home. The day-school we shall carefully organize is certain to be, for months, perhaps years, very small; for around Peterloo there are not, we fear, many parents sufficiently advanced in thought to commit their children to our care. To the average public mind, our school will seem non-religious. The Bible will not be used as a text-book. We regard it as human, a venerable monument of past ages, and although the work it has done, in evolving the conscience of man, and aiding his progress from barbarism to civilization is immense, we perceive that its teaching now is discordant, confusing, partly obsolete, and in no way harmonious with the revealed truths of a scientific age.

"We set it aside, therefore, reverently, and turn to modern books, the highest and best we can find.... [O]ur school will take infinite pains to produce Humanity of a nobler, superior type—men and women eager to do useful work, and capable of doing it intelligently, skilfully, pleasurably; their one aim the general good, their one effort the service of their brethren; and genial, generous love the vital spring of action throughout life.

"Every tendency to dominancy in childhood will be carefully subdued, and the barbarous instincts—anger, revenge, hatred, jealousy, cunning, greed—studiously nipped in the bud. Conduct will be put before cleverness, even culture; and happiness, not wealth, pointed out as the goal of individual effort.

"Our third method of promoting general happiness is by action upon the public.

"There will be no indiscriminate charity, however, with us; no eleemosynary aid that, in supporting individuals, is hurtful to the race.

"We will search for the social forces that are truly remedial, and aid such. We will steadfastly bear in mind the causes of our present evil social state, and its transitional condition, and support such action as deals with these causes alone; whilst, at the same time, we strive to enlighten the public on the principles and practical outcome of Socialism, so as to prepare for the happier future of which this transition epoch is merely the unavoidable, discordant prelude."

To launch a Socialistic experiment in transition surroundings on a basis of non-coercive solidarity,—the task is not easy!

[Source: Jane Hume Clapperton, *Margaret Dunmore; or, A Socialist Home* (London: Swan Sonnenschein, Lowrey, and Co., 1888): 75-77.]

5. Edward Bellamy, from *Looking Backward, 2000-1887* (1888)

[Morris's horror at the utopia imagined by the American writer Edward Bellamy (1850-1898) was an important impetus for his decision to present the quite different vision of *News from Nowhere*. Bellamy identified himself as a socialist, but unlike Morris he saw socialism leading inevitably (and happily) to a state "organized as one great business corporation": centralized, urban, technocratic, bureaucratized. Reviewing *Looking Backward* in *Commonweal* (June 22, 1889), Morris worried that readers of the novel would respond: "If *that* is Socialism, we won't help its advent." In the extract below, the speakers are Julian West, the book's protagonist, and Dr. Leete (who speaks first), his host in the Boston of the year 2000.]

"The records of the period show that the outcry against the concentration of capital was furious. Men believed that it threatened society with a form of tyranny more abhorrent than it had ever endured. They believed that the great corporations were preparing for them a yoke of a baser servitude than had ever been imposed on the race, servitude not to men but to soulless machines incapable of any motive but insatiable greed. Looking back, we cannot wonder at their desperation, for certainly humanity was never confronted with a fate more sordid and hideous than would have been the era of corporate tyranny which they anticipated.

"Meanwhile, without being in the smallest degree checked by the clamor against it, the absorption of business by ever larger monopolies continued. In the United States, where this tendency was later in developing than in Europe, there was not, after the beginning of the last quarter of the century, any opportunity whatever for individual enterprise in any important field of industry, unless backed by a great capital. During the last decade of the century, such small businesses as still remained were fast failing survivals of a past epoch, or mere parasites on the great corporations, or else existed in fields too small to attract the great capitalists.... These syndicates, pools, trusts, or whatever their name, fixed prices and crushed all competition except when combinations as vast as themselves arose. Then a struggle, resulting in a still greater consolidation, ensued. The great city bazar [sic] crushed its country rivals with branch stores, and in the city itself absorbed its smaller rivals till the business of a whole quarter was concentrated under one roof with a hundred former proprietors of shops serving as clerks....

"The fact that the desperate popular opposition to the consolidation of business in a few powerful hands had no effect to check it, proves that there must have been a strong economical reason for it. The small capitalists, with their innumerable petty concerns, had, in fact, yielded the field to the great aggregations of capital, because they belonged to a day of small things and were totally incompetent to the demands of an age of steam and telegraphs and the gigantic scale of its enterprises. To restore the former order of things, even if possible, would have involved returning to the day of stagecoaches. Oppressive and intolerable as was the regime of the great consolidations of capital, even its victims, while they cursed it, were forced to admit the prodigious increase of efficiency which had been imparted to the national industries, the vast economies effected by concentration of management and unity of organization, and to confess that since the new system had taken the place of the old, the wealth of the world had increased at a rate before undreamed of. To be sure this vast increase had gone chiefly to make the rich richer, increasing the gap between them and the poor; but the fact remained that, as a means merely of producing wealth, capital had been proved efficient in proportion to its consolidation. The restoration of the old system with the subdivision of capital, if it were possible, might indeed bring back a greater equality of conditions with more individual dignity and freedom, but it would be at the price of general poverty and the arrest of material progress.

"Was there, then, no way of commanding the services of the mighty wealth-producing principle of consolidated capital, without bowing down to a plutocracy like that of Carthage?[1] As soon as men began to ask themselves these questions, they found the answer ready for them. The movement toward the conduct of business by larger and larger aggregations of capital, the tendency toward monopolies, which had been so desperately and vainly resisted, was recognized at last, in its true significance, as a process which

---

[1]   A plutocracy is a government run by the wealthy. In the popular imagination, the ancient civilization of Carthage in North Africa was associated with plutocratic government (just as Athens was associated with democracy and Rome with imperial rule).

only needed to complete its logical evolution to open a golden future to humanity.

"Early in the last century the evolution was completed by the final consolidation of the entire capital of the nation. The industry and commerce of the country, ceasing to be conducted by a set of irresponsible corporations and syndicates of private persons at their caprice and for their profit, were intrusted to a single syndicate representing the people, to be conducted in the common interest for the common profit. The nation, that is to say, organized as one great business corporation in which all other corporations were absorbed; it became the one capitalist in the place of all other capitalists, the sole employer, the final monopoly in which all previous and lesser monopolies were swallowed up, a monopoly in the profits and economies of which all citizens shared. In a word, the people of the United States concluded to assume the conduct of their own business, just as one hundred odd years before they had assumed the conduct of their own government, organizing now for industrial purposes on precisely the same grounds that they had then organized for political purposes. At last, strangely late in the world's history, the obvious fact was perceived that no business is so essentially the public business as the industry and commerce on which the people's livelihood depends, and that to entrust it to private persons to be managed for private profit, is a folly similar in kind, though vastly greater in magnitude, to that of surrendering the functions of political government to kings and nobles to be conducted for their personal glorification."

"Such a stupendous change as you describe," said I, "did not, of course, take place without great bloodshed and terrible convulsions."

"On the contrary," replied Dr. Leete, "there was absolutely no violence. The change had been long foreseen. Public opinion had become fully ripe for it, and the whole mass of the people was behind it. There was no more possibility of opposing it by force than by argument. On the other hand the popular sentiment toward the great corporations and those identified with them had ceased to be one of bitterness, as they came to realize their necessity as a link, a transition phase, in the evolution of the true industrial system. The most violent foes of the great private monopolies were now forced to recognize how invaluable and indispensable had been their office in educating the people up to the point of assuming control of their own business. Fifty years before, the consolidation of the industries of the country under national control would have seemed a very daring experiment to the most sanguine. But by a series of object lessons, seen and studied by all men, the great corporations had taught the people an entirely new set of ideas on this subject. They had seen for many years syndicates handling revenues greater than those of states, and directing the labors of hundreds of thousands of men with an efficiency and economy unattainable in smaller operations. It had come to be recognized as an axiom that the larger the business the simpler the principles that can be applied to it; that, as the machine is truer than the hand, so the system, which in a great concern does the work of the master's eye in a small business, turns out more accurate results. Thus it came about that, thanks to the corporations themselves, when it was proposed that the nation should assume their functions, the suggestion implied nothing which seemed impracticable even to the timid."

[Source: Edward Bellamy, *Looking Backward, 2000-1887* (Boston: Ticknor and Company, 1888): 72-81.]

6. Oscar Wilde, from "The Soul of Man Under Socialism" (1891)

[Like Morris, Oscar Wilde (1854-1900) believed that philanthropy, legislative reform, and other forms of political or social ameliorism simply helped to perpetuate economic inequality. With characteristic idiosyncrasy, though, Wilde also argues that socialism is of value primarily because it prepares the way for a more fully realized individualism.]

The chief advantage that would result from the establishment of Socialism is, undoubtedly, the fact that Socialism would relieve us from that sordid necessity of living for others which, in the present condition of things, presses so hardly upon almost everybody. In fact, scarcely anyone at all escapes.

... The majority of people spoil their lives by an unhealthy and exaggerated altruism—are forced, indeed, so to spoil them. They find themselves surrounded by hideous poverty, by hideous ugliness, by hideous starvation. It is inevitable that they should be strongly moved by all this. The emotions of man are stirred more quickly than man's intelligence; and ... it is much more easy to have sympathy with suffering than it is to have sympathy with thought. Accordingly, with admirable though misdirected intentions, they very seriously and very sentimentally set themselves to the task of remedying the evils that they see. But their remedies do not cure the disease: they merely prolong it. Indeed, their remedies are part of the disease.

They try to solve the problem of poverty, for instance, by keeping the poor alive or, in the case of a very advanced school, by amusing the poor.

But this is not a solution: it is an aggravation of the difficulty. *The proper aim is to try and reconstruct society on such a basis that poverty will be impossible.* And the altruistic virtues have really prevented the carrying out of this aim. Just as the worst slave-owners were those who were kind to their slaves, and so prevented the horror of the system being realized by those who suffered from it, and understood by those who contemplated it, so, in the present state of things in England, the people who do most harm are the people who try to do most good; and at last we have had the spectacle of men who have really studied the problem and know the life—educated men who live in the East-end[1]—coming forward and imploring the community to restrain its altruistic impulses of charity, benevolence, and the like. They do so on the ground that such charity degrades and demoralizes. They are perfectly right. Charity creates a multitude of sins.[2]

There is also this to be said. It is immoral to use private property in order to alleviate the horrible evils that result from the institution of private property. It is both immoral and unfair....

Upon the other hand, *Socialism itself will be of value simply because it will lead to Individualism.*

Socialism, Communism, or whatever one chooses to call it, by converting private property into public wealth, and substituting cooperation for competition, will restore society to its proper condition of

---

[1] I.e., the East End of London, roughly the portion stretching east from the Tower of London, which contained many of the poorest areas of the city. Most of the philanthropic and social work in London from the 1850s onward was concentrated in the East End. Four years before Wilde's essay appeared, Friedrich Engels had harshly criticized the practice of philanthropy in the 1887 edition of *The Condition of the Working Class in England.*

[2] In characteristic fashion, Wilde here inverts a familiar Christian platitude. The allusion is to 1 Peter 4:8: "Above all things have fervent charity among yourselves: for charity shall cover the multitude of sins."

a thoroughly healthy organism, and insure the material well-being of each member of the community. It will, in fact, give Life its proper basis and its proper environment. But for the full development of Life to its highest mode of perfection, something more is needed. What is needed is Individualism. If the Socialism is Authoritarian; if there are Governments armed with economic power as they are now with political power; if, in a word, we are to have Industrial Tyrannies, then the last state of man will be worse than the first. At present, in consequence of the existence of private property, a great many people are enabled to develop a certain very limited amount of Individualism. They are either under no necessity to work for a living, or are enabled to choose the sphere of activity that is really congenial to them, and gives them pleasure. These are the poets, the philosophers, the men of science, the men of culture—in a word, the real men, the men who have realized themselves, and in whom all Humanity gains a partial realization. Upon the other hand, there are a great many people who, having no private property of their own, and being always on the brink of sheer starvation, are compelled to do the work of beasts of burden, to do work that is quite uncongenial to them, and to which they are forced by the peremptory, unreasonable, degrading Tyranny of want. These are the poor, and amongst them there is no grace of manner, or charm of speech, or civilization, or culture, or refinement in pleasures, or joy of life. From their collective force Humanity gains much in material prosperity. But it is only the material result that it gains, and the man who is poor is in himself absolutely of no importance. He is merely the infinitesimal atom of a force that, so far from regarding him, crushes him: indeed, prefers him crushed, as in that case he is far more obedient.

...We are often told that the poor are grateful for charity. Some of them are, no doubt, *but the best amongst the poor are never grateful.* They are ungrateful, discontented, disobedient, and rebellious. They are quite right to be so. Charity they feel to be a ridiculously inadequate mode of partial restitution, or a sentimental dole, usually accompanied by some impertinent attempt on the part of the sentimentalist to tyrannize over their private lives. Why should they be grateful for the crumbs that fall from the rich man's table?[1] They should be seated at the board, and are beginning to know it. As for being discontented, a man who would not be discontented with such surroundings and

---

[1] An allusion to Mark 7: 25-29.

such a low mode of life would be a perfect brute. Disobedience, in the eyes of anyone who has read history, is man's original virtue.[1] It is through disobedience that progress has been made, through disobedience and through rebellion.... [A] poor man who is ungrateful, unthrifty, discontented, and rebellious is probably a real personality, and has much in him. He is at any rate a healthy protest. As for the virtuous poor, one can pity them, of course, but one cannot possibly admire them. They have made private terms with the enemy, and sold their birthright for very bad pottage....[2]

... Under the new conditions Individualism will be far freer, far finer, and far more intensified than it is now. I am not talking of the great imaginatively-realized individualism of such poets as I have mentioned, but of the great actual Individualism latent and potential in mankind generally. For the recognition of private property has really harmed Individualism, and obscured it, by confusing man with what he possesses. It has led Individualism entirely astray. It has made gain not growth its aim. So that man thought that the important thing was to have, and did not know that the important thing is to be. *The true perfection of man lies, not in what man has, but in what man is.* Private property has crushed true Individualism, and set up an Individualism that is false....

It will, of course, be said that such a scheme as is set forth here is quite unpractical, and goes against human nature. This is perfectly true. It is unpractical, and it goes against human nature. This is why it is worth carrying out, and that is why one proposes it. For what is a practical scheme? *A practical scheme is either a scheme that is already in existence, or a scheme that could be carried out under existing conditions.* But it is exactly the existing conditions that one objects to; and any scheme that could accept these conditions is wrong and foolish. The conditions will be done away with, and human nature will change.

[Source: *Fortnightly Review* 49 (February 1, 1891): 292-96, 315.]

---

[1] Another Wildean inversion: disobedience traditionally is called mankind's original sin. The sentence ironically echoes the opening of Milton's *Paradise Lost* (1667), where "man's first disobedience" in the Garden of Eden is said to have "brought death into the world."

[2] An allusion to Genesis 25: 29-34. Esau sells his birthright to his brother Jacob for a pottage of lentils.

7. Florence Dixie, from *Gloriana; or, the Revolution of 1900* (1892)

[Novelist, essayist, and travel writer, Florence Dixie (1857-1905) was also known for her impassioned advocacy of a wide range of causes, including Irish home rule, African tribal rights, and women's suffrage. Her novel *Gloriana*, set in the very near future (1894-1900), depicts a world in which women struggle valiantly to achieve full legal and social equality with men. That they succeed is due in no small measure to the efforts of Gloria de Lara, who, disguised as Hector D'Estrange, becomes prime minister. The extract below details some of the celebrations that follow the passage of a woman's full suffrage bill under D'Estrange's leadership. Later in the novel Gloria de Lara, her true identity revealed, successfully guides through Parliament a bill ensuring full equality for women.]

In the political world, and in Parliament like everywhere else, Hector D'Estrange has made a stir. His eloquence and debating power are the wonder of all who hear him, and his practical, sympathetic knowledge of the social questions of the day has made him the idol of the masses. He has just succeeded in carrying his Woman's Suffrage Bill by a large majority, thereby conferring on women, married or unmarried, in this respect, identical rights with men. And now to-day, in the monster Hall of Liberty, which he has founded, and which has been erected by the lavish subscriptions of the women of Great Britain, Ireland, and the world at large, he is to preside at the ceremony of its opening. It *is* a monster building. Talk of Olympia, of the Albert Hall—why, they are dwarfs beside it!

In shape it is circular, and towers aloft towards heaven, its great dome pinnacle crowned by a cap of glass, which report declares to consist of a million panes. Around this glass a gilded crown is twined, and holding it there—one in a kneeling attitude, the other upright; with one hand high upraised towards heaven—are two gilded women's forms. They are the Statues of Liberty.

[After the Hall is filled by people of all classes and political allegiances, Hector addresses the cheering crowd.]

"Ladies and gentlemen," he begins, and the clear, exquisite voice thrills through the huge building, "I shall have a few words to say to you before I declare the Hall of Liberty open, but first we will witness the march past of the representatives of all the companies of the Women's Volunteer Force of which I have the honor to be Commander-in-Chief."

A flourish of trumpets and loud cheering greets this announcement. Once more the great entrance doors unfold, the band of the White Regiment strikes up a march, as through the portals, ten abreast, and mounted on grey horses, that regiment advances at a trot....

[A]s each line passes the platform on which Hector D'Estrange is standing [the horses] break into a canter, increased to a gallop, whirling round the broad-spaced horse-ride in magnificent order. Looking along the serried line of horses' heads hardly a hair's breadth in difference can be distinguished, so compact is the position which is maintained throughout the ranks.

The march strains cease, and give way to a flourish of trumpets. Simultaneously the galloping steeds are reined on to their haunches, remaining motionless as statues. Thus they stand until the voice of Flora Desmond [leader of the White Regiment] is heard giving the order to retreat, when they fall into position, and retire at the trot, she riding round to join her chief on the platform.

And in this wise, headed by their respective bands and officers, representative companies of Hector D'Estrange's two hundred regiments march or gallop past him. The ceremony occupies some two hours, but they roll by all too quickly for the spectators, who, spellbound by what they see, watch the revolving scenes with the keenest interest....

Then cheer after cheer rings through the densely packed building as Hector D'Estrange advances to the front of the platform to speak. But he is raising his hand once more, as though appealing to be heard, and again a great silence falls.

"We are here to-day," the bright, clear ringing voice declares, "to open a building the magnitude of which cannot be measured by any other in the world. The Hall of Liberty stands here to-day as a living witness to the desire of woman to be heard. It was six years ago now that I first saw it in my dreams. It is a reality now, and will endure through all time, as a memorial of the first great effort made by woman to shake off the chains of slavery, that ever since our knowledge of men began, have held her a prisoner in the gilded gaols of inactivity and helplessness. I stand here to-day prepared to deny that woman is the inferior of man, either in mental capacity or physical strength, provided always that she be given equal advantages with him. I go further still, and declare that in the former respect she is his superior. You deny it? Then give her the chance, and I have no fear but that she will prove that I have not lied. You have to-day seen passed in review 10,000 representatives of the 200,000 volunteers that in a little more than four years have been enrolled and drilled into the splendid efficiency witnessed on this memorable occasion. Will you pretend or seek to tell yourselves that in warfare they would be unavailing? I laugh such a idea to scorn....

"Men and women who hear me to-day, I beseech you ponder the truth of what I have told you in your hearts. You boast of a civilization unparalleled in the world's history. But is it so? Side by side with wealth, appalling in its magnitude, stalks poverty, misery, and wrong, more appalling still. I aver that this poverty, misery, and wrong is, in great measure, due to the false and unnatural position awarded to woman; nor will justice, reparation, and perfection be attained until she takes her place *in all things* as the equal of man."

[Source: Florence Dixie, *Gloriana; or, the Revolution of 1900* (New York: Standard Publishing Co., 1892): 69-70, 75-78.]

Appendix D: Revolution or Reform

1. Karl Marx and Friedrich Engels, from *Manifesto of the Communist Party* **(1848)**

[The influence of Marx (1818-1883) and Engels (1820-1895) on political thought in Great Britain began only in the 1880s, when several of their works were translated into English for the first time. The following extract is taken from the 1888 translation of the *Manifesto* by Samuel Moore, for which Engels himself provided a preface and explanatory footnotes (here omitted). While not the first English translation of this work, Moore's was (and remains) the most widely known.]

The history of all hitherto existing society is the history of class struggles.

Freeman and slave, patrician and plebeian, lord and serf, guild-master and journeyman, in a word, oppressor and oppressed, stood in constant opposition to one another, carried on an uninterrupted, now hidden, now open fight, a fight that each time ended, either in a revolutionary reconstitution of society at large, or in the common ruin of the contending classes.

In the earlier epochs of history, we find almost everywhere a complicated arrangement of society into various orders, a manifold gradation of social rank. In ancient Rome we have patricians, knights, plebeians, slaves; in the Middle Ages, feudal lords, vassals, guild-masters, journeymen, apprentices, serfs; in almost all of these classes, again, subordinate gradations.

The modern bourgeois society that has sprouted from the ruins of feudal society has not done away with class antagonisms. It has but established new classes, new conditions of oppression, new forms of struggle in place of the old ones.

Our epoch, the epoch of the bourgeoisie, possesses, however, this distinctive feature: it has simplified the class antagonisms. Society as a whole is more and more splitting up into two great hostile camps, into two great classes directly facing each other—bourgeoisie and proletariat.

★ ★ ★

The bourgeoisie, wherever it has got the upper hand, has put an end to all feudal, patriarchal, idyllic relations. It has pitilessly torn asunder the motley feudal ties that bound man to his "natural superiors," and has left remaining no other nexus between man and man than naked self-interest, than callous "cash payment." It has drowned the most heavenly ecstasies of religious fervour, of chivalrous enthusiasm, of philistine sentimentalism, in the icy water of egotistical calculation. It has resolved personal worth into exchange value, and in place of the numberless indefeasible chartered freedoms, has set up that single, unconscionable freedom—Free Trade. In one word, for exploitation, veiled by religious and political illusions, it has substituted naked, shameless, direct, brutal exploitation.

★ ★ ★

A part of the bourgeoisie is desirous of redressing social grievances in order to secure the continued existence of bourgeois society.

To this section belong economists, philanthropists, humanitarians, improvers of the condition of the working class, organizers of charity, members of societies for the prevention of cruelty to animals, temperance fanatics, hole-and-corner reformers of every imaginable kind.... The socialistic bourgeois want all the advantages of modern social conditions without the struggles and dangers necessarily resulting therefrom. They desire the existing state of society minus its revolutionary and disintegrating elements. They wish for a bourgeoisie without a proletariat. The bourgeoisie naturally conceives the world in which it is supreme to be the best; and bourgeois socialism develops this comfortable conception into various more or less complete systems. In requiring the proletariat to carry out such a system, and thereby to march straightway into the social New Jerusalem,[1] it but requires in reality that the proletariat should remain within the bounds of existing society, but should cast away all its hateful ideas concerning the bourgeoisie.

A second and more practical, but less systematic, form of this socialism sought to depreciate every revolutionary movement in the eyes of the working class, by showing that no mere political reform,

---

[1] I.e., paradise.

but only a change in the material conditions of existence, in economical relations, could be of any advantage to them. By changes in the material conditions of existence, this form of socialism, however, by no means understands abolition of the bourgeois relations of production, an abolition that can be effected only by a revolution, but administrative reforms, based on the continued existence of these relations; reforms, therefore, that in no respect affect the relations between capital and labour, but, at the best, lessen the cost, and simplify the administrative work, of bourgeois government.

★   ★   ★

In short, the Communists everywhere support every revolutionary movement against the existing social and political order of things.

In all these movements they bring to the front, as the leading question in each, the property question, no matter what its degree of development at the time.

Finally, they labour everywhere for the union and agreement of the democratic parties of all countries.

The Communists disdain to conceal their views and aims. They openly declare that their ends can be attained only by the forcible overthrow of all existing social conditions. Let the ruling classes tremble at a Communistic revolution. The proletarians have nothing to lose but their chains. They have a world to win.

WORKING MEN OF THE WORLD, UNITE!

[Source: Karl Marx and Friedrich Engels, *Manifesto of the Communist Party* (London: George Allen and Unwin, 1948): 119-20, 122-23, 154-55, 160.]

2. John Stuart Mill, from "Chapters on Socialism" (1879)

[At his death, the liberal philosopher John Stuart Mill (1806-1873) left incomplete a series of essays on socialism, which were later edited and published by his step-daughter, Helen Taylor. In "How I Became a Socialist" (1894), Morris recalled that he disagreed so strenuously with Mill's critique of socialism that it "put the finishing touch" on his own decision to join the socialist cause. Though sympathetic with aspects of socialist thought, Mill argues that it exaggerated both the extent to which capitalism caused society's ills and the extent to which socialism could cure those ills.]

To say the truth, the perceptions of Englishmen are of late somewhat blunted as to the tendencies of political changes. They have seen so many changes made, from which, while only in prospect, vast expectations were entertained, both of evil and of good, while the results of either kind that actually followed seemed far short of what had been predicted, that they have come to feel as if it were the nature of political changes not to fulfil expectation, and have fallen into a habit of half-unconscious belief that such changes, when they take place without a violent revolution, do not much or permanently disturb in practice the course of things habitual to the country. This, however, is but a superficial view either of the past or of the future. The various reforms of the last two generations have been at least as fruitful in important consequences as was foretold. The predictions were often erroneous as to the suddenness of the effects, and sometimes even as to the kind of effect. We laugh at the vain expectations of those who thought that Catholic emancipation would tranquillize Ireland, or reconcile it to British rule.[1] At the end of the first ten years of the Reform Act of 1832, few continued to think either that it would remove every important practical grievance, or that it had opened the door to universal suffrage.[2] But five-and-twenty years more of its operation have given scope for a large development of its indirect working, which is much more momentous than the direct. Sudden effects in history are generally superficial. Causes which go deep down into the roots of future events produce the most serious parts of their effect only slowly, and have, therefore, time to become a part of the familiar order of things before general attention is called to the changes they are producing; since, when the changes do become evident, they are often not seen, by cursory observers, to be in any peculiar manner connected with the cause. The remoter consequences of a new political fact are seldom understood when they occur, except when they have been appreciated beforehand.

---

[1] Prior to 1829 Roman Catholics were barred from holding public office in Great Britain. Pressure for reform came largely from Ireland, which had become part of the United Kingdom in 1801.

[2] The Reform Act of 1832 greatly extended the franchise, though, as Mill notes, nothing resembling universal suffrage was achieved. Nearly eighty percent of the population was still without the vote, including all women and most members of the working classes.

This timely appreciation is particularly easy in respect to the tendencies of the change made in our institutions by the Reform Act of 1867.[1] The great increase of electoral power which the Act places within the reach of the working classes is permanent. The circumstances which have caused them, thus far, to make a very limited use of that power, are essentially temporary. It is known even to the most inobservant, that the working classes have, and are likely to have, political objects which concern them as working classes, and on which they believe, rightly or wrongly, that the interests and opinions of the other powerful classes are opposed to theirs.... It is of the utmost importance that all reflecting persons should take into early consideration what these popular political creeds are likely to be, and that every single article of them should be brought under the fullest light of investigation and discussion, so that, if possible, when the time shall be ripe, whatever is right in them may be adopted, and what is wrong rejected by general consent, and that instead of a hostile conflict, physical or only moral, between the old and the new, the best parts of both may be combined in a renovated social fabric.

... [I]t would probably be found that even in England the more prominent and active leaders of the working classes are usually in their private creed Socialists of one order or another, though being, like most English politicians, better aware than their Continental brethren that great and permanent changes in the fundamental ideas of mankind are not to be accomplished by a *coup de main,*[2] they direct their practical efforts towards ends which seem within easier reach, and are content to hold back all extreme theories until there has been experience of the operation of the same principles on a partial scale. While such continues to be the character of the English working classes, as it is of Englishmen in general, they are not likely to rush headlong into the reckless extremities of some of the foreign Socialists, who, even in sober Switzerland,[3] proclaim themselves content to begin by simple subversion, leaving the subsequent reconstruction to take care of itself; and by subversion they mean not only the annihilation of all government, but getting all property of all kinds out of the hands

---

1   The Reform Act of 1867 further extended the franchise, though women were still excluded. Mill, a Member of Parliament in 1867, had put forward a motion to substitute the word "person" for "man" in the Bill; it was defeated by a vote of 196 to 73.

2   A sudden attack or uprising (literally, "a blow from the hand").

3   Switzerland, home to numerous émigrés and political refugees from Russia, Italy, and Germany, was a center of (mostly theoretic) radicalism in the 1870s.

of the possessors to be used for the general benefit; but in what mode it will, they say, be time enough afterwards to decide.

[Source: *Fortnightly Review* 25 (February 1, 1879): 218-19, 221.]

3. H.M. Hyndman, from *England for All: The Text-Book of Democracy* (1881)

[With *England for All*, Henry Mayers Hyndman (1842-1921) helped introduce Marxist socialism into British intellectual life. Hyndman, like Morris several years afterward, was profoundly influenced by reading *Capital* in French translation, though he neglected to mention Marx in the pages of his "textbook of democracy." In 1881 Hyndman founded the Democratic Federation, which changed its name to the Social Democratic Federation in 1884; Morris joined in 1883. His disagreements—philosophical, tactical, temperamental—with Hyndman led Morris to leave the S.D.F. and found the Socialist League in early 1885.]

Our civilization is in many respects but an organized hypocrisy, filming over as ulcerous places below as ever disgraced the worst periods of past history. But there is something more than hypocrisy or indifference to account for the crying evils of our great cities, and the miserable poverty and bad lodgment which degrade our agricultural population. More general causes than any which individuals can right, are at work. Private enterprise has been tried and found wanting: laissez-faire has had its day.... Bad as is the education of the majority of Englishmen compared with what it ought to be, they have learnt enough to be dissatisfied with arrangements which, when more ignorant, they might have accepted as inevitable. Of the sufferings which the real producers of this great industrial community undergo, the comfortable classes hear but little. They barely talk of their troubles to their most intimate friends. The natural inclination of Englishmen is to bear in silence. Hitherto many have found consolation in religion, which held out to them the prospect of happiness hereafter in return for sorrow and misery here. That resource is now failing, and the bolder spirits—it is useless to blink plain truths—openly deride those "drafts on eternity" which they say are issued solely in the interest of employers and rich men. Their own ills nevertheless they may bear: that they will consent to hand on the same lot to their children is very unlikely. The day for private charity and galling patronage is at an end; the time for combination and political action in redress of social wrongs is at hand.

Such changes as are needed may be gradual, but they must be rapid. In England, fortunately, we have a long political history to lead up to our natural development, the growth of a great nation such as ours has its effect on all portions of the people. Patriotism is part of our heritage; self-restraint necessarily comes from the exercise of political power. Even the poorest are ready to accept the assurance of real reform, rather than listen to those who would urge them to resort in desperation to violent change. Yet these reforms must in the end be far more thorough than the enthusiasts of compromise, and the fanatics of moderation are ready to admit. Hitherto there has been patience, because all have hoped for the best. But longer delay is not only harmful but dangerous.... If the theories now gaining ground all over the Continent, as well as here with us, are to be met peacefully, and turned to the advantage of all, the necessary change of front can no longer be delayed. The State, as the organized common-sense of public opinion, must step in, regardless of greed or prejudice, to regulate that nominal individual freedom which simply strengthens the domination of the few. Thus only shall the England of whose past we all are proud, of whose future all are confident, clear herself from that shortsighted system which now stunts the physical and intellectual growth of the great majority, knit together the great democracies near and far under our flag, and deal out to our dependencies a full measure of that justice which alone can secure for us and for ours the leadership in the social reorganization which will be our greatest claim to respect and remembrance from countless generations of the human race.

[Source: H. M. Hyndman, *England for All: The Text-Book of Democracy* (London: E. W. Allen, 1881): 4-6.]

4. Sergius Stepniak, from *Underground Russia* (1883)

[Sergius Stepniak (1852-1895) was, like Peter Kropotkin (see Appendix B. 8), a Russian aristocrat turned revolutionist. Like Kropotkin, too, during the 1880s he lived in exile in London, where he lectured and wrote. Thanks to works such as *Underground Russia* (1881), *Russia Under the Czars* (1885), and *The Career of a*

Nihilist (1889), Stepniak's name was associated with revolutionary terrorism. Morris called *Underground Russia* "a most interesting book, though terrible reading too: it sounds perfectly genuine: I should think such a book ought to open people's eyes a bit here & do good" (*Letters*, 2:194). In the following extract, Stepniak distinguishes between two stages in the history of revolutionary action in Russia, the propaganda and the terror. The passage begins with a character sketch of the propagandist.]

[E]verything that is noble and sublime in human nature seemed concentrated in these generous young men. Inflamed, subjugated by their grand idea, they wished to sacrifice for it, not only their lives, their future, their position, but their very souls. They sought to purify themselves from every other thought, from all personal affections, in order to be entirely, exclusively devoted to it.... The propagandists wished nothing for themselves. They were the purest personification of self-denial.

But these beings were too ideal for the terrible struggle which was about to commence. The type of the propagandist of the first lustre of the last decade[1] was religious rather than revolutionary. His faith was Socialism. His god the people. Notwithstanding all the evidence to the contrary, he firmly believed that, from one day to the other, the revolution was about to break out; as in the Middle Ages people believed at certain periods in the approach of the day of judgment. Inexorable reality struck a terrible blow at his enthusiasm and faith, disclosing to him his god as it really is, and not as he had pictured it. He was as ready for sacrifice as ever. But he had neither the impetuosity nor the ardour of the struggle. After the first disenchantment he no longer saw any hope in victory, and longed for the crown of thorns rather than that of laurel. He went forth to martyrdom with the serenity of a Christian of the early ages, and he suffered it with a calmness of mind—nay, with a certain rapture, for he knew he was suffering for his faith. He was full of love, and had no hatred for anyone, not even his executioners. Such was the propagandist of 1872-75.[2] This type was too ideal

---

[1] The 1870s.

[2] During this period activists from the cities engaged in a campaign to incite revolutionary fervor among the Russian peasantry. In the aftermath of the campaign's failure a new revolutionary party, Land and Freedom, was formed. Almost immediately tension arose between those who favored a renewed "move to the people" and those who urged more violent action. In 1879 a pro-terrorist group split from the party and took the name People's Will.

to withstand the fierce and imminent conflict. It must change or disappear.

Already another was arising in its place. Upon the horizon there appeared a gloomy form, illuminated by a light as of hell, who, with lofty bearing, and a look breathing forth hatred and defiance, made his way through the terrified crowd to enter with a firm step upon the scene of history.

It was the Terrorist.

★ ★ ★

[The terrorist] is noble, terrible, irresistibly fascinating, for he combines in himself the two sublimities of human grandeur: the martyr and the hero.

He is a martyr. From the day when he swears in the depths of his heart to free the people and the country, he knows he is consecrated to Death. He faces it at every step of his stormy life. He goes forth to meet it fearlessly, when necessary, and can die without flinching, not like a Christian of old, but like a warrior accustomed to look death in the face.

He has no longer any religious feeling in his disposition. He is a wrestler, all bone and muscle, and has nothing in common with the dreamy idealist of the previous lustre. He is a mature man, and the unreal dreams of his youth have disappeared with years. He is a Socialist fatally convinced, but he understands that a Social Revolution requires long preparatory labor, which cannot be given until political liberty is acquired. Modest and resolute, therefore, he clings to the resolution to limit for the present his plans that he may extend them afterwards. He has no other object than to overthrow this abhorred despotism, and to give to his country, what all civilized nations possess, political liberty, to enable it to advance with a firm step towards its own redemption. The force of mind, the indomitable energy, and the spirit of sacrifice which his predecessor[1] attained in the beauty of his dreams, he attains in the grandeur of his mission, in the strong passions which this marvellous, intoxicating, vertiginous struggle arouses in his heart.

What a spectacle! When had such a spectacle been seen before? Alone, obscure, poor, he undertook to be the defender of outraged

---

[1] I.e., the propagandist.

humanity, of right trampled under foot, and he challenged to the death the most powerful Empire in the world, and for years and years confronted all its immense forces.

Proud as Satan rebelling against God, he opposed his own will to that of the man who alone, amid a nation of slaves, claimed the right of having a will.[1] But how different is this terrestrial god from the old Jehovah of Moses! How he hides his trembling head under the daring blows of the Terrorist! True, he still stands erect, and the thunderbolts launched by his trembling hand often fail; but when they strike, they kill. But the Terrorist is immortal. His limbs may fail him, but, as if by magic, they regain their vigour, and he stands erect, ready for battle after battle until he has laid low his enemy and liberated the country. And already he sees that enemy falter, become confused, cling desperately to the wildest means, which can only hasten his end.

It is this absorbing struggle, it is this imposing mission, it is this certainty of approaching victory, which gives him that cool and calculating enthusiasm, that almost superhuman energy, which astounds the world. If he is by nature a man capable of generous impulses, he will become a hero; if he is of stronger fibre, it will harden into iron; if of iron, it will become adamant.

… He fights not only for the people, to render them the arbiters of their own destinies, not only for the whole nation stifling in this pestiferous atmosphere, but also for himself; for the dear ones whom he loves, whom he adores with all the enthusiasm which animates his soul; for his friends, who languish in the horrid cells of the central prisons, and who stretch forth to him their skinny hands imploring aid. He fights for himself. He has sworn to be free and he will be free, in defiance of everything. He bends his haughty head before no idol. He has devoted his sturdy arms to the cause of the people. But he no longer deifies them. And if the people, ill-counselled, say to him, "Be a slave," he will exclaim, "No"; and he will march onward, defying their imprecations and their fury, certain that justice will be rendered to him in his tomb.

Such is the Terrorist.

[Source: Sergius Stepniak, *Underground Russia: Revolutionary Profiles and Sketches from Life* (New York: Charles Scribner's Sons, 1883): 27-29, 39-42.]

---

[1] Czar Alexander II, who was assassinated by a member of the People's Will in March 1881.

5. E. Belfort Bax and William Morris, from "Manifesto of the Socialist League" (1885)

[As its title indicates, this document articulates the beliefs that Morris and others hoped would guide the newly-formed Socialist League. The first version of the manifesto appeared in the inaugural issue of *Commonweal* in February 1885. A revised version, from which the following extract is taken, was ratified by the League and eventually published as a separate pamphlet in October 1885. E. Belfort Bax (1854-1926) was perhaps the first economist in England to make rigorous use of Marxist thought. In addition to dozens of his own articles, pamphlets, and books, Bax collaborated with Morris on a number of works.]

As the civilized world is at present constituted, there are two classes of Society—the one possessing wealth and the instruments of its production, the other producing wealth by means of those instruments but only by the leave and for the use of the possessing classes.

... [T]he necessary results of this so-called civilization are only too obvious in the lives of its slaves, the working-class—in the anxiety and want of leisure amidst which they toil, in the squalor and wretchedness of those parts of our great towns where they dwell; in the degradation of their bodies, their wretched health, and the shortness of their lives; in the terrible brutality so common among them, and which is indeed but the reflection of the cynical selfishness found among the well-to-do classes, a brutality as hideous as the other; and lastly, in the crowd of criminals who are as much manufactures of our commercial system as the cheap and nasty wares which are made at once for the consumption and the enslavement of the poor.

What remedy, then, do we propose for this failure of our civilization, which is now admitted by almost all thoughtful people?

We have already shown that the workers, although they produce all the wealth of society, have no control over its production or distribution: the *people*, who are the only really organic part of society, are treated as a mere appendage to capital—as part of its machinery. This must be altered from the foundation: the land, the capital, the machinery, factories, workshops, stores, means of transit, mines, banking, all means of production and distribution of wealth, must be declared and treated as the common property of all. Every man will then receive the full value of his labour, without deduction for the profit of a master, and as all will have to work, and the waste now incurred by the pursuit of profit will be at an end, the amount of labour necessary for every individual to perform in order to carry on the essential work of the world will be reduced to something like two or three hours daily; so that every one will have abundant leisure for following intellectual and other pursuits congenial to his nature....

The Socialist League therefore aims at the realization of complete Revolutionary Socialism, and well knows that this can never happen in any one country without the help of the workers of all civilization. For us neither geographical boundaries, political history, race, nor creed makes rivals or enemies; for us there are no nations, but only varied masses of workers and friends, whose mutual sympathies are checked or perverted by groups of masters and fleecers whose interest it is to stir up rivalries and hatreds between the dwellers in different lands.

It is clear that for all these oppressed and cheated masses of workers and their masters a great change is preparing: the dominant classes are uneasy, anxious, touched in conscience even, as to the condition of those they govern; the markets of the world are being competed for with an eagerness never before known; everything points to the fact that the great commercial system is becoming unmanageable, and is slipping from the grasp of its present rulers.

The one change possible out of all this is Socialism. As chattel-slavery passed into serfdom, and serfdom into the so-called free-labour system, so most surely will this latter pass into social order.

To the realization of this change the Socialist League addresses itself with all earnestness. As a means thereto it will do all in its power towards the education of the people in the principles of this great cause, and will strive to organize those who will accept this education, so that when the crisis comes, which the march of events is preparing, there may be a body of men ready to step into their due places and deal with and direct the irresistible movement.

[Source: William Morris and E. Belfort Bax, *The Manifesto of the Socialist League* (London: Socialist League Office, 1885): 3, 5-8.]

6. Joseph Lane, from *An Anti-Statist, Communist Manifesto* (1887)

[Joseph Lane (1851-1920) came from a rural working-class family near Oxford. Drawn early in life to radical politics, he was active in various land reform associations and working-men's organizations from the late 1860s onward. Lane left the Social Democratic Federation to join Morris's Socialist League in 1885, where he established himself as the most vehement spokesman against "parliamentary socialism." While Morris agreed that genuine socialism could not be implemented by way of legislative reform, he found Lane's tactics and his taste for political intrigue counterproductive. Lane read his *Anti-Statist, Communist Manifesto* to the Hammersmith Branch of the League and requested a vote of endorsement. Morris joined the majority in defeating the motion.]

Politics properly so-called, that is the science of government or the art of directing men gathered in social community, is entirely based upon the principle of authority, and, it being so, we oppose with all our might the reactionary notion which consists in the pretence that the revolutionary socialists must seek to seize upon the political machine, and to acquire power for themselves. We decline to recognize a divine absolutism because it can only give rise to the enslavery of reason and intelligence. Why, then, should we recognize a human absolutism, that can only engender the material exploitation of the ruled by the rulers? In this argument we are not specially concerned with any particular form of government, for all without distinction had their rise from the same source: Autocratic, Oligarchic systems, constitutional monarchy, plutocracy, the republic, as governmental forms, are all antagonistic to human freedom, and it is because of this that we are opposed to every form of government. If it be admitted that individual man has no right to govern, we cannot admit that a number of men should have this right, be they a minority or a majority....

A certain school of socialists, while sharing our ideas upon the majority of forms of government, seeks nevertheless to defend what they call the democratic state, ruling nations by means of parliamentary systems, but we argue just precisely that freedom does not exist any more in this system than in any of the others, and it is for this reason that we oppose it. Act as it will, this popular state will nevertheless require for its maintenance to appeal to the reactionary forces, which are the natural allies of authority—the army, diplomacy, war, centralization of all the powers which operate in restraint of freedom, and the initiative of individuals and social groups.... In opposition therefore to those who desire by means of parliamentarianism to achieve a conquest of political power, we say for ourselves that we wish to forgo power and monopoly alike.... [P]olitical reforms, as a preliminary to social forms, are a Utopia or a mere trick and an eternal mystification, by which the radicals of every shade, including parliamentary socialists, have up till now deceived the workers. Social science protests against these subterfuges and palliatives; it repudiates every alliance with the policy of parliaments. Far from expecting any succor from them, it begins its work of exclusion by eliminating politics and parliamentarianism. We revolutionary socialists desire to organize ourselves in such a manner as to render politics useless and the powers that be superfluous, i.e., that we aim at the abolition of the State in every form and variety.

[Source: Joseph Lane, *An Anti-Statist, Communist Manifesto* (Sanday, Orkney: Cienfuegos Press, 1978): 28-31.]

7. George Bernard Shaw, from *Fabian Essays in Socialism* (1889)

[A friend and great admirer of Morris, George Bernard Shaw (1856-1950) nevertheless became, by the mid-1880s, the most visible (and vocal) advocate of "parliamentary socialism" in the country. By the time the first series of *Fabian Essays in Socialism* was published, the Fabian Society—with its emphasis on gradualism, legislative reform, and the need to move toward centralization and the state regulation of industry—had long since overtaken organizations like the Social Democratic Federation and the Socialist League in terms of membership and influence. Shaw's account in the passage below of the already-in-progress transition from capitalism to "social democracy" can be usefully compared to Morris's account of "How the Change Came" in *News from Nowhere*.]

It will be at once seen that the valid objections to Socialism consist wholly of practical difficulties. On the ground of abstract justice,

Socialism is not only unobjectionable, but sacredly imperative. I am afraid that in the ordinary middle-class opinion Socialism is flagrantly dishonest, but could be established off-hand to-morrow with the help of a guillotine, if there were no police, and the people were wicked enough. In truth, it is as honest as it is inevitable; but all the mobs and guillotines in the world can no more establish it than police coercion can avert it. The first practical difficulty is raised by the idea of the entire people collectively owning land, capital, or anything else. Here is the rent arising out of the people's industry: here are the pockets of the private proprietors. The problem is to drop that rent, not into those private pockets, but into the people's pocket. Yes; but where is the people's pocket? Who is the people? what is the people? Tom we know, and Dick: also Harry; but solely and separately as individuals: as a trinity they have no existence. Who is their trustee, their guardian, their man of business, their manager, their secretary, even their stake-holder? The Socialist is stopped dead at the threshold of practical action by this difficulty until he bethinks himself of the State as the representative and trustee of the people…. [We now use] the distinctive term Social Democrat [to indicate] the man or woman who desires through Democracy to gather the whole people into the State, so that the State may be trusted with the rent of the country, and finally with the land, the capital, and the organization of the national industry—with all the sources of production, in short, which are now abandoned to the cupidity of irresponsible private individuals.

The benefits of such a change as this are so obvious to all except the existing private proprietors and their parasites, that it is very necessary to insist on the impossibility of effecting it suddenly. The young Socialist is apt to be catastrophic in his views—to plan the revolutionary programme as an affair of twenty-four lively hours, with Individualism in full swing on Monday morning, a tidal wave of the insurgent proletariat on Monday afternoon, and Socialism in complete working order on Tuesday. A man who believes that such a happy despatch is possible, will naturally think it absurd and even inhuman to stick at bloodshed in bringing it about. He can prove that the continuance of the present system for a year costs more suffering than could be crammed into any Monday afternoon, however sanguinary. This is the phase of conviction in which are delivered those Socialist speeches which make what the newspapers call "good copy," and which are the only ones they as yet report. Such speeches are encouraged by the hasty opposition they evoke from thoughtless persons, who begin by tacitly admitting a sudden change is feasible, and go on to protest that it would be wicked. The experienced Social Democrat converts his too ardent follower by first admitting that if the change could be made catastrophically it would be well worth making, and then proceeding to point out that as it would involve a readjustment of productive industry to meet the demand created by an entirely new distribution of purchasing power, it would also involve, in the application of labour and industrial machinery, alterations which no afternoon's work could effect. You cannot convince any man that it is impossible to tear down a government in a day; but everybody is convinced already that you cannot convert first and third class carriages into second class; rookeries and palaces into comfortable dwellings; and jewellers and dress-makers into bakers and builders, by merely singing the "Marseillaise." ... Demolishing a Bastille with seven prisoners in it is one thing: demolishing one with fourteen million prisoners is quite another.[1] I need not enlarge on the point: the necessity for cautious and gradual change must be obvious to everyone here, and could be made obvious to everyone everywhere if only the catastrophists were courageously and sensibly dealt with in discussion.

[Shaw continues by arguing that "we are already far on the road" to Social Democracy "and are being urged further by many politicians who do not dream that they are touched with Socialism— nay, who would earnestly repudiate the touch as a taint." Everything supported by the Social Democrats is already being implemented gradually. The essay closes with the following two paragraphs.]

This, then, is the humdrum programme of the practical Social Democrat to-day. There is not one new item in it. All are applications of principles already admitted, and extensions of practices already in full activity. All have on them that stamp of the vestry which is so congenial to the British mind.[2] None of them compel

---

[1] The Bastille, a notorious royal prison and symbol of the *ancien régime*, was stormed by an insurgent Parisian crowd and its seven prisoners released on July 14, 1789. The "Marseillaise," written by Rouget de Lisle in 1792, is the French national anthem.

[2] Vestries were local administrative bodies organized by parish. For Shaw they stand for the timid and tradition-bound character of British politics. Local governments were substantively reorganized and vestries stripped of most of their authority by the County Council Act of 1888, passed shortly before Shaw wrote this essay.

the use of the words Socialism or Revolution: at no point do they involve guillotining, declaring the Rights of Man,[1] swearing on the altar of the country, or anything else that is supposed to be essentially un-English. And they are all sure to come—landmarks on our course already visible to far-sighted politicians even of the party which dreads them.

Let me, in conclusion, disavow all admiration for this inevitable, but sordid, slow, reluctant, cowardly path to justice. I venture to claim your respect for those enthusiasts who still refuse to believe that millions of their fellow creatures must be left to sweat and suffer in hopeless toil and degradation, whilst parliaments and vestries grudgingly muddle and grope towards paltry instalments of betterment. The right is so clear, the wrong so intolerable, the gospel so convincing, that it seems to them that it *must* be possible to enlist the whole body of workers—soldiers, policemen, and all—under the banner of brotherhood and equality; and at one great stroke to set Justice on her rightful throne. Unfortunately, such an army of light is no more to be gathered from the human product of nineteenth century civilization than grapes are to be gathered from thistles.[2] But if we feel glad of that impossibility; if we feel relieved that the change is to be slow enough to avert personal risk to ourselves; if we feel anything less than acute disappointment and bitter humiliation at the discovery that there is yet between us and the promised land a wilderness in which many must perish miserably of want and despair: then I submit to you that our institutions have corrupted us to the most dastardly degree of selfishness. The Socialists need not be ashamed of beginning as they did by proposing militant organization of the working classes and general insurrection. The proposal proved impracticable; and it has now been abandoned—not without some outspoken regrets—by English Socialists. But it still remains as the only finally possible alternative to the Social Democratic programme which I have sketched to-day.

[Source: *Fabian Essays in Socialism*, ed. G. Bernard Shaw (London: Fabian Society, 1889): 180-83, 200-01.]

---

[1] The Declaration of the Rights of Man and of the Citizen was adopted by the revolutionary National Assembly of France on August 27, 1789.

[2] A conflation of Matthew 7:16 ("Are grapes to be gathered from thorns, or figs from thistles?") and Luke 6:44 ("For figs are not gathered from thorns, nor are grapes picked from a bramble bush.").

Appendix E: Bloody Sunday

[For a discussion of "Bloody Sunday" (November 13, 1887) and its relation to *News from Nowhere*, see Introduction, pp. 40-42. This section gathers together some contemporary responses to the events of that day.]

1. From *The Times* (London): November 14, 1887

THE DEFENCE OF TRAFALGAR SQUARE

SERIOUS RIOTS IN LONDON
(FROM OUR REPORTER IN THE SQUARE)

The organizers and promoters of the great "test meeting" which was to have been held yesterday afternoon in Trafalgar-square have been utterly routed. They were to have vindicated what they grandiloquently described as "the right of public meeting," or, in other words, the right of setting up a bear garden in the midst of the metropolis to the serious inconvenience of peaceable citizens and the dire loss of the traders and hotel proprietors in the neighbourhood. If they are wise enough to know when they are beaten they must this morning confess themselves defeated. There has been no meeting in Trafalgar-square, nor have there even been processions in its vicinity. The right of the disaffected and the turbulent to meet together upon this hereditary possession of the Crown has not been vindicated,[1] but the right of the Ministers and officers of the Crown to prevent such meeting has. Unfortunately, though the Socialists and Nationalists and Radical roughs have completely failed in their attempt to hold their meeting, they certainly succeeded yesterday in gathering in the thoroughfares which surround Trafalgar-square an immense crowd, composed in some part of the most turbulent classes, which was not dispersed until some of the police had energetically resorted to their staves, and until the Life Guards and the

---

[1] An 1844 Act of Parliament made Trafalgar Square the hereditary property of the Crown, the only public space in London to be so designated.

Foot Guards had been summoned to the assistance of the civil forces of the Crown. Fortunately, though the military were called out, their services did not become necessary. The police, admirably handled by their officers and acting according to the well-considered instructions of Sir Charles Warren, proved adequate to the task of clearing the square and restoring order, and a riot, which at one period of the afternoon appeared imminent, was averted.

★ ★ ★

WITH THE SOUTH LONDON CONTINGENT

Battles for law and order in New Palace-yard, in which a vast mob of organized ruffianism, armed with lethal weapons, attacked the police, is a new phase of political agitation, and the struggles which occurred there yesterday presented one of the most remarkable scenes enacted in modern times in the metropolis. The South London contingent, composed of agitators and Radicals, who have "free speech" as their word of order, Home Rulers, who protest that Mr. O'Brien shall be set free, and the Socialists, who desire universal anarchy, made two large forces. They included in their midst a large muster of the elements of disorder between Woolwich and Battersea, with some from Westminster slums, and they attacked the police guarding the streets leading to Trafalgar-square from the Houses of Parliament. The attack was by a vast force, and the police, who were, of course, in a small minority compared with the mob, turned the attack and completely defeated the aggressors. This, unfortunately, was not effected without some of the defenders of law and order being badly injured. Two constables were stabbed, and others were battered with bars of iron by the new apostles of liberty. For an hour and a half the scene was one of the greatest excitement, for disorderly gangs of people were interspersed with multitudes of the foolish ones who came to see a spectacle.

2. Queen Victoria, from her journal and correspondence

(a) From her private journal (November 13, 1887)

There has been a great riot in London. The mob wanted to force their way into Trafalgar Square, and fought with the police. Two squadrons of Cavalry and 400 Foot Guards were called out, and kept Trafalgar Square, where it had been announced the people would no longer be allowed to meet. Fortunately, it all ended well. No lives lost, and no collision between the people and the military. All was quiet before midnight. A Socialist, Burns, and an M.P., Mr. Graham, were arrested.

(b) A telegram to Henry Matthews[1]

Balmoral Castle, 14th Nov. 1887.—Much regret serious riot, but greatly rejoice at the energy so successfully evinced, which put it down, and 2 ring-leaders being arrested. Trust all is quiet today; but, when leaders of Opposition preach disobedience to the law and resistance of the police, one cannot be surprised at such attempts. Trust no serious injury to police or innocent people.

[Source: *The Letters of Queen Victoria: A Selection from Her Majesty's Correspondence and Journal between the Years 1886 and 1901* (NY: Longmans, Green, and Co., 1930).]

3. R.B. Cunninghame Graham, from "Bloody Sunday" (1888)

[Robert Bontine Cunninghame Graham (1852-1936) was a prolific writer of essays, sketches, travel pieces, and short stories. Actively involved in radical politics, he was a key figure in the formation of the Labour Party and later president of the Scottish National Party. In 1887 he was Member of Parliament for Lanark. Severely beaten by police during the Bloody Sunday demonstrations, he was arrested and sentenced to six-weeks' imprisonment. The extract below is taken from a letter written to *Commonweal* (November 10, 1888) to mark the first anniversary of Bloody Sunday.]

I can tell no more of the incidents of the day than can any other spectator. I walked across the street with Burns,[2] was joined by no

---

[1] The Queen sent this telegram in code from her home at Balmoral Castle in Scotland to the Home Secretary, Henry Matthews (1826-1913).

[2] John Burns (1858-1943), labor-leader, trades-unionist, and in 1887 a member of the Social Democratic Federation. Along with Cunninghame Graham, he was arrested and eventually sentenced to six weeks' imprisonment for his part in the day's events, allegedly for assaulting the police and causing a riot.

one as far as I remember, and found myself a prisoner in the Square with a broken head. Whilst in there though I had ample time to observe a good deal. I watched the crowd and the police pretty carefully; I saw repeated charges made at a perfectly unarmed and helpless crowd; I saw policemen not of their own accord, but under the express orders of their superiors, repeatedly strike women and children; I saw them invariably choose those for assault who seemed least able to retaliate. One incident struck me with considerable force and disgust. As I was being led out of the crowd a poor woman asked a police inspector (I think) or a sergeant if he had seen a child she had lost. His answer was to tell her she was a "damned whore" and to knock her down. I never till that time completely realized how utterly servile and cowardly an English crowd is. I venture to say that had it occurred in any other country in the world, the man would have been torn to pieces. But no! in England we are so completely accustomed to bow the knee before wealth and riches, to repeat to ourselves we are a free nation, that in the end we have got to believe it, and the grossest acts of injustice may be perpetrated under our very eyes, and we still slap our manly chests and congratulate ourselves that Britain is the home of liberty.

.... I saw much, too, to moralize on. The tops of the houses and hotels were crowded with well-dressed women, who clapped their hands and cheered with delight when some miserable and half-starved working-man was knocked down and trodden under foot.... As I stood there, as I saw the gross over-fed faces at the club and hotel windows, as I heard the meretricious laughter of the Christian women on the housetops (it is a significant feature of the decadence of England, that not one woman of the upper classes raised her protest by pen or on platform to deprecate the treatment of her unarmed fellow-countrymen; no, all their pity was for the police), I thought yet, still—I have heard that these poor working-men, these Irish and Radicals have votes, and perhaps even souls, and it seemed impossible but that some day these poor deceived, beaten, downtrodden slaves would turn upon their oppressors and demand why they had made their England so hideous, why they ate and drank to repletion, and left nothing but work, starvation, kicks, and curses for their Christian brethren? Somewhat in this style I thought; this I saw as I stood wiping the blood out of my eyes in Trafalgar Square. What I did not see was entirely owing to the quietness of the crowd. I did not see houses burning; I did not hear pistols cracking. I did not see this—not because of any precautions the authorities had taken, for they had taken none, but because it was the first time such a scene had been witnessed in London during this generation.

[Source: May Morris, *William Morris: Artist Writer Socialist*, 2 vols. (Oxford: Basil Blackwell, 1936): 2:262-64.]

4. George Bernard Shaw, from a letter to William Morris, November 22, 1887

[On Shaw, see headnote to Appendix D.]

I was somewhat relieved to see the League march up to Clerkenwell on the 13th without you.[1] The women were much in the way. The police charged us the moment they saw Mrs. Taylor.[2] But you should have seen that high hearted host run. Running hardly expresses our collective action. We *skedaddled*, and never drew rein until we were safe on Hampstead Heath or thereabouts.[3] Tarleton[4] found me paralyzed with terror and brought me on to the Square, the police kindly letting me through in consideration of my genteel appearance. On the whole, I think it was the most abjectly disgraceful defeat ever suffered by a band of heroes outnumbering their foes a thousand to one.

I dont [sic] object to Sparling's article[5] on the ground that it's revolutionary. I deprecate its publication because it is calculated to get him into gaol without doing any good as a set-off. I object to a defiant policy altogether at present. If we persist in it, we shall be eaten bit by

---

[1] Shaw apparently was misinformed. Morris did walk with the contingent from the Socialist League to Clerkenwell Green, where he addressed the assembled protesters before they marched towards Trafalgar Square.

[2] Helen Taylor (1831-1907), daughter of Harriet Taylor and step-daughter of J. S. Mill, women's rights activist, writer, and co-founder in 1881 of the Democratic Federation.

[3] Doubtless an exaggeration. Hampstead Heath, at the northern limit of London, is about four miles from the vicinity of Trafalgar Square.

[4] H. B. Tarleton, a member of the Socialist League.

[5] Henry Halliday Sparling (1860-1924), secretary of the Socialist League, deputy editor of *Commonweal*, and from 1890 to 1899 the spouse of Morris's daughter May. It is not clear to what article Shaw is referring. Sparling's contributions to *Commonweal* during this period include a strongly-worded though hardly revolutionary piece on Irish Home Rule and possibly (the attribution is uncertain) a somewhat more incendiary leader on the execution of the Chicago Anarchists. Shaw perhaps saw a draft version of a pamphlet Sparling published in 1888, "Men versus Machinery," which in places has distinctly apocalyptic overtones.

bit like an artichoke. They will provoke; we will defy; they will punish. I do not see the wisdom of that until we are at least strong enough to resist twenty policemen with the help of Heaven and Mrs. Taylor.

[Source: *Bernard Shaw: Collected Letters 1874-1897*, ed. Dan H. Laurence (London: Max Reinhardt, 1965): 177.]

5. William Morris, from "London in a State of Siege" (1887)

[This account first appeared in the November 19, 1887 issue of *Commonweal*.]

The column in which the comrades of the League were, started from Clerkenwell Green in company with the Patriotic Club and some of the East End clubs, including a branch of the S.D.F. [Social Democratic Federation]. I see the correspondent of the *Daily News* estimates this column at 6,000, but I think that is an exaggeration. Anyhow, we marched in good order through Theobalds' Road, and up Hart Street, crossing Oxford Street and Shaftesbury Avenue without attack from the police, but we had no sooner crossed the latter street and were about to enter the Seven Dials streets to make our way to St. Martin's Lane, than the attack came, and it was clearly the best possible place for it.... It was all over in a few minutes: our comrades fought valiantly, but they had not learned how to stand and turn their column into a line, or to march on to the front. Those in front turned and faced their rear, not to run away, but to join in the fray if opportunity served. The police struck right and left like what they were, soldiers attacking an enemy, amid wild shrieks of hatred from the women who came from the slums on our left. The band-instruments were captured, the banners and flags destroyed, there was no rallying point and no possibility of rallying, and all that the people composing our once strong column could do was to straggle into the Square as helpless units. I confess I was astounded at the rapidity of the thing and the ease with which military organization got its victory. I could see that numbers were of no avail unless led by a band of men acting in concert and each knowing his own part.

What happened to us happened, as I hear, to the other processions with more or less fighting. An eye-witness who marched up with the western column told me that they were suddenly attacked as they came opposite the Haymarket Theatre, by the police rushing out on them from the side streets and immediately batoning everybody they could reach, whether they resisted or not. The column, he said, was destroyed in two minutes, though certainly not quite without fighting; one brave man wrapping his banner torn from the pole round his arm and facing the police till he was hammered down with repeated blows.

Once in the Square we were, as I said, helpless units, especially as there were undoubtedly a good many mere spectators, many of them club gentlemen and other members of the class which employs [Sir Charles] Warren. Undoubtedly if two or three hundred men could have been got to make a rush on the cordon of the police, especially at the south-east-corner, the crowd could have swarmed into the Square, and if the weakest of the column could have reached the square in order this could easily have been done. But the result would probably have been a far bloodier massacre than Peterloo;[1] for the people, once in the Square, would have found themselves in a mere penfold at the mercy of the police and soldiers. It is true that as matters went, there seemed very little need for the appearance of the latter, so completely were the police, horse and foot, masters of the situation; and the great mass of the people also round the Square was composed of Radicals, very angry it is true at the horrible brutality with which they had been treated by Warren's men, but by no means strung up to fighting pitch. So that I was fairly surprised, the crowd being then quite quiet, to see the Life Guards form at the south of the Square and march up towards St. Martin's Church with the magistrate at their head (a sort of country-gentleman-looking imbecile) to read the Riot Act.[2] The soldiers were cheered as well as hooted by the crowd, I think under the impression that they would not act as brutally against the people as the police: a mistaken impression I think, as these gorgeous gentry

---

[1] In August 1819 an estimated 75,000 people gathered for a radical reform meeting in St. Peter's Fields in Manchester. Military personnel, ordered by local magistrates to break up the meeting, attacked the crowd, killing eleven and wounding over 400. The massacre, dubbed Peterloo in derisive allusion to Wellington's victory over Napoleon at Waterloo in 1815, was a rallying cry for radical and liberal reformers throughout the remainder of the century.

[2] Under the Riot Act of 1715, individuals in groups of twelve or more engaged in what the government considered riotous assembly could be arrested as felons and imprisoned for life if they did not immediately disband once the Act itself was read aloud in their presence by a government official. One notorious reading of the Riot Act was at Peterloo.

are just the helmeted flunkies of the rich and would act on their orders just as their butlers or footmen would do. A little after this a regiment of the foot-guards made their appearance with fixed bayonets, and completed the triumph of law and order.

[Source: May Morris, *William Morris: Artist, Writer, Socialist*, 2 vols. (Oxford: Basil Blackwell, 1936): 2:251–55.]

6. Margaret Harkness, from *Out of Work* (1888)

[Margaret Harkness (1854–1921?) was a journalist and activist who in the late 1880s wrote a series of novels of working-class life under the pseudonym "John Law." *Out of Work* tells the story of Jos Coney, a rural carpenter whose move to London leaves him impoverished and unemployed in the slums of the city's East End. In the following extract, Jos and his companion—nicknamed the Squirrel—find themselves inadvertently caught up in the events of November 13.]

The roads about the square now became filled with men and women, who pressed in from all sides, and moved towards the cordon of policemen.

"Pass on, pass on!" said the mounted constables, riding slowly about amongst the crowd.

The crowd kept moving, for it only wanted to see the fun, not to take part in any demonstration. But presently one of the Radical clubs came up a side street, and the policemen received orders to close on it. Banners were seized and broken, a drum was smashed, musical instruments were thrown on the ground and trampled under foot. The club was driven back. But only for a minute. A low angry hiss was heard amongst the men, and they pressed on again, fighting their way with sticks and fists, while the bâtons of the policemen returned their blows with interest. The police hit left and right. Their blood was up. They had been kept on duty day and night for the last few weeks, and this was their first real chance of letting the unemployed know what it is to be overworked. The club fell back once more, hissing....

The crowd of sightseers became filled in with angry processionists, whose anger spread in all directions, when a mounted constable knocked over a man, and the horse trod upon him, when the bâtons of the policemen fell on the heads of men and breasts of women, when man after man, and woman after woman was thrown down and trampled upon. Denser and denser grew the crowd about the square. Louder and louder became the hisses. Nearer and nearer the people pressed on to the cordon of policemen that shut them off from the place which belongs to the public.

The Squirrel and Jos were sucked into the mob, and could not get out again. They felt it moving like one man towards the square, and felt it surge back, hissing. The Squirrel's face was pale as death. But she liked the movement. She crept close to Jos, forgetting her flower-basket that had been torn away by the mob. Her little heart beat fast. She hissed loudly, not knowing why, but feeling the noise a relief in her intense excitement. Then some one said,

"The soldiers are coming!"

The whole scene was like a nightmare, after reading a chapter of Carlyle's "French Revolution."

But the hisses were real enough, for they meant starvation and hopelessness. And since Justice rules the universe, those hisses rise up into the ears of the Lord God of Sabaoth.

The drama was not without a comic element; for certain men and women went to the cordon of policemen, asking to be arrested; and the huge constables, drawing themselves up to their full height, said,

"We cannot do it unless you assault us."

Success is never absurd. Failure is often ridiculous. This thing is certain—if more people had followed the example of those men and women, if it had *really* been a Bloody Sunday, that labour programme which is looming in the distance would now be before Parliament; Lord Salisbury and his party would ere this have vanished into nothingness.

[Source: Margaret Harkness, *Out of Work* (London: Merlin Press, 1990): 198-201.]

THE RIOTS IN LONDON ON SUNDAY, NOVEMBER 13, 1887:
DEFENCE OF TRAFALGAR SQUARE

Illustrated London News, November 19, 1887

Appendix F: Early Reviews and Responses

1. Lionel Johnson, from a review in *Academy* (May 23, 1891)

[Lionel Johnson (1867-1902) was a poet and essayist and a central figure in the London literary scene in the 1890s.]

[A]mong all the Utopian or ideal pictures of a reformed world, drawn for our contemplation by enthusiasts, this book by Mr. William Morris has a singular charm. It cannot, indeed, rank with the great schemes of Plato, More, and Bacon:[1] it has far less perfection of workmanship, less completeness of design, less dignity of tone. But these "Chapters from a Utopian Romance" do not pretend to completeness; they aim at one thing only, the description of an "Epoch of Rest." Life to-day is restless, busy, and troubled; full of sordid cares, and wasted by laborious trifles: we hurry and scramble round the world, pushing and hindering one another, losing all the peace and joy of life. Mr. Morris here shows us, what sort of life he would like to live, what is his conception of the *mens sana in corpore sano*[2]....

But we are not bound to take *News from Nowhere* as a socialist guide book: let us consider it as a vision of the Promised Land. The two chief tenets of this new faith are these: pleasure in work is the secret of art and of content; delight in physical life upon earth is the natural state of man. Whatever interferes with that pleasure, and with that delight, is wrong; work that cannot be done with pleasure, ideas that fill men with despair and gloom, stand self-condemned. We must have no grinding and tyrannous machines of labour; no poisonous and blighting influences of thought. If your factory life make of you a sickly shadow, or a sullen brute; if your subtil introspection turns you into a barren dreamer, or a moping pessimist: then, says Mr. Morris, and surely we all say so too, then away with those manufactures and with those metaphysics! Life has become endlessly complicated by all sorts of interests and of wants, that do not make life happier; we must

---

[1] Plato's *Republic* (4th century B.C.E.), Sir Thomas More's *Utopia* (1516), and Francis Bacon's *New Atlantis* (1627) all outline "great schemes" for "a reformed world."

[2] "Sound mind in a healthy body."

simplify ourselves, and return to 'the primal sanities' of nature.[1] That fine phrase of Mr. Whitman describes the spirit of this book: we are sophisticated, let us go home to the early "primal" sources of simplicity and joy; we are perplexed, let us go back to the sources of "sanity" and strength. Upon the relations of art and work, no one is any longer doubtful, where the truth lies. Although little advance be made towards the perfect conditions of beautiful workmanship, in theory we are all agreed. But the second point is less firmly recognized. What Browning called "the mere joy of the living"[2] becomes less valued every day. Nowadays people seem to pride themselves upon having headaches of body and soul; to relish the sensitiveness of their nerves, their delicate and diseased condition. Effeminate persons give us sonnets upon nature, full of fantastic sentiments, and of refined phrases; but a twenty miles' walk or a sleep under the stars would be to them a painful athletic pleasure. Nor have they that loving and personal regard for the very earth itself, which Mr. Morris so rightly prizes: that sense for the motherhood of the earth, which makes a man love the smell of the fields after rain, or the look of running water. These things, to the modern poet, are so much material for rhyme and metaphor: "rain" and "pain," "stream" and "dream." We have fallen in love with a way of torturing nature into complicity with our vague emotions: we should do well to gain the Homeric simplicity and grandeur of mind, the Lucretian sense of majesty and power, the Virgilian sense of rapture and of glory, in the presence of the natural earth.[3] Mr. Morris, from his earliest poems up to this book, has always shown this rightness of mind, this healthy delight in physical existence, because the world is so exhilarating and so lovely. Man has been distinguished from the other animals in many ways; not the least distinction is this: that man alone takes a double pleasure in his life upon earth, a pleasure of the mind and of the senses....

Only we cannot help having a general impression that Mr. Morris's Utopia or Arcadia, for all its beauty and its energy, would

---

[1] Johnson is quoting from Walt Whitman's poem "Give Me the Splendid Silent Sun" (1872): "Give me solitude, give me Nature, give me again O Nature your primal sanities!" (l. 11).

[2] Johnson may have in mind the phrase "wild joys of living" from Robert Browning's poem "Saul" (1855), l. 70.

[3] The ancient poets Homer (8th century B.C.E.), Lucretius (c. 99 B.C.E.–c. 55 B.C.E.), and Virgil (70 B.C.E.–19 B.C.E.) were often associated with the qualities Johnson ascribes to them.

be a little stupid. Perhaps, in his laudable dislike of everything affected or merely academic, Mr. Morris represents his ideal folk as under-rating slightly the very joy and pleasure of books and learning.... It is merely an excess of zeal, in defence of despised and neglected employments, that so makes Mr. Morris unjust to those which have been exalted with exaggeration. There are too many books in the world; we judge too much by a literary standard; we ignore the culture of the mind and body in other ways; but good books remain the best things in the world, after the hills and the fields.

[Source: *Academy* 39 (May 23, 1891): 483-84.]

2. Maurice Hewlett, from a review in *National Review* (August 1891)

[This highly critical review, titled "A Materialist's Paradise," was by far the longest notice Morris's book received in the years immediately following its publication. Maurice Hewlett (1861–1923) was a popular, prolific writer of poetry, essays, plays, histor-ical novels, and pseudo-Icelandic sagas; most of his work was produced after the time of this review.]

But does Mr. Morris (who may have a sense of humour somewhere) wish to be taken seriously? I pay him the doubtful compliment of believing that he does, and venture to indicate the two fallacies which betray his structure. He has, I conceive, exaggerated the dependence of human nature upon its environment: he is convinced that the conditions of human welfare are physical. Grounding on the first, he would violently overthrow institutions and *compel* free-dom; enraptured with the second, he has allowed his perception to govern his reason. The result is not an earthly, but an earthy, Paradise;[1] and the change of adjective makes all the difference between an honest recognition of rank and a state of blank compla-cency which in a savage or one of the lower animals we should call grovelling. Let me hasten to justify.

When Mr. William Morris went to sleep one night and there-upon began his vision, he found himself in a leisurely country,

---

[1] An allusion to Morris's most popular poem, *The Earthly Paradise* (1868-70).

geographically familiar, but socially incredible. It seemed the difference of winter and summer. He had left behind him a time of repression and mechanical observance, and had leapt into a region of ample growth and a fruity abundance of physical delight. The sun shone daily (although it was but June); all the women were fair; the men were strapping; the buildings, shops, halls, and houses, were intelligently and lovingly built; the trees, the flowers, the birds, the very sky spoke more frankly and enthusiastically to his grateful senses. Everything he had ever loved (and here his speech frequently betrays him) was before his eye—frescoed walls, pictured mythology, bold design in glass and "pot-ware," costly damasks and embroidered webbings, drapery rather than dresses, medieval bridges instead of iron ones; a teeming, expansive growth instead of a concentrated, introspective, fevered struggle. Buxom girls in fresh cotton gowns kissed him for morning greeting; they held his hand as they talked; they leaned on his shoulder as they served him at table. Broad-shouldered youths, in doublet and hose, and metal girdles curiously wrought, acted as his guides and grooms, and opened to him, as they toiled, their light young hearts and enthusiasms.

Humanity at large was an extension of these types: the units of the world kissed freely, and mankind was really akin. So deep-seated, so far-reaching, was this sense of brotherhood that all the watch-dogs of society hitherto known to experience—parliaments, police, soldiers and sailors, priests and newspapers—had vanished or been relegated as curious relics (duly labelled) to museums and national galleries. There were no organizations for national defence: the Continent appears to have shared the lack of things defendable. There were none for mutual defence: every man was coheir of his neighbours. Community of goods, free exchange of husbands or wives, exemption from authority external or internal, of conscience or of police, complete fairly enough the attributes of the new State....

Mr. Morris's inquiries into this bizarre state of things elicited the explanation that it had been forwarded by a Trafalgar Square massacre, a universal strike, and a capitulation of employers so wholesale that there were thereafter no "employed" in the modern sense. With hired labour ceased "forced labour"; and "commercialism" ceased. And, "commercialism" once gone, the conditions of pre-commercial life and that life itself veritably revived. Love was pre-commercial, and love, it seems, was sexual instinct. Beauty pre-commercial, and Beauty was a physical attribute and connoted health. Religion, pre-commercial or not, had utterly vanished from the State and the individual. Man could now conceive of nothing higher than he saw or felt; he asked nothing more than to grow with the plants and birds....

In sober truth, the very pith of the scheme is materialistic, the humanism of a sensuous temperament which sees the beauty of appearance and is too indolent or too indifferent to look deeper. "This world and the growth of it and the life of it!"[1] It is all very real to Mr. Morris, and hence his poem smacks of the soil, "has a kind of taste." This body, glowing with the flush of health or the sun-given graduations of rose-pink, carnation and red-brown,—this body of ample bosom curving and heaving like the waves of a morning sea, supple throat, well-set head, glossy hair inviting homage and caress,—this radiant body he will clothe in silken tissue and cloth of finest web. Its round arms shall be girt with barbaric bracelets of bold design; he will hang quaint chains round its brave throat and circle its waist with a zone of damascened steel.[2] This lovely animal shall be frank and winsome; her mouth shall smile to yours in kisses, her fingers thrill you with their touch. She shall be yours if you will, dwell with you and bear you children as lovely as herself. The prospect would be pleasant, would be well-nigh perfect, if one could so gaily assume a be-all and end-all here. But if the pretty clay which Mr. Morris handles so tenderly and, withal, wistfully, should haply prove no more than mere seeming and the veil of another principle? Other pleasures there assuredly are than the glow of sunshine on the cheek, the light of desire in the eyes. Work, hard work, is good, but not so good as its end, and it may vary in degree. The earth and the growth and life of it, again, signify somewhat other than man and the growth and life of *him*. If thought and consciousness are not the reality of man and the index of his possibilities and origin; if it is more momentous what he feels than what he thinks and (therefore) what he *is*, then Mr. Morris's anxiety to have done with commercialism and caste and class-slavery are natural enough. But he will not abolish slavery by abolishing capitalists and employers (even assuming that every master is a villain and every man a martyr) and the fact that there is another and a worse slavery inherent in every one of us and eradicable only from within, points out that Mr. Morris's cherished remedies are but skin-deep,

---

[1]   Ellen's words in the novel: see p. 241.
[2]   To damascene steel is to incise designs into its surface.

and no permanent remedies at all. Animal love and animal beauty ... are very volcanoes, breeding eruption and riot; burning fiercely, they scorch, and may not always be quenched by being let loose.

And *this* is the kind of slavery which to escape is life indeed. And Mr. Morris knows no way, or hints of none....

Hence Mr. Morris's plan of "Simplicity made easy" pales before the old achievement of "Simplicity shown difficult." In the one case mechanism is exhibited in the very absence of apparent mechanism; in the other case triumph follows as the fruit of strenuous endeavour. Hence we may gather the futility of this "Vision"; hence, too, we may see, if we will, the real remedy and goal of our groaning efforts. It lies, as all that is of value has ever lain, in education and renunciation. Pare off what is clay and clogs aspiration; foster what is ether and strains towards its fount. Now, this will not be accomplished in A.D. 2050, and may not be in A.D. 3050. For this reason alone, perhaps, it will not please Mr. Morris. He is impatient of attainment; effort irritates him. His house at Hammersmith, he tells us, is dingy and irksome. His vision tells him of a sylvan Thames, a spacious architecture and splendid trappings for glorified carcasses; he is in a hurry to begin. But Mr. Morris—poet, artist, seer though he be—must face facts: he must (he really must) read history. And if History tell him that the spirit of the time (not the spirit of a clique or two) is for Socialism and against Individualism; if she tell him that humanity can be transformed by transforming the institutions which are of its own making; if she tell him that free love by the light of Nature and the pampered lives of intelligent animals will stimulate innocence, fine art, and the higher existence; if she tell him that it is possible to revive the accidents of the fourteenth-century without a vestige of the religion which (good or bad, Catholic or Lollard[1]) was its very breath; if, lastly, she assure him that the good of the race has best been served by indulging the appetites of its grosser parts and leaving the soul to find its level in a slough of sensuality and drowsy oblivion—if History tell him this, there's an end of the matter. History cannot lie though Historians can. But history will tell him nothing of the kind. The course of the world tends otherwise.

[Source: *National Review* 17 (August 1891): 820-22, 825-27.]

---

[1]   The Lollards were a dissenting religious sect active in the fourteenth century. They rejected the ecclesiastical hierarchy and doctrinal rigidity associated with Roman Catholicism.

3. Peter Kropotkin, from an obituary notice in *Freedom* (November 1896)

[On Kropotkin, see headnote, Appendix B.8.]

As a poet, [Morris] stood quite alone in modern poetry. Amidst the whining and morbid poets of our own time, who are plunged into self-analysis and self-complaint, and are utterly devoid of energy for struggle, he was almost the only poet of the joys of life—the joys which man finds in the conquest of freedom, in the full exercise of all his powers, in work—the work of his hands and his brain. No modern poet has been known to inspire men with a like love of liberty, and labour with the like vigour, like hope and trust in human nature, like confidence in the happiness that men can find in conquering full freedom and freely associating with their equals. A true poet of the Norse Vikings, of the free labourers, of free men.

These same elements he brought into the Socialist movement.

When he joined it, he, like all really powerful men, did not seek in it the position of wire-puller or a leader. Not even that of a teacher. He simply undertook to express what the masses think and what they vaguely aspire to. He joined the ranks, and brought with him his hatred of oppression in all possible forms, and his love of equality and freedom—which he understood in its broadest sense.

This is why, when he undertook to write his own romance of the future—*News from Nowhere*—he produced perhaps the most thoroughly and deeply Anarchistic conception of future society that has ever been written. As he combined in himself the broad view of the thinker with a wonderful personification of the good practical sense of *collective* thought (the mood of thought of the masses when they occasionally, in revolutionary times, are set free to work)—his ideal society is undoubtedly the one which is most free of all our State and monastic traditions; the most imbued with the feelings of equality and humanitarian love; the most spontaneously growing out of a spirit of free understanding.

[Source: *Freedom* 10 (November 1896): 109-10.]

4. Walter Crane, from an obituary notice in *Progressive Review* (November 1896)

[The artist-craftsman Walter Crane (1845-1915) was a close friend of Morris's. Like Morris, he remained active in the Socialist movement throughout his adult life.]

The practice of his art, his position as an employer of labour, his intensely practical knowledge of certain handicrafts—all these things brought him face to face with the great Labour question; and the fact that he was an artist and a poet, a man of imagination and feeling, as well as intellect, gave him exceptional advantages in solving it—at least theoretically. His practical nature and sincerity moved him to join hands with men who offered a practicable programme, or at least who opened up possibilities of action towards bringing about a new social system.

His own personal view of a society based upon an entire change of economic system is most attractively and picturesquely described in *News from Nowhere, some chapters of a Utopian Romance*. He called it *Utopian*; but in his view, and granting the conditions, it was a perfectly practicable Utopia. He even gave an account (through the mouth of a survivor of the old order) of the probable course of events which might lead up to such a change. The book was written as a sort of counterblast to Edward Bellamy's *Looking Backward* which on its appearance was very widely read on both sides of the water, and there seemed at one time some danger of the picture there given of a socialized state being accepted as the only possible one.[1] It may be partly answerable for an impression in some quarters that a socialist system must necessarily be mechanical. But the society described in *Looking Backward* is, after all, only a little more developed along the present lines of American social life—a sublimation of the universal supply of average citizen wants by mechanical means, with the main spring of the machine altered from individual profit to collective interest. The book did its work, no doubt, and appealed with remarkable force to minds of a certain construction and bias, and it is only just to Bellamy to say that he claimed no finality for it.

---

[1]   On Bellamy's novel and Morris's reaction to it, see headnote, Appendix C.5, and also the extract from May Morris's memoir (F. 6, below).

But *News from Nowhere* may be considered, apart from the underlying principle common to both—of the collective interest as the determining constructive factor of the social system—as its complete antithesis.

According to Bellamy it is apparently the *city* life that is the only one likely to be worth anything, and it is to the organization of production and distribution of things contributing to the supposed necessities and comforts of inhabitants of cities that the reader's thoughts are directed.

With Morris the country life is obviously the most imposing, the ideal life. Groups of houses, not too large to be neighbourly, each with a common guest-hall, with large proportions of garden and woodland, take the place of crowded towns. Thus London, as we know it, disappears.

What is this but building upon the ascertained scientific facts of our day that the inhabitants of large cities tend to deteriorate in physique, and would die out were it not for the constant infusion of new blood from the country districts?

Work is still a hard necessity in *Looking Backward*, a thing to be got rid of as soon as possible, so citizens, after serving the community as clerks, waiters, or what not, until the age of forty-five, are exempt.

With Morris work gives zest to life, and all labour has its own touch of art—even the dustman can indulge in it in the form of rich embroidery upon his coat. The bogey of labour is thus routed by its own pleasurable exercise, with ample leisure, and delight in external beauty in both art and nature.

As regards the woman's question, it never, in his *Utopia*, appears to be asked. He evidently himself thought that with the disappearance of the commercial competitive struggle for existence and what he termed "artificial famine," caused by monopoly of the means of existence, the claim of women to compete with men in the scramble for a living would not exist. There would be no necessity for either men or women to sell themselves, since in a truly co-operative commonwealth each one would find some congenial sphere of work.... I gather that he thought both men and women should be free, but by no means wished to ignore or obliterate sex, and all those subtle and fine feelings which arise from it, which really form the warp and weft of the courtesies and relationships of life.

Now, whatever criticisms might be offered, or whatever objections might be raised, such a conception of a possible social order, such a view of life upon a new economic basis as is painted in this delightful book, is surely before all things, remarkably wholesome, human and sane and pleasurable. If wholesome, human, sane, and pleasurable lives are not possible to the greater part of humanity under existing institutions, so much the worse for those institutions. Humanity has generally proved itself better than its institutions, and man is chiefly distinguished over other animals by his power to modify his conditions. Life at least means growth and change, and human evolution shows us a gradual progression—a gradual triumph of higher organization and intelligence over lower, checked by the inexorable action of natural laws which demand reparation for breaches of moral and social law, and continually probe the foundations of society. Man has become what he is through his capacity for co-operative social action. The particular forms of social organization are the crystallization of this capacity. They are but shells to be cast away when they retard growth or progress, and it is then that the living organism, collective or individual, seeks out or slowly forms a new home.

As to the construction and colour of such a new house for reorganized society and regenerated life, William Morris has left us in no doubt as to his own ideas and ideals. It may seem strange that a man who might be said to have been steeped in mediaeval lore, and whose delight seemed to be in a beautifully imagined world of romance peopled with heroic figures, should yet be able to turn from that dream-world with a clear and penetrating gaze upon the movements of his own time, and to have thrown himself with all the strength of his nature into the seething social and industrial battle of modern England; that the "idle singer of an empty day"[1] should voice the claims and hopes of labour, stand up for the rights of free speech in Trafalgar Square, and speak from a wagon in Hyde Park, may have surprised those who only knew him upon one side; but to those who fully apprehended the reality, ardour, and sincerity of his nature, such action was but its logical outcome and complement, and assuredly it redounds to the honour of the artist, the scholar, and the poet whose loss we mourn to-day, that he was also a man.

[Source: *Progressive Review* I (November 1896): 149-52.]

---

[1]   From the opening stanza of Morris's poem *The Earthly Paradise* (1868-7o).

5. J. W. Mackail, from *The Life of William Morris* (1899)

[The classicist and literary scholar J. W. Mackail (1859-1945), son-in-law of Morris's lifelong friend Edward Burne-Jones, wrote the first biography of Morris.]

It is a curious fact that this slightly constructed and essentially insular romance has, as a Socialist pamphlet, been translated into French, German, and Italian, and has probably been more read in foreign countries than any of his more important works in prose or verse. The romance itself—if it would not be more correct to speak of it as pastoral—is of such beauty as may readily win indulgence for its artificiality. A pastoral, whether it places its golden age in the past or the future, is by the nature of the case artificial, and perhaps as much so, though not so obviously, as when it boldly plants itself in the present. The immediate occasion which led Morris to put into a connected form those dreams of an idyllic future in which his mind was constantly hovering was no doubt the prodigious vogue which had been obtained the year before, by an American Utopia, Mr. Bellamy's once-celebrated *Looking Backward*.[1] The refined rusticity of *News from Nowhere* is in studied contrast to the apotheosis of machinery and the glorification of the life of large towns in the American book; and is perhaps somewhat exaggerated in its reaction from that picture of a world in which the *phalanstère* of Fourier[2] seems to have swollen to delirious proportions, and State Socialism has resulted in a monstrous and almost incredible centralization.

Indeed, a merely materialist Earthly Paradise was always a thing Morris regarded with a feeling little removed from disgust. That ideal organization of life in which the names of rich and poor should disappear, together with the things themselves, in a common social well-being, was in itself to him a mere body, of which art, as the single high source of pleasure, was the informing soul.

[Source: J. W. Mackail, *The Life of William Morris*, 2 vols. (London: Longmans, Green, and Co., 1899) 2:243-44.]

---

[1] On Bellamy's novel and Morris's reaction to it, see headnote, Appendix C. 5, as well as the extract from May Morris's memoir (F. 6, below).

[2] On Fourier, see footnote, p. 112.

6. May Morris, from *The Collected Works of William Morris* (1910-15)

[May Morris (1862-1938) was, in addition to her innovative work in embroidery and book design, the editor of her father's collected works.]

When Bellamy's *Looking Backward* appeared, a Socialist friend remarked that he had accepted the principles of Socialism on the strength of Morris's vision of the future, though he (Morris) had never actually formulated that vision in detail; but now, having read "Looking Backward," he saw how practicable a scheme it would be. This and similar remarks one day stung my father into saying that "if they briganded *him* into a regiment of workers he would just lie on his back and kick." He writes to a Scottish friend, Bruce Glasier, about it: "I suppose you have seen or read, or at least tried to read *Looking Backward*. I *had* to on Saturday, having promised to lecture on it. Thank you, I wouldn't care to live in such a Cockney paradise as he imagines." The same sentiment is embodied in all seriousness and dignity in *News from Nowhere*.... His own unhopeful estimate of its chance of popularity is embodied in the following remark to the same friend some eighteen months later: "I shall now begin to touch up *News from Nowhere* for its book form, and will publish it for 1/0.[1] It has amused me very much writing it: but you may depend upon it, [it] won't sell. This is of course my own fault— or my own misfortune." How mistaken his estimate was can be seen from the abiding place it has in the affections of those who care for England and who understand something of the passionate yearning that peopled her June meadows and gentle river with a happy throng of Dream-folk.

[Source: May Morris, ed., *The Collected Works of William Morris*, 24 vols. (London: Longmans, Green and Co., 1910-15), 6:xxviii-xxix.]

---

[1]   I.e., one shilling—an inexpensive edition.

Bibliography/Recommended Reading

Bibliography

Belsey, Andrew. "Getting Somewhere: Rhetoric and Politics in *News from Nowhere*." *Textual Practice* 5:3 (1991): 337-51.

Boos, Florence S. and William Boos. "*News from Nowhere* and Victorian Socialist-Feminism." *Nineteenth-Century Contexts* 14:1 (1990): 3-32.

Brantlinger, Patrick. "*News from Nowhere*: Morris's Socialist Anti-Novel." *Victorian Studies* 19 (1975): 35-49.

Buzard, James. "Ethnography as Interruption: *News from Nowhere*, Narrative, and the Modern Romance of Authority." *Victorian Studies* 40:3 (1997): 445-74.

Fellman, Michael. "Bloody Sunday and *News from Nowhere*." *The Journal of the William Morris Society* 8:4 (1990): 5-9.

Holzman, Michael. "Anarchism and Utopia: William Morris's *News from Nowhere*." *ELH* 51:3 (1984): 589-603.

Kelvin, Norman. "The Erotic in *News from Nowhere* and *The Well at the World's End*." *Studies in the Late Romances of William Morris*. Eds. Carole Silver and Joseph Dunlap. New York: William Morris Society, 1976. 97-114.

Kumar, Krishan. "A Pilgrimage of Hope: William Morris's Journey to Utopia." *Utopian Studies* 5:1 (1994): 89-107.

Levitas, Ruth. "Utopian Fictions and Political Theories: Domestic Labour in the Work of Edward Bellamy, Charlotte Perkins Gilman, and William Morris." *A Very Different Story: Studies on the Fiction of Charlotte Perkins Gilman*. Eds. Val Gough and Jill Rudd. Liverpool: Liverpool University Press, 1998. 81-99.

Liberman, Michael. "Major Textual Changes in William Morris's *News from Nowhere*." *Nineteenth-Century Literature* 41:3 (1986): 349-56.

Marsh, Jan. "*News from Nowhere* as Erotic Dream." *The Journal of the William Morris Society* 8:4 (1990): 19-23.

McMaster, Rowland. "Tensions in Paradise: Anarchism, Civilization, and Pleasure in Morris's *News from Nowhere*." *English Studies in Canada* 17:1 (1991): 73-87.

Mineo, Ady. "Eros Unbound: Sexual Identities in *News from Nowhere*." *The Journal of the William Morris Society* 9:4 (1992): 8-14.

Parrinder, Patrick. "News from the Land of No News." *Foundation* 51 (1991): 29-37.

Sharratt, Bernard. "*News from Nowhere*: Detail and Desire." *Reading the Victorian Novel: Detail into Form*. Ed. Ian Gregor. New York: Barnes & Noble, 1980. 288-305.

Shaw, Christopher. "William Morris and the Division of Labour: The Idea of Work in *News from Nowhere*." *The Journal of the William Morris Society* 9:3 (1991): 19-30.

Sypher, Eileen. "The 'Production' of William Morris's *News from Nowhere*." *Minnesota Review* 22 (1984): 84-104.

Trilling, Lionel. "Aggression and Utopia: A Note on William Morris's *News from Nowhere*." *Psychoanalytic Quarterly* 42:2 (1973): 214-25.

Recommended Reading

Editions and Reference Guides

Aho, Gary. *William Morris: A Reference Guide*. Boston: G.K. Hall, 1985.

Boos, Florence S., ed. *William Morris's Socialist Diary*. London: Journeyman Press, 1985.

Faulkner, Peter, ed. *William Morris: The Critical Heritage*. London and Boston: Routledge & Kegan Paul, 1973.

Kelvin, Norman, ed. *The Collected Letters of William Morris*. 4 vols. Princeton: Princeton University Press, 1984-96.

LeMire, Eugene, ed. *The Unpublished Lectures of William Morris*. Detroit: Wayne State University Press, 1969.

Morris, May, ed. *The Collected Works of William Morris*. 24 vols. London: Longmans, Green & Co., 1910-15.

———, ed. *William Morris: Artist, Writer, Socialist*. 2 vols. Oxford: Basil Blackwell, 1936.

Salmon, Nicholas, ed. *William Morris: Journalism: Contributions to Commonweal, 1885-1890*. Bristol: Thoemmes, 1996.

———, ed. *William Morris: Political Writings: Contributions to Justice and Commonweal, 1883-1890*. Bristol: Thoemmes, 1994.

———, ed., with Derek Baker. *The William Morris Chronology*. Bristol: Thoemmes, 1996.

Memoirs and Biographical Studies

Much good biographical information on Morris can be found in May Morris's introductions to the separate volumes of the *Collected*

Works of William Morris and *William Morris: Artist, Writer, Socialist*, cited above. Volume 2 of the latter work is also prefaced by George Bernard Shaw's shrewd and illuminating memoir, "Morris as I Knew Him."

Glasier, John Bruce. *William Morris and the Early Days of the Socialist Movement.* London: Longmans, Green & Co., 1921.

Henderson, Philip. *William Morris: His Life, Work, and Friends.* London: Thames & Hudson, 1967.

MacCarthy, Fiona. *William Morris: A Life for Our Time.* New York: Knopf, 1995.

Mackail, J.W. *The Life of William Morris.* 2 vols. London: Longmans, Green & Co., 1899.

Stansky, Peter. *William Morris.* Oxford: Oxford University Press, 1983.

Thompson, E.P. *William Morris: Romantic to Revolutionary.* Rev. ed. New York: Pantheon, 1977.

General Studies of Morris

Boos, Florence S. "An (Almost) Egalitarian Sage: William Morris and Nineteenth-Century Socialist-Feminism." *Victorian Sages and Cultural Discourse: Renegotiating Gender and Power.* Ed. Thaïs E. Morgan. New Brunswick: Rutgers University Press, 1990. 187–206.

Boos, Florence S. and Carole G. Silver, eds. *Socialism and the Literary Artistry of William Morris.* Columbia and London: University of Missouri Press, 1990.

Frye, Northrop. "The Meeting of Past and Future in William Morris." *Studies in Romanticism* 21:3 (1982): 303-18.

Goode, John. "William Morris and the Dream of Revolution." *Literature and Politics in the Nineteenth Century.* Ed. John Lucas. London: Methuen, 1971. 221-80.

Hough, Graham. "William Morris." *The Last Romantics.* London: Duckworth, 1947. 83-133.

Spear, Jeffrey L. "Morris: Revolution as Realized Romance." *Dreams of an English Eden: Ruskin and His Tradition in Social Criticism.* New York: Columbia University Press, 1984. 201-39.

Stansky, Peter. *Redesigning the World: William Morris, the 1880s, and the Arts and Crafts.* Princeton: Princeton University Press, 1985.

Sussman, Herbert. "The Production of Art in the Machine Age: William

Morris." *Victorians and the Machine: The Literary Response to Technology*. Cambridge: Harvard University Press, 1968. 104-34.

Thompson, Paul. *The Work of William Morris*. London: Heinemann, 1967.